Burning
with
Angst

David J. Pedersen

Cover art by:
Alessandro Brunelli

Editing by:
Angela D. Pedersen
Danielle Fine

Acknowledgements

I have great admiration for prolific writers who can produce vast quantities of amazing content that barely needs to be glanced at by an editor. That's not me. I need a team, and mine is amazing.

My wife, Angie, tackles first contact with my drunken ramblings and helps make enough sense of them to share with my beta team. Cristi, Becky, Matt and Mike give each chapter a read-through, often multiple times. They all provide amazing insight, make great suggestions, and sometimes Cristi draws colorful pictures in the margins! My beta team makes it fun, and is always there to give me a boost over any writer's block.

After the rough draft is complete, Danielle Fine gives the manuscript a thorough beat-down in the way only a professional editor can. While she's making me cry, er, I mean making me a better writer, I also work with Alessandro Brunelli on the cover. Let me rephrase that. I provide Alessandro with a description and a sketch that and he turns into beautiful art.

When all that is done, the marketing begins. My muses, Cristi, Marina, and Mayra help me sell books by cosplaying as Berfemmian at conventions and gracing my Facebook page and website. Yeah, I'm the luckiest guy on earth...because I have incredible friends!

I also need to give a quick shoutout to my daughter Joanne and her friend Sarah who have also stepped in to help at cons.

Finally, I have to thank you for taking the time to read my books! As much as I love to write, it doesn't always come easy for me. But, it always seems that when I'm the most frustrated, someone will post a thoughtful review or send me a kind note of encouragement. I couldn't be more grateful for the support.

Dedication

For Sara "Bob" Prideaux

Her life ended too soon,
but her magic will live on.

Books by David J. Pedersen

Angst Five Book Series:

Book 1: Angst
Book 2: Buried in Angst
Book 3: Drowning in Angst
Book 4: Burning with Angst
Book 5: Dying with Angst

Young Adult / Middle Grade Fiction:

Clod Makes A Friend

Map of Ehrde

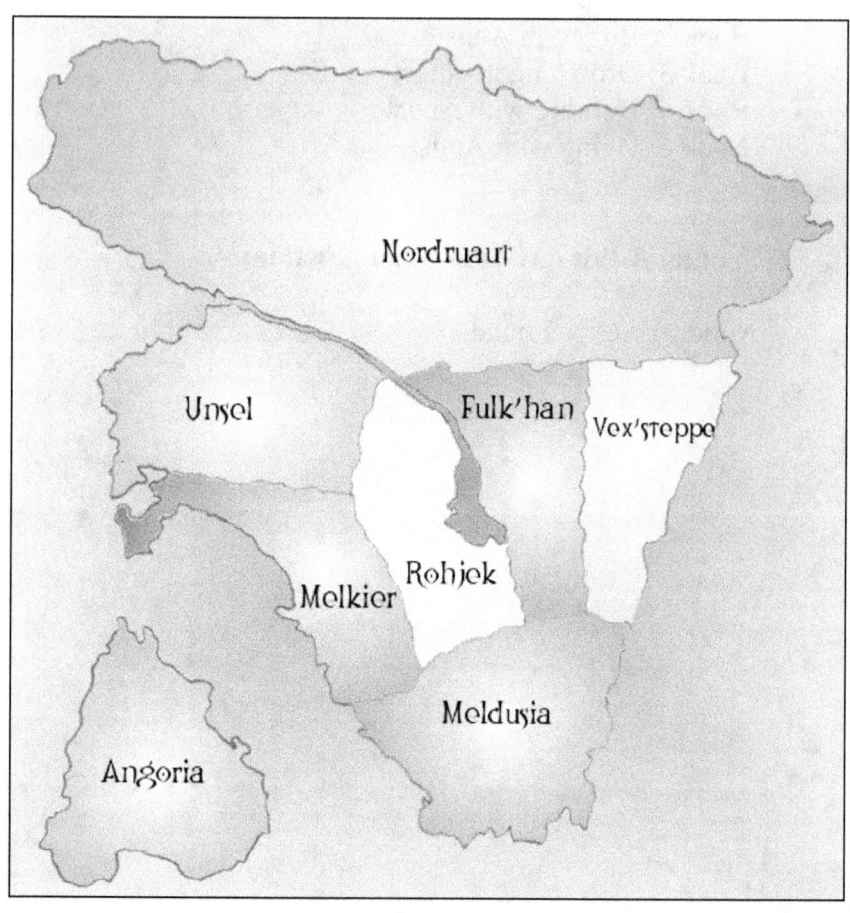

Prelude

The bitter wind was furious, screaming in his ears as hard snow pelted his face. Hector stopped after taking only a few steps through the portal. This had to be wrong, and every instinct told him to go back. He turned around, pushing through knee-high snow. His muscles were already seizing from the cold, each step slower and slower. Tarness appeared—he was the last one through, and the portal began to collapse in on itself.

"Go back," Hector shouted, waving his arms.

There was a noisy sizzle, like bacon frying, and a pop as the cloudy black circle that had delivered them here disappeared. Tarness glanced over his shoulder, grasping at several flickering lights, remnants of the portal that blew away in the storm. He faced Hector and shook his head in confirmation.

"This is the worst rescue ever," Rose cried, her fine red hair whipping across her pale cheeks. "Where are we?"

"This isn't Unsel?" Dallow asked, shielding his face from the winds with one hand.

"Way too much winter to be Unsel," Tarness said, wrapping his arms around Rose and Dallow, a wall against the storm.

"I don't understand," Dallow said, huddling into Tarness. "Describe it to me."

"We're in the middle of nowhere," Rose said, her teeth chattering. "My healing can't keep us from becoming blocks of ice."

1

"A cliff," Hector said. "We're standing on the edge of a cliff. I don't know how high up we are—the snowstorm's clouding the bottom. I can't see shelter from here, and it's almost nighttime. It's going to get colder."

"I hate the cold!" Rose proclaimed, rubbing her hands together and blowing on them.

"It's not that bad," Tarness said with a big grin, his teeth bright against his dark face.

"I need warmth, not smiles," Rose snapped.

"Everyone come close," Dallow said through chattering teeth.

"We're all here," Hector said, grasping arms with Tarness to close the huddle.

Tarness patted Hector's arms amiably.

"No hugging," Hector said sharply.

Dallow's eyes flashed white, and he muttered something to himself. The wind abruptly stopped, snow crashing against the outside of an invisible dome that circled them, the edge within arm's reach.

"Air shield?" Tarness asked.

Dallow nodded, his face wrenched in concentration. The white glow from his eyes was bright beneath the kerchief around his face.

"Nice!" Tarness acknowledged.

"We need another portal," Hector said, vigorously rubbing his arms. "We should be in Unsel. Angst needs us."

"I understand the concept," Dallow grunted, strained by the effort of holding up the shield. "But I don't have that kind of power. It would take a foci, probably more."

"More than a foci?" Tarness asked.

"It's old magic," Dallow said, his hands now shaking. "I don't think I have a chance..."

"Neither do we, if you don't try," he said. Hector looked at his friends; they wouldn't last long in this. Dallow and Rose were so thin, and she was so tiny, they were already affected by the freezing temperatures. Her lips were already blue. Tarness seemed to be holding up, steam rising from his body. Was magic protecting the large man from the storm? If so, how long could that possibly last? If this didn't work, he needed a plan to keep them safe, even a bad plan, even one of Angst's plans. This had to work.

Dallow took several deep breaths, letting them out in measured sighs, as if preparing to lift a heavy weight. After a large gulp of air, he held out both arms and shouted, "Apenn!"

The air shield shimmered, letting in a brief blast of cold and snow before protecting them once again. A slick sheen of sweat covered Dallow's face, which was now haggard with exhaustion.

Hector squinted, broaching the edge of the shield, trying his best to pierce the veil of the storm. Snow battering the barrier completely obstructed his view.

"Nothing," he finally said. "Can you try again?"

"I'm sorry," Dallow croaked, dropping to his knees. His hands shook with fatigue.

The air shield collapsed, and cold wind instantly bit into their skin, rending out chunks of life. Rose pulled herself from Tarness's protective arm to give Dallow a hug.

"You tried," she said, kissing his forehead. She glanced up. "What's that?"

"Describe it!" Dallow shouted over the wind.

"Twenty yards away," Hector said in his gravelly voice. "A rectangle of light in the middle of nothing, like a doorway, and it's getting smaller."

"Did I do it?" Dallow asked hopefully. After a quiet moment, he shouted, "To the light...run!"

Tarness picked Dallow and Rose up and plowed through the burgeoning snow. Hector leaped over mounds and was the first to arrive. Without hesitation, he dove into the light, landing on hard stone and rolling smoothly to one knee. He drew out a staff and surveyed the immediate area for danger. He was on a path, a well-lit stone walkway. It was warm; there was no wind, no storm. The entrance was getting smaller.

"It's safe," Hector called out. "Hurry!"

Dallow flew past Hector as if thrown, belly-flopping on the

path and skidding to a stop. Rose soon followed, folding into a ball and rolling until she crashed into Dallow with a grunt. The doorway was already too small for their large friend. Tarness's shoulder was lodged in one corner as he pushed against the opposite side, struggling to keep it open. He roared in frustration, and the closing slowed.

"He can't fit through," Rose said franticly.

"Tarness!" Hector sprinted to the rectangle. He skidded to a stop at the opening and jammed the staff in the doorway to help prop it open.

The door stopped getting smaller, and Tarness pulled back. Hector faced away from a momentary gust of wind and snow that stopped when Tarness returned.

"Hector," Tarness said through the opening.

They both eyed the staff that shuddered under the weight of the closing door.

"Tarness." This couldn't be happening, he didn't believe in the no-win scenario. He had lost men in hard-fought battles, but had always walked away victorious. Tarness was a close friend, not a soldier, and he didn't know what to say.

Tarness' face looked pained. "Tell Angst thank you."

"What?" Hector asked incredulously. "No, don't give up!"

"Thank him for me, for the adventure," Tarness said. "I'm glad he made me go."

The staff cracked, snapping in half as the opening closed with a thud. Hector took several shaky steps back. He dropped to his knees, frantically searching for a doorframe, eying every inch for a hinge or crack but could only feel smooth wall. He stood up and spun around, stomping to his blind friend.

"Again!" Hector commanded, grabbing Dallow by the shoulder and lifting him up. "Open it again!"

Dallow stood on shaky legs, nodding as he took deep breaths. His eyes flashed dimly as his brow furrowed. "Apenn!"

Hector looked at the wall and waited. He could hear his own heavy breathing, and Rose's teeth chattering. Long moments passed with no sign of the entrance.

PRELUDE

"Again!" Hector yelled.

"Apenn!" Dallow said, the light in his eyes flickering.

"Again!" Hector said.

"Apenn!" Dallow rasped, collapsing to his knees.

"It's gone," Rose said. "The entrance is gone, and so is Tarness."

1

Unsel

Heather was worried. Almost three months had passed, and Angst was still trapped. His face was frozen in an intense look of determination. His gray hair was dark with sweat, his jaw was set, his mouth thin and angry. She'd seen him upset many times, but this was almost frightening. He was mad, and frustrated, and her heart went to him, in spite of it all. She was familiar with that look and could only imagine the effort it took to push his way through the spell that had practically frozen him in Victoria's room.

"He's so close," Wilfred said encouragingly. "This could be the day."

She looked at the short, wide man and smiled appreciatively. Angst's old friend, a former advisor to Isabelle and Alloria, had taken on the considerable burden of leading Unsel while everyone waited. Despite great pressures to step aside for a successor, Wilfred had smartly brought order to Unsel, while dodging weak claims to the throne by miring them down in bureaucracy. Angst had chosen his friend wisely. Not only had Wilfred become a strong leader, he'd also been very supportive of Heather.

"I could probably help," Faeoris offered. "He's almost here. I could just reach in and pull them through."

Heather hadn't heard the Berfemmian come into the hallway. She glanced over her shoulder to see the young woman, who

6

checked on Angst's progress every day. His newest friend was
tall, beautiful, and scantily clad. Heather really wanted to hate
her, with her large dark eyes, over-full lips, and a body that was
too thin to be that curvy. But, like almost everyone Angst was
close to, Heather had become fond of her. She'd been a good
friend in his absence.

"That's probably a bad idea," Heather said, holding out a
warning arm, as if that could possibly keep the strong Berfemmian back. "After what happened to Jaden, I think it's best
we wait."

Faeoris nodded in agreement even as the young woman's thin
brows furrowed in frustration.

Heather turned her gaze back to Victoria's room. It was like a
portrait that changed day to day. According to Jintorich, the
Meldusian ambassador, time had slowed in that room. Angst
hung in the air, both legs poised as if running. One arm was
wrapped around Jaden's waist and the other around what seemed
to be a woman wearing a blue dress. It looked like Angst had
tackled them both, and dragged them along as he fought his way
out of this room now lost in time. Two swords, two enormous
magical foci, stood on their tips at both sides of the entrance,
like soldiers guarding the doorway. After three long months,
Angst had almost reached that door.

It wasn't the frozen room that upset everyone else, nor Angst
making his way through it for what felt like forever. The nightmare was what he seemed to be running from. Victoria rested on
her knees in the gorgeous white gown she would wear for her
crowning as Queen of Unsel. Her hands gripped a golden triangular blade that had been jammed through her chest. Drops of
blood hung in the air, dripping as slowly as time allowed in that
room.

"I'm sure it's any moment now, Heather," Wilfred said. "And
then we'll have some answers."

"Good," she said gruffly. "Because I deserve some."

* * * *

With a final thrust, Angst launched out of Victoria's room. He gasped for breath and staggered into the hall. He tried to remember what had happened, his mind thick with the cobwebs of a fevered slumber. It was a nightmare that had muffled his hearing, clouded his vision, and made his body ache. He remembered only one thing very clearly.

"Where is she?" Angst roared, his throat so dry it hurt.

His arms were stiff and sore. He looked in surprise at two limp bodies pressed against each hip. He could barely remember grabbing even one on his way out and let them go. The bodies fell to the floor in unmoving heaps. They were unfamiliar to him and it was unclear if they even lived. It didn't matter. Spinning about, Angst sought his foci. The giant swords, brothers, five feet tall and two feet wide, were just inside the entrance. They stood guard, keeping his princess safe. His spell only required one sword remain in the room. Angst needed the other, and reached forward.

"Angst, no!" a woman cried. Was that Heather?

Pain like fire and lightning raged through his veins as his arm crossed the threshold. The blade was just out of reach, and he let out a roar of anguish and frustration. Bracing one hand against the doorway, Angst leaned further into the room in until he wrapped his hand around the hilt of Chryslaenor. He pulled the giant sword, *his* giant sword, from the room like removing it from a sheath. The ringing in his ears made it hard to focus, and his arm was almost completely numb, but he had it. Angst faced everyone in the hallway.

"Where is Alloria?" he growled. Lightning from the foci popped loudly, crawling up his arms and surrounding his chest. Its song rang in his mind, trying to tell him something, but he didn't care.

Heather stood before him, her eyes brimming with tears and two blankets rolled up in her arms. His friends Wilfred and Faeoris stood beside her, gawking slack-jawed at the two bodies that remained unmoving on the floor.

"I..." Wilfred said, his tenor voice shaking.

CHAPTER ONE

Their eyes were wide, staring at him as if he'd gone mad. Heather was speechless, her mouth open and bottom lip quivering. Faeoris looked ready to leap forward and hug him, or punch him in the mouth, or both. High-pitched cries clashed with the ringing in his ears. It didn't make sense. They just stood there. Had they all gone crazy? Alloria would escape; he only had seconds to find her. He shook his head, trying to clear away the confusion.

"Where is she?" he shouted.

"I don't know," Wilfred stuttered. The short, chubby man quivered in fear.

With a growl of fury, Angst tore away from them. He blurred through the castle, dodging soldiers, knocking over tables, scaring pages and maids. Doors were knocked off hinges or destroyed completely as he broke into each room. Slowing enough to see faces, Angst checked every single person he could find in the castle. It was taking too long; he drove harder, pushed faster.

Guilt and pain pursued him with every lurch forward. Alloria couldn't have gone far with Jormbrinder, and he needed that other half to save Tori. He ignored Chryslaenor's song, begging him to stop, pleading that it was too late. How could it be too late? Alloria had stabbed his princess only seconds ago. A cook fainted, and everyone else in the kitchen stepped back in fear. Angst gasped for breath, the smell of food cramping his stomach. Nothing made sense. His mind raced to catch up as he fought through thick memories. Alloria had moved as fast as he could, like a blur between moments. Had the young woman bonded with Jormbrinder?

Time was precious. Angst had looked everywhere inside. She must have left the castle, but she couldn't have gone far. He ran as fast as he could to the entrance, weaving through corridors, whirling around people, only knocking over a few.

"Shut up!" he shouted at Chryslaenor. The bells and horns of his foci were too loud, distracting him.

A tempest of harrowing thoughts stormed through his head.

His heart hurt to bursting for leaving Victoria trapped in that room within a hair's width of death. Who were the two people he'd carried out? He didn't even remember grabbing them. Heather had been upset. She'd been holding something. He would have to apologize, again. At least she was safe. He would get answers and give apologies once Alloria was stopped. He rushed out the front gates and skidded to a halt.

The day was bright and sunny, and a cool, damp breeze brushed his cheek. It was warm, the air smelled fresh from rain, and there were new buds on a nearby tree. Winter's snows were gone. This couldn't be right. How could it be spring? The song from Chryslaenor quieted as realization sank in.

* * * *

"He's being stupid," Faeoris said, placing an arm around Heather as she tried comforting the woman. "He's just confused."

"Why was he asking for Alloria?" Heather struggled, sobs sneaking out between breaths.

Faeoris didn't know what to say, and apparently neither did Wilfred. He looked on the verge of tears, apparently affected by Heather's ability to infect others' emotions with her own. He turned away from them, wiping his eyes before gently rolling the bodies over to lie more naturally.

"They're both breathing," he said, his voice catching. "Heather, please try to calm yourself. He'll be back, and we can explain everything to him."

"He can explain everything to us," Faeoris snapped.

Heather nodded and pulled away from her. Faeoris wanted to hunt Angst down and make this right, but even she couldn't keep up with the man. "I'll knock some sense into him," she swore under her breath, making Heather chuckle.

"Thank you," Heather said, taking deep breaths. "I'm sure you're right, that he's just confused."

"He shouldn't wield magic that confuses him," Faeoris said.

CHAPTER ONE

"When he comes back," Heather said, "give him a minute. There's going to be a lot for him to absorb, and—"

There was a rush of air, and Faeoris's long hair brushed her cheeks as Angst blurred into the hallway. He faced away from them, staring into Victoria's room, holding up a fist to the invisible barrier. The barrier sparked, but this time, he didn't push through.

"What is it, Angst?" Wilfred asked. "What happened?"

"The princess and I were talking. Tori asked me if I would..." Angst stopped to take a deep breath. "Out of nowhere, it was there. Jormbrinder, a foci...through her chest. Alloria was standing behind her with the other half of the blade. There was blood, so much blood, and she ran away, fast, like I run with my foci. I wanted to pull the dagger free, I wanted to save her, but Dulgirgraut said I couldn't, not without the other half. So I cast a spell. I cast *the* spell. I tried to relive the day again so I could save her, but something went wrong. I failed. I..." Angst's head dropped, his loss and despair palpable.

The room was breathlessly silent. Faeoris reached out to Angst. His hands trembled, and she couldn't help wanting to comfort him. The beating could wait. She'd been angry at him for months, but this wasn't the time. Before she could think of anything to say, there was a squawk, and then a cry from the blankets in Heather's arms.

Angst's head jerked up. He turned around slowly, and his teary eyes went wide. Chryslaenor fell from his back, clattering noisily onto the marble floor, making both bundles in Heather's arms wail.

Angst took labored steps toward Heather and their babies, his face pale, filled with sorrow and wonder. He looked at his children, tears trickling down his cheeks. His gaze turned to Heather and he swayed on wobbly legs. Faeoris moved behind him.

"I'm so sorry," he said, his voice shaky.

"Oh, Angst," Heather said. She sounded so happy to see him.

"What have I done?" Angst asked.

Faeoris caught him as he collapsed.

2

He wanted to fake it—to just stay on this uncomfortable cot, ignore the growing ache in his back, shut out the noisy room, and pretend to sleep. Like most things these days, he didn't seem to have a choice—there was so much that needed doing. But more than anything, Angst wanted to lie still and pretend to be unconscious. It felt like he hadn't slept in months, but his tiredness wasn't merely a lack of sleep; it was a bone-weary exhaustion, as if he'd spent a week moving a friend's furniture. Couldn't he have just a little more time to understand what had happened? Angst had wanted to be a hero, and then he was, and now wasn't he supposed to be celebrating? Sleep sounded like a great way to celebrate.

So very much had happened since wielding Chryslaenor, he could barely fathom it. Before the foci, Angst had spent a lifetime doing nothing. He'd filed documents for the crown in a castle cellar where even the candlelight had seemed dim. He'd had some friends, including the young princess Victoria. He'd had some foes, including her mother Isabelle. He'd loved his wife, and they'd only argued every third day. It hadn't been a terrible life, except, he'd known it wasn't his.

Angst had longed to be a hero. A knight. Someone who could protect Unsel from monsters and dragons, even if they only existed in stories. Someone who was respected, despite being old, and chubby, and short. Despite being a magic wielder. As a youth, he'd pushed and begged Hector to train him to fight, teach him how to be one of those men in armor. Hector had reluctantly agreed, even though they'd both known it would never happen, because Angst was a wielder. Wielding the magics had been mostly illegal since before memory, and Unsel was the only nation progressive enough to tolerate it even a little. His lifelong goal wasn't against all odds; there were no odds to barter with. It just wasn't going to happen.

On one prophetic night, trying to protect his friend Rose, he'd hefted the giant sword Chryslaenor, which everyone had thought was just a statue. Much more than that, the sword was a foci that enhanced his magic with vast power. When actual monsters began to attack and only "the magics" could stop them, Angst was more than happy to represent. He'd used this opportunity to drag his reluctant friends through an adventure that was filled with hope, and pain, and battle, and sacrifice, and everything required to become a hero.

That win seemed to open doors within doors. The monsters were created by one of the five elements, Magic, who was at war with the other elements, Earth, Air, Fire, and Water. When his father said, "I fought the elements," it meant he walked to school, uphill, in a windy snowstorm. Angst's fight hadn't been that simple. He'd battled physical representations of elements, and each time, it had hurt. A lot. Earth had died protecting Angst and his friends. Air was obliterated when Angst exploded bonding with a second foci, which he'd used to destroy that crazy bitch, Water. And he wasn't done.

He just didn't understand why they even needed to involve humans. This war that happened every two thousand years was like a great game to them, one that usually kept them from engaging directly. Each had their own army to fight for them. Magic created a great river of orange ooze that the Nordruaut called the Vex'kvette. Everything that touched the ooze either died, or changed into a monster. Angst had killed the scariest monster of them all, Sir Ivan. Fire used dragons, great wyrms with wings. Tori had helped him kill the biggest one. Water had an army of gargoyles, and now, maybe an army of merpeople. Air fought with cavastil, giant birds with long steel beaks—he'd killed quite a few of them racing to Unsel after fighting Ivan. Gamlin were invulnerable hedgehog porcupines that used to do Earth's bidding, and now worked for Angst.

Had he actually done all that? Not alone, and not without loss. Soldiers, uncounted heroes, had died trying to protect Unsel from attacks by Water and Magic. Half of Melkier's grand central city was destroyed when Fire dropped a sun on them, or whatever that was. He'd watched Vars slay Victoria's mother, Queen Isabelle, and her Captain Guard, Tyrell. And then, his friends Rook and Janda. And then, Moyra. All of it was his fault. Nothing had happened until he'd touched the sword. These thoughts roiled through his head. He struggled to keep his eyes shut, until he heard it...heard them. A disgruntled "wah" followed closely by another, and his eyes shot open with panic. He was the father of twins. He sat up, and reached out with both arms, making everyone in the room gasp.

"Please." He beckoned.

Without a word, Heather stepped forward and rested the twins in his arms. He could see her face in theirs, and maybe his too. One suckled a thumb before quieting, the other took a minute of rocking. He wasn't sure where the rocking came from, but his body leaned into the cadence instinctively. The little bundles snuggled into the crook of his arms and fell asleep. His children were warm, and comforting, and his shoulders relaxed. For the first time, looking at them, he felt he'd done something right.

He looked at Heather with all the apology he could muster in his eyes. Hers were cool, but she smiled. Her beautiful face was framed with brown, curly hair that had just begun to gray. She was almost his height, and curvy in a way he appreciated more than she did. Neither of them were thin, but she'd kept youth in her face far better than he had, and in his eyes, not much had changed. Heather blushed at his thoughtful gaze, and her look thawed slightly.

After several moments, he realized that his wife and children weren't the only ones in the room. Guards stood at the entrance, both men he recognized, who nodded respectfully. Physician Nynette stood over Jaden as he slept. He breathed slowly in his deep slumber, but at least he was breathing.

Beside his wife stood Angst's tall, stunning Berfemmian friend Faeoris. He couldn't help but be surprised she was still here. How long had it been since he'd cast the spell? It had to have been months, so it was surprising that she'd waited. Faeoris was a far better friend than he'd hoped for or deserved after their brief adventure. She stood a head and shoulder taller than his wife. Her face was pretty, with high cheekbones, full, full lips, and dark eyes that complemented her fine, light brown hair. Like most Berfemmian, she was mostly naked, which was great. She wore a small, armored top that pushed her breasts up and together in a wonderfully distracting way. Her tiny leather shorts had scaled armor protecting both hips, and her legs were covered with shiny leather boots that almost reached her shorts. He smiled curiously at her, and she replied with a quizzical gaze.

"I'm glad to see you," he said. "But surprised that you didn't return to Angoria. Won't they be lost without you?"

"Marisha is leading in my stead," she said. "And I would never leave a friend in need."

"I never doubted you'd have my back," Angst said with a nod, still meeting her gaze.

"Good," she replied curtly. Faeoris nodded at the young woman in a bed to his left. "Who's that?"

Angst turned his head to one side, stretching his neck over the bundle in his arms. His eyes widened. The young woman breathed as deeply and steadily as Jaden. A mane of light brown curls poured over her shoulders. She was beautiful, with a tanned complexion, dark eyebrows, shapely lips, and a little nose. Aerella. They'd met at the cursed mage city Gressmore, which had relived the same day for two thousand years. When Angst killed the man who'd created the curse, her father Anderfeld, his friends had been thrown free from the city, and Aerella with them. She'd adventured with them for a short time before being sucked into a vortex by the monster Ivan. Angst had feared her dead, except that she kept showing up in his dreams to warn him, guide him, and annoy him.

"An old friend," Angst replied.

"I'm not that old," Aerella said in her husky voice, propping herself up on her elbows. "At least, I hope I don't *look* that old."

"You're awake!" Angst said in surprise. He wanted to leap out of bed, but exhaustion and babies kept him in place. "What happened? Where have you been?"

"In time," Aerella said, gently massaging her temples.

"Why wait?" Angst asked. "You can tell me now."

"No, I mean I've been lost in time. I'll explain more later, when the world stops spinning," she said with a thick tongue. "But I think this is it."

The physician brought her a metal cup of water, which Aerella gulped down.

"What's it?" Angst asked.

"It means I've been traveling through centuries to end up here," she said firmly, pushing herself upright and facing him with a stern gaze. "It means that I'm here to stop you from destroying the world."

"Great," he replied.

3

Fulk'han

Guldrich knelt on his mount, placing a calming hand on its back as he looked up at the full moon. He took a welcome breath of the crisp spring breeze—a moment's respite from the stench beneath him. It was worth it; every moment of hard work, and pain, and frustration had all led to this. Four months ago, the Fulk'han leadership had tried to jail him for failing to overthrow Unsel. They'd wanted revenge against Angst for killing Takarn Ivan. Guldrich had, indeed, failed. The Fulk'han had underestimated the wielders in Unsel, a mistake that would never happen again.

Before he was jailed, a purple Fulk'han woman, Felicia, had tasked him to find a champion. The woman had cast a magic portal and pushed him through. He'd appeared in Nordruaut, and spent weeks battling the giants to free himself. Guldrich had even lost his arm during a battle with their champion and been shocked to learn that his new ability to heal was powerful enough to grow another one. He'd learned many things, about himself and about the Nordruaut. More importantly, he'd found something. Something big. Something powerful.

Guldrich had waited three months before returning to Fulk'han. As a general and an experienced warrior, he knew the importance of timing. It was imperative that the arm cut off by

17

the Nordruaut champion, Niihlu, was fully healed and strong. He also needed to collect information, which had been graciously provided by his purple seductress. More importantly, it had taken that long just to come to terms with the monster, their new champion.

He looked down at his new arm. Before Niihlu had sliced it with the giant frozen axe, his bicep and forearm had been covered with scars, a mark for every kill. It now looked naked, and he rubbed at the bony protrusions on his gray forearm, hungering to replace what was missing. He took another deep breath and gritted his teeth before Felicia placed a hand on his shoulder.

"It's time, my general," she said, her voice husky and sincere.

Part of him still wanted to kill her for casting him into Nordruaut unprepared, for making him suffer through the challenge. But without her magic, he would never have discovered how truly weak the Nordruaut had become. He would never have learned that he could heal through the loss of limb. He would never have discovered their champion. She'd been useful, in *many* ways, and she'd been right. Somehow she knew, always knew, what was coming. Her furry purple tail rose seductively up his spine before reaching his neck, wrapping around to brush his cheek affectionately. Guldrich ignored it as best he could, and nodded in agreement.

He stood beside Felicia on his champion's broad shoulders and stepped down hard. "Forward!" he commanded.

The creature let out a wet snort before tromping toward the capital. Light from a thousand torches in the center of the city cast a glow, as soldiers congregated around the remains of Takarn Ivan. Upon their approach, however, he couldn't help but be impressed with how many Fulk'han had gathered to march. Felicia had explained that, without him, they would march to their slaughter. He had to do this, he had to save his people, and the only way was to set them on the right path.

"Slowly," he said to his champion. "We don't want to kill, just scare. For now."

Soldiers gasped and shouted as Guldrich approached. He ignored them and the tension he sensed from men and women preparing to war. Some raised shaky spears, but all scurried away from his mount. A sea of gray men covered in bone armor and beautiful furry women of all colors parted way, making a path to Emperor Gath, General Arbeter, and Sergeant Adviser Beld.

Guldrich scoffed aloud. Gath had the gall to stand at the base of Takarn Ivan. The tree-like husk of Ivan's remains still retained power, orange embers flitting about it like fireflies. Its dark tendrils reached high up into the night. Felicia shivered beside him at the sight, but said nothing.

Gath appeared an easy target, small and weak. Guldrich reminded himself of the plan, that the Fulk'han leadership could still be useful. He didn't want to be a bureaucrat; he was a general. But if they didn't comply, he may not have a choice.

"What...what is this?" Emperor Gath shouted. "Guldrich? Is that you?"

Guldrich let the question hang in the air. "We are at a time of champions, Emperor. Every nation is coming forward with a hero to represent them on the battlefield. It is time for Fulk'han to have a champion of its own!"

He stomped his foot twice, and the creature he called Lurp awkwardly reached over its shoulder and pulled them from its back with a giant hand, setting them down as gently as a hammer. Guldrich winced as his knees buckled, and Felicia yelped in pain. He glanced back at his champion in irritation, and his heart skipped a beat. Even after these months, the beast was horrid to look at.

Lurp wasn't merely a mount or a man; it was something else. It had taken Guldrich days to dig Lurp free of the confines of the Vex'kvette. Like a goldfish placed in a larger pond, Lurp quickly grew. The hand sticking out of the ground that had grabbed his leg had become large enough to lift several men. After setting them down, it rested on its fists—all six of them—like a gorilla. Each fist had a thumb but only three thick fingers, as if there wasn't room for a pinky. Lurp had no feet, merely hands attached to arms the size of old tree trunks. His torso was easily twenty yards in length, covered in wispy hair that hung from his body in patches.

The monster's skin was mottled, a splatter painting of black and olive and peach, as though the Vex'kvette couldn't decide which skin would dominate from the creatures it had combined. Lurp's dark charcoal face was too thin for a 'human' that large, as if someone had squeezed his cheeks until his forehead jutted out in a lumpy protrusion. His right ear was proportionally normal, while his left hung off kilter and rested low like a guilty labrador's. His bottom teeth stuck up in all directions from his jutting jaw, like trees after an earthquake, several almost reaching his large pug nose. But the most frightening thing about Lurp wasn't his six arms, folds of muscles, or terrible smell. It was his eyes. Those eyes that seemed far, far too intelligent and attentive for a nightmare apparition.

Guldrich tore his gaze away and met the emperor's eyes. Eyes that seemed far less intelligent than they should've. Emperor Gath had aged quickly over the last three months. Was it a sign of weakness? He rubbed his bare arm and took a deep, restrained breath.

"Our champion, my liege," Guldrich said with a short bow. "I call him Lurp."

Gath appeared disappointed, as if the bow wasn't enough, but it was all Guldrich would give. The old, gray man hesitated. He looked from the giant to Guldrich, calculating the connection. His awe-filled visage twisted to disgust, as if Guldrich had shown him a pile of feces.

"This is no champion," Gath spat, waving Lurp away like a fly. "This is a Vex'kvette monster. Nothing more. We have no time for your nonsense, Guldrich. We march on Unsel, to finish what you failed to do!"

"You're going the wrong way," Guldrich shouted so all could hear.

Soldiers chuckled hesitantly, looking at each other as if deciding whether the general was just crazy, or actually mocking the emperor. Guldrich needed their attention, quickly. Many were loyal enough to Gath, but marching on Unsel would mean facing wielders they couldn't defend against. As far as he knew, Felicia was the only Fulk'han to wield magic, and nothing she had cast could be used as a weapon. No, one wielder wouldn't be enough to face Unsel, nor was Unsel their true goal.

"You've gone crazy in your absence." Gath shook his head in disbelief. "We know where Unsel is."

"No one here cares about Unsel. You're marching to find Angst," Guldrich said. "The man who killed Takarn-Ivan."

Heads bowed and soldiers muttered in agreement. Spittle formed on Gath's thin lips as he waved one of his advisers forward. The gray man whispered something in his ear.

"Angst hasn't left Unsel for months," the man stated. "We will find him at their capital, and destroy him."

"He will be leaving soon," Guldrich said, surprising himself with patience.

"Where do you think he is going?" Beld asked, swallowing hard as he looked up at Lurp.

Guldrich looked at Felicia. The purple woman's eyes were always hungry seduction, and they peered at him as she nodded in confirmation.

"To Nordruaut," he said firmly. "This is where we must bring the battle."

"Nordruaut?" Gath laughed. "We aren't prepared to face those giants; they would slaughter us."

"The giants are weak," Guldrich called, turning away to speak to the soldiers. "I killed a score of them myself. Stories of their strength are just that: stories. I hunted them like cattle and walked away a free man. They are not the danger. We hunt for Angst, and he heads north."

A strong, bony hand clamped onto his wrist and Gath raised it high for everyone to see. "Then where are your scars?" he called out. "The scars that made you a general."

Guldrich jerked his hand free and held it up high. "I lost this arm in a battle with the Nordruaut champion, a man who wields a weapon as powerful as Angst's. A weak fool, who I defeated!

My arm, this arm," he made a fist and shook it, "grew back, new and powerful. We are immortal, brothers and sisters. We cannot lose. We have nothing to fear from a physical attack. We will defeat the giants, and all other nations will fear us. But first, we hunt for Angst. Join me on the march to Nordruaut."

"Insanity," Gath cried out. "Guards, take this traitor in chains, or kill him now. I'm done wasting my time."

Soldiers closest looked up at Lurp. The giant creature licked its nose thoughtlessly before peering at them. They shuffled back to the safety of the crowd.

"Guards!" Gath commanded again.

"I tried," Guldrich said with a sigh, looking at Felicia, who nodded vigorously in agreement. He pointed at Gath. "Lurp, feed!"

Guldrich turned away as Lurp grabbed the screaming emperor. There was a loud crunch followed by cries from nearby soldiers. Blood and carcass spilled at his feet. He pointed at General Arbeter. Lurp's giant hand scooped him up like a bug, and the general's fearful screams were cut short as teeth gnashed on bone. Guldrich held up a hand and approached Beld. He said nothing.

Beld immediately fell to his knees. "Emperor Guldrich!" Beld cried, touching his forehead to the ground.

Guldrich smiled.

4

Unsel

"Why would I destroy Ehrde?" Angst asked, dumbfounded. "That wouldn't even cross my mind...most days."

"It's not why, Angst, it's when," Aerella said forcefully. "I need to clearly understand what point of time I'm in. What's the last thing you remember?"

"I was talking with Victoria before her inauguration," Angst said, his heart speeding. "Her cousin, Alloria, snuck into the room, stabbed her with a dagger, and ran out."

"Why didn't you just remove the dagger and heal her?" Aerella asked, frowning sternly.

"It's a foci. Actually, half a foci. Jormbrinder the Exception," Angst explained. His words came out thick and heavy. To him, the attack on Victoria had just happened. And now he was supposedly destroying Ehrde? He wanted to pass out again, but his roiling stomach wouldn't let him.

"Jormbrinder...I hate that one," she said with a harrumph. "Yes, I'm familiar. Amongst other things, it dampens magic. A lot. You couldn't have healed her, or even pulled it free without the other half."

"That's what Dulgirgraut told me, so I cast the spell, the same one your father used," Angst explained. "I even uttered the words, 'at all costs.'"

"Good thing you failed," she said.

"What do you mean?" he asked, his stomach gurgling loudly. What else had he done wrong?

"My father's spell cursed Gressmore Towers and its inhabitants to relive the same day for two thousand years. Your spell should've done the same thing. Instead, you slowed time, and only in Victoria's room. It isn't supposed to work like that. I'm not even sure how you accomplished it. Maybe Jormbrinder affected the spell."

"I don't understand everything you're saying," Faeoris said. "But now that you've got two swords, could that have..."

"You what?" Aerella shouted, balling up her fists. "You actually bonded with another?"

"I didn't have a choice," Angst started to explain.

"I told you not to!" Aerella's husky voice became louder, yet her throat sounded dry and scratchy. "Do you know how hard it was to project myself into your dreams from another place...another time? Each time I did, I'd pass out for days. I could've been killed!"

"Well, you weren't very clear about it," Angst said defensively. "You said not to bond with another. I'd just lost Chryslaenor and had to bond with Dulgirgraut or I would've died. Nothing happened...well, other than living. I thought that's what you meant by 'another.'"

"You should pay attention! I meant you shouldn't bond with two at the same time," Aerella snapped. "How did you do it, anyway?"

"Some tall, old wielder was trying to force Chryslaenor to bond with Rose. She was in pain. It could've killed her. So, I did the only thing I could think of to save her. I bonded with Chryslaenor instead. I thought it would kill me, and Dulgirgraut hated it, but Jormbrinder was stuck to me. Half of it, anyway. And Rose was holding onto my leg. I can only guess that between Jormbrinder dampening magic and Rose's healing, I was able to bond with the second foci," Angst said.

"A perfect storm," Aerella said, shaking her head in disbelief.

"Not really perfect. I sort of exploded," Angst said with a shudder. "Not really my favorite thing to do..."

"What do you mean you exploded?" she asked, her eyes wide. "You didn't explode. You're not in little pieces."

"He did," Faeoris said, her eyes glassy. "I saw it. I thought...we all thought you'd died."

"Then...how are you still here?" Aerella asked.

"Because I'm not done yet," he said with finality. "I willed myself back together."

Her eyes widened with fright and awe, her jaw lowered, and she gripped her chest. Angst sought Heather, who was pale and looked sick with worry. This probably hadn't been the best time to tell that particular story.

"What else was I supposed to do?" he asked the room, a little too loudly. "I wasn't going to let anyone die. I had to go be a hero...why are you all looking at me like I'm a monster?"

"You aren't supposed to be able to do that, Angst. Nobody is." Aerella seemed to be breathing very fast.

"Well, I did," Angst said. "See? I've done the impossible; what could possibly go wrong now?"

Everyone moaned, and he couldn't help but smirk at the reaction.

"I've been to the future," she said. "The details of what happened are unclear. Historians believe that being bonded with two foci drove you mad. In your madness, you broke Ehrde."

Heather pulled a baby from Angst's arm before he could reply. He didn't know if his wife was upset or scared until a wave of emotion struck him like a slap. Upset was an understatement. Faeoris hesitantly took the other child, looking at the baby as if it were covered in warts.

"We're going home," Heather said, her cheeks blotchy. "We'll be there when you're ready to talk."

"I'll fetch you after I see them home safely," Faeoris said warningly, spinning on the heel of her tall black boot.

"That should be fun," Angst said with a deep sigh.

"No," Faeoris said over one shoulder, "it won't be."

The guards stepped out of her way as she stomped after Heather, both holding their breath until the Berfemmian was out of sight. Physician Nynette glanced over her patients, shook her head, and followed the parade of angry women and cranky babies. Angst fell back against his lumpy pillow, not knowing if he should chase after them or stay hiding here, wallowing in self-pity. Wallowing sounded safer.

"Is your life always this complicated?" Aerella asked.

"You don't even know," he said.

Aerella got up from her creaky bed and walked barefoot around his to the other side of the room. He flopped his head over to watch as she inspected Jaden. Her small hand glowed a gentle yellow, the soft color of spring tulips, and she placed it on the young man's forehead.

"Hmm," she said thoughtfully.

"Is that your diagnosis?" Angst asked, grouchy at the sudden change in topic. How does one go from 'You're going to break Ehrde' to molesting an unconscious man's forehead without pause?

She ignored him, resting her fingers on Jaden's face, occasionally moving them around as if re-sculpting it. After many long moments, she spoke. "He's fine."

"Then why isn't he waking up like we did?" Angst asked.

"He's fine in the sense that he's still alive," she said, turning to face him. "He's time-locked. His mind is still stuck in that spell you tried to cast."

"How do you know I cast it wrong?" he snapped. "Have you ever cast the spell?"

"No," she said. "I don't have a foci."

"I have two," he replied.

"But the results were different for my father," she said.

"Maybe the spell does what you need it to. Maybe it adapts for different foci," he said, arguing away his grouch. "Or for different people?"

"That's not how magic works," she said, her brows knitting.

"Last time you were here, you said magic changes," Angst

continued. "Are you sure?"

"Yes, that's not how it's supposed to work," she said firmly. She stared into his eyes for a long time before looking at the ground. "No, I'm not completely sure."

The tension in his shoulders eased, and he took a breath. He needed answers more than he needed to verbally abuse someone.

"Why was he even in there?" Angst asked, but he already knew the answer. Jaden and Tori had been falling in love when the princess ran off to adventure with Angst. The idiot had probably jumped in to save her. "Never mind. Will he wake up?"

"When the spell is broken," she replied, walking over to his bed and sitting down. She reached out and placed her hands on his forehead.

He grabbed her wrists and pushed them away gently.

"What is it?" she asked.

"You said you were here to stop me. We aren't going to fight, are we?" He tried to remain calm. She was powerful, her knowledge of magic far surpassing his, or even Dallow's.

"I thought we *were* fighting," she said, her lip curling in a half-smile.

"That's not what I meant," he said, embarrassed. He'd forgotten how cute she was. "I mean, you know, do battle."

She laughed and pulled her hands back. "I don't wield a foci."

"And I wield—"

"Two. I heard you." Aerella grunted. "We just went over this. I even vaguely remember telling you not to."

"Vaguely?" he asked. "It was just a couple months ago."

"For you," she said. "I have a different relationship with time."

"What do you mean, relationship?" Angst asked. So little of what she said made sense, a direct answer would be welcome.

"I'm not usually stuck in any single period for very long," she replied patiently. "Our paths have crossed, or will cross, many times, Angst. But I think, for me, this may be the last time."

"So we are going to battle," he said, unable to hide the concern in his voice. "I don't want to hurt you."

"That sounds like a good idea," she said. "And I have no plans to battle you. I'm here to guide you through the rough journey ahead. If I understand when I am, things are going to get worse."

"Don't they always," Angst said, letting out a deep sigh.

She hovered over him for a second, but seemed to reconsider touching his forehead and instead gave him a friendly hug.

"Thanks," he said, gently returning it.

"It's good to see you again," she said. "You've been one of my closest friends, and an anchor for me. I was angry with you when I was pulled away from my father and Gressmore, but I would've died. Instead, I've lived a lifetime full of adventure, and I..." She clutched her stomach and let out a moan, sitting abruptly on the cot.

Angst shuffled to one side, placing a hand on her shoulder.

She continued groaning and lay down beside him.

"What's wrong?" he asked, inching away to make room on the small bed. "Do you need the physician?"

"I'm not sure." She grunted, her body tense. "I think...there is nothing she can do."

A cough interrupted Angst before he could ask what she meant. General Mirot entered the room, his hands behind his back and shoulders at attention. The general had been one of Isabelle's advisors and had a reputation for voting against any law supporting wielders. He gazed at them with the cool watchful eye of a seasoned veteran who'd lived through many a battle. Mirot didn't sneer or look down at Angst judgmentally, but he watched cautiously. Angst had seen Hector look at people that way, right before killing them.

"Am I interrupting anything?" Mirot asked.

"Just sick people being sick," Angst said wryly. "Welcome to the infirmary."

"Thank you for pointing that out," Mirot said, his cheeks reddening.

"Are you sick?" Angst asked. "Or were you just hoping to see dead wielders?"

"I didn't come to argue, Mr. Angst," Mirot said.

"You're the first," Angst replied.

The tension in Aerella's body lessened. She was shaking slightly, but she still pulled away and sat up. Her forehead glistened with beads of sweat.

"I'm fine now," she said dismissively.

"I'm not sure I agree," Angst said. "There's no hurry to get up."

"No, it's okay," she replied, abruptly standing. Her cheeks flushed crimson. "How can we help you?"

"Right," Mirot said with a wince. It looked like the man was biting his tongue. "Wilfred would like to see you."

"Wilfred the Short?" Angst asked. "How's my buddy?"

"Ahem." Mirot coughed into a hand before replying, his voice heavy with formality. "Your buddy, Wilfred the Wise, seems to be tired from running Unsel."

5

Angst stood in front of the doorway of Victoria's room. A shimmer in the air defined the barrier of time he'd created with Dulgirgraut. He wanted to reach out to her, to pluck her from this prison he'd created. Bonded to both swords, he should have enough power to heal her, and then everything could go back to normal. Whatever that was. A long, triangular dagger stuck out of her chest, and drops of blood hung in the air, their falling slowed by his spell. Angst clutched his fists as the memory flashed before him. He needed to find Alloria. She had the other half; maybe she could remove it. He needed to find her, now.

"Angst," Wilfred pleaded from the hallway behind him. "Unsel is in great danger."

"Exactly why I'm going to leave," Angst replied firmly, turning to face Wilfred and Aerella. "I'm going to help by saving Victoria. Unsel needs her."

"Please, my friend," Wilfred said. "She may already be dead, and our nation could soon follow."

"What do you mean?" he asked.

"War, Angst." Wilfred leaned back against a wall in the hallway. He appeared exhausted; deep circles had burrowed between his thick cheeks and tired eyes. "In the three months you've been...unavailable, the Fulk'han have been raiding our border towns to the east. Civil war has broken out between east and west Nordruaut. Melkier is amassing a new army and getting ready to march on our southern borders, and Rohjek..." The short man grabbed the girth of his belly and looked down, as if trying not to vomit.

"What happened to Rohjek?" Angst asked softly.

"Gone, all of it." Wilfred was pale and shaken. "Burnt to ashes by Fire and dragons."

"No," Angst said in disbelief, waiting for the temporary king to say it was a bad joke. He didn't.

"It's chaos," Wilfred said, breathing in heavily. "We've heard reports that Fulk'han will attack Unsel soon. We believe the raids are merely testing our defenses."

The zealots in Fulk'han hated him for killing their god, Takarn-Ivan, and Melkier blamed Angst for destroying their city, and they were both partially right. Had he actually been a hero, or a catalyst for disaster? Angst avoided Wilfred's gaze, feeling guilty for putting Unsel in the middle of this war that wasn't his. He couldn't even believe that Rohjek was gone. How could an entire nation be destroyed?

"This isn't your fault, Angst," Aerella said knowingly. "This happens every two thousand years. The elements pit humans against each other, distracting us from their war. Weeding us out so we aren't a danger. I've watched this happen, time and time again."

Angst shook his head. It was all too much to take in. Of course, he didn't want to leave Unsel in danger, but Victoria... He faced Wilfred. "So, you're saying I need to hurry."

Wilfred grunted, his hands balled into fists. "You're every bit as aggravating as Isabelle said."

"Well, what do you expect? She hated me," Angst said flippantly.

"No, not really," Wilfred said. "She feared you, respected you, and you pissed her off, frequently. She never hated you."

"I seem to get that from a lot of people," Angst said. "I need to find Alloria and the other half of Jormbrinder. That's our best chance to save Tori."

"How do you propose we do that?" Aerella asked.

"Can't you cast something to find Jormbrinder?" he asked, waving his hand magically.

She shook her head.

A blue glow emanated from Chryslaenor, and Angst listened to the song. It wasn't what he wanted to hear.

"Chryslaenor can't locate it either," he said. "I can't imagine that a spell hasn't been created to locate other foci."

"Maybe," Aerella said hesitantly. "There may have been some knowledge in the Gressmore library, a spell in one of the tomes. But those volumes are lost to time and the dragons who burned them."

"Dallow!" Angst said, snapping his fingers. "Dallow is a reader. He absorbed every book he could find during our visit."

"Then let's ask him," Aerella said with a smile.

"That's the other thing, Angst," Wilfred said. "Rose, Tarness, Dallow, and Hector haven't made it back yet."

"Of course not," Angst said with a sigh. "Why would this be easy?"

"Then we must find your friends in order to find the other half of Jormbrinder," Aerella said.

"How much time do you even have left?" Wilfred asked, pointing at the princess's room. "The puddle of blood from Victoria's wound grows, and you were able to escape. Time has to be passing in that room. How long does she have?"

Aerella inspected the barrier between the hallway and Princess Victoria's chamber. Her hand moved from side to side as if she were washing a window, and the air between the rooms looked like fumes over a campfire that trailed her hand. She squeezed her eyes shut, her tiny nose scrunching, and touched the barrier. Red light flashed with a noisy crack, and she was thrown back into Angst's arms.

"You okay?" he asked.

"Yeah," she said, but she was breathing fast, and her heart raced like it was ready to explode.

He helped her stand and inspected her thoroughly—for damage, of course. It was the first time he'd really taken her in. She had the same luxurious mane of brown hair and sharp green eyes. Her skin had a light olive tone, and she wore the same flowing blue robes. She looked like the Aerella he had first met, except...shorter? Angst had held Aerella while she cried on his shoulder one night at Gressmore Towers. Hadn't she been the same height as him? And the worry lines in her face were gone, as if youth had returned to round out her cheeks. She suddenly looked so young that he couldn't contain his frown.

"What is it, Angst?" she asked.

"Are you feeling okay?"

"I'm fine," she said with a smile. "Thanks for catching me."

Wilfred cleared his throat, as if to remind them he was still in the room. "Can you free her, Aerella? Can you free the queen right now?"

"No," she said with a disappointed sigh. "But he can."

"No, I can't," Angst said. "She'll die."

"She's practically dead now, Angst," Aerella blurted. "You're leaving her in pain."

"She's tough," he said. "She'll manage."

Though flushed from her outburst, she composed herself. She shook her head and looked at Wilfred. "We have about three weeks. Maybe four."

"So you need to find Dallow so you can locate Alloria and Jormbrinder and get back here to save Victoria in three weeks?" Wilfred asked loudly. His arms flailed wildly, as if he were directing an orchestra.

"Yeah," Angst said hopefully.

"And how..." Aerella began.

"You know, I think you're smarter than me," Angst said sharply. "How about more answers and less questions?"

Aerella's lip quivered, and he immediately regretted not reacting more thoughtfully. She seemed so...young, her mood swaying like tree branches in a windstorm. Before he had the chance to apologize, she gathered herself and asked, "How did you locate Rose when she had Chryslaenor?"

"Yes!" he said, and she immediately perked up. "Dallow

found fragments of your father's memndus scattered about the ruins. He gave them to us as gifts. Rose had one, so we were able to track her."

"Of course," Aerella said excitedly. "Hand me the stones. I think together we could cast that spell..."

"Dallow has all of them," Angst said. "He was blinded and discovered he can use one to see. He keeps the extras for back-up."

"Fascinating," she said. "We may be able to find additional stones at Gressmore."

"We?" Angst asked. "I'm not putting your life at risk again. I just got you back."

"We'll discuss that later," she said firmly. "No matter how powerful you are, you can't do this alone."

"You can't do this at all!" Wilfred demanded. "Unsel could be attacked at any moment."

Angst thought for a moment. Wilfred was right; Unsel couldn't be left undefended. Someone had to protect Unsel, and Victoria. His efforts would be useless if the capital was overtaken before he returned. He'd gone away on two separate mission as an Al'eyrn wielding a foci, and both times Unsel had survived attack. He snapped his fingers at the realization.

"You don't need me," Angst said with a broad grin. "You've got a militia of wielders at Rookshire."

"But...but," Wilfred looked panicked, "they hate us."

"Then fix it," Angst said. "Aren't you in charge?"

"I guess," Wilfred said, rubbing his hands together. He shook his head as if tearing away from his thoughts. "But three weeks? How can that possibly be enough time?"

"Hey, all I have to do is find my friends, find Alloria and Jormbrinder, and bring them all back here to save the princess before Unsel is destroyed forever." Angst placed his hands on both hips. "I've got this!"

"Ugh," Wilfred said as if in pain. "I don't know..."

"I'm not asking," Angst said firmly.

"I thought I was in charge," he replied, his cheeks crimson.

CHAPTER FIVE

"With both swords I can do anything now, so I'm the exception," Angst said confidently, unable to hold back a wide grin.

"Of course you are," Wilfred replied with an exhausted expression. "But the Fulk'han are everywhere, and we've heard rumors of Vex'steppe tribesman spying on us, and Melkier... How will you get through all of that in time?"

"I'll cut them down," he said roughly. "I'll make a path if I have to."

"No, Angst," Aerella said, her voice gentle. "That's a lot of killing. Do you really want that on your shoulders? The elements started this. Those other nations don't even realize that they're merely pawns."

"Maybe," he allowed, but something in him itched for battle. It was irrational, and he'd never felt that way before, but he suddenly wanted to cut loose and spill blood until he was king of the mountain. He took a deep breath. "I could try being sneaky."

"With that?" Wilfred jerked a thumb over his shoulder at the giant sword glowing in the corner.

"Look, hold them off for three weeks. That's all I need," Angst said.

"And always make sure a wielder is protecting Victoria," Aerella said firmly. "It's important."

"Once I figure out how to make nice with them," Wilfred said, a bead of sweat trickling from his thinning brown hair.

Angst made his way down the corridor.

"Where are you going?" Aerella asked.

"I need a minute alone," Angst said, grabbing Chryslaenor and resting it on his back. "I've got to plan this out before I leave."

"Maybe I'll do some planning as well," Wilfred called after him.

6

How on Ehrde could he possibly accomplish every goal he'd set for himself in only three weeks? His entire life he'd been overly ambitious. Angst couldn't remember the last weekend he'd finished every project he'd planned. Exercising, and yard-work, and housework, and shopping, and lovemaking, and time with friends, and time for himself...it never came together like he expected. Finding his friends, finding Alloria and the foci Jormbrinder, and then saving Tori seemed like a lifetime's work. All of that in only three weeks? He already felt like he was wasting time. What was he even doing, wandering the halls of Unsel? He should be kissing Heather and the kids goodbye and rushing off as fast as his swifen would take him.

But, deep down, he knew where he was headed and wasn't surprised to find himself at the ruins of the maiden's courtyard. A wide, pink ribbon blocked passage through the overlarge, collapsed doorway, but the ribbon didn't block the view. He took it all in with a gasp. Memories smacked him upside the head as he looked over the destruction created by the battle between Water, her gargoyles, merpeople, and the oldest living creature on Ehrde.

Angst removed the ribbon and walked through the doorway. The maiden's courtyard had been cut in half with all the villainy and vitriol that only an element at war could bring to pass. It was as if Water had purposely destroyed the maiden's courtyard out of spite, picking up half the room and throwing it away. The marble floor ended abruptly at a jagged edge. Water dribbled from the remainders of the fountain centerpiece, droplets falling far to the ground below. Even the bench where he used to sit with Victoria was now in pieces.

This was their place! It filled him with fury that Water had destroyed the spot where he'd first met Victoria, where they'd gathered on so many occasions. It felt like an open wound. It made him angry. It made him want to weep. He wanted to destroy Water again, and again. But she was gone. And she'd taken a piece of him. Pieces. With each labored step toward the ledge, his rage slowly surrendered to a melancholy more exhausting than any illness.

The spring air was cool, and the sky seemed unsure what to do. Dark, threatening clouds were framed by beautiful blue skies, a discordant sight. Would it rain? Would the sun prevail? Angst set Chryslaenor flat on the ground, ignoring its ignoble complaints in his head, and plopped down. He inched forward until his legs hung over the ledge then leaned back on his arms, and wallowed in his despair. A large wet drop landed noisily on his leg, soon followed by several more until rain steadily pelted the dusty marble floor.

"Figures," he muttered.

Angst was sulking, and knew it, but he deserved to sulk. He'd earned the right to sulk, in the rain, in the remainders of the maiden's courtyard. Far below, soldiers guarded the newly formed inlet—a giant sinkhole created by Water that had destroyed the west side of the castle. The guts of the castle were bare for anyone to see; collapsed walls had left open rooms and hallways that jutted out painfully. It was like a tree broken in half, with splinters of marble and foundation sticking out. The sinkhole was connected to another, and another, all the way out to the sea. A new waterway from the ocean, to the capital, all so the element Water could attack Unsel. He'd stopped her, destroyed her, but at what cost?

Moyra.

He'd befriended the mermaid on their trip across the ocean. They'd connected in a way he couldn't rationalize. She'd become his muse by needing him more than anyone had. She'd accepted him, not caring that he was old, short, and pudgy. She didn't seem to care. Moyra wanted him to be Angst, wanted him to be her hero, and nothing more. He'd needed that. Needed someone who wanted just...him. And then she was gone. Killed by Water. His vision blurred, and his throat caught. He couldn't fight the tears, even knowing they wouldn't bring her back.

It wasn't just crying; it was grieving. An uncontrollable feeling of loss for someone loved. It throbbed and ached, and he hated it. Angst would've done anything to change it, anything to bring her back, but that wasn't possible. Not even for him. All this power made the guilt that much worse, and he couldn't talk to anyone about it. He stared off at the horizon and saw nothing as his mind reeled and roiled. He'd beaten Earth, and Air, and, somehow, Water, but the price was too high. He hadn't been there for the birth of his own children. His friends were gone, or dead. His best friend, Victoria, was a spell's breath from dying. His oldest friend, Dallow, had lost his eyes. And Moyra. Despair couldn't begin to describe his loss and guilt.

Wind brushed his graying hair, throwing it forward as Faeoris landed behind him. Angst didn't turn when he heard her gravelly footsteps approach, and from the corner of his eyes saw her shiny boots and long legs hang over the ledge, inches from his own as she sat. Angst quickly wiped his eyes, sat up straight, and sucked in his gut. She inched forward until she could swing her legs back and forth. On any normal day, his heart would be aflutter, and his flirt full on. This wasn't a normal day.

"Hey," he said, hoping his voice didn't sound too shaky.

"Hey," Faeoris replied.

Angst could feel her eyes on him, but refused to look back. His final ounce of pride kept him from completely losing composure in front of the beautiful young Berfemmian, even though he knew she would understand.

"Sulking?" she asked.

CHAPTER SIX

"Yup," he said.

"Is it helping?"

"Nope," he replied.

She sat up and leaned over, looking down the long drop to the sinkhole below. Angst's heart skipped a beat as he grabbed her shoulder and tried pulling her back.

"What is it?" Faeoris asked.

"It's a thing," he said, trying to play it off. From the look in her eyes, she wasn't buying it, so he continued. "I have an irrational fear...when my friends are near heights..."

"But not when you're near heights?" she asked. "The danger is the same for you, and them."

"Eh." He shrugged, only relaxing when she leaned back.

"That seems to be very Angst," she said.

"What do you mean?" he said, trying not to sound defensive.

"You seem to think it's okay that you are in danger, but not anyone else."

"Why would I want someone else to be in danger?"

"Of course you don't," she said. "That's not my point. It's simply that you aren't the only one who cares. You aren't the only hero. You're not alone."

"Oh."

"Your other friends may not be here," she said. "But I still am." She rested a hand on his and slid her fingers between his own.

Angst felt closer to Faeoris than he would've expected in such a short time. Not only had she saved him and been there when he needed her, she'd waited. She waited for three long months for him to escape the spell he'd created. He felt a connection with her, one he knew could grow stronger over time, but he worried that it was fleeting. He'd lost so many, and didn't want to lose her too.

"You don't look so good," Faeoris said.

"Do I ever?" he replied.

"Well..." She let that linger then nudged him with an elbow. "You have your moments."

"Every time I think I succeed, I fail," he tried explaining. "I protect Unsel by destroying the element Water, and not only do I lose my friends, my best friend is almost killed, and then Moyra..."

"I'm sorry for Moyra," she said softly. "I don't completely understand. I think that love and sex are different for Berfemmian, but you are hurting, and I wish it to stop for you."

He merely nodded, trying again not to cry in front of her. He took several measured breaths to calm himself, holding hands with his friend, looking over Unsel's new ocean view.

"Was she your *essent*?" Faeoris asked.

"I don't know what she was," Angst said with a deep sniff. "I'll be fine."

"You need to let her go," Faeoris said, her voice firm. "And you need to speak with your wife."

"She sent you?" he asked, taking back his hand and wiping his nose.

Faeoris nodded, looking at him with worried eyes. Rain splattered the ground more aggressively, but right now he didn't care. It was cool, but not cold, and refreshing, in a way. Faeoris crossed her arms and hunched over, obviously uncomfortable with being rained on.

"She's not happy with you," she warned. "And neither am I."

"She just thinks I'm planning to leave her and the babies to go play hero again," he said with a sigh.

"Aren't we?" she asked.

"Oh, probably." His lip curled in a half smile. "I keep reminding myself that I wanted this. I wanted to be a hero. But now that I've got it, how do I step away from it, even for a break?"

"Death," she stated as if it were as obvious as the rain.

"Oh?" He laughed. "Is that how?"

"In the songs and stories, heroes die saving the ones they love," she said. "At least the stories I've heard. Heroes always die."

"I think I need to write a better story," he said under his breath. "Of course, I've tried dying, several times. It doesn't seem to work out for me."

"Then you don't have a choice," she said. "Rather than feeling sorry for yourself, you should figure out how to do it better."

"Dying?" Angst asked with a grin.

"No," she said sternly. "Being a hero isn't just something to make you feel good about yourself. Lives are at risk. Yours, and everyone who stands with you."

"So I should do this alone?" he asked, feeling stubborn.

"Don't be stupid," she snapped, leaning forward. "Just like I can't rule the Berfemmian alone, you can't hero alone. You need to stop taking on all of the burden yourself."

"But I've got two of these things now," Angst said, jerking his thumb toward his foci. "I should be able to do anything. Nobody else should have to die."

"They will die, I will die," she said. "Everyone knows the cost or they wouldn't stand with you."

"My swords should make this easier," he said, not completely agreeing with her.

"Nothing worthwhile is easy," she said, her words crisp.

Her insight was thoughtful, even if it stung like a slap, but this conversation was becoming something else. Her tone was colder, snappier. Faeoris had shown sympathy for him when she arrived, but something was bothering her. He could feel it.

"You're upset at me?" Angst asked. "How bad is it?"

"You're still alive," she said shortly.

"There is that." He inched back from the edge and stood, clapping dirt off his hands before offering her one. "Are you going to tell me why?"

She took his hand and stood, almost pulling him forward. Faeoris was a head taller and was far too thin for how incredibly strong he knew her to be. She looked down as she brushed off the rubble.

"If there is anything left when Heather is done," she said.

Light erupted from her back, forming into wings of gold, orange, and yellow feathers. The wings were as breathtaking as she was. He barely had time to grab Chryslaenor before she gripped him under his armpits and took off, lifting him into the air.

"I have so much to look forward to," he said dryly, but his sarcasm was almost certainly lost to the wind and rain.

7

Nordruaut

King Rasaol of Nordruaut stood at a crossroads. South was .
home, the capital city Owenqua. A tall cliff to the north loomed
over the wide, snowy valley before him like a watchful parent.
Behind him, thousands of Nordruaut men and women waited
with the impatience of warriors hungry for battle. He'd been
right that they were ready for the march to war, and their blood-
thirst grew with every battle. The remains of the last littered the
valley below the cliff, peeking through snow that had been falling steadily for days. Hundreds of large Nordruaut bodies that
had stained the snow with blood were now almost lost, like footsteps washed away by the tide.

Three months of civil war had aged him. His bright platinum
hair was turning a craggy white, wispy and disheveled more so
than other Nordruaut of three hundred and eighteen. His time
was coming, but if the years didn't finally put him to rest, this
war would. He'd already lost many, but the west had lost more.
He grunted in frustration that Jarle hadn't just agreed to follow
him into battle. A bigger war was coming to Ehrde; the Dark Vivek had told him so. They needed to band together, not fight
each other. It was foolish, and exhausting, and he knew it
showed on his face.

"Why do we wait, Rasaol?" Niihlu asked. "Their loss is three times ours. A final march, and this war would be done."

Rasaol swung back to smash Niihlu across the nose. His hand hurt instantly; there was no doubt he'd done more damage to himself than his target. Once again, Niihlu had stopped using the words King or Majesty. The power of being Al'eyrn was going to the younger Nordruaut's head. Losing respect meant he would eventually lose control, and the brash insolence was unacceptable. Rasaol wanted nothing more than to beat Niihlu into submission, but that would mean one of their deaths. He needed the champion to win the coming war. And if the beating went poorly, Niihlu would kill him. Rasaol didn't fear death, but if Niihlu were to win, he would be in charge. The man couldn't lead himself out of a box, and the east would be lost, even at this late stage of civil war. He stared Niihlu down with a stern gaze and a grimace.

"Your...Your Majesty," Niihlu stuttered, wiping ice from his face where blood should have flowed.

"Don't act the fool. The Dark Vivek has advised us to wait," Rasaol said. "There is a war coming to Ehrde, a war like those in stories. We need our brothers and sisters to survive this."

"If I challenge Jarle and kill him, won't the rest follow?" Niihlu suggested, his voice still shaky.

"You would create a martyr," Rasaol said with a sigh. "We would have to march over there and slaughter them all."

"I should go and fight them all myself," Niihlu said in frustration.

Niihlu obviously hadn't thought past his bloodlust, and he spoke like a reactive child. Niihlu may have been a 'fit' for the foci, according to the strange old man, but he wasn't that intelligent. He was also broken. His face was frozen still, locked in a grimace of pain that may well become a block of ice. The Dark Vivek had forced Ghorfjend to bond with Niihlu. The end result made the old king shudder inwardly. Bonding with the foci had left Niihlu in agony as frost continuously built up on his skin only to fall off in sheets or clumps. His skin was as blue as a frozen corpse. He'd given up on clothes that broke away, choosing to wear only a fur loincloth that needed frequent replacing. Armor of any sort seemed unnecessary. The rare wound Niihlu received quickly filled with ice that eventually fell away. How was the man even alive? Or maybe he wasn't... This made him shiver visibly, something Nordruaut rarely did.

"Don't welcome death so quickly. I give my bond that we will destroy them all if we must," he replied. "But if we want those of the west to follow, they must see you as a champion and not a warlord or murderer."

"How will waiting make me a champion?" Niihlu grunted, wiping more ice crystals from his face.

"They are bait," Rasaol said. Vivek had said to wait with the news, but how else could he restrain the mad hound? "You will soon have to defeat their champion."

Niihlu laughed raucously before spitting ice to the ground. "What champion?"

"Vivek has foretold that Angst is coming, and that he will champion the west," he said. But that wasn't all. Rasaol could sense that the Dark Vivek had held something back, or maybe it was the fact that he wanted Angst alive. Something he needed to understand before explaining the details to this idiot.

Niihlu's eyes went wide, and for a moment, ice crackled across the Nordruaut's body. "I..." Niihlu said, barely able to restrain his excitement. "I get to kill Angst?"

"Beating Angst is how you will prove yourself as champion of Nordruaut," Rasaol said proudly, slapping the young man on the shoulder before jerking his hand back in pain from the cold. "That is the story I was told."

"So we just wait?" he asked through gritted teeth.

"No. They are already downtrodden. Keep them that way," Rasaol commanded. "Go and make your challenge. Shout threats. Spread fear to those who won't join us. Tell them to present a champion."

Niihlu nodded once before taking off through the white sea of corpses. When he arrived at the middle of the battlefield, he roared his challenges, his voice too loud for a mere mortal.

Rasaol nodded, wishing this could've played out a different way, and trying very hard not to question every decision that had led him to this point.

* * * *

Nordruaut was bleeding, and there was nothing Jarle could do about it. He looked down at the valley—a pristine white back-drop painted with splatters of red and brown. Bodies of Nordruaut giants from east and west were quickly being en-gulfed by the snowstorm. It was everything he'd wanted to avoid. He reached down to scratch at the ears of his companion, a fully grown black bear. It lifted a paw, brushing at the gash across its face. The injury had been earned on the battlefield. Jarle had feared the bear would be lost when the axe struck, but he'd endured.

King Rasaol had wanted to turn away from everything they'd worked for so long to change. Over two thousand years, they'd sought peace through the hunt. The hunt was a good way to live, but some still hungered for the march of war. Rasaol had warned of rumbling in the south, said that the only way to be safe was to go on the offensive. While Jarle had his fears, he had to won-der...could Rasaol be right?

Tribesman and dragons had overtaken Rohjek. Berfemmian and merpeople had been spotted battling in Unsel. The Fulk'han zealots were suddenly monsters able to fight off the great Nordruaut giants. Melkier had been silenced after the destruction of their capital city, and the Meldusians were all but washed away by the mysterious Vex'kvette. It was madness. But who could've foreseen this? Jarle feared that a Nordruaut attack on the south would be genocide for any other nation, as it was for the Mendahir. He'd walked away from Rasaol's offer to wage war, and it had followed him. A civil war between his west and the powerful east.

A cry from deep in the valley made him grind his teeth and clench his fists.

"King Jarle," a young Nordruaut said as he approached.

CHAPTER SEVEN

"I said don't call me that, Gose," Jarle grunted over his shoulder. "I am skaadi. No more, no less."

"Their champion is shouting challenges," Gose said.

He took a deep breath of the cold air, and his muscles tensed. Was it truly time? Was he prepared to fight their Al'eyrn? He'd watched the challenge with Guldrich. The Fulk'han monster was ferocious, and cunning. The gray man was covered in armor that seemed to grow from his body. But, even after scarring the champion, Guldrich had lost. Jarle didn't fear death—his life was full from stories and the hunt. There was still strength in his muscles, and he would do what was needed to see his people safe.

"Niihlu," Jarle grunted.

"I will meet his challenge," Gose said. "It is said that their champion is no longer Nordruaut. He is death walking. I would prove them wrong."

"Is that the story now being told?" Jarle said with a grimace. "That Niihlu is death? He is merely a Nordruaut with an axe of power. I have told the story, many times, of how a single Fulk'han almost beat him." He shook his head in disbelief. "No, not death. He has weakness."

"But he has killed so many," Gose said. "He needs to be stopped."

Jarle looked at the young man and nodded. His nephew was covered in furs much lighter than his own, only stained by blood instead of years on the hunt. Jarle was not weak, but Gose had thick layers of powerful muscle. In spite of the cold, he wore only a fur vest, his arms heated by youth and steaming at the touch of snow. His long, platinum hair was pulled out of the way, held together by a feather thong. His tanned face was stern, but his blue eyes were caring. His bed was rarely empty. He was both a fine warrior and good adviser. Jarle's only wish was that the young man's life would yet be full of stories.

"Too many have died by his axe," Jarle agreed, patting his nephew on the shoulder. "What challenge does the mad warrior call out today?"

"Niihlu does sound like a fool." Gose chuckled. "He asked us to join them, like anyone would after *that* battle. He calls out that all will die by his hand but in the same breath says that he will wait to meet our champion," Gose said. "Is he asking for you?"

"I'm no king, nor am I a champion," Jarle said. "But there may be another."

"I don't understand," Gose said. "What do we do?"

"We wait," Jarle said. "Our brothers to the east have already forgotten how to hunt. Hunting often requires waiting."

"Are we hunting, or are we waiting to die?" Gose asked.

Jarle stared into the young man's eyes for a long time. "We hunt."

* * * *

"Have you learned anything?" Rose asked, pacing the small room.

"I believe..." Hector said, taking a deep breath and holding it. His face was pensive.

"What?" she asked, nodding for him to continue.

"I...I think..." he said.

"Hector," she said, her hunger for information being fed by impatience.

"I sincerely believe," he said, turning away from the window, "that we're in Nordruaut."

She slugged his shoulder several times until he held up his sinewy, muscular arms in mock defense. He let out a gravelly laugh, and there was a mischievous twinkle in his eye under those bushy gray eyebrows. It wasn't really funny, but laughter was something they had in short supply, and she couldn't help but smile. They'd become closer over the last three months, and while she didn't always appreciate the older man, she liked him more. He could be callous, and demanding, and raucous, but he was also sharp as an ice pick and just as dangerous.

"You know that's not what I meant!" she said with a last smack to his arm. "You're as bad as Angst!"

CHAPTER SEVEN

A crunch resounded in the small room as Hector bit into a ripe apple. He peered out the window again, his brows furrowing over a gaze that saw far, far beyond her own.

"What?" Rose urged him. "What's going on?"

"You just asked me that," he said with a sigh.

"I can't see what you can," she said, exhausted by his taunting. Rose tugged at her fine red hair, which was far too long for her liking. One would think there'd be scissors in a city so large. She would shave it all off, given the chance.

"They aren't doing anything. The battle has been done for days," Hector replied impatiently. "There are three times as many Nordruaut on the east side of the ravine. This could be over in an hour, maybe two. I just don't understand why they aren't fighting. I only see a speck of a man, from this distance, in the middle of the valley. What could the fool be doing?"

Rose looked around warily, apparently uncertain if this tower had been a good find. It was obviously a lookout, the highest point in the center of the city, with windows circling the room. But, what had it gained them? The knowledge that the world continued outside while they remained locked in this city?

"Aren't you supposed to be gathering dinner?" he asked, taking another sloppy bite of apple.

"How can you think of food at a time like this?" Rose replied.

"First order of business," Hector replied. "Survival."

"There's food in this mage city. Enough to last a lifetime," she said. "If necessary."

"Good," he said, shaking his head as he stared out the window.

"We can't just sit here!" she demanded.

"Oh, yes we can," he replied. After a final nibble of apple, he looked around the room for a place to drop it. "Look, even if we could get out of here, where would we go? How would we get home?" Hector rapped a knuckle against the glass. "And how would we get through that?"

He wasn't referring to the window as much as the shield. They could only assume it was a dome, like the underwater mage city. The shield protected them against the harsh, ongoing winter of Nordruaut, assuming that was where they were. It also had no doors. They'd discovered the entrance, but no exit.

"So, what are you looking for?" she asked. "You come up here every day."

"Lots of things... Anything," he said. "I don't know. After months of looking, we haven't found a way out, and won't be able to until Dallow can find a spell that lets us out. I believe he will, but we need an exit strategy, or at least we need the giants to go away. I'm trying to plan for whatever happens."

"Do you have a plan?" she asked.

"Nope," Hector said, and his ears rose as he smiled. "How could I have a plan when I don't know what will happen?"

"So, Dallow is torturing himself trying to learn a new language, I'm feeding us every...felking...day," she grumbled. "And you're up here making no plan?"

"What else am I going to do?" he asked. "You said we don't need food. I can't read the books here any better than Dallow. It's a gilded cage—nicely gilded, but also boring. At least the mages could've left some alcohol behind, or steak, or..." Hector crossed his arms and looked at her with a frown. "How is Dallow doing? Any progress?"

"He mostly keeps to himself." She grunted in frustration.

"Not the romantic getaway you were looking for?" Hector asked with a wink.

"No!" she said, crossing her arms. "He's just... He's obsessed. Dallow blames himself for Tarness's death."

"Tarness could still be alive," he said, facing her with serious eyes. "Don't give up."

"No," she replied. "And I'm not having this conversation again. You two need to let go."

"Go on," Hector said with a nod. "Dallow?"

"He was at the main library again, before I even woke up this morning," she said. "But last night he mumbled that he might be closer, or something."

"Let's go check on the hermit," he said with a contagious

smile. "He probably needs a break. I certainly do."

"What about your watching?" she asked sarcastically.

"If we hurry, I shouldn't miss too much," he said with a wink.

8

Unsel

It wasn't easy estimating how high up they were when being flown around by his armpits. Angst guessed it had to be halfway between the tree line and the low-hanging clouds, whatever that meant. It was high enough to make his heart race, and low enough that he didn't pee himself. Faeoris hadn't spoken since they'd left the maiden's courtyard, and he'd decided it best, while in her care, not to interrupt her stewing. Her grip under his arms pinched more than necessary, and he wasn't looking forward to the ugly bruising. The young Berfemmian was holding something back, and Angst feared she was a geyser waiting to explode.

His eyes caught a change in the landscape. Treetops opened to a field that, from this distance, looked like a patch of enormous mushrooms. As they approached, he could better make out the stone-formed houses Jaden had created as a refuge for the wielders. Angst missed Jaden, despite the young man's arrogance, and hoped he would wake safely once Victoria was freed. He couldn't stand the thought of losing anyone else, and guilt was a constant reminder.

"Land us here first," Angst asked, loudly enough so she wouldn't ignore him. "Please."

"You're delaying your fate," she said harshly.

CHAPTER EIGHT

"Always," he agreed.

His stomach lurched as Faeoris dove toward the ground, her grip tensing. Angst swallowed a yelp and struggled to lift a hand, pointing to the center of town. They landed by the statue of Rook and Janda, amidst the city of stone houses. They'd agreed to name the city Rookshire in his honor, and Angst had created the statue to recognize their sacrifice. Rook and Janda looked proudly toward Unsel. Rook's arm rested on her shoulder, and a small flame made of stone rose from her free hand. Angst swallowed hard. They should still be alive, married and making lots of beautiful babies.

Was Faeoris right? Was he avoiding Heather's wrath? Her wrath? Angst shook his head at the thought. He had to see this, he had to strengthen his resolve, but guilt and grief were poor companions. Faeoris's long, thin fingers rested on his shoulder. She turned him to face a nearby home and pointed.

A child, no more than five or six, sat near a freshly planted flowerbed.

"Flowers," Angst said, unsure of what he was supposed to be looking at. "So, they're planning to stay awhile. That's good."

The hand quickly left his shoulder to smack the back of his head. It hurt.

"Ow. What was that for?" He grunted, rubbing the back of his head. "Hitting me like that will make me lose hair."

"More hair," she corrected. "Pay attention to the child."

Angst watched closely. The boy was maybe fifty feet away, so it was hard to make out what he was playing with. It looked like a rock—kind of a crappy toy. Were these people that destitute? Had he condemned them to poverty? Why hadn't the wielders returned to Unsel during his three-month absence, at the very least for work? Maybe he could make the kids who lived here some better toys to... He gasped. The rock rose into the air to hover between both hands.

"Keep watching," she whispered.

The stone hopped in an arc, appearing to jump from hand to hand. The child had a mischievous expression, and the rock shot forward to strike a mangy looking dog in its flank. The dog yelped.

"Hey!" Faeoris called out.

The boy must not have realized they were watching. He fled back into the house, calling for his mom.

"I hate kids," Faeoris declared. Rushing over to the dog, she knelt to pet it before checking the spot it had been hit.

"Wait," Angst said, awestruck. He pointed to the spot where the child had sat. "Did he...did he just wield?"

The dog was now licking her, and she had a broad smile on her face.

"Yes," she said, standing up and approaching him. The dog followed closely. "The little bastard was wielding."

"Um, is he okay?" Angst asked, nodding at the dog.

"*She* is fine," Faeoris said.

"Good," he said. "I can go talk to his parents if you'd like. With my sword."

"We'll both go," she said with a wicked smile. "When there's more time."

"But, about the bastard," Angst said. "The, uh, kid. He's so young to be wielding. Is he a prodigy, like Kala?"

Kala was Nikkola's twelve-year-old daughter, and truly gifted. Not only was she naturally adept with animals, especially Scar, she seemed to be able to emulate any magic she saw someone else wield. Kala had ridden Scar to the last battle, saving Angst from being thrown against a castle wall. He was in awe that there could be another child like her.

"Only if they are all prodigies," Faeoris said, holding a hand out to present the entirety of Rookshire. "Almost every kid in this town wields. The people here are trying to figure out how to teach them, to set up a school or something, before the little animals bust the place up."

"But, how did this happen?" Angst asked.

"Graloon says it's because they're free," she explained. "They're far enough away from Unsel, or close enough to your home, that they feel safe. They aren't in hiding anymore, Angst.

They're doing more with magic than they've ever done. It's working."

"I don't know what to say." Angst shook his head. "That's amazing."

"You wanted to come here and stare at your dead friends," she said, her tone cold. "And I'm sorry they died, but it wasn't without purpose. Theirs was a sacrifice, yes. It was tragic, but good things have happened because of it. They were heroes."

She was right. He'd come to wade into a pool of heartache and loss. Angst had hoped anger and hurt would strengthen him to drive forward. The hurt was still there, but this was something different.

"There's more at stake than your princess," Faeoris said. "And you're going to have to choose between pain," she pointed at the statue, "and hope."

Angst didn't know what to do with that. Children wielding magic, free to be who they were meant to be. It was so overwhelming, it was almost hard to grasp. He looked at the statue, and pain clutched at his chest. The pain was so much easier to understand.

"Please take me home," he said.

* * * *

Faeoris practically threw Angst at the doorstep as they landed, and his knee buckled painfully. He grunted but said nothing. Kala and Scar ran up to them, the young girl wrapping her arms around Faeoris's long legs. Scar licked her boot, his tail wagging furiously. The Berfemmian smiled at the lab pup, but only acknowledged Kala with an awkward pat on the head. Angst knelt, not only to rest his sore knee, but to pet his dog.

The black lab puppy sniffed and sniffed, his tail now waggling enough to make his butt rock back and forth. Angst sat and took the puppy in his arms, petting the small animal as it licked his face. Angst couldn't help but smile at the unconditional love. He held the dog out for a moment, and both their eyes flashed red.

"Oooh," Kala exclaimed, kneeling beside him to pet Scar. "He's so glad you're home, Mr. Angst."

"Thank you, Kala," Angst said, smiling at her. She was about three feet tall with long black hair and an olive complexion. Kala still had a little baby fat in her chubby cheeks, and was so cute he immediately wanted to hug her, too. Unlike Faeoris, he loved kids.

"Please, just Angst," he said.

"Mom always told me to call old men mister," she said, looking at him with serious brown eyes.

Faeoris laughed while Angst grimaced a smile.

"But I'm not old," he explained.

"You look old!" Kala said. She stood abruptly. "Uh oh."

"What?" Angst asked, taking Faeoris's hand to get to his feet. Scar scrambled from his lap to stand behind the girl.

The door behind him opened.

"You're in trouble," Kala whispered loudly, her eyes mischievous.

"I'm always in trouble," he whispered with a wink.

Angst turned around to see Heather. His beautiful wife appeared disheveled. Several thick gray and white hairs had sprung free from her formidable brown curls. Dark, tired bags tugged at her disappointed brown eyes. In spite of this, she was still pretty, but he knew better than to compliment her now. He patted his leg for Scar to come, hoping to garner some strength from the pup. Angst looked down to see the dog sitting faithfully next to Kala, looking as guilty as Angst felt.

"Kala," Heather said. "Would you go in to keep an eye on the babies?"

"I told you you were in trouble," she said to Angst before going inside, Scar following close behind.

His wife looked at Faeoris and nodded her head to one side, as if hoping the Berfemmian would pick up on the social cue to leave.

"What?" Faeoris asked. "I'm upset too!"

CHAPTER EIGHT

"Do you have something to say?" Heather asked.

"Your husband wouldn't have sex with me," Faeoris said, sounding genuinely upset.

"Funny," Heather said sharply, looking as if she'd bitten her tongue. "Now he won't be having sex with me either."

"I don't understand humans at all," Faeoris said, frowning.

"Oh? All this, and she's not human?" Heather asked, glaring at Angst.

"She's something more than human," Angst replied.

"Wrong answer!" she snapped. "If you want sex, you're on your own."

"I don't get it." Faeoris looked hurt.

"Not you," Heather said with a deep sigh. "Him."

"It's me," Angst confirmed. "Not having sex with anyone. For some reason..."

"Fish!" Heather screamed.

"Pardon?" He looked at Faeoris for help.

"Yes!" Faeoris said, meeting his eyes with a piercing glare.

"When you came to visit me in the infirmary," she said. "Why did your mouth taste like fish?"

"Because he was kissing the mermaid...again!" Faeoris said with a nod, crossing her muscular arms. "I'm still upset that he wouldn't kiss me, but it was okay to kiss the fish."

"Exactly what we need to discuss." Heather's gaze bored into Angst.

"Agreed!" Faeoris said, her thin brows in a threatening furrow.

His mouth dried, and a bead of sweat trickled down his cheek. Why was it so hot here? He really didn't want to discuss this. Moyra's death still hurt. For him, it had just happened.

"I thought we couldn't do that?" Faeoris asked. "You said we couldn't kiss!"

"You can't!" Heather said sharply enough to make the young woman jump before glaring at Angst. "And neither can you! How could you?"

"You're going to give him a beating, aren't you?" Faeoris

asked excitedly. "Sometimes we have to give the Vex'steppe tribesmen a beating when they get unruly."

"Does it help?" Heather asked, raising an eyebrow.

"It helped me," Faeoris said with a shrug. "Do you want me to hold him for you?"

"No, I should be able to handle this." Heather tilted her head toward the door for Faeoris to follow Kala. "Please."

Faeoris nodded once in confirmation before peering at Angst. She pointed at her eyes with two fingers then pointed back at Angst. "I'll be right inside. There's no escape."

Faeoris bumped his shoulder, knocking him aside, as she entered the house, slamming the door behind her. Dust fell from the roof.

"Heather..." Angst began.

"You were kissing her, right there, in front of Unsel!" Heather screamed.

"Moyra was just overly excited," Angst said, his voice dripping with guilt. Lies weren't right, but what else could he say? This was the last thing he'd expected. He'd thought she was going to yell at him for having to leave again. "We'd just freed her people from a two-thousand-year-old curse!"

"Your curse may last two thousand years," she mumbled.

Tears welled in her eyes, and she held herself close. She wouldn't look directly at him, and he knew he'd broken something. That hurt worse than any damage done by a foci or element. He didn't talk about it, rarely thought about it, but their marriage had been rocky for years—rocky, but not done. It was the excuse that had let him get caught up in Moyra. Although, honestly, he'd come up with a lot of excuses. She was exotic, beautiful, and gave him purpose. She'd needed him to be a hero, and then, just when he'd thought he might be, she'd died tragically. He hadn't been able to save her. It still hurt, but it was a hurt he couldn't share or explain away. Now this. He was out of tears, but he felt old, and tired, and very weak. Maybe honesty was best. At least some honesty.

"I met Moyra, the mermaid, when we crossed the ocean to

save Rose. She brought me to the bottom of the ocean to show me her people were trapped in a mage city. The only way I could breathe...was...well...was through her, when our mouths..."

"I get it," she said crisply.

"They were trapped, Heather. Her people had been stuck in a curse for thousands of years." Angst began pacing, mostly because he didn't want to keep making eye contact. "Moyra tricked me into saving them, but I don't think she knew they were going to attack Unsel. When we arrived at the castle, it was already under attack. She walked to me, on legs. Her fins were gone. She kissed me to say goodbye, because I couldn't...I wouldn't..." He took a deep breath before choking out the words. "I wouldn't go with her."

They were quiet for a long time. Angst fought back grief. He really didn't want to shed tears in front of Heather, not over this. She stared at him, looking sad and lost.

"And then she was killed," he finally said.

"Were you in love with her?" she asked.

"No," he said in a thick voice. "I loved her like I love Tori. Like I love all my friends. But I'm only in love with one person."

There was another long silence.

"I don't know if I believe you anymore, Angst," she said. "I don't feel it."

They were quiet again as he sought forgiveness in her eyes. There was a storm of emotions in Heather's gaze, and any forgiveness was lost in its turbulence.

"I can leave," he said. "If that's what you want."

"Why on Ehrde would you think that's what I want?" Heather crossed her arms, peering at him in disbelief.

"Because I've hurt you," he said quietly. "I've only had minutes to think about this, but you've had months. You must hate me and everything I've done." He was staring at the ground now. "I...I was just trying to be a hero." He didn't know what else to say.

She stepped closer. "I'm so proud of you, Angst," Heather finally said. "You've saved countless lives. You wanted to be a hero, and you are one. But it shouldn't be at the cost of losing us. Our marriage shouldn't be the price."

He could only nod.

"I agree. You need to leave," she said, and placed a hand on his chest.

He looked up, unable to speak.

"But not tonight. Tonight, you'll stay home and be with your family," she said, taking a deep breath. "Tomorrow, you need to go save your princess, and figure out who you want to be. A hero, or a father and husband. And then, if you're ready to come back to our family, you're welcome home."

Angst paused, absorbing all she'd said. "Why can't I be all of those?" he asked.

"We don't get everything we want, Angst," Heather said.

"I've noticed." Angst sighed.

9

An awkward silence hovered around Angst's pending departure like a swarm of gnats. Their unspoken words were just beyond reach of the spoken ones. Should he say something, or had he said too much already? He tried unobtrusively slipping into his rattly chest piece until his arms got stuck, and Heather set a baby down in a cradle to help tug at it.

"I'll do this as fast as I can," he promised. It sounded as hollow as it felt. "I'm worried about you, all of you."

Heather nodded curtly, her eyes cold and her face drawn with hurt. He felt the urge to cry but didn't know if it was her emotions magically affecting him, or his own. She wouldn't say anything; she wouldn't even argue. Had she really given up on them...on him?

"I'll save my friends, I'll save Tori and Unsel, and then I'll come home and be the best father and husband ever!" he said with every ounce of conviction he could sell. "Ever, ever!"

The cute didn't help a lot, but at least she cracked a smile. There was a noisy rattle just outside the door, but Scar hadn't started barking, so he ignored it. He needed to focus on his wife and kids, even if just for this moment. He picked up the baby she'd set down and reached out with his free arm to draw them all into a hug. Heather quickly pulled away, walking to the nearby cribs and putting the other baby down.

He swallowed hard. "Won't you at least tell me their names?"

Angst asked.

"You don't deserve to know their names," Heather whispered sharply, taking the other twin from his arms and resting her in a crib.

He didn't know what to say. For all the pain he'd gone through, this had to rank up there with having his skull split open. Heather chewed on her lip, and took a breath as if preparing to say something, but remained silent.

"I'm alone," Angst explained. "What you don't understand is that I've never been alone. I've always known you would be here for me. Every time I faced death, you were my last thought." He let out a deep sigh. "I've failed time and time again. I'm so bad at being a hero. My friends, all of them, are in danger or dead. Unsel is facing war at every border. My best friend is stuck in time and dying. All I feel is guilt." Angst gently grabbed her shoulders and stared into her eyes. "If I leave, I lose you and my children. If I stay, everyone else dies. I am alone."

Heather rested a hand on his breastplate. She didn't lean in for a kiss or a hug, but there was the tiniest hint of forgiveness in her eyes. It was almost enough.

"Angst," she said sincerely. "You won't be alone."

Heather took his hand, guided him to the door and opened it. His jaw dropped, his shoulders dropped, he almost dropped the sword. A million nos poured from his mind, and he gritted his teeth to hold them back. Faeoris, Jintorich, Maarja, and Aerella stood along their walkway. Just beyond them were two enormous wagons, both with pack horses that looked older than him. He hoped fervently they were just here to see him off, but then her remembered she had said that he wouldn't be alone... The realization struck him, and the nos started tumbling out.

"No," he grumbled. "There is no way they're coming with!"

"Why not?" Heather asked.

"I barely know them," he snapped. "I don't know how they'll fight as a group, or if they'll just end up fighting each other. This isn't like traveling with my friends."

CHAPTER NINE

They stared at him in disbelief. Faeoris crossed her arms, a thin eyebrow rising dangerously. Maarja squeezed meaty hands, her popping knuckles sounded like someone stomping on branches in the woods.

Heather held up a calming hand. "That's not the problem," she said firmly.

"It's also those pack horses, and that caravan," Angst went on. It didn't even make sense. He would move faster alone, and speed was everything. This mess of slow-moving mounts pulling large, covered trailers surrounded by people he barely knew had mistake painted all over it. "I'm in a hurry. What are these even doing here?"

"That's not it either, is it?" she asked.

His heart was racing and his throat felt constricted.

"I already know how much she means to you," Heather said, pointing at Faeoris. The Berfemmian's shoulders lowered from, 'I'm going to kill you before you take another breath' to 'I'm only going to hurt you until I'm done.'

"Yes," Angst agreed.

"And I can already tell how much you care for her." She nodded at Aerella.

"Of course I care for her," Angst admitted, his cheeks warm.

"Maarja has already seen you to safety once," Heather said with a smile. "And you know she'll do anything to protect Tarness's best friend."

Maarja nodded in agreement but said nothing.

"And Jintorich was my mid-wife," she said.

"Wait, what?" Angst eyes went wide, and he stared at the little man.

"Happy to be of service," Jintorich squeaked, bowing respectfully.

Angst looked at them. He was already familiar with Faeoris's fighting ability, and Maarja was a Nordruaut, which almost made her as dangerous as Faeoris. Jintorich was an unknown, but Aerella wasn't—she knew more spells than Dallow ever would. But they were nothing compared to the raw power of the elements. Angst had dragged his unwilling friends along on a simple adventure once already, and now they were missing, possibly dead. And Tori... So many had been hurt because of his decisions, he couldn't stand the idea of losing more.

"I'm bonded to two swords now," he said firmly. "I don't need help. I've got this."

Heather looked at him without saying a word.

"No, this isn't happening!" he shouted. "Everyone who tries to help me ends up hurt, or dead! I can't have that. I can't ask..."

"I asked," Heather said, placing a hand on his shoulder. "They know the risks, and I'll sleep at night knowing you aren't alone."

"But..."

She leaned forward and whispered into his ear.

"O...okay," he said, choking on his words. "That's fair."

She whispered again.

Angst whipped around and hugged her as tightly as he could. Emotion swelled in his chest, and he continued holding her. After several long moments, he let go, setting her back on the ground, and composed himself before facing his new companions.

"Thom." He could barely speak around the lump in his throat. "My son's name is Thom."

"Angst's father's name," Heather explained.

Faeoris was holding a hand up to her mouth, and Aerella smiled knowingly. The others nodded politely, not completely understanding.

"And my daughter?" Angst asked.

"When you come home to me," she said, a hint of smile in her eyes.

"That's fair," he agreed too quickly, even if he didn't feel it was. He clasped his hands together. "Okay, so, I guess we go together."

They all just stared at him, chewing on his insult, which appeared to leave a bad taste in everyone's mouth. Angst had been so caught up in learning his son's name that he'd already forgotten the gaffe. Apparently, they weren't as forgetful.

"Look, I'm sorry if that was rude. This trip will be dangerous, it's just... I just..."

"My husband is an ass," Heather said.

Maarja and Faeoris nodded vigorously.

"He just doesn't want anyone getting hurt," she continued.

"I've lost my friends, literally," Angst said, walking toward them. "I've seen cities and castles destroyed. I've watched titans fall." He began pacing. "I've fought dragons from stories, and dreamed of a war coming that's almost impossible to fathom. I foolishly led my closest friends into this, and we were unprepared. The results have been catastrophic." He looked at each of them before turning away to pace more. "You are all powerful, even more than they were, but it won't be enough. It's not enough to tell you that you might die. It's more accurate to say, you might live."

He stopped long enough to let this sink in. Heather was right, the stakes were too high to do this alone. He really did need help. They were going to face Fire, whom he'd already lost to, and Magic could still be out there. Other nations were rising up to battle each other, and most weren't fans of Angst.

"This trip isn't just to find my friends, or save the princess," he said, balling his hands into tight fists. "This is for Unsel and, if we can avoid starting a war, maybe all of Ehrde."

He sought them out again, and not one looked hesitant. Faeoris appeared hungry for battle, or maybe just battle with him. Jintorich had hopped up on Maarja's shoulder, and both nodded at each other in anticipation. Aerella looked reserved, her face dark and sad, but resolute.

"We need to move faster than these will allow," Angst said, pointing at the caravan. "We only have weeks..."

"No," Wilfred said, stepping out from behind a wagon. "You are taking these wagons out of Unsel."

"Wilfred?" Angst asked, taking a step back.

"The one and only," he replied, trying to bow in armor that fit so poorly Angst was embarrassed for his friend. "That was a great speech, Angst," Wilfred said, his hands behind his back as he approached. "You really are a leader, and a hero. I think many underestimate you."

"Yeah, it kinda sucks," Angst said.

"It's a strategic advantage," Maarja said with a nod.

"So is fear," Angst said to her. "It would really be nice if some of my adversaries were afraid of me instead of wanting a piece of me."

"That's exactly why I'm here," Wilfred explained, his cheeks blotchy red and a trickle of sweat dripping from his forehead. "Leadership in the castle may underestimate you, but Fulk'han and Melkier do not."

"Finally," Angst said. "Maybe that will keep them at bay for awhile."

"It does, because you're in Unsel," Wilfred spoke slowly.

"I told you, I'm not staying in Unsel." Angst was getting irritated. Wilfred was spending too much time selling something and not enough time explaining.

"I'm aware of this," Wilfred said. "Please consider. They know you are dangerous and may not attack if they think you're in Unsel."

Angst sucked in a deep breath as it struck him. "The wagons?" he asked. "You want us to try and sneak out of Unsel, like we're transporting goods. But why two wagons?"

"One is for the sword," Wilfred explained. He jerked a thumb toward Maarja. "The other is for her."

"Will she fit?" Angst asked.

"Barely," Maarja said. She looked like someone had tried pulling out one of her teeth.

"If you are successful, if Melkier and the Fulk'han think you're still in Unsel," Wilfred said, "it may keep them at bay."

"They aren't attacking Unsel because they're afraid of you, Angst," Faeoris said proudly. "And me."

"And us," Maarja said, peering at the Berfemmian.

Angst felt like defending himself from that brief glare of icy daggers shooting back and forth between the women.

"But we're in a hurry!" Angst whined.

"It will only set you back a couple of days," Wilfred said.

"We only have twenty-one!" Angst snapped.

"Now you have nineteen," Wilfred said sternly, crossing his arms.

"That's two whole days!" Angst said.

"You're going on the mission to save five people," Wilfred explained. "This diversion may help save all of Unsel."

Angst looked at his new crew, who waited for his final say. He looked at Heather, who nodded. They were in such a hurry, not only to save Tori and his friends, but he wanted to hurry back and learn his daughter's name. But if Wilfred was right, and lives could be saved, it was worth the effort. Angst sighed deeply.

"Fine," Angst said reluctantly. "Is that all? Did you want us to drag an anchor behind us or anything?"

"Would you?" Wilfred said with a winning smile.

"What about you?" Angst asked approaching his old friend. "I suppose you need a royal escort back."

"No," Wilfred answered. "I'm taking your advice and meeting with the wielders later today."

Angst eyed his obese friend up and down—the man was overweight enough to make *him* feel thin. Layers of expensive armor hung over him like bad drapes. It was like he'd purposefully chosen mismatched sets from the training grounds. Wilfred didn't look intimidating or inspiring, he looked trapped. Angst had no taste, and sought Faeoris, who nodded in confirmation.

Angst moved close and patted Wilfred's back. "We'll do this your way, old friend," he said. "But will you take some more advice?"

"Of course," Wilfred said, frowning curiously.

"Don't visit the wielders. Not yet," he said. "Seek out Teedle. He's the best armorer in Unsel. And Rahvin, the queen's seamstress. Ask them to clean you up. Tell them I sent you."

"I don't really think it's necessary," Wilfred said haughtily.

Faeoris draped a long arm over Wilfred's shoulder and spun

him around. He looked up into her large eyes and went pale, taking a deep breath.

"You would look so heroic in armor that's more...fitting of your prowess, Wilfred," she said, her eyes seductive and voice thick. "So very handsome."

"Oh," Wilfred said, letting only a little air escape. "Do you really think so?"

"Like a leader," she said.

"I can do that," he said, his voice gruff.

Faeoris kissed him on the cheek, and the man shuddered.

Angst choked down a chuckle. There was a long, awkward moment while everyone stared at Wilfred as he attempted to compose himself. It apparently wasn't easy with Faeoris leaning over him like that, but she finally freed Wilfred from her hold. Angst felt for his friend, but this was for the best.

"Uh, so, before leaving, you'll need to change clothes." Wilfred coughed awkwardly. "To be, well, less conspicuous."

"What?" Faeoris snapped, making him wince.

"Into something less, um, noticeable," Wilfred said, his gaze flicking to her bare midriff and thigh-high boots, and everything else. "There are traveling clothes in the back of the wagons."

"This just keeps getting better," Angst said, taking a deep breath.

Aerella didn't need to change and sat in the front of the larger wagon. She remained in her long blue dress, looking tired and older than she had at the infirmary. The Meldusian donned toddler's clothes and an ugly knit hat that hid his eyebrows and long ears. He took the seat beside Aerella and bounced up and down several times, like a child who had just won a prize. Maarja crawled into a ball under the wagon canopy, the wood creaking, but not so loud as her own indignant grunts.

Angst placed his sword in the hold of the second wagon and removed his armor. He reluctantly took off his cloak and rested it gently on the weapon. He slipped into dark oversized pants, an itchy shirt, and someone else's boots.

"Wait," Heather said, scooping up Scar and handing the pup

to him.

"But you'll need him, and Kala..." Angst said, looking around for the kid.

"We're surrounded by powerful wielders. We'll be fine," she said then whispered, "And Kala said you need to take Scar with."

"Of course." How could the girl possibly know that? He was in no position to argue with his wife, though, so he gently set the pup in the back. Scar immediately made a bed of his cloak, turning around several times until it was the perfect nest before plopping down. The dog yawned, its tail wagging lazily.

He sighed before facing Heather. "Please give Thom and whatshername my love," he said, hugging her.

She hugged him back weakly, but chuckled at his joke.

"I hate everything," he said, looking down at his uncomfortable clothes.

"Tell me about it," she said, pulling away.

Heather had always enjoyed his self-mocking humor, but now barely acknowledged it. Leaving under these conditions made his heart ache.

Angst took the driver's seat behind a team of horses that looked as slow as waking up on a Saturday morning. Faeoris plopped down next to him, struggling with a flowery cotton dress that covered more of her than either of them liked. She tugged and pulled at the loose waist as if trapped. He couldn't help but smile at the shiny boots that showed beneath the hem.

"Not a word," she said sharply.

"Maybe a few?" he mocked, but retreated at her fierce gaze. "I'll save them."

They started off at a snail's pace. Angst turned back to wave goodbye to Heather and Wilfred. His friend waved, but Heather didn't. After several long moments, he turned back again, but they'd already gone.

10

Their first day on the road was far, far less than eventful. Angst would've preferred sorting papers in the castle cellar to the arduous ride. Well, not really, but almost. Faeoris was so disgruntled at "being forced to wear this ugly dress," she spoke of little else. Her only relief was that her *essent*, Marisha, couldn't see her. The seamstress deserved some sort of award if the dress made it past the border. It was already losing the battle, with several small tears appearing along the hems. By everyday Unsel standards, she actually looked pretty in her trappings, but even the barest suggestion of this was met with a glare that almost threw him from their wagon.

"Are you upset at the clothes," Angst asked carefully, "or is there something else?"

"I don't understand your marriage and mating," Faeoris said.

"Neither do I," Angst said with a sigh. "Sometimes I just want to be done with it."

"Does that mean we can have the sex now?" she prodded.

"No!" he said, more firmly than he'd intended, before noticing her mischievous grin.

"Heather is a great woman," Faeoris said with a haughty sniff. "She said you shouldn't have been diddling the mermaid."

"I wasn't diddling!" he said.

"She said to keep you from diddling anyone else." Faeoris's face was stern. "What is diddling?"

CHAPTER TEN

"The sex!" Angst snapped.

"Oh," she replied, and paused to think, pursing her lips. "How did you and the mermaid...when she didn't have a..."

"We didn't diddle," he said, unable to hold back his exasperation. "There was no diddling."

"Good," she said, crossing her arms. One judgmental eyebrow raised high enough to lift morality itself. "Let's keep it that way, hero."

Somewhere between his frustration at their slow pace and her frustration of everything, he decided to finish their first day early. At the mere hint of sunset, Angst drove the mounts down an unkempt path so they would be away from spying eyes. After twenty minutes or so, they stopped at a small clearing that had been used as a camp in the past. Before he could even step off the wagon, Faeoris pulled the dress over her head and threw it to the dirt. Angst was surprised, and slightly disappointed, that she didn't rip off her armored top as well.

"I hate wearing so many clothes!" she proclaimed, stretching her long muscular arms outward. She hopped off the wagon, landing on the poor dress, and stared at him.

"As do I," Maarja said, removing layers of furs until there was barely enough to cover her breasts and crotch.

"I say, be yourself." Angst looked at both half-naked women. "Do what makes you happy."

They both nodded, apparently not getting his joke. Angst couldn't help but smile. Sure, Maarja was frighteningly tall, but she was beautiful. And Faeoris was frighteningly powerful, but she was also stunning. His grin subsided as the two alpha females eyed each other up and down in the way only women do. He could almost hear their hackles rise.

"Aerella and I can make a fire," Jintorich squeaked, interrupting the stare-down.

"I'll just go ahead and keep wearing my clothes," Aerella said in a strained voice.

"Shame," Angst said. "I was about to break out the port."

"I'll return with dinner," Maarja said, sternly. She grabbed a spear from the back of the wagon.

"There's plenty of dried meat in storage," Jintorich said.

"I'm hunting," Maarja snapped before running off into the woods, surprisingly silent despite her size.

"Angst," Faeoris said, her voice hungry. "Do you want to?"

Angst glanced at Jintorich and Aerella uncomfortably. Aerella's eyebrows raised, but she said nothing.

"I don't think we should..." he began. "Um, do what?"

"Sealtian," she said over her shoulder. "Would you like to?"

"Yes." He let out a deep breath. "That's the cold bath I'm looking for. Let me check on Scar first. He's been in the back all day."

Fortunately, she hadn't said sex, because Angst certainly hadn't been hoping she would. They were friends, just good friends, there had to be boundaries. Boundaries made of giant brick walls fortified by steel and covered in flame. Angst thought about shopping for vegetables and filing papers and everything else boring as he sought Scar. The pup was still curled up on his cloak, his tail wagging as if on demand. He didn't seem anxious to leave. How was that even possible? Angst had peed four times that day, and Scar hadn't.

"Do you need to go for a walk?" Angst asked politely, not sure if he was understood.

Scar's tail continued to wag, but the pup's only reply was a yawn.

"Come on," Angst said, reaching out. "I don't want you going on my cloak. That was a gift from Tori."

The dog yipped, his hairs bristling.

Angst jerked his hand back. "Fine, stay here," Angst said gruffly. "Just don't pee."

Scar's ears lowered, apparently his loving companion preferred the solitude of this wagon over a walk with him. Angst shrugged and gently pulled his sword from under the surprisingly heavy dog. A blue glow surrounded Chryslaenor in anticipation of their upcoming exercises. The blade was more excited than he was, and sung loudly in his mind. It would be their first time doing sealtian together.

Sealtian was a series of forms and movements that flowed together like a slow dance. Every master of the blade knew most of them. Hector had taught him some when he was younger, but they were boring, or he was too easily distracted. Shortly after their meeting, Faeoris had challenged him to go through the sealtian. How could he possibly have turned her down? He didn't know all the movements, and didn't know as many as Faeoris, but he knew how to cheat. Angst had emulated her movements by sensing the movement of her bones. When she lifted an arm, so did he. When she leaned to one side, he mirrored her. Something about the sealtian had helped him come to terms with Dulgirgraut, which had taught Faeoris and Angst the forms she didn't already know. It became a true bonding with the sword, and an intimate moment of discovery with his new friend.

Angst soon found Faeoris in her short shorts, high boots, and flattering top, already glistening as she stretched. Rather than getting caught staring again, Angst started stretching too. Faeoris' movements flowed like water down an icy mountainside. Each of his jerky motions sounded like he was pulling on an old rope while standing on a pile of brittle sticks. He'd never been able to touch his toes, but tried in vain, hoping she would stop so he could.

Fortunately, he was better at sealtian than stretching. His joints creaked and popped through the first set of movements, and he was embarrassed to be grunting and sweating by the fifth. Faeoris didn't care, she didn't judge, and he appreciated her even more for her lack of attention. This wasn't like practicing with Hector, who called out his every wrong move. He wasn't on display, and this realization helped him relax. When he stopped worrying and let the sword become an extension of himself, he was able to step through each movement without forcing them. The sealtian went pretty well, and Angst remembered all of them, including those movements that were once lost. When they finished, Chryslaenor glowed and sparkled to several *oohs* from Faeoris. He rested the foci on its tip, and his hands on his knees.

"Those last ones," Faeoris breathed heavily, still staring at the sword, "are my favorite."

"Mine too," he said, wiping the flop of sweat from his brow.

Her chest heaved as she approached. He reluctantly stood straight, trying to bury a wince with a smile. It was nearly impossible to arch his back in a stretch while sucking in his gut.

"Angst, I..." Her lips were pursed, and she stood very close.

"Yes," he asked, a catch in his breath.

"I was wondering why you haven't—"

"Make way," Maarja shouted, shoving between them.

Angst and Faeoris jumped apart. The Nordruaut woman hefted a large buck over her shoulder and dragged a doe behind her. Had she had come out of nowhere, or was he just really distracted?

"That's a lot of food for one night," Angst said in surprise.

"I'm hungry," Maarja said.

"It must take a lot of food to feed so much body," Faeoris said.

Angst covered his face with his hand. Should he grab Chryslaenor and tell them to quit? Would he actually be able to hold them both off, even with his foci? Maarja looked back at the Berfemmian, and there was a long pause as both women peered at each other. Finally, with a grunt, Maarja turned away and plodded toward the distant campfire.

"That doesn't help," Angst said.

"What?" Faeoris asked as if nothing had happened.

"We need to work together," Angst said.

"As long as she knows her place," Faeoris said, "we'll work together just fine."

Faeoris walked away. The silhouette of her long legs, one step in front of the other as though she balanced a tightrope, her hips rocking to and fro, was mesmerizing. Angst almost left his sword as he followed her to join the others. He tried to stop gawking at her sultry shadow long enough to think. Why were the two women at odds? It felt like they were marking their territory, but hadn't they just met? It didn't make sense. They lived a continent and an ocean apart, and shouldn't have had any reason to hate each other. He had to do something. He was supposed to be leading this group, but what could he say to make Faeoris and Maarja like each other when he didn't even understand the problem?

Just as Angst opened his mouth to let loose an inspiring speech about banding together, Maarja stopped and drew a knife the length of his thigh. She drove it into the chest of the buck with a nauseating crunch and efficiently stripped and prepped the deer. Before long, she was roasting kabobs of venison over a fire that blazed way too high for cooking.

A fire this large would've set Hector to cursing and leaping into the trees on watch for anyone who might have spotted the blaze. Chryslaenor sensed nothing. Angst sought out his gamlin friends, who'd mostly been silent since he escaped Tori's chambers. They seemed distant, but their buzz of communication warned of nothing, so he relaxed.

Jintorich added some expertise to the cooking with seasoning, making it much better than anything Angst had tasted from Rose, though he would never admit it to her. The Meldusian spices the small man had used only made Angst hungrier, and he ate until his belly was more distended than usual. He reached for another plate, but his hand fell in exhaustion. The only thing that would've made this meal better was a draft of port, a cigar, and his lost friends. He sighed.

"Jintorich, Maarja," he said. "That was just amazing."

Maarja belched noisily, pounding her sternum. Faeoris scoffed but said nothing.

"Thank you." Jintorich bowed his head, his large ears lowering respectfully. "Thank you both. I used to be a chef—"

"What exactly is the plan?" Maarja interrupted.

"Find my friends, hunt down Alloria, save the princess," Angst said pointedly.

"You really think these things out," Aerella said dryly.

"Okay," Angst drawled. "Then I retire and spend the rest of

my life apologizing to Heather. Is that enough?"

"I doubt it," Faeoris replied. "You're going to need more apologizing, to more people."

"Probably," Angst said, prodding lazily at the campfire with a stick.

Everyone looked up at the sound of a branch cracking nearby. They all glanced toward the wagons and waited long moments for another sound. Angst focused on Chryslaenor, listening for a warning, but heard only the steady song of his foci.

"We're fine," Angst said. "Promise. The sword would warn us."

"The plan, Angst," Faeoris urged.

"We should arrive at Gressmore in a day or two," he said. "Once we find the memndus stone, we ditch the wagons and head to...wherever."

They all nodded somberly and nobody said anything further. The day had taken much more out of him than he'd expected. Angst looked around to the three tents already set up.

"I'm beat," he said. "I should pitch my tent."

"We're in that one," Faeoris said casually, nodding toward the nearest one.

"Oh," Angst said in surprise. "Uh, good. Thanks."

Everyone else remained silent, uncaring. Hector didn't admonish, Dallow didn't scoff, Tarness didn't snicker—and Angst missed all of it. His old friends were sometimes the conscience he didn't want, but often needed. This crew didn't care an iota who slept with whom, but why not? Was it indifference or beliefs he wasn't familiar with? He knew so little about them, and they hadn't offered anything. This wasn't a night of stories or experiences; it was a night of strangers.

"I'll keep watch," Maarja said.

"That's not necessary," Angst said. "Chryslaenor will warn me of any problems."

Maarja stared at him with untrusting eyes.

"I'll take second watch," Jintorich stated in his high-pitched voice. "Wake me when you are ready."

"Of course, my friend," Maarja replied huskily, staring at the fire.

"Ooookay," Angst said as he stood. "Well, thanks."

Aerella entered the third tent, and Jintorich the second. Angst walked to the first, kicked off his boots, and crawled in. He paused for a moment to appreciate the pillows and blankets already laid out before quickly shuffling over to the farthest side of the tent to make room for Faeoris. She unbuckled her boots then pulled off her noisy shorts with their scale sides, and finally removed her scale top before entering the tent. The campfire left little to the imagination as she crawled in. He pulled the blankets over his crotch as she crept into place beside him. She tugged at them, covering herself until his left leg was exposed.

"Thank you," she said.

He really wanted to say something clever and charming, but instead Angst remained on his back, not thinking of her thin young curves or voluptuous bare breasts. Shouldn't she be wearing clothes? Not that it would've helped, much; she looked amazing clothed too.

"For what?" he asked.

"I've never slept alone in the woods," she said. "I'm glad to be here with a friend."

And with that, she rolled to her side, her breasts squished against his shoulder, not that he noticed, and kissed him on the cheek. There was a brief pause as she waited for something that didn't happen. Faeoris sighed and returned to her back. He wasn't sure if the covers actually covered anything, and did his best not to check. Angst lay there for a long time, staring at the dark canopy of his tent, thinking about vegetable shopping again. He hated vegetables.

11

Rohjek

SMyket briskly rubbed his dark muscular arms as if that was enough to fend off the spring morning chill. He longed for the warm sands of the Vex'steppe desert. This cold was yet another reminder that he did not belong in this foreign place, and nor did the tribes, but in this he had no say. Instead, he hovered over the fire, hoping it would cook life back into his muscles. It was a very small fire.

"Why don't you kill him as he sleeps?" DEdin asked, glaring at a large tent.

SMyket froze at the suggestion, and the chill stiffening his back was not caused by cool air. Of course he'd thought of killing ANduaut, but refused to even utter the words. Their leader had become far too deadly since his return from Angoria. Since his change. SMyket scoffed at his friend for even suggesting it, shaking his head to release the image of DEdin slowly dying at ANduaut's hands.

DEdin might have been one of the few physically strong enough to beat their leader. The man was a head taller than ANduaut and covered in thick muscle. His chest was the definition of barrel, and his arms and legs were made of raw power. DEdin's head was shaved to his smooth dark skull, his only hair a thin line of beard tracing his jawline. He looked both fierce and battle ready, but that wasn't enough. DEdin was also slow. His bright green eyes weren't dull; he just didn't move fast enough. He was the type of man who would kill you with one blow, if he could hit you.

"You know the truth of it," SMyket whispered, unable to keep defeat from his voice. "If he heard you right now, you are already a dead man. You've watched him. You aren't as fast, nor as merciless."

"That's why I said *you* should kill him," DEdin said. "You are the only one he trusts alone in his tent."

"Trust is too strong a word," SMyket said. "He is always alert when I enter."

"It's not as though he sleeps with one eye open," DEdin replied with a fierce smile.

"Ha." He coughed to cover his chuckle. "As if he had two eyes."

"The man who crushed his skull did a poor job." DEdin looked down, rubbing his hands fiercely. "How is it possible to live like that?"

"The Dark Vivek," SMyket said, unable to keep the hatred from his voice. "He is...unnatural. After returning with ANduaut's carcass through a dark circle in the air, he healed him to full with the magics."

"Magics!" DEdin's thick jaw jutted outward as he clucked his tongue in disapproval. "And not to full!"

"Oh?" SMyket whispered loudly, hoping DEdin would pick up on the hint that he too should speak more quietly.

"He's an aberration! His head is broken!" DEdin said. "His skull half crushed! How can he even think?"

"He thinks enough," SMyket snapped, his body rigid. "Enough to kill any who attack, enough to take over this nation we are in, and enough to lead! He came back a changed man. Twice the danger and undefeated."

"You are the only one remaining from the counsel of three," DEdin replied, crossing large arms across his dark chest. "All believe it should be you who faces him then takes his place."

"I am far from ready," SMyket replied. "And I owe him my life."

"Because he didn't kill you?"

DEdin soaked in that slight for uncomfortable moments. Was fear the only reason he refused to face their leader, the Iroquai? No, there was also the Vivek. He had returned ANduaut to life, and directed their leader to come to this place. If SMyket actually killed ANduaut, they would not only have to fight this Vivek, they would be surrounded by monsters. He would be responsible for the end of the tribes. No, it wasn't fear, it was wisdom—he struggled to convince himself of this.

"It's not time," SMyket said.

"You fear him," DEdin snapped.

"Fear does not make me a coward," he replied firmly. "You've seen the dead who challenged him."

"And that's all?" DEdin asked.

"No, there is more," he said darkly. "It's this place."

"This place we don't belong!" DEdin whispered loudly. "Tending creatures that aren't natural!"

"It's too late now, and you know it's true. Could we defend ourselves against him?" He pointed all around at surrounding camp. "Against all of them?"

"Can we defeat this Vivek? I thought there were two. A Dark Vivek, and one of the light," DEdin said. "Maybe we misunderstand."

"Maybe they are one and the same," SMyket whispered, unable to keep the concern from his voice.

"Your delay will doom us all," DEdin said.

"I should see to the Iroquai," he said dismissively, gritting his teeth.

SMyket left his friend with no other words. He approached the large, open tent, which rested in the middle of their settlement. The ground was soft, the moist ash and dirt sticking to the sweat of his bare feet. The air was cool enough to numb his nose, but a dry heat rising from the ground warmed his legs. It felt like a sickness, and DEdin was correct, they didn't belong

CHAPTER ELEVEN

here.

He entered the tent and bowed his head respectfully. It didn't matter that the Iroquai was meditating and his courtesy went unnoticed, it was respect for tradition that he bowed to. Their leader was lost to meditation, with his legs crossed and his hands resting on the two-daggered staff set across them. His breathing was steady and his remaining eye shut.

ANduaut never seemed to sleep like everyone else. He merely sat, like this, whenever he felt it necessary. Usually, this came on their leader at night, but it could happen at any time. In the middle of counsel, at the beginning of a meal, he would say, "It is time," and fall deep into meditation. Their leader would make his way to this tent, sometimes stumbling like a drunkard, and rest here. Tribesmen would flock around the tent to protect it in hopes of being recognized by the Iroquai, even if they never were.

SMyket shook his head in confusion. Never in the history of the tribes had a murderer remained leader. While running away with his lover, ANduaut had killed his father, the former leader of the Vex'steppe. His first action as their new Iroquai was to reject Faeoris and her Berfemmian during their mating cycle. The Berfemmian left furious, with more than a few dead in their wake. The tribesmen had remained furious. ANduaut had destroyed the natural order of things, including their cycle of reproduction. He had turned away their sex, and everyone had hated him. How could the fool say no to Faeoris? The man had to be blind in both eyes. ANduaut had then disappeared like a coward. Weeks passed, and when the Vivek returned with his body, the tribes had gathered a representative of the young, the old, and the middle-aged to choose a new Iroquai. In a way, a new leader did come forward. When ANduaut woke, he immediately killed the young man, and the old, leaving SMyket alive as a servant. Yes, more than anything, SMyket wanted the Iroquai dead.

ANduaut had returned a different man. He was grotesque to look on. His forehead was caved in over the right eye, like an apple smashed against a wall. The eye was always shut, bulging out behind an eyelid that occasionally leaked thick, orange tears. That half of his face hung like honey dripping from rye.

But it was more than appearance. SMyket had always considered ANduaut weak, indecisive, and cowardly. These concerns were crushed with his head—their leader was now cold, thoughtful, and ruthless. He always looked like he had a plan, even at rest. Even now, in his trance, ANduaut's good eye fluttered, wincing in pain or concern, lost in dreams and insight. The tribal leader's breath caught and calmed in a torrent of unknown thought.

Since his return, nothing had been the same. They had migrated to the lands beyond, ending in a place filled with ash and lava. The Iroquai announced that there would be no more Berfemmian, and if they wished, men could sleep with men unhindered. Which did nothing for the majority who still wanted to mate. Those few who could wield magics would be held in the highest regard. They were no longer just warriors; they now tended smaller tribes. All those who argued met a quick demise, usually at ANduaut's own hands, and, occasionally, at SMyket's.

"You are looking at me again," ANduaut said, his eye still shut and his voice puzzled. "Is this more than curiosity?"

"No, Iroquai," SMyket said in fear. He didn't want the gaze to be mistaken as hate, or anything else.

"Is our nation whole?" he asked.

"We are one, my Iroquai," SMyket said, biting his tongue. It was true nobody was fighting, but almost everyone hated ANduaut. That certainly brought them together.

"I hear you speak of me in whispers," he said darkly, his eye still shut. "Is there danger that I need to address?"

"No, I promise," he said quickly. Was it possible he had heard them? "We merely wonder what the Iroquai dreams."

There was a long pause, and ANduaut squeezed his eye tight. A grotesque orange tear leaked from the bulging mass of deformity. He caught his breath several times before speaking. "I dream of my love, ENdear. I dream of my father, and his mistakes. I dream of Rose."

"The flower?" SMyket asked.

"Yes," ANduaut said. There was an awkward silence before he continued. "How are my eggs?"

"They haven't hatched," he replied, his throat tightening. "But there is movement."

"Finally." ANduaut smiled, his eye opening.

12

Unsel

Angst's eyelids opened suddenly, the unexpected consciousness making him gasp. His swords sang in his mind, not quite harmonizing. Dulgirgraut sounded muffled, like a horn under blankets. Were they warning him or talking to each other? His heart was racing, and he felt...angry? He was struck by a wave of anxiety, as if something was terribly wrong. Maybe it was a foci dream he'd already forgotten? But they rarely faded from memory this fast, and had never left him feeling so upset.

His nose itched, as did a small spot under his back. He felt trapped in the closeness of the tent. One arm was tucked under Faeoris, who'd rolled back to her side and fastened herself to him, an arm over his chest and a leg over both of his. Why wasn't he loving this? It was inappropriate cuddling at its best, and Angst should've been sound asleep.

His mind tried racing past the discomforts, but they were like deep ruts in an already rocky path. Two days on the road, and it felt like they should've already found his friends. The large wagons had slowed their progress like a lazy summer day. It didn't help that they also took the road less traveled, which was as unkempt as Heather's hair after an argument. He'd have to thank Wilfred for the suggestion.

Sleep. He needed sleep. The first night on the road had been filled with trepidation, so maybe the second was too. Maybe if he willed it hard enough, his brain would turn off and he could sleep, this time without crazy dreams. Thinking about sleep always helped, right? It wasn't just that they were in a hurry, or the unknowns of these new companions, there was definitely something else. It was as if the front door had been left unlocked or the windows were still open. The storm of concern wasn't restful, and his worry took constant precedence. Sleep was hours away, and then hours still.

Drops of rain gently pelted the tent's canvas. Dry dirt hungry for spring showers made the air smell earthy. He was just starting to drift when his ears were struck with noise. Chryslaenor rang in his mind like bad performance art. A song that blurted with horns and rattled with drums. His heart sped, racing faster as he dragged himself from a cloudy haze. It made his anger flare once again. Then, another buzzing tickled his mind, which was just what he needed. The gamlin were nearby, their noises warning him. Fulk'han. According to the gamlin, Fulk'han were everywhere. They were surrounded. A child cried out, and Scar barked in fury. A child? Was he still dreaming?

Anger raged anew. Lying in the tent, cuddling with Faeoris, listening to the rain—this moment should've been perfect, and it was being taken from him. He reached out with his mind and felt their approach. Bones shifting, moving slowly forward, footsteps in the fresh mud. They were surrounded; the Fulk'han were near and approaching fast. The heat of fury overwhelmed his reason. Those creatures had attacked Unsel and were now trying to stop him from saving his friends.

He took deep breaths as he sought the gamlin with his mind. Earth's creatures waited for his command to attack, and let Angst know where each of the twenty Fulk'han stood. Like thieves in the night, the Fulk'han circled their camp and crept closer. Angst urged the gamlin to hold. The Fulk'han were his.

He jerked himself from Faeoris's embrace and grabbed Chryslaenor as he left the tent, blurring past Jintorich on his watch. Faeoris cried something in surprise as he ran toward the first target. The gray man ignored Angst and his giant sword covered in blue lightning, instead staring in awe at the enormous monster dog. Scar had grown, the lab puppy now towering ten feet tall. His fur had become metallic protrusions that looked like daggers, and his six eyes glowed a bright red. The wagon behind Scar was destroyed. His growl shook the earth, and his steely fur hackled.

Angst's bare feet slapped against the mud, rain pelting his face as he struck out with his great foci towering five feet above him. He paused over the first Fulk'han target after splitting it in two across the waist with Chryslaenor. The Fulk'han's eyes were wide with surprise as it collapsed into a pile of itself. The gray man hadn't cried out, but the attack had been loud enough to alert the others and wake the camp. He could feel the steamy breath of Scar on his shoulders, and hear the tiny whimpers coming from an unknown voice behind his dog. He wouldn't let them be hurt. Frustration and anger became a maddening rage as he blurred to the second Fulk'han, slicing the enemy's head off before sprinting to the third without pause.

His head rang with sounds. Fulk'han cried out warnings to each other. Chryslaenor sang loudly, demanding he attack, urging Angst to hold the monsters still with magic. His traveling companions, his new friends, shouted at each other to wake up. Scar barked loud enough to rattle his eardrums. The gamlin chittered in his mind, offering help he didn't need or welcome. And somewhere in the middle of it all was a child's cry. It was maddening. And Dulgirgraut. Far away, the distant song of his other foci urged him to defend. He did.

Angst could feel his targets, now stuck in the mud as he willed their bones to anchor them, just as Chryslaenor had advised. He ran to each target in a blur, a red fury rushing through him as he destroyed them all. His was a berserker rage that took over every movement, but he didn't care. He wouldn't let these new friends die. He wouldn't let them hurt Faeoris. He had to protect everyone. Bodies dropped in smoldering heaps, splayed by his sword and burnt to a crisp by the lightning. Angst ignored their cries, ignored warnings from the camp, ignored warnings from his foci and gamlin. There was one left, and he raced toward it. He sliced down at the dark shadow, and his blade struck something solid.

The sound was like striking a bell, and Angst was thrown back in a flash of white light. Landing on his rear, he skidded several feet in the mud. He blinked away blinding spots in his eyes and shook out each hand. Both were numb, as if he'd struck a tree trunk with a board. Angst blinked until his vision cleared enough to see Jintorich standing before a crouched Fulk'han woman, his tiny staff held in front of her protectively. Angst took a deep breath and stood, lifting Chryslaenor to attack again.

"Stop!" Aerella cried. She moved to stand before the pink, cowering woman. "Angst, please stop. You don't murder. You don't kill, not like this."

"Get out of my way," he growled.

"Please, Mr. Angst," said a small voice. Kala stepped out from behind Scar's enormous leg to stand beside the Fulk'han. She placed a hand on the woman's head. "Please don't hurt the pretty, pink woman."

What was she doing? They shouldn't stop him. Not now. Something in his mind urged him to kill them all. His hands shook with rage as he stared into Kala's eyes. Her gaze pleaded for him to stop. A wave of exhaustion and guilt struck him, and Angst shuddered as the madness abated. He was standing in his undergarments, drenched in rain, his legs covered in mud. Aerella stood before him, pale yellow aura of magic surrounding her. Jintorich held out a tiny wooden staff. Kala looked up at him, her large dark eyes brave yet sad. He glanced over his shoulders to see Faeoris and Maarja behind him, both ready to attack. Tiny gamlin faces popped out of the muddy terrain, peering at him with curious eyes.

"Move!" Angst shouted. He was exhausted, but knew he wasn't done. Cold blue lightning forked about his arms, crawling around the blade. The lightning popped noisily at the touch of every raindrop.

"No!" Aerella said defiantly.

Jintorich shook his head, his long brows dripping heavy in the rain. Angst held the giant sword high, but they didn't budge. Kala squeezed her eyes shut and faced downward.

"This isn't you," Aerella said. "You're not a killer. You don't murder."

"I won't let them hurt you!" he replied. "Not any of you. I've lost too many already because I wasn't enough. Now, move so I can finish this!"

"Please," Kala said, shivering, perhaps from both cold and fear. She continued facing downward, her tiny fists shaking.

Angst stared down at the Fulk'han. A pink woman who looked far, far more seductive than dangerous. He wanted to be free of them, all of them. He wanted to keep everyone safe. But now that he looked at her, now that he'd peered into her eyes, how could he kill this woman? She wasn't just some thing. The Fulk'han wasn't an "it," she was a person. He lowered the tip of his giant sword to the ground.

"Go," he thundered, pointing off into the woods. "And tell your people that I protect all of Unsel."

She stared in awe, her gaze darting from Angst and his sword of lightning, to the nearby gamlin, to the giant monster dog behind him. Panic froze her in place, and her breasts heaved with every deep breath.

"I said go!" he shouted.

His words were followed by a crack of thunder, and that was enough to shake her from her trance. The pink woman hissed at him like a cat before running off into the dark woods. Part of him wondered if that wasn't the worst mistake he'd made yet.

13

"No," Angst said, as firmly as he could. "Absolutely not."

"Please," Kala pleaded, her lower lip trembling with the sincerity of any child. "It's okay for me to come with. I left a note with my mom!"

And how much trouble would Angst get in for that? "Dear mom, I ran away with Angst and Scar to save the world. Your only twelve-year-old daughter, Kala." Heather already hated him, he couldn't keep his friends safe, and they were about to face the very definition of danger. His eyes widened in fear, and he sought Faeoris for help.

His beautiful Berfemmian friend was naked. Not the mostly-naked of her armor; she was naked-naked. Angst hadn't really thought of it in the tent—it was just sort of cozy—but now, slick rain on her skin reflected the blue hue of his glowing hands like a beacon. He reluctantly concentrated until the light went out, the image of her amazing body burned into his mind's eye. Aerella whispered something, and a soft yellow glow emanated from her hand. Yup, still naked. Really naked, and she didn't care. Not a bit. Neither did anyone else, including Angst. Mostly.

"I agree," Faeoris said then her voice became hesitant. "I guess I could try to fly her back to Heather."

"But Scar needs me!" Kala cried.

"How long would that take?" Angst asked Faeoris, struggling

to keep eye contact. His cheeks felt so warm, the rain must've been evaporating on contact.

"She won't make it," Maarja said with a smug smile.

"What do you mean she won't make it?" Angst asked, turning to Faeoris. "You fly so fast..."

In the light of Aerella's glow, he could see Faeoris covering her mouth. Not her breasts, or anything else, just her mouth. Was she embarrassed?

"It's the reason she stayed in Unsel," Maarja said, crossing her arms. "She couldn't find Angoria."

"I'm not great with direction," Faeoris said, staring angrily at the Nordruaut.

"But you fly back and forth to Vex'kvette every year," Angst said in disbelief.

"Instinct, Angst," Aerella explained.

"After you got stuck in Victoria's room, I tried to find my way home," Faeoris said, not making eye contact with anyone. "I got lost and was barely able to make it back. I just wanted to check on my people. I would have come back for you, I promise!"

"It's okay, Faeoris," he said. "I know you would have."

"I could return the child faster," Maarja scoffed and rolled her eyes.

Faeoris glared, her hands balling into fists.

"Please, no," Kala said, running behind Aerella. She was pale, shivering, and her eyes widened in panic. "No more fighting! Please!"

"I won't hurt you, child," Maarja said, taking a step toward her.

Kala screamed. Scar barked, his monstrous head lowering to the Nordruaut. Maarja took a step back. Faeoris smiled and crossed her arms.

"No!" Angst shouted. "That's enough!" He placed a calming hand on Scar and nodded to Maarja, who looked confused and slightly hurt that the girl was scared. "Thank you, Maarja. I think we'll have to find another way."

"I can help!" Kala pleaded. "I'll feed Scar, and walk him, and help cook."

"Kala," Angst said. He was suddenly very aware that he was dripping wet in his undergarments. Unlike Faeoris, this made him very uncomfortable, and he dropped to a knee in the mud, hoping to look less imposing and creepy. "This trip is going to be very, very dangerous."

"I want to come with! I want to be a hero, like you," she said, her voice filled with shaky confidence. "And I couldn't let Scar go alone. He said come with! He needs me!"

What had he done? He'd tried leaving the dog with Heather, but gave up that argument almost immediately. Heather had been beyond upset, and Angst would've agreed to painting the house pink if she'd asked. Distracted by so many different things, he hadn't thought it through. Heather had mentioned the two were inseparable, that they had a connection. This didn't occur to him when Heather handed the pup over and said, "Kala said you need to take Scar with." The kid had planned this, and Angst couldn't help but smile.

He completely understood her desire for adventure, and probably would've done the same thing when he was twelve. Kala would make a great companion, in about five or six years. She had the ability to emulate any magic she saw, and the extent of her powers were just coming to fruition. But she was far too young to put in danger's path. He looked to the others for help, and they all looked back at him, waiting for an answer he didn't have.

Angst gazed on the prodigy. The rain had flattened her dark hair, which was far too long for traveling. Her olive cheeks were puffy with baby fat, but her thin dark eyes and determined lips in full pout mode made Angst smile. Her perseverance was moving, and who was he to argue with someone who wanted to be a hero? There was something he could do; maybe it would be enough.

"You can stay with us," Angst said.

"What?" "No!" "You can't be serious!" Protests rang like a

chorus from all around him.

"Yes!" peeped out a little voice still behind Aerella. She jumped up and down in the mud before running to Angst and hugging him.

"But," Angst said, holding Kala back and looking her in the eye, "only until we reach Oakhaven. I have a friend there you can stay with. She can see you home safely."

"Oh," she said, her excitement deflating. "But what about Scar?"

"Scar can go home with you," he said, smiling. "Bring him to Heather so you can both keep her safe. It would mean a lot to me."

She nodded sincerely, with a bit of win still in her eyes. She was getting her adventure, and she got to keep Scar. Angst sighed in relief as she gave him another hug. It seemed he'd finally done something right. Hopefully, Marissa was still at Oakhaven. The innkeeper was the only one he knew in the area who could be trusted with her safety. There were no further arguments, everyone else seemed more agreeable, or at least less upset.

"To bed then," Angst said with a sigh. "We have a long day tomorrow."

"Where will I sleep? You broke the wagons," Kala said, looking at the pile of boards and muddy tarp. "I know! I can stay with Faeoris."

Faeoris shook her head vehemently. Angst had the impression she didn't love children. Who knew if Kala would make it through the night alive?

"Actually, she's sharing my tent," Angst said.

Kala's thin eyebrows furrowed. "Won't that make Ms. Heather upset?"

"Uh," Angst said, his cheeks warm from being struck hard by this disclosure. "Well, I don't know..."

"Oh?" Faeoris asked. Her cheeks were apparently red for a different reason, and she glared at Angst darkly. "Why didn't you say Heather would be upset?"

"You, uh, you said you didn't want to sleep in the woods alone," Angst said. His sincerity was overshadowed by another scoff from Maarja and the cluck of Aerella's tongue.

"But I didn't know about Heather. She's my friend," she snapped. "Why did you think that would be okay?"

"Because you thought it was okay," he said. It felt as if his argument was becoming less valid by the second.

"It's not okay if your Heather would be angry...angrier!" she growled. "I don't understand your messed-up customs of one partner and no bed sharing. Humans are stupid." And with that, she sloshed angrily to the tent and crawled in, still naked, and now naked without Angst.

Kala covered her eyes as if suddenly realizing Faeoris wasn't wearing clothes. What a great story this would make for his wife. "I guess I'll just go home now," Kala said, looking at the muddy ground. She sniffed loudly and clasped her hands together.

"I'm sorry, Kala," Angst said. "Things are more complicated than they need to be."

"It's not complicated that you want to sleep with Faeoris," she said.

Angst covered his face with a hand and sighed.

"You can share my tent," Aerella said, peering at Angst while steering the young woman toward the other end of the campsite.

"I'm not sure where I should sleep." Angst looked from Jintorich to Maarja.

"In the broken wagon!" Faeoris shouted from inside the tent. It sounded as if she was crying.

"For once, Faeoris is right. Humans are stupid," Maarja said with a nod. "I'll be on watch."

"You can join me, Angst," Jintorich said. "I hope you don't mind. I sleep naked too."

Angst looked from Jintorich to the broken wagon, considering his options.

14

Wilfred enjoyed being a kingmaker far more than being king. Management was not in his blood. It felt much more natural to specialize in something and be appreciated for it. As Queen Isabelle's advisor—he was busy without being overwhelmed, the compensation was excellent, and almost nobody in the general population knew who he was. He now longed for the person who didn't recognize him, or even better, ignored him completely. Wilfred had always loved his work, but didn't realize how much until it was too late. So here he was, on the other side, and the grass wasn't greener at all.

General Mirot entered the great hallway that was currently the makeshift throne room. His burgundy cape flowed behind him, and a plain steel helm was tucked neatly under an arm. He walked toward the throne with an efficient stride and stern determination. His gray hair was swept back as if brushed by the wind. The man always seemed to be in a hurry. He was almost too thin to be a soldier, much less a general, as if he no longer had time for eating. Mirot consistently spoke to the point, in clipped sentences that didn't banter creatively or bureaucratically. He was a storybook without descriptions, who provided a service to Unsel but not much else. Much like a well-made faucet, he served a purpose.

"Is there something wrong with your throne?" Mirot asked, his blue eyes cool and intelligent.

"Just stretching my legs," Wilfred said, feeling his throat tighten.

Mirot placed his hands behind his back in a way that didn't really appear at ease. He said nothing, staring at Wilfred, his expression impatient.

"It's not my throne," Wilfred said. And it wasn't. The throne had been Isabelle's, and was now Victoria's. Sitting on it felt wrong. He wanted nothing to do with pretending to be royalty. More than anything, he dreamed of handing over a clean and healthy kingdom to Victoria, and being rewarded for that. Rewarded well.

"We've been over this," Mirot said. "In Her Majesty's absence, the leader of Unsel must take the throne. The people need to see you as a leader, and you need to act like one."

Wilfred rolled his eyes and sat at the edge of the large throne, worried that if he leaned too far back he might not be able to escape. "Better?"

"Almost," Mirot said, his gaze still disapproving.

"Next you're going to tell me how to eat," Wilfred said.

"You seem to excel at that," Mirot said, his cheek lifting in the barest of smiles before returning to stoic.

"Are you actually here to banter?" Wilfred asked, impatience tickling his hackles.

"A Fulk'han army has gathered," he replied. "They are preparing to march."

"To Unsel?" Wilfred asked, his mouth suddenly very dry.

"Possibly," Mirot said. "It's too early to tell. We will know in a day. The Fulk'han have become dangerous, and our spies are being cautious."

"If they are marching toward Unsel, how long before they arrive?" Wilfred asked, calculating scenarios.

"Two weeks, at best," Mirot said. "Speculation is that they move much faster than they used to."

"Angst said he can be back in three, which seems unrealistic," Wilfred said, rubbing his chin. "What if we send most of our troops to the east? Can we hold them off for a week or two?"

"Maybe," Mirot said, his tone unsure. "But the Fulk'han aren't our only problem."

The general handed over a rolled parchment adorned with the wax seal of Melkier. There had been no official communication from Melkier since Angst's visit, or notice from any spy who worked for Unsel. The only information Wilfred had was uncomfortably sketchy. Word of mouth reported that a dragon had laid waste to half the capital. Another rumor claimed that a giant, made of fire, had destroyed the city. Wilfred had also heard that all the damage had been wrought by Angst. Not only had he stolen a giant sword, but destroyed all their soldier's armor, and then their city. He shuddered. Was Angst really a hero, or a calamity?

"Maybe..." Wilfred began. "Maybe they are accepting our offer of aid."

Mirot shook his head again, and Wilfred's mouth grew dryer yet, transitioning from cotton ball to desert. He opened the document and skimmed its contents, inching forward, as if ready to leap from the throne he wanted no part of.

"Is it as bad as I fear?" Mirot asked.

"Maybe worse," Wilfred said, skimming it again. "They want Angst within a month or they will formally declare war. Actually, let me be more specific. They want his head."

"You should have made him stay," Mirot said sternly.

"Right," Wilfred said. "I'll be sure to task you with that job next time we see him."

"I would have taken his family hostage," Mirot said.

"And he would have taken you apart, along with the castle." Wilfred shook his head in disbelief. "We aren't barbarians, try to remember that. Well, at least I'm not. And he's no longer just some lone wielder. He can destroy this castle, this city, with a sneeze. Remember that, too." He tapped his temple with a finger. "So...Fulk'han could be at our doorstep to the east in about two weeks, at about the same time Melkier starts attacking our southern borders."

"That's not all," Mirot said.

CHAPTER FOURTEEN

"Of course not," Wilfred said, rolling his eyes and slumping deeper into his seat.

"There is another claim to the throne," Mirot continued. "And this one is legitimate."

* * * *

Wilfred felt the weight of his years, or maybe it was just his weight, as he struggled up the stairs to the royal hallway once more. He needed to exercise, but who had time when everything was an emergency? How was it possible for people to rule and be thin at the same time? It must be a magic undiscovered, and one he was sure would be lost to him.

A distracted staff had sent him from hither to yon looking for this newest throne-seeker, and it was a big castle. A sheen of sweat slicked his forehead, and the humidity hovering under his arms would mean another change of clothes before the next big match...er, meeting. Was this why Isabelle had changed clothes so often?

He stopped before the hallway entrance, gasping for breath, just in case someone was waiting for him. He looked up from resting on his knees to see two guards standing at attention along the wide hallway. The soldiers watched over two men, one in his fifties and the other in his twenties. Both faced the entrance to Princess Victoria's chamber. The visitors stared slack jawed at the scene before them. Wilfred understood; the image was shocking. Princess Victoria unmoving in her white gown, a large triangular, golden dagger emerging through her chest and dripping blood that hung in the air. It was so disturbing, they couldn't help but gawk. He couldn't.

Wilfred recognized the older man immediately. Lord Ranson was well dressed in rich crimson and ivory. His jacket and pantaloons were of the finest velvet, and his dark patent leather boots came up to his knees. A flouncy ivory shirt thrust out from his thin chest. At a glance, the man's willowy frame appeared that of a youth, but his slight hunch suggested that his thinness was caused by poor health. Ranson's face was stern, with a jutting forehead, weak jaw, and a nose long enough to hover ominously over his narrow lips. His pale eyes bespoke of intelligence and cunning. Wilfred had met the lord on many occasions, and despite the man's weak demeanor, he had a sturdy inner resolve. Isabelle had adored her cousin, and he'd supported the queen without question. Many respected the lord. He was not a fool, nor one to be trifled with.

Ranson coughed before Wilfred could speak, grabbing his chest and leaning against the stone wall. The young man beside him placed a hand on Ranson's chest. He looked like kin, with a similar longish nose and thick chin. Unlike Ranson's peppered flowing hair, his was brown and unkempt all the way to his shoulders. Mud caked the hem of his dark, burgundy leggings. They both appeared travelworn. Ranson nodded in response to his concern and mechanically turned to face the veil between the hallway and Victoria's timelost room. The young man placed a careful hand on the barrier and moved it around like Aerella had.

"Wait," Wilfred said between breaths. "Be careful, it's dangerous."

He jerked his hand back and both turned to Wilfred in surprise. Ranson flashed him a political thin-lipped smile and stood up straight as if the wracking cough had never happened. He left his companion and walked to Wilfred with an open hand.

"You must be the man in charge," Ranson said.

"So I'm told," Wilfred replied, taking the lord's hand in a firm grip and trying his best to make his smile genuine.

The handshake was professional and surprisingly firm. Wilfred met Ranson's eyes and frowned until the lord looked away. On closer inspection, those hungry blue eyes were filled with concern. Was this a practiced worry or the real thing?

"I apologize for the late welcome," Wilfred said. "To what do I do the honor, my lord?"

"Please, Wilfred," Ranson said. "This isn't the time for honoraries. I'm here to see to my cousin."

"Oh?" Wilfred asked.

"Is she still..." he replied, hesitantly. "Is the princess still alive?"

"According to Angst, she is," Wilfred said after a long pause.

"And do you believe him?" Ranson asked, frowning critically.

"Yes," Wilfred said sincerely. "Always."

Lord Ranson studied Wilfred's features, staring for several moments before nodding. "That's a relief," Ranson finally said, his shoulders loosening slightly. He looked at the young man, who bowed. "This is my son, Mika."

"Master Mika," Wilfred said before turning to Ranson. "Is it? Is it a relief? It's my understanding you are here to claim the throne."

"If Her Majesty doesn't survive, I am next in line," Ranson replied. "Unsel needs a king or queen if Victoria passes."

"So, you're not here to demand the crown?" Wilfred asked. "Then why are you here?"

"We're here to help Unsel," Ranson said, spreading his hands in a way that seemed welcoming, but practiced. "Of course."

15

Fire stood at one end of the long stone table, his blazing fists pressed into it as he leaned over to glare across. Black smoke rose from the pits of his eyes. The element looked tense as a bowstring, and the stone beneath his fists boiled and crackled as small pools of lava formed beneath them.

"You know, I just made this table," the tall, bald man said from the other end. He rested leisurely in his highbacked chair, rubbing his chin with a forefinger.

"I blame you," Fire's voice rumbled as he slammed a fist into the table. Hot stone popped up and landed on the ground with a sizzle.

The Dark Vivek appeared mostly bemused, and unconcerned. "And how is that going to help us?"

Fire flared brightly, his heat almost too much to bear, the light from his flame reflecting off distant cliffs. Embers drifted lazily to the stars, hissing away their short life in the cool spring air.

"What is it?" Vivek said with a mocking pout. "Why is Fire so angry?"

"You think you can just keep breaking the rules?" Fire asked, his voice crackling.

"We have rules?" Vivek asked.

"We are supposed to use avatars to keep from destroying this planet. It's always been that way."

"If you really need to blame someone, point the finger at Earth," Vivek suggested. "She took direct action against Air's avatar, opening the door for new rules."

"After that Al'eyrn destroyed your avatar, Ivan," Fire said, pointing at the man. "You did this because you didn't want to lose to a human. That's never happened before."

"Semantics," Vivek said, waving a hand. "Go ahead and blame Angst if you'd like."

"You said I could kill him!" he shouted. "You said it would be easy!"

"It should have been," Vivek said.

"He killed my dragon, the mother of all!" Fire flung out his arms. "I've had to create them the old way, and that uses up my power!"

"And did I argue once over Rohjek?" Vivek asked. "I even provided help to tend your new flock."

"What about this?" Fire said. "Look at me! Angst almost destroyed me!"

In spite of the element's rage and power, Fire looked like he had been on a diet. His frame seemed more like that of a runner than a weightlifter, his arms almost wiry beneath the flames. Like the Dark Vivek, it was as if something, or someone, had taken its toll on him.

"It's not *that* bad," Vivek said, looking the element up and down. He tsked, shaking his head. "Angst really did do a number on you, though, didn't he?"

A blast of flame shot out from Fire's extended hands, crashing against an invisible barrier in front of Vivek. The flames roared, cooking the stone table into a twisted mass of boiling lava rock. Long moments passed before the attack ended.

"Done?" Vivek asked. "Or did you want to end the war here and now?"

"I hate you," Fire said.

"Me?" Vivek asked, placing fingers on his chest, feigning innocence. "I didn't attack you, did I? I only told you where you could find the Al'eyrn. You were the one who took on Angst and

Earth."

"You always have to twist things..."

"It's not twisting," Vivek said calmly, pressing his long fingers together and resting them on his chin. "It's called a plan."

"Do you have a plan for him?" Fire said, sounding worried.

"I did," Vivek snapped. "He should have been killed by Ivan, or you."

"Or you," Fire snapped back. "He was a risk before, when he had one foci. Now that he's got two, he thinks he's one of us."

"The element human," Vivek spat and looked away. "Either way, you are right, the rules have changed, again."

"He destroyed Water! What if he kills us next?" Fire asked. "It's unfathomable."

"He does, indeed, need to die." Vivek looked over the element. "But you are in no condition to face him alone, and I don't care to either. He is at the height of his power, but his confidence is in question."

"How do you know this?" Fire asked, burning brighter.

"I know," Dark Vivek said with a wry smile. "I watch, I listen, I plan. You could too if you weren't burning with anger all the time."

"You mock me even now?" Fire snorted, slamming a fist on the table. "I hate being mocked!"

"Just my point," Vivek said, smiling wryly.

Fire stood, pacing along the length of the table until the dark clouds of smoke around his eyes and mouth subsided. "Doesn't it frighten you, just a little?" Fire asked. "He has so much power. Angst has broken time! Twice!"

"Of course it scares me," Vivek replied. "That's why he needs to be stopped, before he destroys everything by accident."

"If we are both...reluctant to attack him directly, what is your next great plan?"

"I've already taken away his friends, and hurt someone he loves. That should slow him down a bit," Dark Vivek said. "So we continue to throw the impossible at him until he's exhausted. He will be crossing into what's left of Rohjek soon enough."

"My dragons aren't ready," Fire said. "It's too soon."

"Your dragons and my tribesmen don't have to kill him," Vivek said with a malicious smile. "If he dies by accident, great. But if not, just wear him out. Chisel away at his resolve. Make him question everything."

"That sounds too easy," Fire said warily.

"It won't be. We have hours left to plan and mere weeks to execute," Vivek explained. "The only way we will succeed is to destroy him emotionally. Remember, he is only human."

"And then lure them all here?" Fire asked.

"I've already planted those seeds," Vivek said smugly. "The final battle will take place here, as always. We will wipe them all out and start from scratch. We will win Prendere together. It will be our vision."

"What do we do with her?" Fire asked, his burning glare finally falling on her. "Or should I say *it*?"

Alloria shivered, despite the great heat billowing from Fire. She looked from the Dark Vivek to Fire, hoping they wouldn't hurt her anymore. Her failure to kill Victoria had been met with unending punishment. The elements hadn't been able to kill her, but Vivek seemed to relish in her torture. Days and days were lost to pain Alloria felt like she couldn't endure, and when she would finally collapse he would haunt her nightmares. More than anything, Alloria wanted to hide from these monsters, but was unable to move, unable to speak. She could only hover in the air and tremble.

"Calling the young woman 'it' is a little cold," Vivek teased.

"She is half alive," Fire said. "And that half is broken enough to hold a foci."

"But not bond with it. Just use it a little," Vivek said, walking toward her. He snapped his fingers, and she could move again.

"Was that part of your plan?" Fire asked, pointing at her.

She glanced down at the half of Jormbrinder attached to her palm, trying once again to shake it free. The triangular golden blade of the half-foci wouldn't budge, and her arm quickly tired from its weight. She looked into the Dark Vivek's eyes as he lifted her chin. He inspected her as if she were an object, turning her head to one side and looking down at her body. It made her feel disgusting. Tears streamed down her cheeks, but she refused to cry out loud.

"No," Vivek said, his voice and gaze filled with interest. "What she did was unexpected. Humans always tend to be more resilient than I expect."

"Your pet is a danger. We should be done with her," Fire spat. "You said she was nothing more than a pawn. You should let her finish dying."

"Tut tut." Dark Vivek raised a finger. "She was a pawn. But with a foci in hand, even half a foci, she has become a bishop. Maybe a queen. And after what I've put her through, she will do anything I command."

Alloria couldn't bring herself to speak. She could move but was petrified with fear. It was humiliating. Even worse, the constant buzzing in her head wouldn't go away. When she concentrated enough, the buzzing sounded like a distant song. There was power in that song, just beyond her reach, and it was maddening.

"Do you want to live, young Alloria?" Vivek's mocking voice asked. "That has always been your driving force, hasn't it? From the look in your eyes, you do."

Of course she wanted to live. All she had ever wanted to do was live and enjoy life. And rule Unsel. And have everything.

"It's simple," Vivek crooned. "Kill his friends. You will be rewarded a nation for each one who dies by your hand. When Rose dies, you are ruler of Unsel. Kill Hector, and Melkier is yours. And so on."

The song rang louder in her mind. Had the Vivek found a new way to torture her, or could it be Jormbrinder? Angst had told her the foci sang to him. She didn't understand what the blade wanted, and tried shaking the blade free from her hand. The half-foci remained attached to her palm, and the song subsided, but her fear didn't.

"Just to be clear, either they die, or you will meet your final

CHAPTER FIFTEEN

death." He waved a long, thin arm in a circle. "And it will hurt far beyond anything I've put you through."

A void appeared before them, dark mists swirling into nothing. Her heart raced like a rabbit being chased by a fox as her body floated toward the dark vortex.

"This is going to sting, but from what I've seen, it's nothing you can't manage," he said with a smirk. He placed a hand on the small of her back and pushed her into the darkness.

She screamed as she fell.

16

Oakhaven

"Why are we stopping so early in the day?" Maarja asked, her low voice rumbling with discontent.

"We're dropping off Kala," Angst answered, trying to sound positive for the young girl.

Angst had other reasons for visiting Oakhaven, even if it meant losing a half-day of travel. He was familiar with this place, having been here with his friends once before. This town had seemed prepared for the unexpected, welcoming those who wield magic and even defending against Vex'kvette monsters. There was a good chance his new companions would be accepted. While Faeoris could get by as human, it was obvious Maarja was a Nordruaut, and, of course, Jintorich was something else entirely.

"Are you certain you don't want Maarja and I to camp nearby tonight, Angst?" Jintorich asked politely, as if reading his mind. "I'm sure it will be less disturbing for the town's inhabitants."

"That's thoughtful, Jintorich," Angst said. "But I wouldn't leave you behind. I'd also rather sleep in a bed with my friends."

"I've noticed," Faeoris said darkly.

"I...I mean..." Angst said, his back rigid and his cheeks warm. "You know what I meant."

"Ms. Heather is going to be angry again, isn't she?" Kala

asked hopefully.

"Probably," Angst said weakly.

Everyone else laughed, and he didn't know what to say. Fortunately, the distraction of their surroundings made the mocking easy to ignore. The barricade that had encircled Oakhaven during his last visit was gone, and the town was bustling. They passed a busy spring farmers market filled with early near-ripe vegetables and skinned rabbits that looked thin of meat. People glanced and, to Angst's pleasure, smiled or ignored them as they made their way through town.

They approached a large building near the center, the smell of greasy bar food wafting through the air. It made him think of Tarness, who loved bar food more than anyone, and he smiled. He missed his friends, and hoped they were safe. Angst and Faeoris dismounted his ram, and he turned to face everyone.

"Wait here. I'll only be a few minutes," he said.

Faeoris followed him to the door, despite his request. He sighed, but she was already upset, and he didn't want fight with her now. The inn was dark to his adjusting eyes, and even before he could see clearly, there was a squeal, a bracing hug, and wet kisses on his cheeks.

"Really?" Faeoris asked with a sigh.

"Hi, Marissa," Angst said, leaning away as politely as he could.

By the time she'd freed him from the embrace, his vision had cleared. Angst took her in, and she was as beautiful and full of life and confidence as he remembered. Long curly blond hair poured over her shoulders, tumbling around her full breasts, which were accentuated by an incredibly thin waist. She was curvy in all the right ways, and wore a soft red leather corset that made him stare for a lingering moment. His gaze finally rose to her pouty lips and green eyes that sparkled with excitement. She was genuinely happy to see him, and her welcome warmed him.

"On another adventure?" she asked.

"Always," he replied with a smile.

"Who's the hottie?" she asked, eyeing Faeoris up and down

with a broad smile.

His friend blushed.

"I'm Faeoris," she said, reaching out to shake hands.

"I'm a hugger," Marissa said, bringing the Berfemmian in for an embrace.

"I see why you like it here," Faeoris said, slow to release the hug.

"You haven't replaced Heather already?" Marissa teased.

"No," Angst replied, not daring to glance at Faeoris.

"Good," Marissa said, with a little too much sincerity. "I'm hoping you aren't here just for a nice hug."

"It was a very nice hug," Faeoris said, making Marissa smile.

"That's the main reason," Angst said with a wink. "Do you have some rooms?"

"The usual crew?" she asked.

"Not exactly," Angst said, his voice low. "There are six of us, including a Nordruaut, and a Meldusian."

"Oh?" she replied in excitement. She glanced over his shoulder, calculating. "I need to meet them."

She walked back to a desk, her hips swaying seductively below a long skirt. Angst glanced at Faeoris, who was watching Marissa walk with every bit of concentration he had been. She looked at Angst, shrugged, and continued looking on hungrily. A burly man stood near the desk, exuding an air of impatience.

Marissa handed gold back to the man.

"We're out of rooms," she said.

"But you said I could have two," he snapped.

"I misspoke," she replied. "There was a reservation I'd forgotten."

Before Angst could interrupt and offer to stay in a tent, the man raised a fist. Faster than he could blink, Faeoris grasped the man's wrist.

"Let go of me, bitch," he barked.

There was a loud crack as she jerked his wrist back, snapping the bone of his forearm. She twisted, and he collapsed to his knees. He writhed, his cheeks pale and eyes wide with shock.

Chatter in the tavern was loud and full of surprise.

"How would you like to be my bitch?" she asked darkly. "Do you want that?"

"No," he whined. "Please, stop."

"Faeoris..." Angst cautioned.

She let go, and the man grasped his broken arm. He choked several times, obviously trying not to throw up.

"Marissa, I'm very sorry," Angst began.

"Faeoris, thank you," Marissa said, ignoring Angst. "He's always been an abusive ass."

She walked around the desk and pulled the man up by his broken hand. He screamed loudly enough to quiet the inn.

"You are no longer welcome here," she announced. "Ever. Do you understand?"

He nodded, whimpering as he staggered out the door. As if nothing unusual had happened, the audience returned to their conversations.

"I now have two rooms," she said brightly. "Thank you, Faeoris."

"My pleasure," the Berfemmian grunted, glaring toward the door.

"We're a little tight on space," Marissa said, apologetically.

"We'll make it work," Angst replied. "Though, I'm not sure what to do about Maarja, the Nordruaut."

"Oh, yes! I need to meet her," Marissa said. "But first, I have an idea. Manst!"

After a long moment, a tall, thinnish man stumbled in through a door. His eyes went wide when he saw Faeoris, taking her in quickly. "Ma'am? Hey...it's Angst!"

Marissa turned to him and spoke quietly. He nodded several times before rushing out the front door.

"Introduce me to your friends, Angst?" she asked, taking his arm.

"My, uh, traveling companions are right outside," he replied.

He immediately felt like a jerk for correcting her, but they weren't his friends. Acquaintances, maybe buddies... Angst just didn't feel close enough to call them all friends. He led Marissa outside into the brightness of midday. Once their eyes adjusted he introduce everyone, and he enjoyed watching Marissa gawk in awe at the Nordruaut. She looked her up and down, a crooked grin on her face. "What?" Maarja snapped, apparently not enjoying being on display.

"I..." Marissa began, holding a hand to her chest. "I expected you to be large and frightening, but you're so beautiful."

Marissa stepped forward and did her best to hug the larger woman. Maarja patted Marissa but seemed very uncomfortable, her eyes wide at the unexpected compliment.

"Angst?" Marissa went on, not skipping a beat. "Are all your friends stunning?"

"I have good taste in friends," Angst said with a winning smile. Maybe it *was* okay to call them friends.

"I'm glad I'm one of them," she said, winking back at him.

"I can see why we're here," Aerella said, reaching out to shake Marissa's hand.

"It's not for the food," Marissa said with a wink. Her face suddenly lit up, and she squealed like she'd just won a new puppy. The innkeeper dropped to her knees before Jintorich as if preparing to hug him, but thought better of it and placed her hands in her lap.

"I am Jintorich of Meldusia," he said sincerely.

"I've never met a Meldusian," she said, bowing her head. "It's an honor."

"The honor is mine." He bowed politely, his long eyebrows drooping to the ground.

"No wonder you wanted to come here," Faeoris whispered in his ear.

"She's nice," Angst agreed, smiling as he watched the interaction.

"She likes you much more than your wife does," Faeoris said.

"Doesn't everyone?" he asked.

"Almost everyone," she said gruffly. Her eyes flashed with anger.

He frowned, but she stared at him so intently, he knew apologies wouldn't be enough. She couldn't just be angry about the naked tent sharing thing. She'd already been upset with him before he escaped Tori's room, but then he'd assumed it was frustration. Was she angry on Heather's behalf? He'd barely flirted with Marissa, and even then, only out of courtesy. Mostly.

Kala shyly came out from behind the Nordruaut's leg with Scar at her heels. Marissa's face went from amazement to warm and welcoming. Smiling softly, Marissa reached into her pockets with both hands. She held out two fists, palms down, and winked at the young girl. Kala and Scar approached, staring at the hands curiously. Scar sniffed at one, his tail immediately wagging as he licked her knuckles. Marissa turned her hands over and opened them. Scar gobbled up the treat like he'd never eaten before. Kala grabbed the piece of candy from the other before Scar could get that, too.

"Thank you!" she said, not wasting any time stuffing it into her mouth.

"You're the youngest adventurer I've met," Marissa said, patting the girl's shoulder warmly, yet unable to hide the worry on her face.

"Someone has to keep Angst in line," she said between vigorous chews.

"Then I'm glad you're here," the pretty innkeeper said as she stood. "Please, come in. Eat some real food and get some good rest."

Maarja eyed the small door, her head tilting to one side as she tried to figure out how to fit.

"I'm sorry, dear, you're right," Marissa said. "Manst is preparing space in the storehouse. You'll find it warm, and there are casks of ale. I'll have food brought to you as well. I hope that's okay."

"It was a good decision to stop, Angst," Maarja said with a nod.

"Ale, you say?" Jintorich squeaked. "You don't have to eat alone, Maarja. I'll join you."

"Manst will show you the way shortly," Marissa said, taking Kala's hand and leading the others inside.

"Do you always have candy and dog treats in your pockets?" Angst asked under his breath.

"A small courtesy with great return. We get a lot of repeat business," she said. "It helps keep this place running."

"Oh, yeah," Angst said, feeling dumb as he pulled out a pouch of gold. "How much..."

"Nothing," she said. "Heroes stay for free."

"No." Angst shook his head. "Please let me."

"You can help with something later," she said. "The hot spring has been acting up. Some days hot, some cold. Maybe you can..." She wiggled her fingers in a way Angst took to mean magic.

"I'd be glad to try," he said.

"Hot springs?" Faeoris asked hungrily. "We can take a bath?"

"Sounds fun," Angst said with a grin.

Faeoris's excitement washed away, and her eyes became cold.

"If Angst can fix it, you're welcome to use it," she said. "I would be happy to join you."

"That would be much better," Faeoris said warmly.

17

"That was amazing," Angst said, trying not to burp again. "I'm going to have the worst food hangover."

"How many times have you eaten like that since escaping the, uh, spell?" Marissa waved her hand as she took a long draw of her ale.

"Um, this was my first," Angst lied with a lazy smile. The port wine was as thick as his head, which felt much better than it would in the morning.

The bar was mostly empty. An old man snored at a nearby table, clutching an empty bottle for dear life. Manst wiped the table around him, occasionally eying them. Aerella and Marissa sat across from Angst and Faeoris. Aerella sipped hot tea, her eyes drooping heavily. She looked exhausted, older in a way, but it was hard to tell in the firelight. In spite of Faeoris's strength and prowess, she listed slightly, leaning against him. Angst was surprised how much the alcohol had affected her, but drunk was much better than angry.

"Your story...that's a lot of adventure in such a short time, Angst," Marissa commented. "You really did become a hero. I knew you would."

"Some days I'm a hero, maybe, but not all of them," he said with a sigh. He certainly didn't feel like a hero, but the port melted his self-loathing into a puddle of mere disappointment.

"So, you're really a Berfemmian?" Marissa asked, her pretty

green eyes wide with drunken wonder.

Faeoris smiled as she stood on long, wobbly legs. She squeezed her eyes shut in concentration, and her wings of light appeared in their shining glory. Manst dropped a dish, which broke on the floor, before stepping back against another table.

The drunkard lifted his head and looked at the wings and smiled. "Sexy birdy." His head wobbled before thudding back to the table.

"Wow," Marissa said, her shoulders tense. "So beautiful!"

"Isn't it cool?" Faeoris slurred, the feathers fading away as she slid back into the chair and threw a heavy arm around Angst.

"I love your armor too," Marissa said.

"Do you want to try it on?" Faeoris said with lusty eyes.

"That sounds like a great idea," Angst said. "But you should probably get to bed."

Faeoris shot him an angry look that was mostly tired. She slurred, "You're jussss trying to get rid of me."

"Let's get her upstairs," he said to Aerella.

"I'll help. You stay here and drink, hero," Marissa suggested. "I'm not letting go of our evening this early."

"It is getting early," Angst said, stifling a yawn.

Marissa threw Faeoris's arm around her shoulder. Aerella took the other arm, mostly leveling the young Berfemmian.

"Which room are we going to?" Marissa asked.

"I'll be naked in Angst's room," Faeoris's words sloshed out. "If you want to join us."

Angst sighed, his cheeks warming to the point of burning. She wouldn't wake up happy being naked in his bed, and he looked at Aerella, who shrugged.

"Kala is sleeping with me," Aerella said. "Faeoris doesn't seem...comfortable around kids."

"Bah," Faeoris blurted out. "I like puppies! Where's Scar?"

"Probably with Maarja in the stables," Marissa said.

"Is he all right?" Faeoris stopped, making everyone stumble or bump into her. She was too sturdy to budge, even in this drunken state. "I'll beat her again if I need to!" she said, raising a triumphant fist before collapsing in a drunken heap.

"Again?" Angst asked.

"Maarja challenged her when you were stuck. It didn't end well," Aerella said in frustration, trying to pick the Berfemmian up. "You just stay there, Angst. We'll be fine." Her tone was dry, but she said nothing further as they wrestled Faeoris out of the bar.

"Good, I'd hate for this port to go to waste," he slurred to himself as he poured just a little more, almost to the brim.

"Is that port?" asked a melodic voice. "It looks delicious!"

"I think it's him, finally," another whispered.

"Shush," said the first.

Angst wanted to ignore the voices but something about them sounded pretty. He took a deep breath and looked up.

"Whoa," he said, immediately sitting up. His mouth felt like cotton rolled in dirt, and he longed to know the spell that would make him sober again. At least a little soberer.

At first, he only caught a blurry glimpse of curvy figures flowing gracefully into the seats across the table. He concentrated until his eyes focused. This was obviously important, and he was elated to discover that he wasn't seeing double. A young woman with long, platinum blond hair giggled beside her twin with auburn hair, who rolled her eyes, elbowing the blonde. They were so incredibly perfect, maybe they were Berfemmian. He mustered up every remaining ounce of sobriety and charm to blurt out the well-thought-out, charismatic greeting, "Hi!"

"Hi, Angst," the blonde said in an accent he didn't recognize. The redhead glared at her, and she stared back, their duel entirely too cute to be fierce. The blonde came to some realization and said, "Oh, I mean, you must be Angst, right?"

"Yeah," he replied, the word drawing out much longer than he'd intended.

The twins glanced at each other with round eyes that seemed filled with intelligence and cunning. They both smiled mischievously with very pouty lips, and he took that moment to really focus. He'd never seen anyone who looked quite like them. They were pale, as if hidden away from the sun since birth. Both wore heavy makeup around their eyes, and those thick, seductive lashes couldn't possibly be real—not that it mattered. The blonde's hair was big and alive, tied up with a dark, leather bandana before flowing back far below her shoulders. The right half of her sister's head was shaved, the rest of her red hair pulled into a tight braid that hung neatly over her shoulder and draped down her chest. His eyes lingered far too long on those chests, which was okay because booze. Ample cleavage poured out of the blonde's brocade corset. Her sister wore a crisp white top that tucked neatly into a tight vest of wide brown and burgundy stripes. His drunky eyes lingered on their buttons of brass and silver, each intricately carved and unlike anything he'd ever seen. They had fine notches around the edge and...

"Angst?" the redhead asked snappily.

His head jerked up, and he smiled. "How can I be of service?" he asked, and unfortunately continued. "Not that I'm of much service to anyone, I'm reaaaaally drunk. It's been a long year, a tough week, and not the best day. But that's another story, and I'd love to service both of you."

Even before he could take it back, the blonde woman burst out in laughter. Her sister's eyes peered dangerously, but it was more like Rose peering at him. Friendly and familiar as opposed to upset.

"You never change," she said, her lip pulled back in a tight curl.

"You know what I mean," he slurred, not understanding her comment. He'd never met them before; even this drunk he would've remembered. "Wait, how could you know that? We just met."

Angst reached to take a sip from his carafe, but the young blonde grabbed it first and drank, and drank, and drank before her sister seized it.

"Lush," she admonished, not quite chugging the remainder.

"I could get us more." Angst raised two fingers.

"No," the redhead said nervously, glancing around the room.

116

"Uh...is Faeoris around?"

"That one doesn't like us much," the blonde whispered. "Not yet."

"What?" Angst asked. "I'm confused."

"That's because you're drunk, silly," the blonde said, winking at her sister.

They both rose from the table, one dragging a chair around so they could sit on both sides of him. They rubbed his chest. At first it was nice and made complete sense, thanks to the empty bottle, but then the rubbing became rummaging.

Angst reached down to pull a hand out of his pocket. "Not that I want you to stop, but what are you doing?"

"It's not here," the blonde said in frustration.

"Of course not," the redhead replied. "We were told it was too big for his pockets."

"But it was fun to make him blush!"

"A little." She smirked. "Maybe his room?"

They leaned in, far too close. Their breath smelled like mint laced with alcohol, and he steeled himself poorly.

"Or maybe you could ask," he said firmly. "I don't even know who you are."

They were still leaning over him deliciously as they looked at each other, as if communicating without words. His eyes slowly tracked from side to side. Angst was surrounded by breasts. It was impossible to be upset, but some dim part of his brain really wanted to know what this was about.

"I'm Bella," the blonde said, kissing him on the cheek.

"We weren't supposed to tell him," the other one said. "Fine. Angst, I'm Karina."

"That's a good start," Angst replied. "And cheek kissing is good." His head was spinning.

"We're looking for a foci," Bella said.

Angst's back went rigid, and he sat up quickly, bumping something soft in the process. "What?"

"Too much," Karina said, placing a calming hand on his chest.

"What's this?" Marissa called from the stairs.

"Hurry," Bella whispered.

"Do you have a horn?" Karina asked. "A silver horn?"

"A horn?" Angst asked in reply. "I...no, I don't."

"Let's check his room," Bella suggested.

"Where is it?" Karna pleaded. "Hurry!"

"Up the stairs," Angst replied, dizzy from the scent of a flower he didn't recognize. "First on the right."

They both kissed a cheek. Cheek kissing was still good.

"Don't forget us," Bella whispered in that delicious accent.

"How could I?" Angst said, turning to face her.

They were already scrambling up the stairs. Angst stood, watching them rush past Marissa and Aerella.

"The twins!" Aerella shouted. "Stop them!"

"Not so loud!" Marissa called after them. "Don't wake my patrons!"

Angst lurched from the table and stumbled up the stairs as quickly as he could with more than a little railing help. He slammed into Marissa on the way, and wrapped his arms around her so she wouldn't be knocked down. She didn't seem to mind.

"Who are they?" he asked, trying to pull away.

Marissa seemed reluctant to let go. "They've been coming here for weeks," she said. "I assumed you'd know."

"No," he replied. "But I'd like to."

She answered with a grunt and followed him to his room. Angst shook the door handle; it was locked.

"I can unlock it," Marissa said, digging into a pocket and pulling out a large ring of keys.

They heard rustling in the room while Marissa failed to unlock the door with wrong keys. She finally opened the door to see the room in shambles. Bags were opened, clothes everywhere, and the twins stood over a passed-out Faeoris. He wanted to ask what they were doing, but was too drawn into those large eyes, and pouty lips, and curves he couldn't even believe. Bella blew him a kiss, and Karina winked at him playfully. They held hands, and light flashed so brightly Angst was momentarily

CHAPTER SEVENTEEN

blinded. When his vision returned, the twins were gone.

18

"Really?" Angst shouted. "Again?"

He held his arms out and crouched slightly to steady himself from the sudden shock of being in the middle of a large field. He turned around slowly, warily scanning for oncoming hordes of, well, everything. Every step crunched noisily underfoot, and a warm, gentle breeze brushed his cheeks. Angst took in a full, calming breath and sighed deeply. The field was empty of dragons and gargoyles. Mermen didn't clash with Tribesman, nor did Nordruaut fight with men of Unsel. In the far distance, easily a mile away, stood tall cliffs that encircled the valley like a giant salad bowl. Maybe that was why he hated being here—he hated salad; there couldn't be anything worse than vegetables.

Angst shielded his eyes from the high noon sun and sought the others who typically attended this dream. The last time he was here, representations of each element stood at five points of the valley. Fire blazed like an enormous human volcano, throwing balls of flame the size of his house. Earth, the large stone maiden, lobbed boulders across the chasm as though tossing the top of a mountain was nothing. Water had drowned the entire valley, and Air stood in a dark, cloudy mess of tornadoes. At the far points, directly across from each other, were two broad beams of light—one so bright it hurt Angst's eyes, leaving spots in his vision after he glanced at it, and the other so black it chilled him to the bone. It should've been horrifying, but this was a dream, and what could possibly be scary in a dream? Other than everything.

Unlike past dreams in this place, this was boring. There were no battles being fought, no lessons to be learned, and even worse, he stood here alone, in the middle of all and none. That was what he hated the most. The last time he'd stood here, in this particular dream, was with Tori. Amidst the chaos of battle, as every nation on Ehrde warred with each other and all the creatures the elements could muster, they'd argued. Throughout their adventure, Victoria had been trying to guide their dreams to confirm whether or not her mother, Queen Isabelle, had been killed. Their last visit to this field had been a foci dream, where he had some modicum of control over what they wore and what they discussed. He had, more or less, forced her to admit being in love with him.

Angst had only ever wanted to be friends, but she was so forward, and it felt so right, and Heather was always so upset, that Angst couldn't help but wonder if there was something more. There was, and when he finally realized it, he also realized that relationship wasn't for him. He loved Tori as a friend, as family. A part of him wanted her, but he also knew that she was meant for someone else, and certainly someone younger. But yet, there it was. And before Alloria had stabbed her through the chest, she'd said, "I want you to be my..." He longed to know what those words were. The memories wrenched at his heart, and he wished more than anything she would appear so he could hold her and tell her how much she meant to him. How sorry he was that she was hurt because of his failure to protect her. But, she wasn't here.

Why wasn't she here? This was his dream. He shook his head, trying to clear his mind. This wasn't right. He could barely remember his dreams, and was now remembering all of them. If this was his dream, he would've looked more fit, and heroic, and thin, and there would've been a beautiful woman nearby, probably lots of them, and they wouldn't have been wearing much. Because, you know, dreams. Angst took a step forward and something else crunched underfoot. Sound. He wasn't floating. This wasn't a foci dream; it was something else.

"What's this?" he called out. "I've got to go save the world soon, and I need some sleep!"

Nothing, not even the kacaw of a bird or gurgle of a dying monster.

"Okay, now I'm bored," Angst shouted.

Energy crackled loudly behind him—it sounded like the lightning that spewed from Chryslaenor. He spun about. The wide beam of dark light appeared in the distance, reaching high into the sky, approaching faster than Angst on his swifen. In spite of the distance, there would be little time to step free of the charge. Angst reached out and wielded...nothing. His hands didn't glow blue, he couldn't feel earth or air around him, and he suddenly felt powerless.

"I'm not bored anymore!" Angst cried out.

Angst squeezed his eyes shut and covered his face with both arms to block the dark beam, but nothing happened. He opened his eyes and jumped back at the sight of a tall, ageless, bald man.

"I'm glad to hear that," the man said, in a voice unexpectedly high for his height. "I'd hate to be blamed for being boring."

Angst lowered his arms and stood up straight, though he hadn't realized he'd been crouching, and was pretty certain that wouldn't have helped much if the dark beam had actually crossed his path. The man stood very close, making Angst look up, way up, as he tried making eye contact. His opponent was easily a head and a half taller than Angst—his height rivaled Tarness's. Unlike his enormous friend, though, this man was thin and gangly, with long arms, and long legs, and long fingers. His movements were exaggerated, unnatural, as if he were still figuring out how his limbs worked. His head was shaped like an egg, with the wider part at the top. Everything about the man was awkward and made Angst's stomach roil with discomfort.

"Um, hi," Angst said with a nod. "I'm Angst."

An empty laugh accompanied a wide smile that felt as fake as this dream. "I am well-aware of who you are," he said in a haughty voice.

"And you?" Angst urged.

The man's forehead crinkled, and his lack of eyebrows raised curiously.

"Are you the bad guy?" Angst asked, placing his hands on his hips. "It really feels like you're the bad guy, and let me tell you how I feel about bad guys these days."

"I'm aware of this as well," the man said.

"Are you?"

"What constitutes being this 'bad guy'?"

"Killing people is a start," Angst said. "Manipulating people."

"You kill people, Angst," the awkward man replied. "And don't you manipulate?"

That stung. It was completely untrue. Mostly. A little.

"You aren't going to use 'a means to an end' as justification, are you?" the man asked.

"Probably," Angst said.

"You may call me Vivek," he said.

"As in, 'by the Dark Vivek'?" Angst asked.

"Dark Vivek, Vivek, what's in a name?" Vivek said slyly.

"Well, if your name was Jackass, I'd say a lot," Angst said, feeling clever.

"Or if your name is Angst," Vivek replied darkly.

"I think that's already been established," Angst said. "Or maybe you forgot and you're older than you look?"

"Maybe you aren't as old as you look," Vivek said. He made a flourish with his hands. "I wish to sit, and chat."

Angst hadn't noticed the long table and chairs appear beside them. The table was made of a dark marble, and parts of it were melted away.

"I guess I don't have a choice," Angst said cautiously. "I seem to be at a disadvantage."

"Oh?" Vivek asked.

"I'm without my foci...you know, Chryslaenor and Dulgir-graut?" Hopefully, reminding the Dark Vivek that he was bonded to two foci would make him appear formidable. "It makes it harder for me to clean up like I did with the others."

"The others..."

"You know, Earth, Air, Water," he said, flippantly. "I hear she used to win..."

Vivek winced. "There won't be any fighting today," Vivek said.

"So, what's this about?" Angst demanded. "I really do need to start saving Ehrde tomorrow."

Vivek walked to one end of the table as Angst approached the other. This felt like a negotiating table, and he didn't feel like negotiating.

"And why here?" Angst asked, unable to hold back his impatience. "Again!"

"Because this is where it will all end," Vivek said, crossing his arms. "Or, where it all could end. But you already knew that."

"Tori is a seer. This was the future she saw," Angst said. "Are you a seer too?"

"Isn't everyone who wields the magics?" he said mockingly. "Haven't you had the occasional glimpse in your little dreams of things that could be, and they eventually come true."

It was true, he had. Throughout his life, things happened that felt like he'd experienced them before—little, inconsequential things he'd dreamed about came true. Angst had never considered this seeing the future like Tori could. He'd called it coincidence, or maybe even fate, if there was such a thing.

"All who wield are seers," Vivek said, his high-pitched voice drawn out and sounding wise.

"So it's true?" Angst questioned. "That all wielders can use all forms of magic?"

"On some level. It's all about how you channel magic, Angst," he said. "Sometimes the river flows down a different path, but it's still a river."

It was poetic, and made sense, but didn't help.

"What do you want?" Angst asked. "I'm getting tired of this

place."

Vivek placed his long fingers on the table and leaned into it. "Please, join me," he said. "We have much to discuss."

Angst really wanted to lift a leg over the back of the chair to be cocky and threatening, but he was too short and instead shuffled into it. The chair was heavy, and scratched on the limestone ground. When he looked up, the valley was gone, no battle had taken place, and he was in a large room. The room was mostly dark, with the fire crackling in the distant fireplace illuminating the side of Vivek's face. The tall man waited patiently.

"Neat," Angst said to the sudden change.

"I've been doing this for awhile." Vivek nodded politely, lifting a chalice.

Angst picked up his own and smelled its contents. He eyed Vivek suspiciously.

"If this was about killing you in a dream, I would be much more creative," Vivek said, and Angst took a sip.

It was unlike anything he'd tasted. Sweet to his tongue, thick on his palate, and heavy in his stomach. A familiar warmth filled his body as the alcohol immediately took effect, and he wished to be lost in a dance with Tori on tables. He took several long draws before returning the chalice to the table.

"It should always be this good," Angst said with an acknowledging nod.

"Few mortals have tasted this fruit," Vivek replied graciously. "I'm glad you enjoy it."

Angst studied his opponent for long moments without gleaning any insight. Vivek was so awkward looking, there was barely an indication of his temperament, much less his age. He had the cool, stoic face of an experienced gambler, with only the barest of thin-lipped smiles. Angst felt like the man, the creature, would have waited forever. But Angst wouldn't.

"What's this all about?" Angst asked.

"Winning, of course," Vivek said.

"If you aren't an element, why do you even care?"

"Who said I wasn't an element?" The Dark Vivek looked uncomfortable. "Either way, let's just say I have a stake in matters."

"Then you're all doing it wrong," Angst blurted, drinking from the chalice again. The booze was strong, and his inhibitions quickly waned. "Rather than going to war, why don't the elements work together? Why do so many people need to die? Ehrde could be even more amazing if it were in balance!"

"It's always been the way of things," Vivek replied, his face curious. "Erosion, volcanoes, tidal waves, tornadoes, earthquakes...the battle always goes on."

"But at what cost?" Angst said too loudly. "So many lives lost. I'm done with people dying."

"That's why we are here," Vivek said. "So I can ease your conscience."

"Oh?" Angst asked, taking another drink. The chalice should've been empty, but it remained full, which was his favorite.

"You've done your duty, Angst," he said. "You've sacrificed everything to be a hero."

"Not everything," Angst replied.

"No, not your life," he said. "But why that? You have a family now who needs you. A wife who needs her husband. Two beautiful children who need their father. Don't they want you home? Aren't you tired?"

Vivek was right. He wanted it to be done. Angst felt tired in his bones, as if the burden were too much, as if his losses were too great. He felt old, and didn't he deserve a break? This heroing thing wasn't what he'd expected. It was so much harder, the cost was so much greater, than he'd ever thought.

"I can promise their safety," Vivek said smoothly.

"But what about my missing friends?" Angst asked, his tongue feeling unnaturally thick. "Dallow, Tarness, Hector, and Rose?" He struggled to focus, the words seemed reluctant to leave his tongue. "And Tori is still trapped!"

"All of them," Vivek said.

"That's all I ask," Angst said. "I want the people I love to be safe."

"I can make that happen," Vivek promised.

"What do I need to do?" Angst asked, licking sweet drink from his lips. He was so thirsty, his hand gripped the chalice firmly.

"Lay down your sword," Vivek advised. "Step away from the battle. Just as your wife has asked, it's time to stop being a hero."

Angst sighed in relief as though this was the answer he sought, even if he couldn't remember the question. "That's it?"

"Nothing else, Angst," Vivek said. "You will see your friends home tomorrow. Your princess will be alive and safe. Life will go on."

"It seems too good to be true," Angst said. He drank again from the chalice and felt more than a little spinny. "What about the others?"

"The others?" Vivek asked.

"Everyone else," Angst said, throwing an arm in a wide arc. "What about my not-friends? The Nordroot? The Fulkinn? What about the people of Melkeerr?"

"I can't promise you everyone will survive what will come to pass," Vivek said.

"I can't leave them unprotected," Angst slurred.

"Haven't you lost enough? Haven't enough friends died?" Vivek continued. "How many more deaths do you want on your conscience?"

His thoughts were thick as sludge. He wanted his friends safe, and somehow knew Vivek could deliver. But, someone else had a Tori, or a Hector, or a Rose. They were just as important as his friends were to him. What kind of hero was he if he abandoned everyone? If he abandoned anyone? He knew he couldn't save everyone on Ehrde, but he couldn't just walk away from them either.

"Your offer is fair, and gracious," Angst said, forcing the words out around his thick tongue. "But I decline."

"What?" Vivek asked.

"This is bigger than me, and my friends. They would all give their lives to save innocents." Angst said sincerely. "What kind of hero would I be if I traded their lives for me and mine?"

"But your friends will die if you don't," Vivek said. "You will die! Your wife and children..."

Angst stood, the chair flew backward, and he slammed his fist on the stone table. A wide crack appeared, reaching across the marble to Vivek, who stared down in surprise.

"Don't you dare threaten my family!" he said, his hand glowing a bright blue.

Vivek stood. "Tell me, boy, is this your choice? Do you sacrifice your friends and family just to be a hero?"

"No," Angst declared. "I'll save them, and I'll save everyone! I choose to do the right thing!"

The room shook, and the distant fire blazed and grew, shaping into something almost human. It approached the table, raw heat emanating painfully as it closed.

"I told you this was a waste of time!" Fire's voice crackled.

"Are we doing this now?" Angst snapped. "As I see it, three down, two to go!"

Fire grew, and Vivek stood defensively.

"Wait! You're not the Vivek, or the Dark Vivek," Angst said. "I know you!"

"And you will barely remember any of this!" Vivek snapped.

"We can't fight here," Angst said, realization dawning. "Or you would have killed me already."

Neither creature said a word. He was safe! Angst smiled, reached for the chalice and took a deep drink. He set it down and wiped his mouth. Pointing at Fire, he said, "Let's start with you. I'll take you out first!"

Fire roared, but Angst ignored him, facing the one who called himself Vivek.

"And then you," Angst said to Vivek. "Tell me, what happens when I win? Is that when I become an element?"

"Like we discussed," Vivek said to Fire. "Kill everyone he loves, starting with his friends."

19

Angst's eyes drew open slowly, as if he were trying to peel an orange that wasn't ripe. His head didn't merely throb, but rather made a thudding sound like a trapped monster anxious to get free. He foggily thought through his various discomforts and wondered if this hangover would be the thing to finally kill him. His burning stomach wanted nothing more than to empty its contents. Angst hated throwing up, for any reason, and began to take deep, soothing breaths. The bed was entirely too warm, and he wiped slick sweat from his face with his free hand. Wait...why was only one hand free?

His other hand was numb and tingling painfully under Faeoris' neck. Her firm breasts were once again nicely squished against his chest. He looked down to see her long, dark hair that smelled like fresh rain over a field in springtime. One of her legs was wrapped over his stiff knee, which popped as he shifted his weight. Angst's concerns became far more powerful than his burgeoning hangover. What had he done last night, especially with Faeoris? How could he uncouple himself to go use the bathroom? Weren't there twins involved in this dream? Why hadn't beautiful young women crawled into bed with him before he got married?

Angst vaguely remembered chasing twins to his room before they disappeared. That was neat. All he'd wanted to do was sleep, and dream of them, but Aerella had made him repeat everything about the twins. She was mostly concerned about the buttons on Karina's fitted vest, of all things, referring to them as gears. Angst had said goodnight to a nagging Aerella, sort of promising to stay away from them. They didn't look dangerous, though; they looked delicious. Perfect, even. He hoped he hadn't sounded like an idiot. Aerella had been right about one thing: they were there for a reason. Beautiful young women never just sought him out. He always had to woo them, even into friendship, and convince them he wasn't just a dirty old man. Well, not a threatening one. So, who were they? Twins were so rare, they were almost magic, and the only ones he'd ever met were his own children. Until now.

He drifted, thinking about Thom and whatshername, and winced. It must've been a very good port, or at least a lot of mediocre port. Either way, it had soothed his worries and ailments for the night, even if it was already punishing him. Something popped in his back, and he sighed. He didn't remember it hurting, but it felt better now.

Angst tugged at his numb arm, hoping to be gentle. Faeoris rolled over as if done with him, providing an amazing view from the top of her back down to everything curvy. The view brought him to his senses. After freeing his arm, Angst clenched his hand until blood flowed again. He sat up slowly and lolled to one side. Bracing himself with one arm, he drew shaky fingers through his sweaty, graying hair with his other. His gaze lingered on the back of Faeoris's fine torso. She really was incredible. How did she end up with him naked, again, after being so angry? He winced and avoided thinking on that further. Hopefully Kala didn't know, or there would be even more explaining to do. She was a constant reminder to behave himself, like he needed *that* in his life.

The only thing that really made sense right now was bacon. A lot of it. Angst needed food more than air, and the greasy kind that only inns like this could provide. His stomach growled anxiously at the thought before clenching in pain. He covered his mouth and let out a small burp.

CHAPTER NINETEEN

"I just want to eat then return to the blanket cocoon," he mumbled. Seriously, why had he had so much to drink?

Faeoris cooed something far too welcoming, and Chryslaenor sang something that almost sounded judgmental. Angst really wanted to sink back into the cool sheets until the throbbing in his head went away. It wasn't right, but Faeoris was probably too drunk to care if he accidentally curled around her again. After a long, deep sigh, Angst covered her up, because in a guide to chivalry that someone else must've written, it was the proper thing to do.

Angst braved standing, glad to see he was still wearing pants. They were drenched, and he leaned over to sniff, hoping it was sweat. Had he really had that much to drink? He must've passed out on the bed then she'd crawled in naked next to him. He smiled. That meant it wasn't his fault, right? Mostly? He leaned over to pick up a tunic, which was a mistake as his stomach revolted. He slipped it on with moments to spare before rushing out the door.

* * * *

As a boy, Angst had read a lot about heroes. Great knights doing great deeds, dragon slaying and maiden saving. There wasn't a single story that included peeing. Maybe it wasn't heroic to pee, or throw up, or break into a cold sweat and the shakes from too much booze, but he couldn't imagine being the only one. After his brief experience with this heroing nonsense, he truly believed a lot was left out of those stories. He wanted his money back. Nobody sang about friends reluctant to adventure, rowdy nights of drink and naked women the hero wasn't married to, or stumbling down the stairs. In his mind's eye, every knight from stories was seven feet tall with bright shining armor and the indelible disposition of perfection. They lived without err, they were always young, and so were their fair maidens. And skinny, don't forget skinny, and fit as if they didn't eat food to get all those muscles. He'd bought into a beautiful bill of goods, and thought he did his best to live up to it. But the truth was, this may've been the best pee of his life.

After returning to the inn, Angst could smell something greasy cooking, and used the walls of the hallway to guide him. The quiet was broken only by the sizzling sounds of breakfast, which probably meant it was early. His mind worked through the possibilities. This meant he could scarf down a disgusting breakfast, drink a jug of water, and crawl back into bed for a few naked hours. Of course, maybe he should sleep on the floor. He stopped and shook his head. Even this drunk, sleeping on the floor made no sense at all.

The main room was dark, fortunately, and empty, more fortunately. A dim light shone from the kitchen, and Angst crashed in more violently than he'd planned. The skinny, awkward-looking Manst spun to face him, holding up a dark, greasy pan dripping with soap. Not quite a foci, Angst thought, grinning to himself.

"Oh, Mr. Angst," he said. "You're still up."

Still? He was afraid to ask what time it was. He nodded, a little irritated that Manst was being so rude. Couldn't the funny man stay in focus a little?

"Not breakfast?" Angst asked.

"Um, did you want me to make you something?" Manst asked, his voice wary.

"Bacon?" Angst asked.

The younger man looked toward a plate on a nearby table. "This was wrapped around some of our beef for cooking. It's cold, but I'm sure it's fine to eat."

Angst eyed the small pile of dark, oily strips. He nodded and grabbed a handful. The bacon was cool and greasy, but it smelled amazing. He bit into the mass like a wild animal and nodded gratefully around a cold, tasty mouthful of sloppy meat. Even as he swallowed, his stomach gurgled loudly, which made Manst wince.

"Hank ooo," Angst mouthed. "Wa-er?"

Manst nodded slowly, handing him a carafe. Angst accepted with his free hand and chugged the water until he was too full. He slowly turned about to stumble out the door.

CHAPTER NINETEEN

"Um," the young man said. "Mr. Angst?"

"Mmm?" he asked around another biteful.

"Ms. Marissa," he said, his voice strained. "She was looking for you?"

Angst swallowed several times, and it was painful, his mouthful being too large. Suddenly, the bacon was sort of disgusting, and he turned around to return it to the plate. His hand was oily, and Manst handed him a towel.

"Thanks," he slurred, hoping it made sense. "Is everything okay?"

"She said there was something wrong with the hot springs," he said, his face tightening like the string on a bow. "That maybe you could magic them..."

"Oh, uh, sure," Angst said, his stomach clenched. His eyes were heavier than Tarness, and his brain begged for bed. "I'm not sure how much help I can be, a mess something like this, but if she's waiting, I'll let her know I can help tomorrow." It was so frustrating; he was certain none of his words made sense.

Manst seemed apprehensive, maybe even upset. He held a pan up high, almost defensively.

"I'm sorry," Angst said, not really understanding. "I probably seema mess right now too. It's been tough and, really, I'm just trying to help."

"Right," Manst said dismissively. Angst could make out wide eyes. "Just go to her."

Angst didn't know what that meant, but took it as his leave to leave and stumbled out of the room.

The night air was brisk, refreshing, and needed. He took in several deep spring breaths. Bed would still be a much better idea, but Marissa was waiting, and he wasn't rude. How could hot springs even break? He sighed. A quick look wouldn't hurt. He walked an unsure path to the rear of the inn and found a double door to the basement springs wide open. Angst stumbled down the curving stair, following a torchlit path to the bottom, where his knee buckled. He leaned over to rub it when he heard a pleasant *ahem*. His eyes slowly tracked from his knee and along the stone floor, all the way to the heady pool and beautiful woman in it. His eyes widened, and his mind sobered for but a moment.

Marissa stood in the distant hot spring pool, the water rocking low below her waist. Steam wafted from her naked body. Candles around the room reflected off her pale, glistening skin. Her breasts were far more than a handful, and her tiny waist stretched taut from the cool air that followed him in. Goosebumps formed as she shuddered, making everything jiggle seductively. Marissa's firm, wet nipples begged for attention. Long, blond, wet hair was pulled back from her round face. Her eyes were dark and seductive, enticing him to join her. His clothes suddenly felt very uncomfortable. She cupped the hot water in both hands, pouring it over her breasts in steamy wonder. Angst took it all in like a starving man, not shying away once from the beautiful vision. He became dizzy, and suddenly remembered to breathe.

"I came to, uh, I'm here to fix the hot spring," he said thickly, not daring to take a step forward. Not daring with every ounce of his waning strength.

20

Nordruaut

"Dallow's still in there?" Hector asked, leaning against a tree and rubbing the scar along his chin with a thumb.

"He won't leave," Rose said, unsure what to do. "He's obsessed with opening that door again. It's as if he thinks Tarness could still be alive."

"Maybe he is," Hector said.

"It's been months," Rose reasoned. "Out there, in that cold...you two need to accept what's happened. Tarness is dead."

"I would've believed that a year ago," Hector said. "But now, after what we've seen? Angst's head was split in two. I watched what look like a sun destroy a large city. I've seen dragons. Dragons! We were in a city that was stuck in time. And another city that was underwater. I just don't know what to believe anymore."

"I do," Rose said, her vision blurry with tears. "I believe Tarness is dead. It breaks my heart, but we aren't going to get out of here unless you two focus on what's real." She wanted to smack reason into Hector until he accepted the truth. It was frustrating, and Rose longed for a win in this conversation. "And why aren't you helping him?"

"Helping him what?" Hector asked, clearly dumbfounded.

Rose rolled her eyes. Maybe smacking wasn't enough, but

even if it was possible to knock him senseless, she would just end up healing him, absorbing his injuries into her. It always hurt, so talking would have to do.

"You seem more upset today than normal," Hector asked. "What gives?"

"I feel like we're waiting to die," she admitted, slumping to the ground.

"I'm not going to die here," Hector said confidently. "I'm going to die on the battlefield, against all odds, doing the impossible. There will be songs, and stories...though, not as good as my stories."

She couldn't help but chuckle. Hector could always make her laugh. She looked at the old soldier, who was even older than Angst. His military crop of short white and gray hair had grown into a mess over the last several months, almost hanging to his shoulders. He would sometimes pull it back into a top knot that made her scoff, but it kept the mess out of his stern face. His eyes were caring and yet intense, gray and wolf-like under thick lashes. Hector crossed his bare arms, all wiry muscle, and frowned at her. He wore light brown leather breeches and a sleeveless tunic. He held no weapon, but always had one in hand when needed. His magic, other than the weapon thing, was inside. Who knew, maybe that was where the weapons were too? He was strong, fast, and could climb trees like a monkey. He could stand incredibly still, like a cat, and then move so suddenly it would startle everyone nearby. It was said Hector was one of the few men who had been able to beat Captain Guard Tyrell in a duel. He was dangerous, and Rose was glad they were on the same side.

"There won't be any stories if we don't get out of here," she said sharply.

"Consider it a vacation before we return to battle," he said with a grin.

"We should be doing more," she tried arguing.

"Dallow is obsessed enough to find a way out," he said. "And if he doesn't, you and I will continue to explore until we do."

"But it's been months," Rose said with a sigh.

"Then why are you sitting there pouting?" Hector asked with a hand out.

Rose cursed his charm and rolled her eyes, but couldn't hold back her smile. He was right about this being a vacation. This vast city was far from awful; it was actually paradise. They were protected from the freezing Nordruaut winter. They'd discovered an abundance of trees overgrown with fruit, nuts, and crops of vegetables. Every home they'd entered was pristine and new. It was as if the inhabitants had cleaned before leaving. It was so unnerving that she couldn't sleep in the same home for more than a week, and left them all in the same condition in which she'd found them. Something didn't feel right. The other two mage cities they'd visited were cursed, so what had happened here?

She took his hand and stood before brushing herself off. He smiled, turning in a direction they hadn't explored. After two steps, Rose heard a shout from the library behind them, followed by several curse words she recognized. They were some of her favorites. She turned about to see Dallow burst through the library doors, trying to tear a hardbound book in half. He roared like a giant, but the book seemed to be winning the battle. Dallow's eyes flickered several times, like twinkling stars in a cloudy night, before going into hiding. His light blond hair was matted, sweaty against his forehead. Princess Victoria's blue sash covered his eyes, but it wasn't wide enough to cover all of the scars. Rose approached him and gently took the tome from his hands She set it on the ground before giving him a reassuring hug.

"Something goes wrong every time I think I'm close," he said, barely returning the hug. "Every time."

"What made you think you were closer?" Hector asked hopefully.

"I thought I figured out a word," Dallow said.

"Really?" Rose asked. "That's great!"

"What word?" Hector asked encouragingly.

"The," Dallow said. "I thought I successfully translated 'the,' but after looking at this book, I'm probably wrong."

After a moment, Hector burst out laughing. Rose covered her mouth, grateful that Dallow couldn't see. Dallow forced a terse smile, pretending to appreciate the humor, but not really.

"I should be making more progress," Dallow said in frustration. "It's been months."

"You'll get there," Rose encouraged.

"It feels almost like Acratic, but not really." Dallow sniped. "I'm going to call it Ughcratic."

Rose finally let herself laugh. Even if the joke wasn't funny, it made him smile.

"Join us for a walk?" Hector asked, reaching into a pouch and tossing him an apple.

"Sure," Dallow said, catching the apple and biting deeply.

"You're getting better," Hector said.

"It's not like being in Azaktrha," Dallow explained. "The memndus stone didn't work in the underwater city. While there's obviously some sort of shield here, I don't seem to have any problems outside."

Rose held hands with him, even if he didn't really need help getting around, and they followed Hector. Everyone assumed they were in another mage city. How else could this oasis exist in the middle of a blizzard? It was smaller than the others, but more colorful, as if trying to counterbalance the harsh conditions outside. Red brick roads and pathways edged by deep blue flowers wound through the city like an aimless path through the woods. Dallow had once suggested it actually was just one path, but would take weeks to follow. Tall quadratic buildings, mostly diamond shaped, rose high into a blue sky. The roof of each building angled like a hill with only one side. Several trees high, a second set of pathways connected buildings, though none of them had braved the sky paths. Who knew how old and well-kept this place really was? Dallow longed to see them more than anyone, to which Hector would often reply, "Leave flying to the Berfemmian."

"What do you usually look for?" Dallow asked.

"A way out," Hector said, his tone mocking.

"I know that," Dallow said, his smile fading into a grimace.

"We mostly walk along the edge," Rose explained. "We look for a door. Hector tries to cast your spell, Apenn."

"Rose!" Hector snapped, spinning about and trying to stare her down.

"Really?" Dallow asked, sounding impressed.

"I don't do spells," Hector said sharply, still peering at Rose. "But I want out, too."

Rose stuck her tongue out at Hector. She was impressed that he'd tried, and hadn't intended to mock him, much.

"I'm glad you're giving it a go," Dallow said with a nod in Hector's direction.

"At least we aren't trying to smash our way out!" Hector said. "Do you remember the time Angst was still figuring out how to wield and got stuck in the kitchen cellar with that serving girl...what was her name?"

"No way," Rose exclaimed, shaking her head.

"She was showing him the wine stores, and he tried showing off. He couldn't control his magic back then, and there was a small quake. The entrance collapsed. After a day of tunneling, he figured out how to escape, and made the room twice as large," Hector said.

"He must've been in so much trouble," Rose said.

"It's my understanding that the queen had wanted the room expanded, so Angst got away with it. They said all the wine they drank was his reward for helping!" Dallow laughed. "Though, I remember there being more than one woman stuck in there with him."

Rose shook her head in disbelief. "He really hasn't changed, has he?"

"No," Hector said. "He's put himself through a lot, but he's still the same Angst."

"What's that?" Dallow asked, pointing toward a building.

"It looks like another library," Rose said.

"Or something equally boring," Hector muttered.

"Sorry, I'm looking farther ahead." Dallow stepped faster. "Not the building. I think I see something behind it, floating in the air... Wait, boring?"

There was a scream followed by a distant thud. They followed the blind man as he took broad steps with his long legs. He led them down a smaller pathway, each of them panting as he moved faster. Dallow stopped abruptly at the entrance to a dark alley, possibly the only one in this city. A body lay on its side, curled up in a ball and hidden in shadows. Hector approached first, a small dagger in his hand, his other held out, urging them to stay back. He placed a hand on the body and shook it gently.

"It's a woman," he said. "I can barely make her out."

"Sorry," Dallow said, muttering something under his breath. A bright blue globe appeared in his hand, illuminating the dark corridor.

"No," Hector said. "It can't be."

Rose took several steps forward, her eyes slowly adjusting to the light. A young woman lay on her back. She wore a dark corset that was cut away at her midriff, her large breasts practically falling out with every breath. Her leather pants were sliced along each leg, showing multiple abrasions. Honey brown hair framed a face that would've been beautiful if it weren't sallow and gaunt. The young woman's arms rested at her side, and in one hand she held a very long, golden, triangular dagger. Rose reached forward, careful not to touch the woman, wary that she would start healing without being prepared. She instead rested a hand on the dagger.

"*JORMBRINDER*" echoed in her head, bringing to life a song that wouldn't stop, a ringing that wouldn't go away. She pressed both wrists to her ears but still the song jangled about inside her skull. The dagger wanted her to take it, wanted more from Rose than she was willing to give. A panic seized her. It was the nightmare all over again. Along with the song, her mind filled with flashes of the odd, tall man forcing her to bond with Chryslaenor. Rose jerked her hand away as if that dark lightning would reach out to her again.

"It's Alloria!" she said to Dallow, grasping his sleeve. "And she...she has a foci!"

"A foci?" Dallow exclaimed. "That's exactly what we need to get out."

21

Oakhaven

"The hot springs don't always work," Marissa said, her voice entrancing. "Sometimes they're cold, but tonight they're fine."

"Fine is a good word," Angst croaked. His mouth was very, very dry. Water would probably help. There was a lot of water in the bath. "Then, uh, you won't be needing me."

"I need you," Marissa said, reaching for another handful of water.

Where was this attention twenty years ago? She was like a magnet to his legs, but the more he felt drawn in, the more tense his shoulders became. Hadn't Heather kicked him out with an ultimatum? *The* ultimatum? Marissa's heaving breasts didn't take into account that he was a dad now. He should've been at home with his kids.

Her lips curled into a smile like a cat on the prowl.

He hadn't come here for this. Or had he? Angst was frustrated with his crappy heroing, but hadn't he done the job? At least a little? It shouldn't all be about the work, shouldn't some of it be about the attention, too? Yet Heather had been so upset, and for good reason. She didn't deserve any of this. At this point, Faeoris would probably be upset, too. He whipped his head about to make sure the Berfemmian wasn't marching down the stairs behind him.

"Angst," Marissa called. "I never should've let you go."

CHAPTER TWENTY ONE

"What?" he asked, looking back at Marissa.

"It's been so long since since I've met someone I like as much as you. I've been so lonely," she said. She pulled more water over her naked torso. The glistening didn't help. "Please. I don't want to be lonely."

"Felk," he cursed under his breath. Every fiber of his body wanted to touch her, to join her in that warm pool of wet nakedness. Nobody had ever tried seducing him. Certainly not like this. He was short and stubby. Women didn't want short and stubby. But there she was, with her curvy, really, really naked body. Perspiration from the hot spring, or alcohol, or indecision formed at his brow and dribbled down his cheek. He was wearing way too many clothes. He couldn't tear his eyes away. He wanted this. He deserved this. Hadn't he fought hard enough, hadn't he heroed well enough for a moment like this? She was so...very...perfect and so...very...right now. A beautiful naked woman lay upstairs in his bed, and another was longing for him in this hot spring, and his wife didn't want him at all. He really wasn't doing it right.

"Uh, Marissa, I uh," he said, looking around as if someone were watching, guilt thick in his throat. Where were the hero stories now?

"It's so hot," she said, but something about her voice didn't sound quite right.

A bubble popped in the spring, and she dropped to a knee. More bubbles appeared, and she reached for the edge. Sound filled his head. Gamlin, his gamlin were warning him of something. The sound had been there all the time, but drink and nakedness had distracted him. Everything was all drunken fuzzy, and when his focus returned, he heard Marissa scream. Angst scrambled forward, but time seemed to slow. The room was suddenly lava hot, and his legs felt covered in molasses, every step a struggle. She screamed again, reaching for him. She was just out of arm's reach, within a finger's breadth, before he was blasted away.

Dragonfire filled the room as an enormous diamond-shaped

head drove up through the ground. Her screams abruptly stopped as the hot spring, the entire side of the inn, and Marissa were just...gone. Angst grabbed for the sword over his shoulder, the one that was in his room with Faeoris. Cries from the inn's occupants filled his ears. He reached deep down for earth, but before he could attack, the dragon roared in anguish. Angst watched as gamlin dove into the monster's chest, boring through it like angry worms tearing into an apple.

The dragon writhed and thrashed until its head was directed at Angst. It lashed out with a burst of flame that rushed toward him. His lungs emptied in a surprised gasp as he was lifted up and away. What had him now? This was madness. He had to get to Marissa. He had to stop the dragon.

"Got you," Faeoris said thickly, gripping him hard around his back. He could only see her hair and wings of light in their embrace. He glanced down to see she was still naked. She didn't seem to care and held him tight.

"Let me go," he slurred, pushing away from her, trying to twist from her hug. "Got to save her! Kill the dragon."

They rose high into the night, finally hovering over the burning inn. He couldn't break her hold physically and couldn't bring himself to wield magic to escape.

"It's done, Angst," Faeoris said. "It's already too late. The dragon is dead."

"I need to see!" he shouted.

She tossed him up in the air to turn him around. His stomach lurched, but at least he could see what was going on. Patrons scrambled from the inn, running through the door or hopping out windows. The wyrm thrashed in its death throes before melting away. He could feel a great satisfaction from the four gamlin who'd killed it. There was a loud crunch as wood tore, and half the inn collapsed. A fury built in him, making him want to lash out and destroy the creature. He wanted to destroy everything! The madness blurred his vision and thoughts. Everything was dark and red. Faeoris held him like a cocoon.

"Let me go!" he roared.

CHAPTER TWENTY ONE

"This was a trap," she said, her voice heavy. "Heroes don't die in traps. I won't let you go this way. Not until it's clear, and not until you calm down."

"Marissa," he said, reaching out.

He felt so incredibly helpless just watching. Aerella was already moving from person to person, the soft yellow glow from her hand healing every burn. Kala stood beside Jintorich, holding Scar in her arms. Villagers ran toward the fire with buckets, following Maarja, who dumped rain barrels onto the flames.

"Please, Faeoris," he said, the anger subsiding. "I can put out the fire faster, and they'll need me if another dragon shows up. Trap or not, this is my job!"

"Fine," she said crisply, lowering him to the ground.

Aerella rushed to him. "I'm not sure you deserve this," she said, appearing old in the firelight. She placed a cool hand to his forehead. His mind cleared and the storm in his belly subsided, all signs of inebriation gone.

"I don't," he replied.

It was the clarity he'd needed. "Everyone back!" Angst shouted, waving them all away from the building. He reached deep into the earth as quickly as he could until he located an underground spring. The ground shook as he opened a seam wide enough for the water to geyser up. He formed a quick air shield over the geyser that redirected water toward the burning inn. When the fire was out, he sealed off the spring so it wouldn't do more damage.

He turned around to check on everyone. A soft glow from smoldering wood gave a clear view of tired faces. Maarja was covered in dark soot. The people of Oakhaven were exhausted and upset and Angst felt all their blaming eyes upon him. He'd apologize later. They weren't done yet—he could feel bones moving under the rubble.

"Maarja, Faeoris, with me." He waved them forward. "There are people alive under there, and you two are strong enough to remove the rubble without hurting them more."

Thirty minutes later, they'd found everyone—three who'd

lived and two who hadn't. They were also able to salvage most of the gear, including their armor and his sword. After they'd done everything they could, Angst approached the crowd.

"There aren't any more dragons nearby," he said, having confirmed this with the gamlin. "It's done."

"She's dead, isn't she?" Manst called out from the group of people. "Because of you!"

"Yes," Angst said wearily, suddenly tired to his bones. "Marissa is gone."

Manst ran to Angst, his fists high in the air. Faeoris stood before him, but Angst gently pushed her aside. The man tried to beat on him, but Angst merely held him in a bear hug until the flailing stopped. Angst didn't have tears, it was too fresh, but Manst seemed to have enough for both of them.

"She deserved better than you!" Manst cried before collapsing to the ground.

Angst placed a hand on Manst's head and tried to comprehend all of it. The dead woman he'd barely known. The upset, confused people of Oakhaven. His distraught companions. This had to stop. Death had to stop being the outcome for this nonsense of war between the elements. Manst was right; Marissa had died because of him. Being here had put her in danger, and he should've known better.

"She did!" Manst sobbed. "She deserved better."

"You're right," Angst said, pushing the man to stand on his own. "She did. You do. You all deserve better." He looked at his traveling companions, making eye contact with each of them. He suddenly felt very cold, and very angry. "Every single one of you. And I'm going to give you better."

They all stared at him like he was supposed to apologize, or mourn. He looked at Faeoris, jerking his head in a way that suggested it was time to leave.

She nodded in firm agreement.

"Let's summon our swifen, and get out of here," Angst growled, his throat dry from smoke and resolve. "We've got work to do."

22

Angst and Heather's cottage

"I really should be on watch," the young man said apologetically before stuffing another honeyroll into his mouth.

"Even brave guards need to eat, Mehta," Heather said with wink.

She couldn't remember the last time she'd made Angst's favorite rolls, but it would be rude not to feed her guest. It had to take a lot of food to sustain that sort of physique, and it was her duty to be a good hostess. Making those rolls had absolutely nothing to do with the fact that Mehta was cute. But Heather felt a sense of justification for feeding this cute young man in her home when Angst spent so much time gallivanting around with so many beautiful young women. This twenty-something, with his tousled black hair, dark eyes, and chiseled jaw, was the thing of dreams. The collar of his tan homespun shirt opened wide enough to tempt her gaze with a hint of collarbone. Not that she'd ever fantasize about olive complexion, or bulging muscles, or friendly disposition, or the fact that he was a flirt. Was it flirting? It had to be—some of the things he said really made her blush. Like "hi."

"I'm sorry," she said, hoping the makeup wouldn't melt off her burning cheeks. "What was that, dear?"

"Did you always know Angst would be a hero?" he asked,

while making funny faces at the twins. They both giggled, each grabbing a hand, making his forearms flex. He was a natural with children. "Or did it just sort of happen?"

And he had to bring up her husband. It was like a splash of cold water, washing away daydreams. Daydreams she really didn't have, because that would be inappropriate for a married woman. "He always wanted to be a hero," she said. "All his life. He even trained to be a soldier, but they wouldn't have him because of wielding. Once he decided to take that giant sword, it all fell into place."

"You must be proud," the young man said excitedly. "Especially at his age."

She stopped pouring honey as the word 'age' struck her in the ego. "You realize that he's only a year older than me, right?"

"No," Mehta said, looking up in surprise with those dark pools. "I assumed you were much younger than him."

The flirting made her heart race like she was being chased in a park. He was just so, very pretty. How did Angst get anything done with young women like Faeoris and Victoria around? She suddenly realized she was stirring his milk and honey with a finger, while she stared into his eyes. After jerking it out of the mug, she licked it without thinking, and then realized she'd licked it, and then really wanted to leave the room.

"What is it you do, exactly?" she asked, taking a deep, calming breath. "Why were you put on guard?"

"I can create—"

There was a grinding crunch of stone, and the house shook violently. Both twins cried, and Heather rushed to cover their baskets. Mehta stood, holding both fists out as if ready to box. A cloud of dust fell from the ceiling, making sunlight visible in thick beams. She tried to calm the babies while fighting back a sneeze.

"I do this!" Mehta said heroically, pressing his wrists together, spreading his hands, and aiming them toward the hallway. Soapy bubbles poured from his palms, and a gray-blue misshapen orbs of light quickly surrounded them. It smelled like sulfur.

148

CHAPTER TWENTY TWO

"You may feel queasy. I'm working on that. They will be enough to protect your entire home in...just...a...minute"

The house shook again, and again. Mehta grunted with each attack. There was a scream of anguish from outside as the ground rumbled. A cabinet filled with dishes rocked forward and then back again, the smelly bubbles keeping it in place. Heather held her babies close, concentrating on keeping her fear in check so Mehta could focus.

"Where is Kala?" Nikkola cried from outside the house. "Where is my daughter?"

"Nikkola, what are you doing?" Heather shouted.

The house shook again, and Mehta took a step back. His face was strained, veins bulged at his temples, his eyes pinched in concentration.

"Kala!" Nikkola cried. "Where is she?"

"I haven't seen her since Angst left," Heather said, and then it struck her. "Oh, please no..."

"Where is she!" Nikkola shouted again.

"Mehta, let the shield down," Heather said.

"What?" he asked, panting heavily. "No way!"

"Please," she said, placing a hand on his arm.

He looked at her with eyes that, under other circumstances, would've melted her. She nodded, and he lowered his hands. Their soapy protection slowly disintegrated as bubbles popped.

Nikkola entered the room, her face filled with the rage of a thousand volcanoes. Darkness surrounded her hands, and hundreds of tiny black orbs circled her forearms, each growing until they exploded with an electrifying snap. Her eyes were mad and wild, looking from Heather to Mehta. She raised clawed hands toward them, the flurry of dark orbs spinning faster around her forearms. Nikkola's breath hastened, and Heather placed a calming hand on Mehta's shoulder to hold the young man back.

The kitchen now smelled of rotten eggs and moldy books. The crackling from Nikkola's hands sounded like a forest fire in a lightning storm. The twins screamed as if they'd never eaten. Kala's mom saw the babies, and her heaving chest slowed. Her lip quivered as she lowered fists, the darkness flickering away like a candle out of wax.

"Nikkola," Heather said. "Please tell me she hasn't gone with Angst?"

The poor woman looked frail and disheveled as she reached into a pocket and pulled out a note. She handed it to Heather with a shaky hand.

Mom,
   I went on an adventure. I wanted to keep Scar and Angst safe. I'll be home soon, promise.
   Love you!
   Kala

"No," Heather whispered.

Nikkola collapsed to her knees, and Heather knelt beside her. She took the woman in her arms and instinctively patted her head.

"I'm so sorry," Heather said. "I didn't know."

"She's all I have," Nikkola said between sobs. "After my sister, Janda, passed, Kala is my only family. My daughter."

"This is my fault," Heather said. "I didn't think. She and Scar are inseparable. I told Angst to take Scar, I wanted him to be safe. I didn't think Kala would try to sneak along. I'm so sorry."

Nikkola sobbed into her shoulder, dampening it with tears. Heather focused, taking deep, calming breaths, and the twins stopped crying.

"I don't even know where she is," Nikkola said, choking on her grief. "I've never felt so lost."

Mehta handed Nikkola the mug of milk and honey. She took a deep draught and spat it onto the stone floor.

"Ugh," she said, handing back the mug and wiping off her mouth. "It's so sweet!"

"I like it that way," Mehta said with a shrug, finishing the mug.

Nikkola glared at Heather.

"What?" Heather asked.

"You're as bad as your husband!" she said loudly.

"I don't understand?" Heather asked.

"Angst drags these young women on adventures to who-knows-where doing who-knows-what," she said, her face curled in a sneer. "And here you are, with your own young man, offering him milk and honey and whatever you and Angst promise!" Her glare turned on Mehta. "What were you promised? Adventure? Sex?"

Mehta avoided making eye contact with either of them, wringing his hands, his muscular shoulders tensing.

"Well?" Nikkola shouted.

"They didn't promise me anything," he said with a long sigh. "I volunteered to be here because, well, I like it here. Heather is nice, and pretty, and Angst has always been kind to my family. And..."

"Tell the truth!" Nikkloa said.

"That *is* the truth," Mehta snapped. His eyes were glassy. "But you're right, there's more."

"Finally," Nikkola said, her shoulders dropping.

"It was a long time ago, like twenty years," he began.

Heather and Nikkola winced.

"My parents were in the Wizard's Retreat," he said.

"The Wizard's Revenge," Nikkola corrected.

"Back then," Heather said, "it was called Wizard's Retreat."

"My parents were married at the bar," he went on. "They said Angst was there with a pretty young woman named Izzy. Just as the ceremony ended, the Wizard's Retreat began to burn. Izzy said she could make it stop forever, but she would never be able to see Angst again. She kissed Angst, and they said goodbye. Even though it was illegal, he used his power to keep the building stable until my parents could escape. He saved them. He saved everyone. Ever since they told me, I've wanted to be a hero like Angst!"

It was apparently not what Nikkola had expected to hear, and she sobbed freely. Mehta looked at Heather with the blank expression of an innocent puppy. She nodded to let him know it was okay before looking at the door, urging him out of the room.

"Just...just please tell me he'll bring her back home," she said, her face filled with desperation. "Alive."

And it struck her. Was this what it was like for her husband? With beautiful young temptation at arm's reach, she was forced to make snap decisions to keep everyone safe. Every decision was a sacrifice, and every promise made a half-truth. What had Angst given up to be a hero? What had she done holding back their daughter's name?

"I promise," Heather said resolutely. "I promise Angst will keep your daughter alive."

* * * *

Unsel

Wilfred's freshly minted mage armor was the definition of "something is better than nothing." Not because of how it looked, or how he looked in it. For the first time since tending the throne, he felt, *dare he think*, kingly. Teedle the blacksmith had somehow squeezed weeks of work into days, without any loss of quality—at least not that Wilfred could tell. The suit felt solid, and despite his girth, it wasn't cumbersome. The armor fit snug around the front of his legs and arms without chafing. He looked in the mirror, attempting to adjust the breastplate, but it wouldn't budge. He rapped it with his knuckles, like kicking a wagon wheel for durability, and felt nothing beneath. He grasped onto that false sense of security, knowing that in spite of everything the armor was, there was plenty it wasn't.

The plate armor that knights of Unsel wore covered everything. Layers of steel like an onion—that probably smelled as ripe on the inside—surrounded soldiers in a metal cocoon. It was the reason they were all so mighty; they needed all that muscle just to walk around, and even more to swing those swords. Wilfred's new armor protected his heart, the tops of his arms, and the front of his legs, but not much else. Throw on a cloak, though, and nobody would know it was half a suit of armor.

Whoever had provided Angst with his cloak had excellent fore-sight.

"I feel pretty good," he finally said, admiring himself in the mirror. While the armor didn't hide his dark wispy hair or heavy cheeks, it covered enough of everything else and was made to fit. Angst and Faeoris had been right; he only hoped they continued to be. "I should wear this all the time."

"You certainly look less frumpy," Mirot said. "I suppose more like a leader. It was good advice, except I'm not sure the style you chose was wise."

The style of armor was his idea. The armor of zyn'ight, a wielder's armor similar to what Angst wore. The armor Teedle had fashioned for Angst was a dusky black, supposedly because he'd been in a hurry. Wilfred's was the bright silver of a polished sword. It didn't look as tough, but that wasn't his goal.

"They'll recognize it as one of their own," Wilfred said confidently.

"Everyone will," Mirot warned, his nostrils flaring and lips curling downward. "There haven't been zyn'ight for centuries. The very thought of magical knights, of a militia who can wield is... It's just..."

It was the first time Mirot had shown emotion since positioning himself as second. The general normally defined stoic, but his prejudices were showing today like a gaudy brothel sign. Anger surged through Wilfred, and he spun on the man, pointing a finger at his face.

"It's time!" Wilfred shouted as loudly and sharply as any slap in the face. Mirot stepped back. "Bigotry will not be accepted while I am in charge. If that's what you have to offer, you can step down right now!" He took a step forward, and Mirot shuffled away, his eyes wide with surprise. "That look of disdain you wear when you say wielder will no longer be accepted in Unsel, especially in this castle!" Wilfred said loudly. "The champion of Unsel wields magic. The people we are asking, once again, to defend Unsel wield magic. And by the Vivek, when our queen is saved, she will wield the most powerful of magics."

"I..." he said, looking about wildly with as much discomfort as a scolded child.

"Princess Victoria reads minds," Wilfred explained. "She knows what you think. She sees the future, your future! Tell me, what future will she see for you?" He hadn't even realized his finger was pounding on Mirot's chest piece. Wilfred lowered it as if withdrawing a broadsword. Nearby soldiers shuffled in place, glancing at each other, but remained quiet. The general hadn't backed down, but he swallowed hard, his face pale and cheeks flushed.

"I will serve my queen with my dying breath," Mirot said. His voice sounded dry, and he smacked his lips as he spoke.

"Even a queen who wields?" Wilfred asked.

"Without question!" Mirot said proudly.

"Don't you see, man?" he said. "If you accept one, you have to accept all of them."

"I..." Mirot sighed deeply. "I just..."

"Do you believe it's the right thing to do?" Wilfred urged.

"I hate you," Mirot said between gritted teeth. "And I hate this conversation."

"Do you hate Heather, Mirot?" Wilfred asked. "Do you hate Angst's wife?"

"No, of course not," Mirot said, his cheeks red. "She's a love-ly woman."

"Do you hate Princess Victoria?" Wilfred asked. "Do you hate our queen?"

"By the Vivek, I love my queen," Mirot swore. "I have said as much! Why do you keep riding me?"

"Because I'm trying to get it through your thick skull. Heather is a wielder, her husband is a wielder, Princess Victoria is a wielder," Wilfred said patiently. "If we treat them as equals or our betters, then we must treat all wielders the same."

Mirot nodded once, briskly, but looked to be struggling through his own internal battle.

"We are facing too many unknowns to rely on one man who isn't even here," Wilfred said. "Angst has requested we put a wielder on guard at Victoria's chamber. That's easy enough, but how do we defend against a Fulk'han army without magic? Do we bring back the zyn'ight or let our soldiers muscle their way through monsters?"

Wilfred gave Mirot a moment to toil and tangle with this conundrum. It took a while. The Unsel military was set in their ways like a tile floor. It took a leap to recognize that the tile was broken.

"You are right," he said, his voice tight. "We need the zyn'ight."

Wilfred looked into the general's eyes, staring the man down even while his own heart raced away. Those dark gray eyes were filled with questions. There was a sadness, or the type of hurt that comes with change, with admitting you are wrong. But, slowly, those eyes submitted.

"And our queen will see that," Wilfred said with a gentle smile, patting the man on his arm.

"Thank you." Mirot lowered his head, albeit briefly. It was enough.

"Heather has coordinated a meeting at Rookshire in the town hall. Now that I am presentable," he slapped his breastplate, "maybe I can convince them to join us."

"What is your plan?" Mirot asked, wringing his hands.

"We will reinstate the zyn'ight!" Wilfred proclaimed proudly. "We will have wielders as protectors, once again, officially recognized by the crown."

"What will the citizens of Unsel say?" Mirot asked.

"Nothing, if they are dead," Wilfred said. "This isn't just any war. This is *the* war! Our soldiers won't be able to fend off the zealot Fulk'han, not alone. If we're asking wielders to defend us, to die for us, they deserve that title."

Mirot wasn't as intelligent or cunning as himself, but he had a sort of wisdom, a street-smart that came only from experience. Mirot seemed as upset as Wilfred's stomach after skipping two meals. The general was lost in thought and calculation. This was it; this was the test. Mirot was deep in the throes of bigotry, but he was also a planner. If Mirot accepted his plan, there was a greater chance the citizens of Unsel would follow. The battle wasn't only with the Fulk'han, it was here at home. And who would win? Bigotry or the will to survive?

"We also need the zyn'ight to work as a part of the military, not alongside it, doing their own thing, or we risk putting everyone in danger," Mirot said. "That is a reason we can share with our people."

"Yes," Wilfred said, unable to hold back a smile. "You should join me at Rookshire."

"If you wish," Mirot said, "but it may be best for me to stay behind. My opinion is well known."

"Exactly why you should be there," Wilfred said. "But it has to be your choice."

"Then I will join you," Mirot said, wiping his palms on his legs.

Wilfred nodded, sighing in relief. One down, thousands to go.

23

Unsel – border of Grayhollow Forest

To his surprise, Angst felt cold, but not tearful. He'd thought of Marissa as a friend. Not a close friend, like Victoria, or something else, like Moyra, but a buddy he could talk to. Someone he could count on. He couldn't imagine what had overtaken her to try to seduce him. Maybe her eyesight was bad. His wasn't. Angst had seen clearly, even through his cloudy drunkenness, how incredible she'd looked standing in that pool. His stomach cramped with the vision of the dragon tearing into her, a memory that would leave scars. It hurt, but he didn't feel like mourning. This fresh wound made him itch to fight. Anger simmered at the base of that pain, a slowly boiling pit deep in his gut. As if fed by his fury, the songs of Chryslaenor and distant Dulgirgraut clashed in his head like an orchestra terribly out of key.

"Angst!" Faeoris shouted, smacking the back of his head.

"What?" he lashed out. Had she been talking? She really didn't deserve his anger, but he hated everything right now, and she smacked hard.

"Fine," she said sharply. "If you aren't going to listen, you don't need me here."

Faeoris shoved down hard on his shoulders as she launched from the back of his steel ram swifen. She was upset, her voice filled with worry and fury. It had been thoughtful of her to ride with him after Oakhaven, but his mood was shrouded in darkness, and he couldn't have been worse company. Angst had never felt so bitter. Everything was falling apart. His marriage was all but over. His friends missing. His best friend, Victoria, almost dead. And now Marissa? The more he tried to be a hero, the more he put people he loved and cared about in danger. He only wished there was a way to go back and change it. To set everything right. The only way out of this mess was to destroy everything that threatened him and his, or die trying. And right now, buried somewhere in his gloomy thoughts, he also worried about what he was leading these people into. And what in the world was he going to do with Kala?

"We are close to the forest," Maarja said, as if answering his unasked question. "We should make our way through it quickly."

"Carefully," Aerella corrected, holding tight onto Kala. Even though Kala could summon her own swifen, they'd all agreed she would be safer traveling with an adult. The young girl could quickly be lost if she were to race off in panic. "There are reasons people avoid Grayhollow Forest, and not just because of the terrible stories."

"What terrible stories?" Kala asked, clutching the lab pup closely.

"Last time I was here, Scar had been affected by the Vex'kvette, but that didn't turn out too badly, did it?" Angst asked, winking at Kala. He didn't feel like being positive, but, in a way, he was responsible for her being here, and she needed hope. "And we saw a Mendahir Rise. It was very pretty."

Maarja peered, gripping so tightly to her longbow that the wood creaked. She looked as upset as Faeoris. Why not? Everyone was angry at him for something. But she hadn't reacted until he'd mentioned the Mendahir Rise.

History was not Angst's best subject—that was Dallow's job—but he vaguely remembered that Grayhollow was home to the Mendahir. Something had happened long ago between the lost race, the Angorian, and the Nordruaut. A history that Dallow would've been excited to explain in such infinite detail that Angst would've had to struggle to listen. Who knew, maybe his oldest friend had explained it once already. He should pay more attention, maybe not to history lessons, but to his friends. Faeoris deserved his attention now just as Dallow had deserved it.

"Angst?" Jintorich asked in a squeaky voice, his ears perked up excitedly.

He'd already been nice to Kala. Did he really have to be nice to Jintorich, too? But, hadn't he also just chided himself about being a better listener?

"Yes?" he asked through a gritted smile.

"Would you tell me about bonding with your foci?" Jintorich asked.

Angst turned his head to face the Meldusian. Jintorich and Maarja rode together on a creature he didn't recognize. It had six thick legs and a wide dog-like head with horns. The swifen was made of red gravel and was large enough for them both to ride. Angst hadn't considered the fact that it meant Jintorich could wield magic, or was maybe magical like Hector.

"We should eat," Aerella said. "It's well past lunch."

She and Kala dismounted her swifen before it disappeared. Aerella placed two fingers in her mouth and blew out a piercing whistle. Within several breaths, Faeoris landed with a thud that shook the ground, cracks appearing beneath her feet. She wouldn't make eye contact with Angst, walking swiftly to Aerella to speak in whispers. Angst shook his head in dismay. Had being ignored made her angry enough to break the ground, or was it still that tenuous strain he'd felt between them since escaping Victoria's chamber? He was the last one remaining on a swifen, so he patted the shiny steel ram before it disappeared, dropping him and his satchel.

"Fine," he said, frustration building. Had they forgotten about being in a hurry? "Is there anything I can help with?"

"No," Aerella and Faeoris said in unison as they broke apart bread and cheese. "Kala, please come help."

The young girl grunted, reluctantly placing Scar on the ground. She stomped over to Aerella but didn't say no.

Angst sighed and looked from them to Maarja. The enormous Nordruaut sat on a boulder, tearing apart a dark, fibrous root and shoving pieces into her mouth. She glared at Faeoris briefly before looking off into the distance. Was this what he should expect from the next several weeks, or was his dark mood tainting his expectations? Were they possibly feeding off his own poor attitude? Scar barked, his tail wagging furiously as he leaped at a tall blade of grass, grabbing it in his jaws. He tugged and rolled around in fierce battle until he was wrapped in grass. The puppy looked at Angst helplessly and yipped in fear.

"The most powerful dog on Ehrde defeated by a blade of grass." Angst chuckled. He couldn't help but smile as he freed Scar from the evil confines of foliage. Scar barked fiercely at the grass before Angst scooped him up and petted out the hackles. "I'm just glad you're here to protect everyone. Thank you for keeping us safe."

"Ahem," Jintorich coughed politely.

Angst looked down, making eye contact with the Meldusian. The tiny, black marbles that looked up at him were impossible to read. Jintorich's long brows dangled over his heavy eyelashes. He seemed sincere, and Angst returned Scar to the ground. The pup ran off toward Kala.

"Right," Angst said, clapping dust and puppy off his hands. "Sorry. You were asking about my foci."

"If you don't mind," Jintorich said, sitting on the ground and placing his tiny staff across his knees. "I traveled for months, all the way from Meldusia, to discuss your experience with Chryslaenor. Now that you are bonded to Dulgirgraut as well, I'm very hungry to learn."

"Oh, I didn't realize that's why you came to Unsel," Angst said, unable to hold back his surprise. He removed Chryslaenor from his back and set it on its tip. He sat slowly, unsure which creaked louder, his joints or his armor. "A lot has happened over the last six months... Well, I guess it's actually nine months. I'll do my best."

"Please, tell me about the first time you held your foci," Jintorich said.

"I'll start with the first time I picked up my foci," Angst said firmly.

Jintorich smiled around his great, bulbous nose and nodded vigorously. Angst couldn't help but return the smile. The Meldusian was always so kind, and so patient. Not only had he been Heather's midwife, which was still shocking, but he was here, helping Angst face the unknown. All of this to learn about his sword? The man deserved to know everything he could remember.

"I first picked up Chryslaenor at a party," Angst began. "Every fall, the queen threw a party for the staff. It was a way of saying thank you for all our hard work. Thinking back, it was a generous thing for Isabelle to do. I never thought she cared, but she must have. Anyway, I was a member of that staff, and held the awesome and respectable position of paper shuffling. Every law passed came into my small office for filing in the cellar of the castle. It wasn't a glorious job, or heroic, but none of my friends got killed or went missing."

Jintorich looked ready to interrupt, but instead sucked in his puffy lips.

"Sorry," he muttered awkwardly. That had sounded much funnier in his mind.

Faeoris dropped a plate onto his lap so forcefully a hard roll bounced to the ground. He grabbed the bread and brushed it off before looking at her. She ignored him, and he worried. How many apologies would it take to make things right?

"Please," Maarja urged. "Continue your story."

"Sure," he said. This had to be the first time she was actually interested in something he was saying. Nordruaut did love stories. "So, the party was held in a courtyard. In the middle was a monument with a giant sword that everyone thought was a statue. All new employees were encouraged to try to lift the sword. It was a game. A joke. If anyone could lift it, they would be knighted. No one ever did, and it was mostly considered to be hazing. Anyway, as the party wound down, a knight, Sir Ivan, was harassing my friend Rose. She can handle herself, and typically I wouldn't have interfered, but he wasn't alone, he was in armor, and he was drunk. I don't know what he said, but it was bad enough that she poured wine on him..."

"Good," Faeoris said.

"He deserved it, but it probably wasn't the best idea. Ivan was a large man, and Rose is tiny," he said, looking at Jintorich, "and human. He picked her up by a wrist and was going to strike her. When he reached back, his hand hit the sword. He looked back to see that I was holding that thing, which was supposed to make me a knight. It was enough to make him stop attacking."

"And then you killed him?" Faeoris asked, frowning.

"No," he said.

"And then you bonded with the sword?" Jintorich asked, his voice high and excited.

"No," Angst replied. "I brought it home and went to bed."

"So, you didn't bond with it?" the Meldusian asked.

"And you didn't kill him?" Faeoris asked, frowning in confusion. She tore angrily into her roll.

"Not yet," Angst said to both of them. "But Chryslaenor still gave me great power."

"How could you use the sword without bonding?" Jintorich asked.

"I guess it sort of wanted me to," Angst struggled to explain. "Chryslaenor wanted me to bond, and shared power with me until I would. I didn't completely understand at the time. I had no control over the power at all, but it seemed to work best when I was emotional."

"When you were angry," Aerella interrupted. "The foci would give Angst bursts of great power, but only when he was driven by strong emotion like anger, or, uh, angst. Sometimes he was even more powerful than an Al'eyrn, and sometimes it would kill him."

"Kill him?" Faeoris asked in concern.

"I tend to die," he said. "But my foci, somehow, always brings me back."

Maarja barked out a laugh. "You couldn't have been so very dead."

"He was!" Kala said defensively. "Scar said so!"

"Please," Jintorich said, looking up at his tall friend. His pale cheeks were blotchy, and he seemed upset. "Let him continue."

Maarja nodded respectfully, her lip raised in a disbelieving curl.

"A lot happened. We traveled to Gressmore Towers and met Aerella's father, Anderfeld. He wielded the foci, Dulgirgraut, and had cast the spell 'at all costs' to protect the mage city from a dragon attack. The spell cursed the city to live the same day over and over for two thousand years. To break the spell, he tricked me into killing him. We were cast out with Aerella, and the city was returned to the past. At least, that's what we assumed. When we woke, everything was in ruins."

"What? Angst...he killed your father?" Faeoris asked, looking between the two of them. She thoughtfully placed a hand on Aerella's.

Aerella blinked rapidly. Guilt welled up in him, and he swallowed hard. Killing an innocent man was his first, great failure as a hero. The Gressmore wielders had made Angst see an illusion of Anderfeld murdering Rose, and he'd lost control. His fury, and the power he wielded from Chryslaenor, drove him to kill, but there should've been another way.

"I used to be upset with Angst, but he was tricked," Aerella said, her face contorted in a wince. "He really had no choice."

They shared a long gaze, her eyes holding back fire and bitterness, but not at him. Did she feel the same? That it should have gone another way? She nodded, either in agreement, or to continue. Either way, it didn't help his guilt.

"Even as we were being kicked out of Gressmore," Angst finally went on, "Ivan got lost in the Vex'kvette."

"Ooh," Maarja said, leaning in as if a jouster had been struck with a lance.

"Yeah, it wasn't good," Angst continued.

"Didn't you beat him first?" Aerella asked.

"I slapped him senseless." Angst grunted. He met Kala's frown and rolled his eyes. "It wasn't my proudest moment, but the man was crazy. Something in the Vex'kvette drove him mad. Eventually, it changed him into a giant, a monster. Somehow, he mutated all Fulk'han into whatever they are now. I fought him, and he beat me by splitting my head open with Chryslaenor."

"What?" Faeoris asked, leaping to her feet, her plate dropping to the ground. Scar rushed over to lick it clean.

"That's not possible," Maarja said in shock.

"Almost in half," Angst clarified, rubbing at the spot on his forehead. "I don't remember much. I was told they dragged my body to a dungeon so my companions could watch me die. I didn't, not completely, Chryslaenor wouldn't let me. I just re-member pain, all of the pain."

"You couldn't have survived this." Maarja shook her head.

"My friend Rose is a healer who could absorb injuries. Rose was attacked by two guards and grabbed my ankle. She trans-ferred the damage Ivan had caused to one of them. His head exploded, and mine knit back together. I woke up and immedi-ately bonded with Chryslaenor. It's a longer story, but I eventually destroyed Ivan."

"Yes!" Faeoris said, still standing.

"Fascinating," Jintorich said, his black eyes wide. "And Dulgirgraut?"

"Well," Angst said. "Ivan had actually been taken over by the element Magic. It became a beam of light that reached high up into the sky, but it was black. I chased Magic to Unsel. We trav-eled from Fulk'han to the capital of Unsel so fast, it only took the night. Magic threatened to kill the people I cared for most, the ones I love. I had to stop it no matter what, and the only way I could trap it..."

"Was to break the binding with Chryslaenor," Jintorich fin-ished his sentence, his voice filled with wonder. "That...that must have been awful. How are you still alive?"

"Dulgirgraut," Angst said, frowning at him thoughtfully. How could Jintorich know all of this? "Removing the bond almost killed me. One moment I'd be flush with more power than ever, the next I'd be sick and weak. It took a while, but we found Dulgirgraut in Melkier. This time I bonded immediately. It saved my life."

"But, how did you find Chryslaenor..."

"I don't know the full story of what happened to my first foci," Angst explained. "Rose stole Chryslaenor from Unsel while it still trapped Magic. She somehow ended up at the bottom of the ocean in Azaktrha, which was an old mage city filled with cursed mermen. When we found Rose lying on a stone, Chryslaenor was hovering over her, some old guy was casting a spell, and she was in a lot of pain. I had to save her. The only thing I could think of was to bond with it again."

"How is that even possible?" Jintorich asked.

"Jormbrinder," Aerella explained. "A foci made of two daggers. Among other things, it muffles magic."

"And I think Rose healed me, again," Angst said. "Rose and the dagger made it possible to bond with another foci. I saved her, and now I have two."

Faeoris rushed over and picked him up, holding him in a bone-crunching hug. Her eyes glossy with tears, she sniffed loudly. "You are so stupid."

"I've got to be good at something," he wheezed.

She let him go but didn't leave his side.

"But...but, how do you do it?" Jintorich asked, his voice filled with concern. "Being bonded to two foci, both in your head? How do they not drive you mad?"

"I just do it," Angst said, very aware of both songs he always heard. He gritted his teeth. "What choice do I have?"

Jintorich stood and looked back and forth between Aerella and Angst, his eyes wide.

"Is this what you were looking for?" Angst asked.

"Mostly," Jintorich said. "For now."

"Then why?" Angst asked. "Why did you travel all the way

from Meldusia for this story?"

Angst and Jintorich made eye contact for an uncomfortably long time. The Meldusian looked ready to loose the words resting on his tongue when they heard a high-pitched wail. A distant cry, the pain of ages.

"What was that?" Angst asked, scanning the path ahead.

"Mendahir," Kala whispered.

24

Scar growled a ferocious puppy growl until barks burst out of him. Tall hackles rose from the nape of his neck and along his rear, and Angst wondered if he would grow into the large monster dog he'd first met in these woods. Looking into the thickness of trees, he saw nothing and heard less. Gamlin provided no warnings, and Chryslaenor's song sounded like it was trying to teach him how to magically boil pasta. He wished Hector was here, not only to see and hear what he couldn't, but the old man's advice would've been welcome. Scar was still barking, and both his eyes and Kala's were glowing bright red. He rushed to the pup and knelt, petting the length of his coat. Angst wouldn't presume to read the mind of a dog, which was probably full of chasing butterflies and eating other people's food. The one thing he did know about dogs was that they could be trained. Experience taught them good from bad, and for Scar, this place had to be the worst.

"Shh, it's okay," he said, urging Kala over. "Help me calm him."

Kala blinked several times and, dragging her eyes away from the distant woods, scrambled to Scar. She cooed and coddled until the lab stopped barking.

"I hadn't thought about this," he said.

"What, Angst?" Jintorich asked.

"Scar was a monster when we found him, transformed by the

167

Vex'kvette," he began, trying hard to soothe out the hackles. "He was dragging forest creatures toward him in bubbles, everything that could be eaten. Eventually, his magic captured us, pulling us to the large bubble he waited in. We fought. I won. He almost died, but I cauterized his wound with Chryslaenor, leaving him with a scar, and his name."

"I would like to hear that story," Maarja said, tugging at her long, platinum hair. "The long version."

"When we have time," Angst replied with a smile. "It's a good one."

"But the Vex'kvette is no longer a concern," Jintorich said, his long eyebrows and longer ears pulled back. "Is it?"

"No, but being here is going to be more frightening to Scar than bringing him to the vet," Angst warned.

"And the Mendahir," Kala said softly, her voice quavering.

"Bah," Maarja and Faeoris said simultaneously before stabbing each other with ferocious glares.

"The Mendahir are mostly dead in this time," Aerella said softly, her husky voice soothing. "They don't make noises. That was just the wind."

"Mostly dead?" Angst asked.

"What does that mean?" Maarja snapped.

"They are alive during other time periods," she said. "Just not this one."

"I saw a Mendahir Rise last time I was here," Angst said. "They were beautiful, ghostly things that rose from the ground."

"They are like a rainbow, Kala, which is made when water filters sunlight," Jintorich said. "A Mendahir Rise is a reflection of memories that are formed through the graymowl trees. They are nothing to worry about, and certainly aren't alive."

"Then why did they talk to me?" Angst asked.

"No," Aerella said. "That's not possible."

"They told me Scar was my guide," Angst said. "And they weren't wrong."

"I thought you could handle your liquor," Maarja snarked. "How much did you have to drink that night?"

"Not enough," Angst said. Despite the lack of concern from his sword or the gamlin, something made his own hackles rise. Maybe it was just Scar. He didn't trust his intuition enough these days; it was too clouded by frustration and anger. But anger had never given him goosebumps.

"Well," Maarja barked out laughter, "I promise not to drink in Grayhollow Forest."

Jintorich chuckled, and Faeoris covered her mouth. Aerella looked at him like she'd found him drunk on a street corner, which wasn't encouraging. Kala seemed to be the only one who believed him. Scar glared into the woods like a pointer dog hunting pheasant.

"It'll be okay," he whispered to the young girl. "Let's mount up. We'll ride fast."

"Can we ride with you, Mr. Angst?" Kala asked. "Will your girlfriend be upset?"

"I'm not his—" Faeoris began.

"Of course you can," he said, holding up a hand. This wasn't the time. Though, for a brief second, he wondered about the stories Heather would hear. Would he ever learn his daughter's name? With a sigh and a spell, Angst summoned his swifen. The creature still caught his breath—a solid steel ram that shone brightly in the sun, moving and snorting like the real thing. After fastening his leather satchel, he mounted the swifen and waved Faeoris over to help.

Faeoris lifted the girl and puppy, setting them both in front of Angst. Kala's concerns seemed washed away by the adventure as she wrapped her arms around Scar to pat the swifen. The puppy grunted, his tail wagging under her arm.

"What's his name?" Kala asked.

"Scar?" he replied, dumbfounded.

Kala's long black hair whipped across his face as she looked over her shoulder and flashed him sincere eyes. "I know who Scar is."

"Right," Angst said delicately. "My bad."

"Your swifen? What is his name?" she asked. "My swifen is

Bubbledeath."

Angst barely held back his shock and laughter. He didn't know what to say.

Faeoris shouted, "Yes," and Aerella said, "Oh my."

"Isn't that great?" Kala asked.

"Yes," Angst said, not knowing if he should laugh or be frightened. "Bubbledeath is probably the greatest name I've heard yet."

She nodded in agreement. "I'll think of a good one for your swifen, too," she promised.

"It will be the best name ever. Well, almost as good as Bubbledeath," he said. "Maarja, can you lead us through here?"

"Better than anyone," she said proudly, holding out a hand. Jintorich leaped up, bounced off her hand and landed deftly on her shoulder. His long-nailed toes wrapped around Maarja's broad shoulder like a monkey.

"Faeoris, not so tight," Aerella wheezed.

"Sorry." Faeoris grunted.

Angst drew in power from Chryslaenor. It may not have been necessary, but he wanted to prepare for the unknown. Like that was even possible. As they followed Maarja into the forest, color washed away as if the blood had been sucked out of their bodies. In a way, he found it relaxing. Sure, it was disconcerting that all color was gone, but there were no distractions. Everything was black, white, or shades of gray. There was a certain clarity to this he appreciated. They paused as Maarja took note of their location.

"Fascinating," Jintorich said. "The stories are true. Everything changes without color."

"Not everything," Faeoris said with a wry smile. "Angst's hair hasn't changed color."

Angst shook his head as they laughed at his expense. It didn't really bother him. They needed the laugh, and it wasn't like he could do anything about his thinning grays. He flashed her a look of mock-anger, and she blew him a kiss. Then the sound came again, that high-pitched cry. It was filled with pain, and

Angst sensed longing, and blame. During his last visit, when the Mendahir Rise had approached, it was silent until it spoke. This was different; this sounded dangerous.

"Go," he urged.

Maarja ran at a horse's gallop. The pace was much slower than the swifen could ride, but after an hour, Angst was amazed that the Nordruaut had kept it. The cries followed, becoming louder as they progressed through the thick forest. The path brought them around enormous graymowl trees, easily ten feet across. How old must they be to grow so large? Was that why everything was black and white? Were they so starved that they had to eat color as well?

Another cry, but this time in front of them. Maarja skidded to a halt. Jintorich yelped, holding tight to a handful of hair as he flew from her shoulder. He scampered back up as she freed her bow and nocked an arrow. She jerked to the left, aiming her bow at another sound, and then to the right as something else moaned in the distance. Wailing came from all around, and Angst drew Chryslaenor from his back, gripping Kala tight with his other arm.

A cloud of thick fog formed at their feet, covering the forest floor like frosting on a cake. Thin lines of dark blue light rose from the fog, illuminating shadowy figures that slowly grew. At first, the shapes bobbed up and down like fish peeking out of a lake. As the blue light intensified, the shapes formed into tall, human-like figures. Unlike his first visit to Grayhollow when the Mendahir Rise had flowed in one direction like a river, this time they approached like a whirlpool. The party was surrounded by hundreds of apparitions. Bright blue hands with long fingers reached out from beneath shadowy cloaks. Angst sought them with his mind, but couldn't feel any bones to lock them into place. He listened for music from his foci, pleading for spells, begging for advice. Chryslaenor and Dulgirgraut were both completely silent.

"We need to keep moving!" Angst said firmly. "Maarja!"

"Right," she replied, her voice nervous, an oversized arrow

171

still nocked.

Angst checked on Faeoris and Aerella. Both were wide-eyed and pale, Faeoris looking all around in jerky motions, her long-sword at the ready. Scar whined, and Kala petted him, but she was breathing so fast Angst worried the girl might pass out.

"Do you want Scar and me to ride with you, Miss Faeoris?" Kala asked nervously. "We can keep you safe."

Faeoris said nothing, merely shaking her head.

"You may have to," Angst said quietly.

"This is your fault," Faeoris accused Maarja.

"Mine?" Maarja snapped, her eyes wild. "This is because of the Angorian! You Berfemmian and your tribesmen!"

"Argue later. Run now!" Angst interrupted. Nobody moved. "You can both blame me for everything when we get away. I don't mind. I'm used to it. We need to go!"

"Angst," Aerella pleaded in a wheezy voice.

Scenarios ran through his head. He would wield Chryslaenor and maybe hold the ghost-light-thingies at bay with an air shield while Faeoris flew overhead with Kala and Scar to keep them safe. Maarja was frightened, but Jintorich could help her focus so she could pick him up and run. There was a thud, as if something solid had fallen to the ground. A thud? There wasn't time for a thud. His eyes flicked down to make sure his arm was still wrapped tightly around Kala and Scar. Jintorich remained on Maarja's shoulder. Aerella's mount was riderless, fading in and out of view like the ghostly Mendahir until it was just gone.

Faeoris knelt beside Aerella, who was curled in a ball on the gray forest floor. The fog rolled in, and blue lights appeared like pinpricks in clouds. Angst dismissed his own swifen, landing on his feet and setting Kala on the ground. He knelt beside Aerella, who was incredibly still. He gently shook her shoulder. She wheezed.

"Aerella?" he asked. "Aerella, are you okay? What the..."

The woman who looked up at him was an Aerella he strained to recognize. To say she appeared older was flattering. Her skin was mottled with marks of age, her cheeks now wrinkled jowls that hung loosely. Her entire face was covered in fine lines that looked like a dry clay field, baked in hot summer sun. She covered her face with emaciated hands that shook with age.

"What did they do to you?" he asked in a rage. He could feel the power of his foci flowing through him, fueled by a sudden rage. The ground around them began to rumble. Mendahir surrounded them, as if shaken free from the forest floor, once again pointing at them. "I'll destroy this whole forest to make it right."

"Not the Mendahir Rise, Angst," she said, her voice soft and scratchy as if she hadn't drunk water for a year. "You did this to me, a long time ago."

25

Rookshire

Wilfred's four-hour ride to Rookshire was unacceptable. He was strangled by the gamy smell of horse. That fresh air everyone spoke so fondly of leaked freely from his nose. The sunlight was practically blinding him, most likely forever. The fact that he'd insisted on wearing the armor that made him appear so noble and heroic was one of many mistakes. With every trot, the armor became heavier, and when he adjusted his chest piece, fresh air was replaced with a blast of his own sweat and oily metal. And then, *and then*, there was the dire possibility he might not walk again, since the only feeling he had below his waist was throbbing pain. If it were possible, he would go back and slap Isabelle for "rewarding" Angst with land so very far away. He was a castle dweller, and spent little time on a mount for a reason. This was the second time in a month he'd visited, and he was still sore from the last ride. More than anything, he wanted to weep, and then eat pie. He deserved pie.

"Shall we stop to rest?" Mirot asked, his lips pulled up in the barest curl. "Again?"

"No." Wilfred did his best to make his grunty whine sound regal. "We're already late."

"Good news," Mirot said. "I'm sure the refugee camp is only ten or fifteen minutes away."

"Refugee camp?" Wilfred asked.

"What else should we call it?" the general asked with a shrug. "These wielders escaped the capital under duress and built these temporary shelters to hide away in."

"Have you seen them?" Wilfred asked. "What you call temporary shelters?"

"I've only heard stories," Mirot replied, looking forward, his nose a little higher than normal. "Huts of stone that look like mushrooms or some such."

"Huh," Wilfred said, shifting his rear to another uncomfortable position. "They're proud of this place, as they should be. It's more impressive than you've heard, and they're trying to make it into something."

"What could that possibly be?" Mirot asked, his snide showing.

"Home," Wilfred said softly.

Those ten minutes passed slowly and noisily in his rattling armor. Anticipation sweated out of his hands as worry jumbled the thoughts he'd prepared last night. Wilfred's heart thrummed quickly against his armor, which felt clammy inside. Maybe only a few wielders would show up, and they could meet at Graloon's over some cold mead. Maybe Graloon would have something good to eat, like pie.

"Are you all right?" Mirot asked, handing over a flask. "You look pale."

"Just nervous," he said, taking a deep gulp from the flask and wincing. It was water, and he handed it to the general with a disapproving gaze.

"I'm not Angst. I drink water," Mirot said. "You'll do fine."

"Do you think I should have a sword?" Wilfred asked. "I want to look like a leader."

"Only if you want someone to think you know how to use it," Mirot said slyly.

"Good point," Wilfred said.

"Oh," Mirot said in surprise as they approached the first chatlen, homes of the wielders. He brought his great stallion to a halt.

"Everything okay, General?" one of the four accompanying soldiers asked.

Wilfred could understand why the gray, bulbous buildings were compared to mushrooms. The chatlen looked like bubbles of stone that had risen from the ground only to get stuck halfway. Several round windows were positioned about the circular wall, and a kept stone path led to an arched doorway with a stone overhang.

"Not very camp-like, is it?" Wilfred taunted.

"It's larger...more durable than I'd expected," Mirot said. "More like a bunker." He pointed at smoke that drifted gently from the rooftop.

"It's my understanding that each one has a fireplace," Wilfred explained. "For heat, cooking, and campfire songs."

Several soldiers chuckled.

"You can stop that now," Mirot muttered.

"I'll try," Wilfred said.

Mirot pointed once again.

"Flowers," Wilfred explained with a smile, admiring early spring blooms placed evenly along the path.

"I know what flowers are," the general snapped. "I just...it just looks like they're here to stay."

"What's that?" a soldier asked, tilting his head.

There was shouting followed by the unhappy grumbling of a crowd. Mirot shot him a worried glance and reached for his sword. Wilfred shook his head.

"Let's go see," Wilfred said. "Ask first, kill later."

With a grimace, Mirot led them at a painful trot off path. They rounded several chatlen until they reached a wide road leading to a much larger stone structure at the center of town. Wilfred couldn't help but grunt in pain at every lurch forward, but the general was correct—something in that sound of discontent wasn't right. The jeers became louder as they approached.

Wilfred swallowed hard, and the blood drained from his face. Surely this had to be a bad dream. This wasn't just a few people who'd shown up with mead in hand to join him at Graloon's. The entire town was here—every man, woman, child, cat, dog, and goat filled the open space before the town hall and makeshift bar. He scanned a sea of scowls and raised fists held high. Under normal circumstances, Wilfred would've expected pitchforks and torches, but instead many of those fists were glowing bright with power in every color imaginable. Everyone at Rookshire glared at two men standing on a makeshift stone pedestal. Ranson, and his son Mika.

"You misunderstand. This is for the good of all Unsel!" Ranson held out two shaky hands, as if that would be enough to stop fireballs, or lightning, or any other act of unbelievable power. Mika, the gangly young man, stood tall by his side, with the death-defying bravado of youth emboldening him.

At this sight, Wilfred had two thoughts. What were these two men doing here, and what could they have possibly said? In spite of the urgency, he dismounted his horse with all the delicacy of a pastry chef student trying to pass their final exam. Everything that wasn't numb was sore or itchy. A soldier led the smelly beast away to reveal Heather, who'd been standing behind it with a baby in each arm.

"Hurry," she urged. "Before it's too late."

Wilfred followed her to the podium, his armor chafing with every step. How could she possibly move faster than him with those two squirmy bundles in her arms? Both men on the pedestal looked relieved at his approach, and Ranson pointed to Wilfred as if he were completing introductions. As if this were planned.

"And here to tell you more about the draft," Ranson said firmly. "The King Regent himself, Wilfred."

"Draft?" Wilfred snapped, ignoring the rumblings of the crowd. "King Regent? What are you talking about, man?"

Cries and shouts erupted around them. The sky darkened, thunder rumbled, the ground shook, and something hit Wilfred's cheek. He wiped off a papery, wet glob and met eyes with a young woman, who shrugged unremorsefully.

"Calm down!" Heather called out. "Or I will calm you!"

The great storm of Rookshire became a mere squall.

"Who invited you?" Wilfred asked. "And what is this about a draft?"

"According to law 215, page 9, paragraph 4," rolled off Ranson's tongue, "Unsel can recruit by draft any man, woman, or child over the age of twelve who could potentially aid or assist Unsel at a time of war in any capacity by said leadership or by those designated to represent. And, as I have explained to these good people, they must serve Unsel at her greatest time of need, under your command, King Regent Wilfred."

The wielders hushed, looking at them with accusing eyes that threatened life and limb.

"You are correct about law 215, Duke Ranson," Wilfred said apologetically.

A rainbow of raised fists shook, brighter than before. Heather moved away, holding her babies close. Wilfred shook his head no at the soldiers who reached for swords and put his hands behind his back. He looked sternly at the crowd until they quieted.

"I'm no King Regent, nor King, and nor do I wish to be called one," Wilfred said as loudly as he could. "We have a princess waiting to be crowned queen. Her name is Victoria, and she wields magic!" Angry fists lowered, and lights dimmed. "I am merely a servant of the crown, and a defender of Unsel, like our friend Angst!" More nods. "I am merely waiting for her return, just like you!"

"And until her return," Ranson cut in, "we need—"

"Heroes," Wilfred said firmly. "People of Rookshire, it's true—Unsel needs your help. Your queen needs your help. I need your help. Unsel needs soldiers who can wield magic. They were once called zyn'ight."

"Just one minute," Ranson cried, placing a hand on Wilfred's shoulder and jerking him around. "These people are obliged to help, by law. They have no choice."

"By law, page 1, paragraph 1, sentence the first, who is in charge?" Wilfred asked firmly.

"The royal family," Ranson stuttered.

"And who shall make decisions in their stead?" Wilfred egged on.

"The person designated to represent the throne," Ranson said, defeat thick in his voice. "You."

"Me," Wilfred said. He pointed to the crowd. "But I have no real control. Simply put, these people have a choice. What you don't understand, what many don't understand is that they always have had a choice. No matter the law, they can say no, and have the power to stand behind it. Let me say that again, they have the power to say no. Do you understand?"

Ranson glared at him with hatred and vitriol, but after glancing over the crowd, he reluctantly nodded.

"Citizens of Unsel," Wilfred said. "And you *are* citizens of Unsel. You have come to Unsel's aid time and time again, but now, finally, it will not go unrewarded. Long, long ago, before my time, even before Graloon..." Laughter, tension breaking laughter. "...wielders represented the crown as zyn'ight. They wore armor like Angst, like I wear now! I will not recruit you by force or by draft. I *will* offer you equality, and it is your choice to protect our people as soldiers of Unsel."

Wilfred had hoped for cheers, but was met with silence. He looked around to see less angry people muttering to each other. He waited.

"If I may ask, what can I do to prove that we want wielders to be seen as equals?" Wilfred asked.

"Equals?" Ranson scoffed.

"Please remove him," Wilfred said with a wave.

"Rookshire," Graloon said in his gravelly voice, looking around at the other wielders. "We want Rookshire to be recognized as an official town of Unsel. A city, a mage city."

Cheers erupted from the crowd, and Graloon raised a fist triumphantly in the air. The people of Rookshire were still hot with anger from Ranson's foolish demands, and the barkeep had stirred them into a flurry.

Wilfred made himself look as worried as possible, writhing

his hands and looking at the ground in apparent calculation. When the clamor finally subsided, he coughed.

"That's a lot, what you ask," he said hesitantly, giving the crowd time to grumble. "Unsel hasn't recognized a new city in a hundred years." Wilfred waited for the grumbling to grow before holding up a hand. The noise subsided. "But, as Duke Ranson confirmed, I guess I'm in charge, and it's the least I could do for friends."

Cheers, the right kind, erupted from the crowd. Heather stood beside him again, which he took as a sign that they probably weren't going to be burned to a crisp or turned into candy.

"In order for this to happen, we need you," Wilfred said sincerely. "We need wielders willing to be zyn'ight."

Many hands raised in the crowd, as if it were that easy to become a knight of Unsel. Wilfred nodded, clasping arms with Graloon and helping the large, old man onto the platform. He had done it. What would Faeoris have thought? His chest heaved proudly. It may have even earned him a kiss on the cheek. Those cheeks warmed at the thought.

"Graloon," he began. "Do you have any pie?"

"The best roogdibar pie you've ever had," Graloon said with a wink.

"Let's bring our zyn'ight in for some pie, and port," Wilfred said. "On the crown."

"Not only our leader, now you're *my* hero too," the barkeep replied, slapping him roughly on the back.

He was glad to be wearing armor.

26

Grayhollow Forest

The needles of blue light rising from the ground became broad and bright. Shadowy faces of the Mendahir Rise formed into something from nightmares, with wide, open mouths and eyes like angry blue pits. Angst couldn't move, as if held in place by his own trick. But it wasn't his trick. Cold hands reached from the ground, pulling at his legs, dragging down his arms. Faeoris and Maarja both cried out and collapsed, rocking back and forth. Scar's eyes flashed bright red, but the dog seemed unable to grow, howling in frustration.

"I've got you, Scar," Kala said, grasping the pup away from the reaching hands. "Mr. Angst, help!"

The same hands that held him in place shot up into Maarja and Faeoris. His companions had stopped making noise, but their eyes showed their pain. Maarja was locked in a silent scream while Faeoris's face looked strained as though ready to burst. They were dying.

"You're not killing anyone!" he bellowed. Lightning flickered around his arm, and he wrenched it free, holding Chryslaenor high. He let anger overtake him, and power flowed from his foci.

The rage-fueled lightning poured down his chest and bit at the restraining hands around his legs. With a loud crack, the ghostly

181

limbs returned into the ground. Cascades of blue lightning flowed from him, snapping and popping as it leaped to each companion. The Mendahir released their hold and backed away. Faeoris and Maarja coughed between gasping breaths. Kala rushed to Aerella, setting Scar down. The lab instantly grew into his larger form, his fur becoming angry steel daggers. The dog's six eyes glared menacingly at their opponents. He barked, making the trees shake as if nervous they would become a chew toy.

The foggy shapes avoided the lightning so Angst directed it into a circle around them. Grass and leaves flashed, instantly burning to ash as the ring grew. They stood in the middle of the blackened circle, still surrounded, but now at arm's length from the horde of the Rise. Setting Chryslaenor on its tip in the center of the circle, he willed it to remain on guard. The sword continued to feed lighting into their line of protection as Angst approached the edge.

"I know you can speak," Angst shouted. "Tell me what this is about before everyone calls this a Mendahir Fell!"

The Mendahir parted, making a path for the tallest of their shadows. It floated slowly toward the lightning's edge, its horrific features washing away as it got closer. The other ghosts dimmed even as the tallest one became more opaque. The echo of life transformed into something more recognizable. It appeared tangible, more human, but barely. It hovered at the edge of the lightning, waiting, looking on them all sternly, but at least the anger appeared gone.

"I'm Angst," he began.

"I remember," it said in a low, hollow voice. "I am Kitecor."

"What is this?" Angst asked, pointing all around. "Why did you attack us? And why are you still alive?"

This made Kitecor smile, maybe—Angst had never seen a shadow smile. The figure nodded toward Faeoris and Maarja, and both looked at each other guiltily.

"Your friends destroyed us long ago," he whispered. "The Mendahir are forever lost to this half-life, neither fully alive nor completely dead. Because of their treachery, you shall all perish."

"Probably not," Angst snapped. "I'll finish whatever it is they started if I have to."

"Or you could try bringing them back," Jintorich said positively, staring on in awe.

"That's not possible. At least not for an Al'eyrn," Aerella said. "Those in a state of half-life are forever lost."

"You can explain that later," Angst said over his shoulder. He pointed directly at the shadow. "You, Kittycat, tell your people to back off, or this gets ugly. You have no idea what my sword and I can do."

"I am *very* aware of what Chryslaenor can do," he said in a haughty tone.

Angst's heart skipped, but he hoped it didn't show on his face. He felt the need to appear strong, and intelligent, and couldn't bear losing any sort of verbal fencing. But, how did this ghost know the name of his foci? Kitecor must be ancient and, in spite of his condition, maybe he had retained a lot of knowledge. Or maybe the ghost was just a know-it-all trying to make him look like an idiot.

"And Dulgirgraut?" Angst asked.

Kitecor looked around for long moments, as if he'd lost his keys. Finally, he said, "I see no Dulgirgraut."

"I don't like carrying both my foci at the same time. It scares people, and ghosts, and everything." He lowered his head and peered at Kitecor. Very slowly, he said, "I'm bonded to both foci."

"Oh," the Mendahir said, sounding surprised.

Angst wanted to cheer for himself and point and say, "Who looks like an idiot now?" There was something about surprising a gaggle of ancient half-dead ghost creatures that felt like a small win. The thin blue lights shooting up from the ground became brighter and then dimmed, again and again. Before he could prepare for an attack, it stopped, and all lights diminished save the ones around Kitecor.

"You can leave," Kitecor said. He pointed at Faeoris and

Maarja. "But there must be justice. We will have one."

"I'll stay," Faeoris said sadly, sheathing her sword.

"No, you won't," Angst snapped.

"This is my responsibility," she said, placing a hand on his arm.

"I don't believe this." How hard would it really be to burn their way out with lightning? "What could you have possibly done?"

"You're right," she said. "*I* didn't do anything."

"Then how is this your responsibility?" he asked, crossing his arms. "Wait, I can barely hear anything." He willed the sword to stop spewing lightning. The noisy circle faded, and he faced Kitecor. "Don't think you can haunt your way over here fast enough to hurt anyone. With my last breath, I'll destroy everything before I let her, or any of them, be harmed. Got it, cloudy?"

It almost looked like the Mendahir grimaced, but he nodded in agreement, and nothing approached.

"Go on," Angst said to Faeoris. His heart skipped at her wolfish smile. Apparently, she liked his threats.

"Thousands of years ago, all of Ehrde was at war. That was when the Berfemmian and the Vex'steppe tribes lived together in Angoria," she said with a longing sigh. "The Mendahir had refused to fight. They believed their magic would be too destructive for the world, but the Nordruaut attacked everyone. My people joined the Mendahir to stop Nordruaut, but soon learned that the Mendahir were planning to turn on us after the Nordruaut were destroyed."

"So, you defended yourself," he said.

"We killed them, Angst," she said, looking ashamed. "In our bloodlust, we killed all of them."

"But that wasn't you," Angst said.

"It was my people," she said, dabbing the corners of her eyes. "And it's time someone took the responsibility for their actions."

"Not you," Maarja said, now standing beside them. "That responsibility is mine."

"Really?" Angst asked. "You two don't need to compete over this. Let me just blaze a path out of here..."

"You won't burn down this forest, Angst," Maarja said fiercely. "Not when my people have worked so hard to tend this world. It has been our penance for letting the Mendahir die. I've heard the story many times. We were trying to stop the madness that had taken over Ehrde. My people were warriors, barbaric at times, but we stayed in Nordruaut until it became too much. We learned that the Mendahir were the catalyst for the great war, and that they merely waited until other armies were mostly defeated before striking. We attacked the Mendahir first and were winning, but were forced to retreat when they allied with Angoria. The Angorians, our fiercest rivals, turned on what remained of the Mendahir. We stood by and watched. The Nordruaut could have stopped them. Instead, we let them all die. This was our fault, and I will stay behind."

"You are both mistaken, and so are you, dear Kitecor," Aerella said in a wheezy voice, looking up from her kneeling position. "Angst, come here and help an old woman stand."

To Angst's surprise, Kitecor waited patiently, almost respectfully. Angst helped Aerella up slowly; she seemed very frail. Was she continuing to age? Her hands shook so violently, it was as if her body was failing before his eyes. Could he heal her? Was it possible to will life into her before she died in his arms? He began summoning power, but she abruptly shook her head no.

"We don't want him to feel threatened, and even if you could heal me, it would weaken you too much to protect the others," she said, taking tired, wheezing breaths. "This will take me a minute, but I'll be fine. Now isn't my time—"

"But..." Angst interrupted.

"I've read how I am to die," Aerella said, squeezing his hand gently. "You have to trust me, my oldest friend."

"Hey," he replied with a half-smile. "I'm not that old."

"I've got this," she said, patting him on the face. She stood up straight, gathering not strength or magic, but something else. It

185

was as if wisdom and experience had their own power. Whatever this was, it was enough, and her voice sounded stronger. "I'm the oldest human who has ever walked Ehrde, and only one will ever be older," she began. "I have danced through millennium like a bee to flowers. I have been to the future and the past. So much has happened I don't remember it all, but I have walked among the powerful Mendahir of old. Remember, if you can, because I was there."

Kitecor nodded once, but otherwise said nothing.

"Faeoris, Maarja, you are both right, but you don't quite have the full story. Thousands of years ago, the Mendahir stood as the most powerful beings on Ehrde," she explained. "A kind and benevolent race of creatures who wielded magic like no other. They lived long, and were aware of the element wars that took place every two thousand years. They taught all peaceful races how to protect themselves through magic, built cities where they could stay safe, and forged weapons of great power."

"The foci," Jintorich said in wonder.

"No," Angst said in disbelief.

Kitecor nodded again, smiling at Angst's shock. Did the ghostly figure wink at him like he had gotten ahead in their verbal battle?

"The elements feared what the Mendahir could create, and most avoided confrontation," she went on. "Magic felt they were his greatest threat, and worried they could make a person dangerous enough to destroy all elements. They couldn't, the Mendahir weren't able to make weapons more powerful, so some tried to wield more than one foci. A ring and a dagger, armor and—"

"I had that dream! Right after I first wielded Chryslaenor," Angst said. "Some guy tried to wear armor he wasn't supposed to, but it...broke him."

"No one was meant to wield another, Angst," she said, her old face dour. "Semiya's attempt pushed Magic into action. He is the slippery one, the element with a plan, and he connived. Alone, he wasn't powerful enough to destroy the Mendahir and all their Al'eyrn."

"But the Angorians and Nordruaut were powerful enough," Maarja said, her eyes wide with horror.

"He tricked us?" Faeoris asked, her fists shaking.

"Magic first drove the Nordruaut to war and sent them to battle the Mendahir. Later, Magic tricked the Angorians into believing that the Mendahir would turn on them." she said. "After the war was over, the realization that they'd committed genocide was too much. The Nordruaut changed their ways, becoming hunters and tending to the land. The Angorians agreed to live on separate sides of Ehrde, only coming together once a year to mate."

"Magic is the reason I didn't get my sex!" Faeoris cried out. "That bastard is the reason I live on an island with all women!"

"I love that island," Angst said, not thinking before speaking.

Everyone turned to look at him, including Kitecor. Angst frowned and looked at Faeoris as if she were the one who'd farted. Her cheeks flushed, and she crossed her arms.

"You're right. Magic is the reason your people killed the Mendahir," Aerella said. "And the reason Nordruaut let it happen."

"Well...right," Faeoris replied, her cheeks a deeper crimson. "That's awful, all of it."

"How could they possibly kill the Mendahir if they were so powerful?" Angst asked, struggling to grasp it all.

"It's a longer story," Aerella said. "But their last battle was in the mage city Enurthen. The city had a powerful shield to protect them against all manner of creatures, including the Nordruaut. It is said a curse drove them out of the city. They were slaughtered on a field at the foot of Enurthen, and those who tried to sneak back into the mage city were never seen or heard from again. It was assumed they were dead."

"Or half-dead," Jintorich said. "And cursed to live here, where it's said they originated."

There was a moment of silence as the stories sank in like the first spring rain. Even the poor, half-alive Mendahir seemed lost in speculation.

"Mendahir," Aerella called out, her loud voice only crackling slightly with age. "You were killed by the Angorians and Nordruaut, but this death was not the fault of these two children. Their people were misled by power well beyond their comprehension. It is Magic's will, above all others, to pit nations against one another. He tricks them into battle so they do not threaten the elements and their play at power over Ehrde. You cannot blame these two for the transgressions of their races when all were misled by one so powerful. Not when they are trying so hard to make it right. Don't push them further away. Do not create martyrs of yesterday's children. Show them that power comes from peace and wisdom, as you always taught."

Aerella sagged into Angst. He held her shoulders with both hands, his mind whirling to understand everything she'd said. But deep down he seethed in anger that living beings on Ehrde had always been merely objects for Magic and the other elements to use. It was as if everyone was merely a pawn, especially to Magic. It had to stop. He had to stop it, at all costs.

The blue light of Mendahir that surrounded them glowed increasingly brighter. They moved, gathering, coalescing to become a singular point of light too bright to look at directly. Angst turned away, blinking spots from his eyes and burying Aerella's face in his chest protectively. Something about the light made him happy. His mind wandered, thinking of his wife, thinking of Thom and his daughter, imagining a lazy future of walks through pastures and teaching his children magic. Euphoria overwhelmed him, and he was smiling when a weight pressed gently on his shoulder.

Angst blinked away happy thoughts to see a very tall man standing before him. He was beautiful. In all his life, Angst had never before said a man was beautiful, but this man was perfection. If you could combine the best features from every human and make them glow a dim shade of blue, it would've been this lone Mendahir. His light faded in and out like the moon behind clouds.

"Who are you?" Jintorich asked.

"I am one," the man said. "One of many."

Jintorich's black eyes went wide, and the hair on his ears stood up. He said nothing else, merely watching the Mendahir glide to Faeoris and Maarja.

"You are forgiven," he said to Maarja then faced Faeoris. "As are you, my child."

"I don't deserve it," Maarja said.

"No, you do not," he replied sternly. "But we forgive you, because it is time to move on."

Faeoris looked at him, her face filled with disappointment, her mouth poised on the edge of words.

"We are sorry about your sex," the Mendahir said. "Our mating cycle was similar to your own. We are sorry you are hurting even now."

Angst wanted to laugh but managed not to. Really? Sex? They were talking about sex?

"It's not your fault," she said with a grimace. "Thank you for understanding."

The Mendahir floated to Angst and Aerella. Angst looked into the deep, ocean-blue globes of the creature's eyes and saw...something. Intelligence, sadness, and an unknowable wonder that made his breath catch.

"We did, indeed, make the foci," he said. "And I made your swords myself."

"Oh fine," Angst replied, rolling his eyes. "You win."

Kitecor smiled a gentle, knowing smile that was infectious. Angst had a sudden longing to know him better. Something in that smile, and those blue orbs that must be more than eyes, made him wonder. Under other circumstances, in another world or another time, could they have been friends? He could sense a mentor in that face, and would've loved the opportunity to learn more. It gave him hope, which felt so much better than anger.

"You can wield two?" he asked, his voice like steel striking rock in an empty canyon.

"I can," Angst said, surprised at the question.

"They are at war?" he asked. "In your mind?

"Like you wouldn't believe," he replied, exasperated. "Always at odds, always striving to be noticed, always wanting to be better than the other. They are so different, but so similar."

"Like siblings," he said.

"Yes!" Angst said. Finally, someone understood. "They offer so much, often too much information that I have to ignore them both. But I feel, sometimes, if I don't hold them back, I might...I might go—"

"Mad," he said knowingly, the corners of his mouth tight.

"Yes," Angst whispered.

"It is too much power for any one person," he said sternly, his voice becoming deeper. "You must release one or you will go insane and break Ehrde in half."

"The last time I released one, I almost died," Angst said.

"It can be done in one place. Seek Prendere before it is too late. It is a place from dreams where all is possible, and you can set things right," the Mendahir said before turning his focus to Aerella. "We remember you with honor, and your actions have saved your friends. As have your words."

"Thank you, *maiestatem*," Aerella replied, bowing her head low.

The being placed his long fingers on her head and uttered words Angst couldn't recognize.

"You are welcome to leave," he said. "You can pass through safely, but you must go and not return."

"We will," she said. "But know this. Your time will come again. Your magic is strong, too powerful to let you die completely, and you will rise. I can now remember that a Mendahir Rise is not an anomaly, like a rainbow. It is a prophecy of what is to come."

27

Eastern Border of Unsel

Guldrich sat by a roaring bonfire, gnawing on the last chunk of raw beast from the end of his long hunting knife. He wiped the blade on his lap before looking at his too-bare arm forlornly. It had grown back and was once again at full strength, maybe even stronger than before. He should've been grateful to Takarn Ivan for this miraculous gift, but still wished that the kill scars had returned as well. It was one of the few things that made him stand out amongst other gray men, who were all practically identical. He would have to replace those scars, but at this rate, it would take a very long time.

The familiar tickle of Selina's purple tail crept over his shoulder and along his cheek. Guldrich threw the knife into the muddy ground before jerking the tail hard. Selina screamed as he dragged her over his shoulder and threw her to the ground. She rolled away and stood, ready to attack with her clawed hands.

"Where have you been?" he shouted, unable to hold back a smile.

She struck him across the face with her claws, carving away skin and leaving behind three lines of blood. She swung again, but Guldrich caught her small hand.

"Don't you ever, ever treat me like you can do this without me!" she shouted.

He was taken aback, having never seen this side of her. She'd always been seductive and conniving, yet, despite her great power, Selina had never shown backbone. It made little difference—she had always been correct in her premonitions, and that was all he cared about. This was something different. She was very aware of her value, and so was he. Up until now, she'd been a means to an end, but could she be more than that?

"You missed the first three raids," he said, less demand in his voice.

"You're still alive," she said, jerking her hand away.

"As is everyone else." He grunted in frustration. "Almost everyone."

"Almost?" She sounded concerned.

"A raiding party found Angst," he said. "He let one of them go. She confirmed that he's leaving Unsel, like you said he would."

"But how did they die?" Selina demanded.

"He butchered them, or burned them with lightning," Guldrich said dismissively. "What difference does it make?"

They were interrupted by the noisy rattle of bone-laden armor as two Fulk'han approached, dragging a third. They threw his body to the ground, both spitting in disgust. Guldrich kicked the body over. The gray man wheezed and coughed, dark blood flecked from his toothless mouth. He'd been beaten senseless, both eyes wide but staring at nothing. Many of the protruding bones that had formed his armor were cracked or completely torn off.

"This is the one," a soldier said. "He killed a dozen villagers before we could stop him."

"Lost to a blood lust," the other soldier said. "I've seen the look in others' eyes, but he's the first to give in."

"I couldn't help myself," the beaten man lisped, sitting up on his elbows.

Guldrich's arm had taken a month to grow back, and months again to become strong. This man was healing before their eyes. Bones crunched as they once again covered his body in armor.

CHAPTER TWENTY SEVEN

There was a grotesque squishing sound as sharp teeth grew out from his gums. The focus that returned to his eyes quickly turned to worry.

"It was Takarn Ivan, my liege," the man said. "He hungered for blood, demanded revenge, and I lost myself to his cries."

"I've heard others whisper the same," a soldier said in a hushed voice. "Is a sickness coming over us?"

Guldrich had no answer, and Selina wouldn't make eye contact, her gaze mischievous. Was it more frightening that the man healed so quickly, or that his soldiers were losing their minds to battle?

"We have the strength to kill everyone in these towns," the man lying on the ground said. "But instead we pick like carrion."

"If we kill everyone, there will be nobody left to beg for help," Selina said, her voice purring. "Even now, a town hero is racing to Unsel. They will march with their armies before we attack again."

"It is cowardice," he argued.

"These...were...my...orders!" Guldrich stomped on his chest over and over.

The others moved away as new bones splintered and the man's chest caved in. When the light in his eyes was gone, Guldrich jerked out his blood-covered boot. Wiping his foot on the grass, he drew out his hunting knife and carved a scar into his forearm. "I don't care about dead Unsel villagers," Guldrich barked. "I only care that you do what you're told. Make sure this is clear to the others."

The other two men nodded quickly, their eyes wide as the moon.

"No more kills!" he shouted. "We continue north, to the next border town, and do it again."

"Guldrich," Selina said, her voice filled with excitement. She pointed at the corpse. "Look!"

The body jerked and seized as its chest began to reform. The soldier's eyes snapped open, wide with fear as he tried to breathe without lungs. He scratched at his chest then looked at his blood-soaked hands.

"What is this?" Guldrich looked at the men, who now seemed more like frightened children than frightening warriors.

"It's wonderful," Selina said melodically. "You're becoming more powerful every day."

Guldrich dropped to his knees, wrestled the soldier's hands away, and chopped at the neck with his hunting knife. Blood splattered his face with every swing until the blade finally struck stone, and the head rolled to one side. Like creeping vines, tendons and muscle grew from the body, reaching for the head. They crawled to the skull, grasping at it like bloody fingers.

He jerked the head away from the body with a snap and handed it to a soldier. The gray man took it reluctantly.

"Burn it in a fire, on that side of camp." He pointed far to the south. "And wait until there is nothing left."

The man ran off with the skull, which he held at arm's length.

"You," Guldrich said to the other soldier. He kicked the writhing mass, neck muscles still grasping for something that wasn't there. "Take the body to a fire at the other end of camp. Burn it before another head grows back."

The soldier seemed reluctant. Guldrich bared his teeth like a hungry wolf and pointed his knife at the body. The man grabbed a foot and dragged it away.

"More...powerful?" Guldrich said. "Is that what we've become?"

"I promised you revenge on Nordruaut," she said. "How could they possibly beat you now?"

He nodded reluctantly. "And Angst?" he snarled.

"We will both get our revenge," she said.

* * * *

Rohjek

SMyket approached ANduaut's tent with the same caution one would take sneaking up to pet a wild panther. His measured

194

steps and forced calm came from a combination of fear and respect. There was no actual sneaking—the tent was wide open and ANduaut sat in the middle, cross-legged with his stadauf resting on his knees. The man was as still as an ice-covered tree on a windless day. SMyket stopped before the entrance and watched, waiting for the broken man to breathe, hoping he wouldn't.

It was impossible not to stare at the caved-in corner of ANduaut's forehead. He may have been magicked to continue living, but it was so unnatural it felt wrong. ANduaut squeezed his eyes in concentration until a thick, orange tear leaked from the damaged one. He finally gasped as he took a deep breath.

"Why have they gathered?" he asked in a low, dangerous voice. "Is this treason? Do we need more examples?"

"It would take a lot of examples. They have questions," SMyket said, licking his salty lips. He was sweating, and it wasn't from the heat of this place. He steeled himself. "I have questions. And if you wish, I'll be the example."

"Oh?" ANduaut's eye opened, his one eyebrow raising in surprise. "Feeling brave?"

"Just because I chose to live when you killed the other two does not make me a coward," SMyket said defiantly, his words braver than his heart.

"Then why do you follow my lead?" ANduaut asked.

"Because you have become a leader, my Iroquai," SMyket said sincerely. "Your injury has changed you. You are suddenly bold and decisive. Though I don't agree with all your decisions, you have become what the tribes need."

"But you challenge my decisions?" ANduaut asked. He remained seated, but the grip on his stadauf tightened.

"I haven't," SMyket said, sweat now trickling down his cheeks. His knees were locked, and his muscles would soon join them. He would lose a battle with a squirrel if attacked. "I've followed you, but if you are leading our people to death, then yes."

To his surprise, ANduaut didn't rush forward and slice out

the contents of his stomach. Instead, the Iroquois of the Vex'steppe tribes stood and stretched. The man's forehead was the only thing broken. He wore nothing but the barest of leather loincloths and a large ruby ring. Everything else was dark skin stretched over sinewy muscle. He had neither an ounce of fat or a drop of sweat, and looked as dangerous as that panther. He approached SMyket calmly and smiled, which was almost as frightening as the fight he had half expected.

"Bring me to my people," he said, his voice a little tired. "And I will tell what I know."

SMyket nodded once and turned around, leading the Iroquai to a great bonfire. ANduaut followed uncomfortably close, a mere half-step behind, still within peripheral vision. They approached the fire surrounded by a thousand men, all waiting with the impatience of toddlers. Angry toddlers ready to pounce, shifting anxiously from side to side on muscular legs or moving their weapons from one hand to the other. Their loud voices subsided on ANduaut's appearance. In the distance, a large, shadowy form loomed beside a jagged structure that SMyket wished with all his being didn't exist.

"The tribes of Vex'steppe fear nothing," ANduaut began, his voice booming. "We do not fear Nordruaut or Fulk'han or any creature on Unsel, nor do we fear death."

Those closest nodded pensively, as if more worried that they were the front line than in total agreement.

"When I was injured, I learned a fear I had never experienced," ANduaut said, placing a hand on his dent. "Not fear of death, for I fought knowing I would die to protect our people. Instead, the fear I learned is that a war is coming that could end our tribes forever."

A great muttering came from all around, and ANduaut raised his hand for silence, surprisingly patient as he waited for the voices to quiet.

"My father Maudusta hid from the truth. My father, our Iroquai, tried to stop me from protecting our people." He covered his eye with one hand. "To my shame, I was forced to kill him. It was a great loss to the tribes, and to myself, but had I not escaped, it would have been far worse."

More shuffling, eyes looking to and fro, but nobody spoke.

"What my father did not understand, what he foolishly ignored, put us all in danger. I learned that all nations are gathering forces to battle. Some have champions of great power, wielders of magic, and others have been gifted power beyond comprehension. Many nations have changed who they are and what they believe, all for something far more insidious than mere war," he shouted. "At great personal cost, I have learned that there is a weapon of power that appears once every two thousand years. A weapon so devastating it can eradicate nations, entire races, leaving behind nothing but memories."

Raised weapons lowered and jaws dropped as all became entranced by his recounting.

"I wish this weapon did not exist, but we will not be the ones destroyed by it," ANduaut said. "To prepare for this war, I have aligned with creatures of such raw power that none will stop us. With these allies, we will march on Nordruat, Unsel, and any other nation that gets in the way of our prize."

The cheers were so boisterous and rowdy that SMyket expected fireworks. Did this weapon really exist, or was ANduaut buying their people with false hope?

"We will soon face our first challenge," ANduaut cried out, slamming his stadauf into the ash. "I need one hundred men who will follow me to glory, or death!"

Everyone raised their weapons, even his nearest, DEdin.

"SMyket, my first, will choose one hundred of our best to clear a path," ANduaut said. "Prendere, the prize, will be ours, and I pity those who choose to stand in our way!"

28

Grayhollow Forest

"Why are you old?" Angst demanded.

"Angst," Faeoris admonished gently.

"I could ask you the same," Aerella rasped with a dry cackle.

She was, indeed, older. When Aerella had collapsed in front of the Mendahir, Angst had guessed her to be sixty, maybe seventy. It was hard to gauge since that was ancient for humans in Ehrde. But Aerella now appeared older still. He held her frail form close as they rode through Grayhollow. She felt like dry sticks held together by a thin veil of supple satin. Her ears had lengthened, and her face was covered in a cobweb of fine wrinkles. It was hard to discern her hair color, since the graymowl trees gobbled color up like food. But her skin was blotchy, and he could see spotting around her hands.

"I'm not old," he muttered.

"No, you're not old. You're not old at all," Faeoris mocked, like she was speaking to a baby.

Faeoris, Maarja, and Jintorich all laughed. Great, now that everyone was buddies, they were teaming up on him. Was he the only one taking this seriously?

"Should I remove my armor?" he asked, looking at her bruised hands, worried that the steel could injure her back.

"I'm not young enough for you, am I?" Aerella teased.

More laughter. It was as if she'd saved up this teasing for, well, a millenia. His mouth was dry, and he itched all over, like he could use a hot bath. Pacing, or a long walk, would be infinitely better than a slow ride out of this depressing forest.

"How much farther?" he asked for the umpteenth time.

"Almost there," Maarja said, her voice filled with mirth.

"You never answered my question," he said, slowing his swifen to keep the ride gentle.

"I believe you're old because of how Angst plucked you out of time," Jintorich squeaked. "Your body isn't adjusting properly to this time period."

"That sounds like a good theory. One of many," she said with a wink.

Jintorich's black eyes went wide.

"I remember your story, Meldusian," she said, clearing her throat. "Maybe I'm old because it's what Angst needs to see."

"Pardon?" Angst asked, trying not to roll his eyes.

"Earlier today, I could've easily been in my twenties, and you enjoyed that," she said, her tone mocking. "Now, I'm possibly older than one hundred. Am I still Aerella?"

"Of course you are," he said with a frown. "But you aren't actually older. You haven't changed on the inside, just on the outside."

"That isn't true at all," she said, coughing weakly into a shaky hand. "I've known you for more years than I will admit. You are my oldest, dearest friend. My memory isn't what it should be, but I remember glimpses of our adventures. That night in Gressmore Towers when you held me as I cried. The moment I found you nearly dead in the maiden's courtyard. Those felking twins you love so much. More than they deserve. And the terrible choices you have yet to face."

"I remember the maiden's courtyard," he said, reeling from the sudden impact of a deeply buried memory. "It was just a dream, or a vision. The courtyard was mostly destroyed, just like it is today. Instead of a sinkhole filled with water, the Vex'kvette flowed from the castle. Dragons flew overhead. It was madness, and you were there. You said it was my fault. You said not to wield another."

"I did," she said.

"Aerella, what else can you tell me?" he pleaded. "What was that? How can I keep it from happening?"

"I'll tell you what I remember," she said. "That was the future, or a possible future. The reason I told you not to bond with another is because I've seen the results of your madness. Not only will you destroy Ehrde, your actions will kill half the people on our planet."

He heard gasps from the others.

"I wasn't there when it happened...happens...anyway. These are legends I've learned that were passed down for thousands of years. Stories that became history, and then myth," she said. "But it is said you suffered a terrible loss, and in your madness, with all the power from two foci, you cracked Ehrde in half. You broke our world."

"What loss?" he said, his heart skipping several beats. "Was it Tori? Was it Heather? My children?"

"I don't know," she said, squeezing his hand weakly. "I...I remember your children grown, and your wife older, but only glimpses."

Angst nodded, but his mind was racing. Since escaping Victoria's room, he'd felt a growing anger, but had assumed it was because of Victoria being stabbed. Did this mean she was the one destined to die? Aerella had struggled to explain what had happened—at this age maybe she wasn't remembering everything. He stopped his ram swifen, unable to catch his breath.

"We're almost there, Angst," Maarja said, but not too firmly.

He dismounted and paced, squeezing his hands, desperate for this overwhelming sense of helplessness to pass. Doubt. He was filled with doubt. He was going to fail someone, again, and he didn't know who. He paced, unable to control his anxiety. Angst stopped when shiny black boots crossed his path. He slowly looked up those black boots, up very long legs, pausing at a delicious torso and round breasts until he saw Faeoris's pretty face.

Her eyes were sad, but her face was stern.

"Snap out of it!" she said.

In a blur, she reached up and smacked him across the mouth. He flew back, crashed against a tree, and collapsed into a heap.

"I'm sorry, I'm sorry," Faeoris said, suddenly kneeling beside him.

It took a moment for the darkness and bright spots to go away. Angst winced at the muscles knotting between his neck and shoulders. His head was spinning, and his jaw felt locked into place. Had she broken it? A soft, warm hand touched his cheek. A wave of comfort washed away his pain. Aerella drew her hand from his face and stood up. He was surrounded by his traveling companions. How long had he been there? Had Faeoris knocked him out?

"Did I...did I say something wrong?" he asked. "Why are you crying?"

"You were pacing for a long time. You were lost to us in your worry," Faeoris said hurriedly. "I couldn't get your attention, and I didn't know what else to do. I was getting frustrated. I didn't mean to hit you so hard."

She held him close, kissing his cheeks over and over. He waited for her to calm down, and waited longer because the kissing and hugging was nice. His hand was damp, and he realized Scar was licking it furiously.

"Thank you," he said sincerely.

"You're...you're welcome?" Faeoris said questioningly, her face still wrought with worry.

"Aerella's story was probably the most frightening thing I've ever heard," he said, picking up the lab pup and petting him. Scar's tail fought through his hold to wag in a frenzy. "I always thought my greatest fear was heights...well, other people near heights. It's actually losing people I care about, and not being able to do a thing to save them. Heather, the kids, Victoria...you." He looked at Faeoris, and she met his gaze before looking at the ground. He sought Aerella. "You. All of you. It's why I didn't want you here. Not because I don't like you, but because I love my friends and don't want to lose them."

Kala wrapped her arms around him, and he felt a tugging on his side as Jintorich hugged him too. Maarja stood away from them, looking sad, or defeated, or guilty. It was hard to tell. Angst took in the hugs before reaching up to Faeoris, who helped him stand. He approached Maarja and held his arms open. She hesitated but finally kneeled. Her hug emptied his lungs.

"I'll try to be a friend," she said, looking more worried than he would've expected.

"Before I become young and forget, Angst," Aerella said. "Thank you."

"For what?"

"For this." She gestured with her arms and looked at all of them. "I've lived a hundred, hundred lifetimes and enjoyed adventures no human ever could. I've seen so much of the past and future. I've saved countless lives. I've had adventures throughout time that you couldn't dream. It's been quite wonderful, and it will soon end. Moments like this mean everything."

"Don't talk like that," he said.

"I'm tired, Angst," she said. "At this age, I'm exhausted. I have no regrets, and just wanted you to know that I'm grateful you pulled me from Gressmore."

"You're welcome," he said, not knowing what else to say.

"But," she said, as if trying to sneak in the last word. "You missed my point, when I asked if I'm still Aerella."

"I didn't miss anything," he said definitively. "You're Aerella, whether you look twenty or one hundred...no offense."

"None taken," she replied. "Mostly."

"I get this, because I've always been Angst," he explained. "Whether I'm twenty, or forty, or want to be twenty. I'm still...well, I'm still me."

"You do get it," Aerella said in surprise.

"You missed my point, though," he said.

"How so?"

"I asked why you're old. Not because of how you look, or

who you are, but because it puts us in danger, like it did," he said firmly. "You've known about this condition since you were in Unsel, and said nothing. I remember you writhing in pain in the infirmary. The Mendahir could've eaten us alive or tossed us into space..." The worry in Kala's face told him to stop, but she needed to know—they all did. "We need to reassess. We've had it easy. So far, we've had a few Fulk'han sneak up on us, seen one town destroyed by a dragon, and we've been attacked by a race of beings that are supposed to be dead. We haven't faced an element. We haven't faced Fire. You don't even know the dangers ahead."

"That's scary, Mr. Angst," Kala said. "I'm scared."

"Then you're the smartest of us all," he said sincerely.

"I know that!" she replied, taking Scar from him and holding the puppy close.

"It's just that we can't have any more unknowns," Angst said firmly.

"I don't know why my age fluctuates," she said. "I was trying to communicate with you from the future when you pulled me to your time."

"Uh, sorry," he said, staring at his feet.

"It happens," she said. "Is it enough to know *that* I get older sometimes?"

"It helps! We now know your...condition. Everyone has a good idea of my fears and weaknesses. Does anyone else have any secrets they'd like to share?"

Nobody wanted to be first to bare their hidden truths, and who could blame them? Angst hated this more than anyone, but this was what had made things work so well with Dallow, Hector, Tarness, and Rose. They knew each other. They understood each other's capabilities and knew how to make up for any failings. It made them stronger as a whole, and these new companions needed to come together before they faced something unprecedented.

"Please," Angst urged.

Kala raised her hand. Angst smiled, kneeling to be at eye level.

"I stole cookies from Miss Heather," she said.

Angst sucked in his lips, and his heart swelled. If only all their problems could be so big. It was serious to her, so he frowned. "Is that all?"

"I gave some to Scar," she said, her voice thick with guilt. Scar appeared less remorseful with his tongue hanging out and tail wagging.

"Oatmeal with chocolate?" Angst asked.

She nodded but looked down.

"Thank you for telling me, Kala," he said. "I promise you, it wasn't stealing. She knows when I've taken them too. They're really good, aren't they?"

She nodded vigorously, smiling as if the weight of the world had been lifted from her shoulders. Angst was a little jealous.

"Um," Faeoris said nervously, glancing at Kala and raising a hand. "My mating cycle was broken by that ass." She coughed into her hand. "By ANduaut, and now I really need to make babies."

"I like babies," Kala said.

"I don't," Faeoris said under her breath. She was blushing furiously, staring at Angst with a frustrated gaze.

"We know," Maarja said. "It's okay."

He didn't completely get it, but the Berfemmian's shoulders dropped about a foot as the tension abated, as if the words had meant more coming from Maarja than anyone else.

"Aerella already said it," Jintorich replied. "I am one, one of many."

"I don't know what that means, my friend," Angst said as gently as he could, glancing to the others for help.

Jintorich's face was wrenched in pain, as if he wanted to explain but couldn't. His ears were pulled back in a way Angst had never seen, and his eyebrows drooped to the ground. The Meldusian didn't say anything further and looked like he couldn't.

"It's okay," Angst said, placing a finger on the small man's shoulder. "We'll figure it out. We're in this together."

CHAPTER TWENTY EIGHT

Maarja concentrated on the ground and her shuffling feet. Angst stared at the tall woman until she met his gaze. The Nordruaut was hard to read, her face stoic.

"I'm ready to go," she said.

"Okay then," he replied. "So am I."

29

Gressmore Ruins

"I've been here many times throughout my life," Aerella said, her old hand gripping Angst's shoulder for support. "I'm always excited to visit great memories, but they leave me with a heavy heart, and a sense of..." Her voice quavered as it trailed off.

"Regret?" Angst continued for her, his own voice quiet. He remembered the several awe-inspiring days he'd spent in Gressmore Towers—a mage city in the clouds, resting on tall pillars designed to protect them from wyrms, dragons without wings. When they grew wings, and began attacking the city in the sky, Anderfeld was out of ideas. Desperation drove him to cast a spell that locked Gressmore in time, making them relive the same day again and again. To free the city, Angst had been tricked into killing the man, Aerella's father. Angst and his friends were cast out, with Aerella. Being here reminded Angst that he'd killed an innocent man. He had regrets too.

But, if it hadn't been for Anderfeld, Angst would never have cast the same spell now keeping Tori alive: "At all costs." Those three simple words, coupled with pain, desperation, almost un-limited power, and will, were enough to change time. Angst had only wanted to go back in time one day, to protect Victoria. In-stead, the spell had only slowed time, and only in Victoria's room. He couldn't begin to fathom how it was possible that the spell had affected time, but why had it reacted differently for him than Anderfeld? Neither Chryslaenor nor Dulgirgraut would feed him information, not even table scraps, but he had to know: was the spell broken, was it him, or was it something else entirely? Aerella looked as weary as she did old. Returning to this sort of destruction, to the remnants of an empty home, couldn't be easy. But maybe she retained more knowledge when she was older...if she could remember.

"I'm sorry to bother you with this now," he said, as delicately as he could. "But when I cast the spell 'at all costs' it turned out differently than when your father cast it. Young Aerella said I did it wrong, but I was wondering if you still feel that way now."

"That's a good question, Angst, but one I may not have the answer to," she said. "It's not actually a spell. At least, not like the one we use to summon swifen. Saying *at all costs* is more of a plea for the foci to try to fix everything. They are incredible tools, but their interpretation of your plea will have random results. I don't advise you to cast it again. It won't always work out the way you hope."

"Thank you," he said respectfully, not wishing to push any more.

She nodded gratefully at his understanding and patted him gently. "Let's get this over with," she said, her words thick and heavy.

Gressmore ruins showed little sign of the majestic city it had once been. The black pillars that had held it up appeared to be smashed into the ground as if by an enormous hammer. The earth was littered with black stone shards and broken clay pottery. Aerella pulled back old vines that clung to a marble statue but shook her head and let go of nostalgia.

"My father was in the process of creating a memndus," Aerella said.

"Oooh," Jintorich said in wonder. "I used to teach my students about those when I was a professor. They were living maps that provided a bird's eye view of Ehrde. With a foci, one could concentrate enough to see closer, like viewing the top of a house. Did it work?"

"Until I broke it," Angst said.

"Father was so upset." Aerella chuckled.

"Why did you break it?" Maarja asked.

"I was using it to see my wife," he said.

"And your princess," Aerella said, nudging him.

"Well..." Angst said with a cough. "I may have concentrated a bit too much. I guess it wasn't quite finished yet, and it crashed to the ground."

"You break everything," Faeoris said sharply. "Don't you?"

"It's a gift," he said, trying to turn his wince into a smile. Was she still upset? Knocking him out should've helped a little. He continued with a sigh. "Dallow has pieces of those memndus, which allow him to see. If we can find more, Aerella and I can cast a spell on the stones to locate him."

"Where do we begin?" Maarja asked, opening her arms wide.

"We need to find a needle in a haystack," Angst said.

"Why would someone put a needle in a haystack?" Faeoris asked, looking at Maarja. The Nordruaut shook her head. At least they were agreeing on something.

"He means this will be difficult," Jintorich squeaked, his ears flicking away gnats. "The glass rocks of the memndus will be hard to locate in these ruins."

"Why didn't you just say that?" Maarja asked Angst.

"He's dumb," Faeoris stated, her bright wings unfolding. She launched into the air and called out, "I'll look for reflections from above while there is still daylight."

"It sounds like your other mate is still angry," Maarja said as she watched the Berfemmian fly ahead.

"She's not my other mate," Angst said in frustration.

"Maybe that's why she's angry," Maarja said, sitting down. She took out a knife the size of Angst's leg and began sharpening it on a curved stone.

"Why are you sitting?" Jintorich asked. "Are you all right?"

"You don't need me stomping around," she said stoically. "I'm not here to find little things."

"You found me," he teased.

Maarja dropped the knife and scooped Jintorich into a hug. Muffled squeaks snuck out from somewhere between large arms and giant Nordruaut breasts. The hug lasted a little too long, and she finally set him back on the ground. His cheeks and ears were red as an apple, making Angst wonder if he'd been suffocating. It wouldn't be the worst way to die.

"You made my entire head blush!" Jintorich spluttered. "I hate it when you do that!"

"No, you don't," she said, casually. Maarja picked up her knife and sheathed it. "Maybe I'll go hunt for dinner."

"Thanks," Angst said.

She nodded once in reply, but said nothing else. He had a terrible time reading the Nordruaut woman. She seemed distant, cold, but she obviously cared. Maarja was always tense around Faeoris—they weren't exactly on the best of terms—but was something else bothering her?

"Call out if you run into trouble," Angst offered.

Her face wrenched into a snarl that made him swallow hard, a reaction he could read very easily.

"Or how about we call you if we run into trouble," Angst said, failing to remove his foot from his mouth.

"I hate it when she does that," Jintorich muttered, the Meldusian's red face becoming less ripe.

"No, you don't," Angst said with a wink.

"I believe I can identify where the memndus would've been," Aerella said.

"That'd be a great place to start," Angst said, following her around marble outcrops. He couldn't get out of his head the fact that—

"Go ahead," she encouraged.

"You know me well," he said. "Okay, fine. You said I go mad, after bonding with the two swords."

"I said too much." Her voice was shaky, and she stopped to lean on her knees and cough.

"I don't understand," he said. "Why was that too much?"

Long moments passed, as did her racking cough. She stood upright, still older than him, but not quite as old as before.

"I don't believe in fate," Aerella said, her voice firmer. "Although I've seen one future, I think it can change. I don't believe that you're destined to walk a specific path. You have yet to make choices that you may regret. I fear that telling you what will happen will make it happen. Even now, I worry that if you become mad, it is because somewhere inside you feel you have no choice. It's why I left Jaden asleep. He knows too much. If I tell you the future, if he does, it will be inevitable. Maybe it already is."

"What?" Angst asked, spinning around as her hand left his shoulder. "Jaden knows my future too?"

His mouth opened wide as he stared in disbelief at the twelve-year-old Aerella standing before him. She was thin and wiry, but it was still her. He recognized her olive skin and mane of brown hair. Kala rushed up to hug her like a long-lost friend.

"I'm sorry, Angst," she said, returning Kala's hug. "I don't remember anymore. I only remember what I've experienced at that age, mostly."

"You did that on purpose," he admonished.

She winked before running off with Kala to play. Angst wanted to be upset, he wanted to know more about this dark path he should avoid, but seeing the girls run off hand-in-hand made him smile. Kala deserved a break from the seriousness of world-saving, and didn't Aerella as well? There was still time for moments. There had to be, or what was the point?

Faeoris landed with a thud, eyeing the girls at a distance. "Great, more children," she said with a grunt. "I couldn't see anything from above."

"Everything must be buried from years of rain and mud," Jintorich said.

Angst gently smacked himself in the head. "I should start using this thing."

"What's that?" Jintorich asked.

"My brain," he said, holding out his hands.

CHAPTER TWENTY NINE

"Maybe try hitting yourself harder next time," Faeoris snapped.

"I'll leave the hitting to you," Angst replied. "Maybe that way you'll stop being a bitch all the time."

A blue glow surrounded Angst's hands as he reached out with his mind, surfing through the dirt for clues. The earth felt cool, like letting sand sift through his fingers. There were large stones and indigenous rock of all sizes. He wasn't really sure what the memndus should feel like—he'd never searched for glass. Maybe he should just look for something little, and smooth. He heard a high-pitched roar and dismissed it; it had to be the girls playing.

Air left his lungs, knocked out from a blow that lifted him into the sky. His mind whirled as it was yanked from his search. Was it another dragon? Was this a cavastil bird? Were the others in trouble? Soft hands gripped his armpits as he desperately gasped and coughed. His focus into the ground faded, and his captor smelled nice. Angst opened his eyes and could almost make out her pretty face through his wind-blasted tears.

"Faeoris?" he asked.

Without answering, she flung him high into the air, flew over him, and punched him hard in the chest.

30

Unsel

Wilfred paced and fumed and paced before the empty thrones. How could Ranson have tried to institute a draft without coming to him first? If he could wield, he would've turned the man into a squirrel.

"We don't need a draft," he said to himself, the guards, and his assistant Jenna. "Once they learned Princess Victoria was in danger, the people of Unsel have been lining up to join the military. We even had to turn away wielders. They love our queen, just like we do."

He faced Jenna and nodded, expecting the young woman to nod in surprise. What he saw made him stand upright and tug down on the chainmail of his armor.

"You...you're not Jenna," he said, not sounding regal at all.

The gorgeous redhead kicked something under the desk before shaking her head and smiling with blood-red lips. She was pale, as though she only went out at night. Her full lips and large eyes almost distracted him from the fact that the side of her head was shaved. She wore a dark vest with thin stripes that buttoned below her voluptuous chest in the most amazing way. The white silk blouse with puffy sleeves that tucked neatly into that vest covered everything and yet left nothing to the imagination. She wore dark makeup around her large eyes, with thick lashes that couldn't possibly be real. If it was somehow magic, it was the good kind.

"I'd enlist," she said, in an accent so sultry he couldn't have cared less that he didn't recognize it.

"I...uh...I," he said before impressively closing his jaw. "Where is Jenna, young lady?"

"She had to step away," the young woman said with an endearing smile. "She asked us...me to cover for her."

"Good choice," Wilfred said, his mouth dry. "I mean, thank you for helping. I'm Wilfred, and you are..."

"I'm Bella. Ouch," she said, kicking again. "Is Mr. Angst expected to arrive soon?"

"Angst...of course," he said with a sigh, his shoulders drooping. What was it with that man? "I'm hoping he arrives within a week or two."

"Oh," she said, her eyes downcast.

Wilfred really wanted to cheer her up when his pending heroics were interrupted by footsteps.

"Fulk'han are raiding the borders," General Mirot said as he stormed down the hallway. "Their army is only days away. Our army is on the march, but we need your zyn'ight, all of them."

Wilfred struggled to drag his eyes and focus away from Bella, only to find Mirot now staring at the young woman. He coughed to get the general's attention.

"The zyn'ight aren't trained in the ways of the military, but they are ready to help," he said.

"How many?" Mirot asked hungrily.

"There are roughly a dozen wielders. Mostly those who fought alongside Rook," he said with a sigh. "Everyone else is too young, or their magic just won't help."

"Fine," Mirot said. "When can they leave?"

"I need three to stay behind and guard Princess Victoria," Wilfred said.

"What?" Mirot said, spitting out the word. "You said there are only a dozen!"

"I promised a wielder would be on guard," Wilfred said, running fingers through his wispy hair.

"As much as I want Victoria to be queen, as much as I want her to be safe," Mirot said in a somber tone. "We need to protect all of Unsel, not just one person."

"You're right," Wilfred said, feeling defeated.

"Is there anyone else who can help guard her?" Mirot asked.

"I'll see if I can find someone," Wilfred said, already thinking through the lists of wielders and their abilities.

"If you don't mind me asking," Mirot said, his face stern, "who did you make this promise to?"

"I promised Angst and Aerella that a wielder could help stand guard," Wilfred said.

"Angst?" Bella asked, quickly covering her mouth.

"Pardon?" Mirot snapped.

"This is the second time you've mentioned his name," Wilfred said. "Do you know something about Angst?"

"Bye," she said. Bella reached under the table and, in a flash of bright light, disappeared.

Guards drew weapons as Wilfred and Mirot stepped back. They looked at each other with wide eyes and slack jaw.

"They're everywhere," Mirot said in dismay.

"Don't start with me," Wilfred said, staring at the empty desk, hoping she'd come back.

* * * *

Nordruaut

"There is no way I'm healing her!" Rose whispered, practically spitting out the words. "Not with that thing attached! Not until she's awake, and we can find out how she got here!"

"That's a lot to ask of someone who seems half dead," Hector said gruffly.

Goosebumps spread across her arms as if tickled by cold fingers, and Rose hugged herself tightly. This wasn't right. Nothing about Princess Alloria being here made sense. Hector had carried her to his temporary home in the mage city and placed her on a cot. She hadn't moved for hours; the only indication that

Alloria lived was her quick, shallow breathing. One of Jorm-brinder's blades remained firmly attached to her hand. Neither Hector nor Dallow could remove it, and Rose refused to try, even after the songs quieted in her head.

At one time, Alloria had been so beautiful that a part of Rose had sort of hated her. Actually, she'd really hated her. Rose had only seen her a couple of times in the castle, but had heard stories of Alloria's flirtings with Angst. It was beyond inappropriate since he was married, and she was only sixteen. The young woman radiated naïve innocence while wearing clothes best left in the bedroom. Someone else's bedroom.

Alloria wasn't looking so pretty now. She looked more like a harlot someone had roughly tossed out of a brothel. Her face was sunken in from malnourishment, making her typically full lips protrude unhealthily. Her red and black leather leggings and corset appeared battle worn, cut randomly around her legs. The midriff of her top was completely torn away. Chunks of honey-brown hair were gone, as if torn from her scalp. Rose may not have been a fan, but nobody deserved to be treated like this.

Hector knelt, looking closely at her legs, torso, and ample breasts. He pulled at the rips in the leggings, peeking beneath each one before gently placing his hands on her bare torso. Hector scratched at dark splatters that covered her corset, finally leaning in to smell Alloria's cleavage.

"Really?" Rose asked, placing fists on her hips and leaning in. "They're not that impressive."

"You're just saying that because you don't have any," Hector said with a twinkle in his gray eyes.

She slugged him in the shoulder, wishing it was harder.

"Oh, be careful, I may need healing," he said with a pained expression, rubbing the spot on his arm.

"Are you done gawking at the half-naked teenager's boobies?" Rose asked.

"I'm studying," he said, unable to hold back a smirk.

"I see that," Rose said dryly.

"Help a blind man, brother?" Dallow said, his voice half teasing, half pleading.

"Well," Hector began. "Her breasts are still enormous, and they're barely tucked into a leather number Angst must've picked out."

"Good," Dallow drawled, scratching at his stubbly chin.

"You two are terrible," Rose said. "How can you joke? She's obviously been attacked or something."

"Or something," Hector said seriously. "Her corset and leggings have been shredded, but I don't see any fresh cuts or scars beneath. She's also covered in blood."

"What?" Rose asked, standing back.

"I don't think it's hers," Hector said. "It's all over her, and caked on dry, like it happened weeks ago. Maybe longer. It just doesn't smell right. I can't put my finger on it."

"Because you generally go around smelling young princesses?" Rose asked.

"They usually smell nice," Dallow said.

"They do," Hector agreed. "She doesn't. Alloria's pretty ripe. She hasn't bathed in a very long time. I'm also not sure if she's really been attacked, if her clothing was cut for show, or if she was just partially healed but forgot to change."

"And why did she suddenly arrive here, where we happen to be trapped?" Dallow added. "Holding half a foci that Rose can...sense."

The song was muted, but she could still hear it, hungry for her, practically begging to connect. Wishing it would stop was as effective as forcing herself to nap.

"Maybe someone on Ehrde wanted to give us a change of scenery?" Dallow said with a broad grin.

Hector's chuckle was cut off by Rose's frustrated roar.

"Answer me!" Rose shouted. "How can you joke about this?"

"We have to," Dallow said. "This is the worst kind of joke, because we have to be the punchline."

"What do you mean?" Rose asked, her frustration quickly replaced with quieter worry.

"This is some sort of trap," Hector said. "She's either here to kill us, or somehow use the foci to help us escape and lead us to our deaths."

"Not mine," Dallow said. "I'm too pretty to die."

Rose sighed. They kept bantering, egging each other on even as the danger of Alloria's appearance seemed to increase with every theory. The young woman appeared haggard. But had she been attacked and tortured like her clothing suggested? It was really nothing to joke about, and Rose tried changing the subject.

"Why do you think the foci can help us get out?" Rose asked, nudging Dallow in the ribs with two fingers.

"I hate that," he said with a frown, jumping away defensively. "Jormbrinder could be the key to unlocking Ughcratic so I can learn a spell that opens the door," Dallow said, his face tightening at the mention of the lost language. "I've absorbed so many volumes, but I can't understand any of them."

"That's a pretty big if," Hector said. "Maybe she can just poke a hole through the shield. Look at everything Angst can do with Chryslaenor and Dulgirgraut, and he barely knows what he's doing."

"Is she even a wielder?" Dallow asked. "That's what I don't understand. Angst would've told us. He's terrible at keeping secrets, especially when Victoria blurted them out."

"Like the kiss?" Hector asked.

Both men's smiles were quickly wiped away by Rose's frown.

"Victoria read Angst's mind and found out that Alloria had kissed him," Dallow said.

"Or he kissed her," Rose corrected.

"There's a difference," Hector said, running fingers through his mane of long gray and white hair.

"Not really," Rose said, her frown winning the argument. "Not to mention, how did Victoria not know? The entire castle knew."

"I think they run with different crowds," Hector explained. "Less gossipy, more ruling Unsel-y."

"When she did find out, Tori was furious," Dallow said with a satisfied grin.

"I don't care about Angst and his cheating ways," Rose said

sharply. "I care about getting out of here. What do we do?"

"Maybe we cut the hand off," Hector said, rubbing his thumb thoughtfully along the scar on his chin. "And use the hand to poke a hole through the shield."

Rose and Dallow faced him, and she tried her best to pierce his jokes with her glare.

"Fine," he said, not laughing. "We'll wait until she wakes and question her."

"That could take forever," Dallow said.

Rose approached the cot and leaned over until her mouth was mere inches away from Alloria's ear. "Wake up!" she shouted.

Alloria's eyes sprang open, and, like a frightened animal, she scrambled to the far edge of her bed. She held her knees up to her chin and pulled the dagger in close to her face. The princess wasn't screaming or barking orders like royalty. She looked petrified, and a bit ridiculous with that giant, golden triangular dagger. Had she actually been through that much trauma? Rose didn't know what to believe anymore. Should she console Alloria or throw peanuts at her?

"It's all right, Your Highness," Hector said, his gravelly voice far from soothing. "We aren't going to harm you."

"She already knows that," Rose snapped before focusing on Alloria. "If we wanted to hurt you, or kill you, you wouldn't be in Hector's room, lying safely on his bed."

"Rose, be gentle," Dallow said, inching to the bed and feeling for the corner before sitting at the opposite end.

"Maybe she *has* been through a lot," Hector agreed, his voice filled with worry.

A pretty young female fell out of the sky, and despite the potential danger, they suddenly wanted to be heroes again. Rose hadn't seen this much energy from them since she'd told them she'd located a frozen stash of steak. That prank had kept them from talking to her for days, which sounded nice right about now. She rolled her eyes, but they were too engrossed in bosomtastic to notice.

"Where am I?" Alloria asked, her voice grating painfully as if she had swallowed a desert.

Hector rushed out of the room, returning just as fast with a flask of water. He offered it, but she just stared as if it were a trap. He took a drink before setting it on the bed and stepped away. Alloria picked it up and gulped down the contents, trickles of water streaming through dirt along her chin and neck. She sucked the flask dry before throwing it to the floor. Wiping off her chin brought a sudden realization, and her face wrenched in disgust at the filth on her fingers.

"We believe we're in a mage city, somewhere in Nordruaut," Dallow said.

"A mage city. That's good," she said, lowering the dagger. "Is there...is there anything to eat?"

"If you like fruit," he replied wryly, pulling an apple out of his pocket and gently setting it on the bed. She plucked it up and began devouring it.

"Why?" she asked around a mouthful of the fruit.

"Why what?" Rose asked impatiently.

Alloria swallowed hard, twice, as if fighting her dry throat to get the food into her stomach. "Why are you here?"

Rose and Hector looked at Dallow, who was blushing furiously.

"That's sort of my fault," he said. "We were with Angst, in Angoria. He'd just finished destroying Air, bonding with another foci, saving Rose, and exploding."

"He... Angst exploded?" She sounded near tears. Her lip quivered, and she clutched the blanket on the bed.

"He's okay," Rose said, surprised at the young woman's reaction. "I saved him, again."

"I don't understand," Alloria said, her breath catching.

"Rose is a healer, and Angst doesn't seem to die," Dallow continued. "He's fine. He flew off with Victoria and a Berfemmian. There was a portal left behind by a tall, odd-looking wielder."

Alloria's eyes went wide, and she gripped the dagger so tightly her knuckles whitened. She nodded for him to continue.

"We went through, hoping to end up in Unsel. We ended up

here instead."

"Go on..." Rose urged. "Maybe confession will help you feel less guilty."

"Well," Dallow said, reeling on the corner of the bed. "I'd been reading about other mage cities in Azaktrha, a different mage city that was underwater. We were supposed to focus on Unsel when going through the portal, but I may've been thinking of this city. We aren't sure what it's called. It's the only explanation I can come up with for ending up here."

"In short," Rose said with a scowl, "it's Dallow's fault."

"How long are you going to be mad at me?" Dallow asked.

"Until we're back in Unsel," Rose said, kissing him on the cheek. "Not to mention, you're cute when you look guilty."

"Victoria flew off with Angst?" Alloria asked, her voice shaking with worry. "When did this happen?"

"Best guess?" Hector asked. "Three months ago."

The young woman cried. Not the fake cries of a spoiled princess, but the racking sobs of someone who'd been to a dark place and was now back. She held herself as if waves and waves of pain were crashing on her shores. Rose sat on the bed and placed a hand on the young woman's knee. The princess looked a mess. Against her better judgment, Rose tried to heal her, drawing some of Alloria's wounds into herself. There was a loud crack, and searing pain coursed through her hand. Rose leaped from the bed, holding her arm, which was now numb, as if she'd slept on it wrong.

"Rose?" Dallow asked, standing and reaching out. "Are you okay?"

"I tried to heal her," Rose said through gritted teeth. "I can't feel my arm."

The teenager looked up at Rose with large, sad, eyes. She tried covering herself with her arms awkwardly, as if hiding how terrible she looked, the weapon hanging limply from her hand.

"I'm sorry," Alloria said. "I didn't know what you were doing. I would've stopped you."

"What was that?" Rose snapped. She wiggled her sore fingers

CHAPTER THIRTY

as feeling slowly returned to her hand. "Why can't I heal you?"

"Because I'm already dead. I was killed by the Dark Vivek," Alloria said through her sobs. "And he sent me here to kill all of you."

31

Gressmore Ruins

"Are they going to be okay?" Kala asked, holding hands with her new best friend.

"They'll be a little bruised, but better for it," Aerella said calmly. "They really needed to get this out of their systems."

"Why are they fighting?" the young girl asked.

"They're flirting," Aerella said cautiously.

"Does flirting always have to hurt?"

"Sometimes," she said. "They're...complicated."

"If you become old again," Kala said, "can I call you grandma?"

"No," Aerella said firmly.

* * * *

The blow should've crushed his ribcage, but his armor and a hastily created air shield had mostly protected him. Everything was great, except for not being able to breathe and the quickly approaching snowbank. Mere inches from impact, she grasped his ankles. The sudden jerking stop made his back pop and crack all the way to his neck before she threw him up into the air again.

They'd fought once before. He'd thought she was relieving

sexual tension after being torn from her normal mating cycle, but that was months ago. This couldn't be about mating. Something had been bothering her, he'd felt it, but fighting? Here? Now? He had to end this quickly without hurting Faeoris, or dying.

Just as he reached the apex of her throw, he placed an air shield platform beneath him to rest on. His stomach caught up several seconds later as he hovered, and waited. He was still winded from her first blow, and there was a formidable dent in his chestpiece the size of a small fist. He looked around until he finally spotted bright wings in the distance, approaching fast.

At the last second, he willed the shield to drop him down far enough that she passed overhead. He grabbed onto her ankle, thinking he could stop her. Or not thinking. Big mistake. He dangled from her foot as she dove toward the mountain. Faeoris leveled out to swoop in and out of branches. They were the small kind at the top of trees, the ones that poked and scratched instead of skewered. His mind raced. He could stop her. He could throw a shield in front of her, but he didn't want to hurt her...much.

They approached a cliff, and he sighed. This would have to be it. She flew along the face of an outcrop, kicking her feet to shake him free, and close enough that he could anchor himself to the mountain. Like a hinge, she smashed into the stone, landing on her face and shoulder. Faeoris skidded alongside the cliff face to a stop. Before she got up to attack again, Angst lunged forward, tackling her. They rolled and rolled until he was on top.

"Let me up!" Faeoris roared, unable to move her arms or legs. Angst had anchored her bones to the ground and was straddling her stomach. "Get off me!"

"What, can't you breathe either?" he asked, struggling to draw in air. Maybe humor would shake her fury. "I know I'm fat, but a strong, muscly Berfemmian like you should breathe fine. Your lungs look nice to me."

Faeoris wasn't laughing, even a little. Tears of frustration streamed through dirt and blood on her cheeks. This didn't feel at all like flirting, or playing. She was genuinely upset. Wait, blood? He immediately jumped off her.

"I didn't mean to hurt you," he said. "Are you—"

She swatted him, and Angst flew back fast. Berfemmian. Temper. Got it. He bounced off something that looked like a mountaintop, his shoulder wrenching painfully as the bounce hadn't slowed his flight. As if she'd been skipping stones in a pond, he bounced again, his leg twisting the wrong way with a wincing crunch. That one hurt. He continued flying back until he landed on something soft enough, at least, that he was sure it wouldn't be the worst way to die. Faeoris's arms were wrapped around his chest, the same one that was struggling to breathe. She brought him to a snowy mountaintop and set him down. Everything throbbed, a severe precursor to pain. Tomorrow was going to suck. His companions only seemed to remember he was old when they thought it was funny.

"Goodbye, Angst!" she shouted as she rose into the air.

"Where are you going?" Angst coughed.

"Home!" she shouted, looking around helplessly.

"Do you know where home is from here?" Angst asked.

He lay in the cold snow for a very long time before she landed beside him. He should've had the right words. This probably should've been one of those chivalric moments mentioned in that crappy heroing guide he'd never received. Sitting up made him gasp for breath, and everything popped or stretched wrong and then popped again. The only reason he wasn't screaming had to be the cold, numbing, delicious snow. Why couldn't he suddenly become younger like Aerella? He'd been able to deal with pain when he was younger.

Angst stood on one leg to face Faeoris. She turned away, holding herself.

"What's this about?" Angst asked, holding back a potentially embarrassing cough. "You startled me when you attacked. I think I peed a little."

She chuckled, finally.

"That's not my favorite way to pee," he continued. "Getting knocked into the air by a pretty woman. But now we know it works, in case of peeing emergencies."

"Don't make me laugh when I'm angry at you," she muttered, wiping her cheeks.

"I'm sorry," he said.

She spun on a heel, her fist reeled back.

"What?" Angst said, holding up his good arm defensively. The other arm was supposed to defend him too, but instead chose to hung limply by his side. "I'm...not...sorry?"

"You just don't get it! You say sorry, and you don't even know what for."

"I've been married a long time," Angst said. "I'm well trained."

"That doesn't fix anything!" she screamed.

"Then tell me," he said. "I care, Faeoris, but I won't understand until you tell me. I'm a man."

She covered her face with both hands. "I was stuck in Unsel for three months. I waited for you, and you never once said thank you!" she said behind her hands. "When you found out I didn't know how to get home, you didn't once offer to help. Not once!"

"Oh," he said, carefully lowering his injured leg for balance.

"I was trapped—with your wife, who hates what I wear, and Maarja, who hates me for being Berfemmian. I had to beat her insults into submission, which made everyone else afraid of me," Faeoris shouted. "I agreed to travel with you because you're my friend, only to learn from a child...a child...that we aren't supposed to sleep naked together."

"I..." he began, raising a finger in his defense.

"No one in Unsel would mate with me. No one! They look at me like I'm a freak," she cried. "And then, nobody made me feel more like a freak than you did."

"What?" he asked. "What are you talking about?"

"You would kiss that fish. That human-fish-mermaid. You would kiss her, but not me, Angst," she said. "You have no idea what I'm going through. Our time to mate came and never left. It's still here!" She beat on her chest. "I don't want children, but I'm driven to make them. It's maddening. You're the only one I care about, the only person I love, and you turned me away. It's the most embarrassing thing I've ever experienced. Tell me why, Angst. Am I a freak? Am I really so awful?"

Angst could only wish that the cold crawling up his legs would reach his heart, which ached for his friend. She didn't understand, and he'd done a terrible job of explaining. It was just that, Faeoris was his friend. Despite her insane beauty, he wasn't looking for a new wife. He'd chosen her to be his friend. It had to be so different from how she lived, where women were friends and lovers, and men were for mating. Distracted by everything and more, he'd really neglected her, and she deserved better. But first, she had to know.

"Kiss me," he said.

"No," she snapped.

"Please," Angst said, as sincerely as he could. He genuinely wanted her to try. "I love you too, Faeoris."

Her head jerked around to make eye contact, and she sucked in her lips.

"I'm serious, I really do love you," he said, reaching out. "Please kiss me."

She took several steps, closing in. He could feel her heat, smell her skin. Even after beating the crap out of him, she smelled great. Faeoris wrapped her arms around his neck and moved closer. Her eyes closed lustily, their noses bumped, and she stopped. Seconds passed, and her eyes opened once again.

"I...I don't get it," she said. "I want to mate so badly, and you're a man, but I can't with you. I can't even kiss you."

"Now you understand," he said, only hating this a little. "You may be one of the few who does."

"What do you mean?" Her arms were still around him, but she pulled back.

"You can't kiss me because we're friends," he said, holding up a hand and crossing his fingers. "We're like family. I do love you, totally and completely. But we're friends. We don't kiss, or anything else. I'm sorry if you thought...if I led you to believe... Faeoris, I'd do anything for you."

Her hug made more things pop, and he was awareded with many wet kisses on his cheeks. Angst wanted to hug her back, but was locked into a Berfemmian straightjacket, which was pretty nice. When she finally let him go, he took several moments to catch his breath.

"I'm sorry," he said. "Now that I realize some of what I've done, I'm really sorry. You deserve so much better, and so much more from me."

Faeoris sniffled, but said nothing and stood very still. She didn't even shiver. He did, almost uncontrollably, and it felt like they may be here awhile. He sought help from Chryslaenor, who hummed from a distance, giving him just enough of a spell. Angst created a fire that burned air instead of wood. That spell didn't make sense to him, but he would just have to ask someone smarter when this was done. Snow quickly melted onto rough shale, and he slowly regained feeling in his legs.

"My closest friends have always been women," Angst said, as he gave up standing and sat down awkwardly in his armor. "Always. It's been that way my entire life. I've had some friends who are guys, but not many. Most of the women I'm close to are beautiful, and needy. Sometimes it works, like with my friend Rose. She's kept me on the straight and narrow, especially after wielding Chryslaenor. There were never any misunderstandings with our friendship. I thought it was the same with Victoria. I was always drawn to her, too much, but we were friends. I never thought we crossed the line, but we jumped on it a lot. When I realized she'd fallen in love with me, I felt like I'd done something wrong."

"What about Moyra?" Faeoris asked, sitting beside him.

"I don't know," he said honestly. Angst sighed deeply, and his heart chilled as he swallowed a deep lump of sorrow. "Maybe we didn't have time to learn to be friends. Maybe I finally crossed a line I shouldn't have. Maybe I'm just a terrible person." He covered his face.

"She was pretty, your Moyra," Faeoris said. "I would've kissed her."

Angst looked up and smiled. Her reply wasn't forgiveness, or pity, or even understanding. It was acceptance, which he needed more than anything. "That would have been great."

She smiled in a way that made her seem older, and wiser. "Why did you let me sleep naked with you, if it would make Heather mad?"

"She's always mad," he said in frustration, and quickly saw that wasn't the right answer. "You're young, and beautiful. Did I mention that you're beautiful?"

"I'm not sure I remember you saying that," she teased.

"You are," Angst said, his cheeks very warm. "The attention is nice. But it was selfish. I didn't mean to hurt you, just to make myself feel good."

"I'm older than you," she said.

"You look younger," he replied. "It still counts."

They both stared into the fire that burned from nothing. As the snow continued to melt, so did the numbness that masked his pain. His breathing became shallow, and spots began to appear before his eyes. She'd really worked him over, but he would do anything not to show it.

"Would you save me?" she finally asked.

"What?" Angst asked.

"Like your princess," Faeoris explained. "Would you save me like you're trying to save her?"

"I'd fight through time to save you," he snapped. "I'm not going to lose anyone else I love."

She launched at him for another bone-crushing hug. It hurt in the best way possible.

Faeoris pulled away, frowning at him. "Yeah, you're right, no kissing," she said firmly.

"Of course not." He sighed then grinned mischievously. "What about the sleeping naked together thing?"

"Only when I'm drunk!" She laughed.

"That's fair," he said.

"And I'll try not to make you mate with me."

"What?" His heart skipped a beat, his question lost to her

228

CHAPTER THIRTY ONE

laughter.

32

Angst and Faeoris landed gently at Gressmore Ruins, and he wanted to thank her. But the first step away made him wince, and the second made him wince more. The snowy mountaintop no longer numbed the injuries from Faeoris's thrashing. He struggled to breathe and hunched over with his hands on his knees; his ribs didn't feel right. Faeoris helped him remove his plate and chainmail chest piece, and then the padding beneath to reveal his pale torso covered with dark purple blotches.

"Oh no," Faeoris said, shocked at the sight.

"That looks painful," young Aerella said with a wince.

"That was a lot of flirting," Kala said, swallowing hard as she stared at his wounds. "Miss Heather's going to be very upset."

"Not with this type of flirting, she isn't." He groaned. His whole body was throbbing in pain, and he dropped to his knees.

"I'm sorry, Angst," Faeoris said. "I guess I was a little upset."

"More than a little," he wheezed, feeling dizzy. "Aerella, can you heal this?" He waved at his entire body.

"I don't know if I remember all the spells. I'm still too young," she said apologetically. She squeezed her eyes shut, her nose scrunching. "I'll concentrate."

"I think I can mend the bones." Angst awkwardly threw out his cloak and lay in a sprawl, stretching out his arms and legs. He tried to focus, but just couldn't catch his breath. "Then we can look for the memndus stones."

"I was a physician, Angst," Jintorich said, bounding next to him. "I'll fix you up, and then see to your armor. I'll need a hot fire."

"On it," Maarja said, rushing away, the ground shaking less with every step.

"A physician, and a blacksmith?" Faeoris asked. "And a midwife?"

"I am one," Jintorich said sincerely. "One of many."

"Thank you," Angst said. His little friend had said that several times, but before he could ask what it meant, Faeoris was hovering over him in the best way possible, and he was too tired to even try making eye contact.

"I'll stay right here, Angst." She sounded worried. "I'll take care of you."

"That sounds like a great idea," he said, before everything faded away.

* * * *

Angst woke to a crackling fire, laughter, and the distinctive horting of gamlin. He opened his eyes and took in deep, full breaths with working lungs. It was night! How long had he been out? As delicately as one would pet a newborn pup, he felt along his ribs. They weren't even sore to the touch. Concentrating, he sought broken bones with his mind, but everything seemed connected and whole, though old. He'd never healed so quickly before... Would it be possible to rebuild the squeakier parts of his knee, or even reinforce his tired back? Glorious laughter interrupted his thoughts, and Angst rolled to one side.

A slightly older Aerella, a sweaty Kala, and a tail-wagging Scar chased a gamlin who dove in and out of the ground like fish in water. The giggling didn't stop as a human-like face popped out of the dirt, smiled, and returned to hiding. Little puppy hackles rose from Scar's neck and back, but his tail wagged vehemently. Jintorich lay nearby on a bedroll, snoring loudly, hair from his eartops occasionally twitching. Maarja and Faeoris sat beside each other, staring at the fire, sharing a jug of something that seemed large for the Berfemmian but small for the Nordruaut. Maarja laughed at something Faeoris described with her hands, before deftly placing one on the Nodruaut's knee.

He shook his head and blinked hard several times. This couldn't be right. He felt well-rested and healthy. The kids, or whatever Aerella was, were playing and happy. Maarja and Faeoris weren't killing each other; they were acting like friends. Nobody was being mauled, burned alive, or attacked by something unrecognizable. Completely out of his control, his worried frown curled into a smile. Maarja nudged Faeoris and nodded her head in his direction. Both women wore the scantest of tops and bottoms, making Angst grateful for raging fires that showed everything in the night. The tall, lovely Berfemmian approached him, her long legs walking an uneven path and her hips swaying deliciously. She *fwump*ed onto his cloak, handed him a roasted leg of something that made his mouth water, and took a long swig from the jug. The drink smelled tart, and strong. Faeoris set it down, wiped her chin, and looked at him with a sleepy smile.

"Meldusians make some fine booze," Faeoris slurred. "Itsa bit spicy, like me!" She laughed.

Angst couldn't help but chuckle and reached for the jug, but she pulled it away teasingly, and then again, before holding it over his mouth. He opened wide, and she poured more than he could handle. It was thick and tasted like pepper and oranges, burning all the way down. She stopped when the booze covered his face, pouring over his tears that streamed from the liquor's spices. He sniffed loudly and blinked as she sloppily wiped off his mouth.

"Spicy," she declared.

"Like you," he agreed, already feeling the warmth in his belly relaxing everything. "What is it?"

"Narankur," she said softly.

"You better save me more of that," he said.

She drank deeply, and he took that moment to devour the leg of beast in his hand. It may have been the best, fastest, most fulfilling meal of his life. The meat was also spicy, making his eyes and nose run freely. He tossed the meaty remnants to his dog, which brought an approving nod from Faeoris.

Scar seemed torn between gamlin-chasing fun and a bone that shouldn't be shared. The decision was made quickly as the lab pounced on the bone and brought it to a safe spot for a quick gnawing, far away from thieving gamlin. After a quick pee and ground-scratching that would certainly keep evil at bay, he returned to the frolicking chase.

Angst laughed before leaning his head back so Faeoris could fill his mouth with the spicy liquor. She smiled as it splashed onto his bare chest. Making a poor attempt at wiping his face and chest, her hand landing on the ruby ring that hung from a chain around his neck. She leaned in to inspect it, rocking only a little as she squinted.

"Wasss this?" she asked, her tongue thick from drink.

"A gift from someone I thought was a friend," he said, not wanting to say who for fear of a long round of questioning.

"Is she pretty?" she asked then smiled. "Never mind. All your friends are pretty."

"They are," he agreed.

She beamed as she returned to a somewhat upright position. Firelight danced across the tanned skin of her taut stomach, ample cleavage, and pretty face. Her full lips and large eyes smiled at the gamlin's game of hide and seek for a long moment before she looked back at him again. Her expression went from ecstatic to concerned, in the way only someone drunk can manage. Faeoris took a breath to say something when she was interrupted by a panting child.

"You drink a lot," Kala said, suddenly in his face. Her thin brow frowned with curiosity as her eyes darted between Angst and Faeoris.

"Oh?" Angst asked, surprised at her sudden appearance. Faeoris did not look amused at the interruption.

"Heather says you drink a lot, too," she said with a parental frown.

"Huh," he said, not remembering much more than a wife-look

233

after one of his outings.

"Why do you drink so much?" she asked.

"Well, I only drink when I don't want to be sober," he said.

"When is that?" she asked, very sincerely.

"Right now," he said, and he meant it.

"Oh," Kala replied. She smelled of fresh air and youthful sweat, and her long black hair was damp around her face. "Thank you for letting me come with."

"You didn't give me much of a choice," Angst replied, feeling a bit too buzzed to be sincere. He tried to speak soberly. "I wish we could've gotten you home safe. This *adventure* is going to be a tough way to learn about heroing."

"I'm learning so much!" she said excitedly. "Today I learned about healing, and fixing armor. I think...I think I could even..."

"What?" he encouraged.

"I bet I could pick up Chryslaenor!" she said firmly.

"I bet you could!" he said with the enthusiasm he would've given any child.

Kala's eyes were disappointed, as if the answer hadn't been sincere enough. Before he could say more, she was distracted by Aerella's beckoning. "Gotta go!"

The twelve-year-old ran off in a fit of giggles. Angst smiled, but wondered through his quickly growing haze of drink what she'd learned. Was she talking about his interactions with Faeoris? Was Aerella teaching her powerful spells? Could she actually pick up a foci?

"I'm sorry I hurt you," Faeoris said.

"What?" he asked.

"Are you angry?" she said, leaning over wonderfully.

"You brought me booze and food," he said with a wink. "You brought your beautiful self over here to check on me. How could I be angry?"

"Flirt!" she said, preparing to pour more booze into him.

It was too late to say no, and the alcohol burned all the way down.

"Jintorich said it would help us rest, or something," she said.

"Oh, it will," he said, feeling dizzy. "What happened when I was out? I feel so much better."

"He fixed you, and your armor," she said around a yawn. "Said something about being a blacksmith once."

"Really?" Angst asked. The fire was feeling warmer still, and prickles of sweat formed on his brow.

"I almost forgot," she said, resting her hand on his bare chest. Once again, he didn't notice, really. "Your gamlin found some memb-dust stone things."

"Aren't they great?" he said with a surge of pride.

"They're so cute!" she squealed.

"I feel like I'm dreaming," he said.

"Is this what your dreams are like?" she said lustily, winking at him with those long eyelashes.

"The ones I can't remember," he said, rolling to his side. "They have to be."

"You promise you're not mad, Angst?" she said, the smell of alcohol thick on her breath. She settled in, her bare back resting against his stomach. Not that he noticed any of this, because that would be inappropriate, right?

"You had every right to be angry," he said. "I'll be a better friend."

"You better," Faeoris said, her eyes suddenly dangerous. She laughed and drank deeply before leaning to her side.

"Why is that?" he asked with a smile.

"You love me," she blurted.

"Oh, I do, do I?" he teased.

"You love your princess," she said. "Who really isn't that pretty, you know."

He choked down a laugh, assuming it was the booze talking, encouraging unashamed candor.

"I do love Victoria. She's my friend," he said.

"You are fighting through time for her," she continued.

"I guess I am," he said. It was very drunken logic, which meant it made sense.

"You said you'd fight through time for me," she said, lying

beside him, making the jug of Meldusian booze her little spoon. "That means you love me too. It's the nicest thing anyone has said."

"Indeed, I do," Angst said softly, petting her fine, brown hair. She was already snoring. Faeoris may not have heard, but it didn't matter. She knew.

"It's time for bed," Maarja said, in a surprisingly motherly tone.

"Awwww," the girls replied in unison.

Scar scrambled off and came back with his bone. The lab promptly walked around so everyone could see his winnings before returning to the shadows, ensuring once again that no one would steal his kill. Dogs.

"You promised a story," Kala whined.

"You did," young Aerella said, nodding in agreement.

"I am not as good as others at telling stories," Maarja said, holding up a hand to quell disappointed moans. "So I will tell you the first I learned, about The Great Hunter."

The girls sat together on the ground, cross-legged with hands in their laps. Both stared at Maarja intently. The Nordruaut's tanned complexion glistened as she paced before the fire. Her platinum blond hair flowed over her taut leather top. Angst would've thought her size made her frightening, but the girls just looked on with trust and anticipation.

"The Great Hunter captured Fire first and put it in the sky, making Fire the sun and the stars. The next day, he hunted Water, catching it, and making her into lakes and oceans and rain." She raised her hands up high and wiggled her fingers as they fell. "Earth was very strong and powerful, and when she was defeated, The Great Hunter made her into the very ground we stand on."

The girls looked down, shifting uncomfortably.

"Air was quick and elusive, but was captured by the Great Hunter and shared with all to breathe and live," she whispered, spreading her arms and hands expansively. "But the hunt was far from over. Magic is always the hardest to capture, and always the last to be caught. It is everywhere and nowhere, hiding under Water and behind Earth. Becoming one with Air and then lashing out with Fire."

Maarja reached out with clawed hands, leaning over the girls, who both gasped. She winked at Angst as she pulled away. "But the Great Hunter was patient and cunning and captured Magic, only to find it could quickly escape. He tried different prisons—objects and animals and people—but Magic was too clever to be trapped for long. Only the Vivek could balance Earth and Fire and Air and Water, and only the Vivek could capture Magic."

Maarja stood tall, as if the story were done. Both girls looked at each other with the same wonder Angst felt.

"And then?" Angst asked, as Faeoris snuggled deeper around the bottle.

"It's another story," Maarja said, almost apologetically. "But Vivek trapped Magic, until someone released it."

"Who would do such a thing?" Kala asked.

Aerella looked back at Angst as if not knowing how to answer.

"An idiot," he said. "A total and complete idiot."

33

"Lord Ranson," the page announced, bowing with a flourish.

Wilfred winced as he glanced up from his parchment, an engrossing stipulation on the control of bovine mating in the western province of Unsel. It was requests for laws like these that made him question what sort of nonsense went through people's minds. But, everyone had the right to be heard, even if they were wrong. There was the off chance Wilfred could be convinced he was wrong. It may have happened once. Maybe.

The actual throne room was still under repair after the damage Angst had done saving the queen and everyone. This temporary throne room was the great hall, a place typically reserved for the largest of gatherings. Soldiers stood beside tall, round pillars spread twenty feet apart along a marble walkway that led straight to the makeshift throne. Empty chairs were set in neat lines on the outside of the pillars for lengthier meetings.

Ranson walked stiffly toward him, his long crimson coat flaring at his sides as he made his way past the tall pillars. Wilfred returned his gaze to the boring document, wishing it were interesting, or at least distracting. He needed a distraction to control his temper. Right now, he loathed this man, and glared at the document as if it were the cause of all his troubles. Anger and frustration seethed out of his eyes, and he wouldn't have been surprised if he suddenly wielded magics that burned a hole in the parchment. Unfortunately, the results weren't that dramatic. Nothing caught on fire, spewed lightning, or turned into a swarm of bees. Just a little shaking. Lord Ranson coughed politely, and Wilfred stared down, gazing at the document as if it required his full attention. Long moments passed then he handed it to the young woman standing attentively nearby.

"Bring this to the council for review," he said. "It's far too important to be ignored."

"Isn't it about cows?" Jenna asked, her face screwed up in confusion, immediately deflating the importance he'd feigned.

"We have many cows in Unsel," Wilfred said, every single curse word floating through his mind.

"Yes, sire," she said with a quick bow before setting it on a nearby table.

"What can I do for you, Lord Ranson?" Wilfred asked formally.

"I came to discuss what happened at the, uh, at the refugee camp," Ranson said, the old veins and tendons on his neck strained tight as if he were picking up something heavy. He looked down his prodigious nose haughtily.

"You mean Rookshire?" Wilfred asked, keeping his voice cool.

"Respectfully, sire," Ranson said. "It's not a city recognized by the crown. It's merely a band of refugees gathered together. Some could contest how legal it actually is..."

Wilfred sat on the edge of his seat and snapped his fingers several times, pointing at a table of documents. Jenna sorted through the nearest pile and drew one toward the bottom. She handed it to Ranson. The lord's eyes danced across the page quickly, his face becoming rigid as he finished.

"I see I am mistaken. You have declared the camp a town." Ranson sounded disappointed. "You will give them whatever they want, won't you?"

"You left me with little choice," Wilfred said. "But this is a small price to pay."

"The price is already too high!" Ranson snapped.

"Do you hate wielders that much, Ranson?" he said, hoping the lack of formality would reflect his level of irritation.

"No, I don't hate wielders," Ranson said, looking away.

"You almost turned them all against us," Wilfred said, fury rising in his chest. "When we need them the most."

"I've seen things you haven't," Ranson said. "I'm trying to protect them."

"We need *them* to protect *us*," Wilfred snapped. "Drafting them would've been like making them indentured servants. They need to be rewarded for their work, recognized for their efforts. How could that possibly help them?"

"You're putting them in more danger than you realize," Ranson said sincerely.

"What on Ehrde are you talking about?"

Ranson coughed into his hand, so much that Wilfred left the throne to hold the man's shoulders. Wilfred wanted to knock the fool out so he would stop, but instead stood vigilant. After long moments, Ranson waved him off.

"I was very concerned for my son when he was younger," Ranson began. "He was slow to learn, always distracted, unable to focus. His studies were late or ignored, his swordsmanship was poor. I thought he was lazy."

"It happens to the best of us," Wilfred said, completely understanding.

"That would've been okay, but as he grew older, my son often seemed withdrawn, almost without emotions," Ranson continued. "He was quick to temper for any reason, and I would often find him arguing with himself. It was odd."

"That doesn't sound very...healthy," Wilfred said, looking for a polite way to say mentally disturbed.

"It was my fault, not his," Ranson said, a bit of sweat trickling down his brow. "I misunderstood until it happened. One day, Mika was wandering the village when he came on a teen boy bullying a younger boy. Mika stepped in, and...it didn't end well."

That would explain it. Mika must have been clunked in the head, several times, and that made him...odd.

"I'm glad that Mika recovered," Wilfred said politely.

"Mika was never hurt," Ranson said, sounding confused. "The bully barely lived through the ordeal. Mika almost killed him...and nobody saw it happen."

"I don't understand," Wilfred said.

"Neither did we," Ranson said, staring at the ground as if it would give him confidence. "After some convincing, Mika explained that he could manipulate time. He could slow it, even freeze it for short periods."

"That sounds like a useful gift," Wilfred said, feeling uncomfortable.

"It could be," Ranson explained. "But people began to question how he defeated the larger bully, and why nobody saw him attack. They concluded it was magic and were furious. It didn't matter that this bully was a terrible, terrible person. They truly feared my son, and I didn't realize how much. One afternoon, a group in the nearby village rallied, knocked him senseless, and burned him at the stake."

"Okay, now you're making things up," Wilfred said. "Because I'm pretty sure I saw him with you, unburned, at Rookshire."

"Somehow he lived, but he has provided no explanation," Ranson said. "I was just grateful to have him back."

"I rarely understand how magic works, but I'm glad to hear your son lived through the ordeal." Wilfred shook his head. "But to your point, you feel responsible for his safety."

"I should never have let him go freely about after learning of his infliction," Ranson said. "Had I controlled him, and limited access to him, he never would've been put into danger."

"And that's why I'm in charge." Wilfred stabbed the man's chest with a finger.

"Wh..what?" Ranson stuttered.

"Have you ever tried to make it a safe place for wielders?" he asked.

"No."

"So you blindly accept things as they are rather than enforcing tough changes," Wilfred said. "And now you're on the run?"

"Not exactly," Ranson said, tugging at his collar. "Mika convinced me that we need to be here. He worries for his cousin's safety. He's always felt very strongly about her."

Royalty, Wilfred thought, rolling his eyes. "I appreciate your concern, but Angst has convinced me that she's safe until he returns."

"Maybe," Ranson said, caution in his voice. "My son is worried that the spell may not last if Angst is delayed."

"A fair concern," Wilfred allowed. "What are you suggesting?"

"Mika merely wants to stand guard and maybe study the spell," Ranson said. "He would like to find a backup plan."

His first thought was to say no with a side of no and two more helpings of no, but it would solve a problem. Angst had requested that wielders help guard Princess Victoria, and they had, but they would soon be leaving to fight the Fulk'han. Others had offered to help, but they were too young or had passive abilities. If the princess was harmed because the wielder guarding couldn't do more than summon up a vat of chocolate pudding, Wilfred would get the sharp end of a foci. Despite his reservations, and he had many, Mika could supposedly manipulate time.

"Do you think your son could make the time-shield-whatever-it-is last longer?" Wilfred asked hopefully.

"I can ask him to try," Ranson offered.

Maybe, sometimes, things actually do work out. The thought gave Wilfred the tiniest bit of hope. Not only could he protect Unsel against the Fulk'han zealots, he could do Angst's bidding and maybe even help save his queen. Not to mention, it was unlikely that Mika could do much anyway—he was a kid, and Angst was Al'eyrn with two giant magic swords. What could possibly go wrong?

"Under guard," Wilfred said. "Someone will always be there to watch."

CHAPTER THIRTY THREE

"Of course," Ranson said with a nod. "Thank you."

"As for your other concerns, I believe I understand now," Wilfred said with a deep breath. "You fear that people will turn on the wielders if we let them use their magics freely."

"Precisely," Ranson said. "We can't treat them like normal people. It's too dangerous for everyone."

"Sire," his assistant said. "It's time."

"Good," Wilfred said, smiling at her. "Ranson, come with me. I need to show you something."

* * * *

Wilfred could hear Lord Ranson's crisp steps from behind as he rushed forward, insistent on staying a shoulder's width in front of the man with much longer legs. He turned sharply on his heel, and Ranson scrambled to keep up. There was no way he would let the man lead, especially when Ranson had no clue where they were heading, on so many levels.

He stopped abruptly before a wide, wooden door.

"What is this?" Ranson asked.

"Hope," Wilfred replied, the door creaking loudly as he swung it open.

A dozen soldiers stood in a smallish hall that led directly outside. Each of them wore steel armor with shiny plate that covered their chests. Chainmail dangled below the plate, covering full bellies or tight stomachs. The armor was like Angst's, and every one of the wielders wore a red cloak that hid their very unarmored backsides.

"Wilfred," Andec said with a smile as he approached.

"Thank you for coming together so quickly," Wilfred said, shaking the man's hand. "It was a lot for us to ask."

"Anything for our queen," Andec replied with a nod.

"This is Lord Ranson," Wilfred said.

"A pleasure, my lord," Andec said, bowing his head.

Ranson bowed his head graciously, but said nothing.

"What did you decide, Andec?" Wilfred asked.

"We're splitting into groups of three," he replied. "Each party will consist of at least one wielder who can attack, and another who can defend. We will make our stand at the four towns nearest the highway. "

"And you're all aware that the Fulk'han can regenerate?" Wilfred asked.

"Hopefully they can't regenerate without heads!" Tanden called out. The middle-aged bookkeeper cupped his hands together as if choking someone's throat.

Wilfred laughed with them, grateful for the confidence, hoping Tanden was right.

"Is everything set right, my lord?" a young woman asked. She couldn't have been older than sixteen, with dark caramel skin and large bright eyes full of life.

"I ratified Rookshire as a city this morning, Amay, which means I get to start collecting taxes tomorrow," Wilfred said to laughter and a little back-patting. "It should've been done sooner."

"You would make a good king," Andec said proudly.

"Victoria will make a better queen," Wilfred said. "It's time for a wielder to take the throne."

They cheered, and Wilfred's chest filled with pride. He knew this was their future, and was excited to be part of it. Though not everyone seemed enthusiastic. One stood apart, buckling her boots for the umpteenth time. She was a striking forty-something with sharp features and long hair black as night.

"Nikkola?" Wilfred asked, placing a hand on her shoulder. "I heard that Kala is with Angst. Why are you here?"

"My daughter went with Angst to be a hero," she said, her face taut as if holding back tears. "I would be doing her a disservice if I didn't do the same. And, I want a safe Unsel for when she comes home."

"You'll both come home safe," Wilfred said. "I believe it."

Her mouth smiled at the sentiment, but her eyes bespoke pain and anger.

"Kala?" Ranson asked, frowning in confusion.

CHAPTER THIRTY THREE

"I think my daughter snuck onto Angst's caravan," Nikkola said. "She wanted to go on an adventure, to be a hero. I don't think they had time to return her and save the princess. Kala is too young to be out there. She will only be thirteen in a few months."

"Oh...well I'm sure Kala will return home safely," Ranson said, his voice smooth but his eyes squinting with worry. "I hear she is in good hands."

"The best," Heather said.

Wilfred hadn't seen her. She'd been facing away from them, kneeling before a pale, curly headed boy, who Wilfred hoped with all his heart was older than fifteen. The boy's cheeks were flushed and his eyes filled with pride, as if ready to take on the Fulk'han by himself. Heather finished clasping the red cloak and ruffled his hair before standing.

"Heather," Wilfred said, his eyes dancing around the room. "Please tell me you aren't going with. Please."

It took a moment to gather his wits and realize that Heather wasn't wearing armor. She wore a brown leather corset that was very flattering, and a dark tapered skirt that hung over her black riding boots. The forest green traveling cloak was almost hidden by the full mass of brown curls that teased a few grays, which draped over her shoulders. She looked radiant, and everyone stood at attention as she approached Wilfred. She smiled broadly, and the room practically glowed with encouragement and bravery.

"Who...who is this woman?" Ranson asked, slack jawed.

"Angst's wife," Wilfred said over his shoulder.

"Oh," Ranson said, standing up straight. He bowed slightly. "My lady."

"Lord Ranson," she said with a gentle bow of her head. "No, Wilfred, I'm not going with."

"Good," he said in relief, sweat pouring from his hairline. "I worried for the enemy."

"Well said," she replied with a coy smile. "My children come before Unsel, always."

"Of course," Wilfred replied sternly. "I was just surprised to see you. Are the twins okay?"

"They are wonderful," she replied, gushing with happiness. The entire room seemed elated, which wasn't a surprise since she never completely controlled her ability to sway other's emotions with her own. "And safe. I have an entire city more than happy to protect them. Isn't it wonderful that Rookshire is a city, Lord Ranson?"

Every eye in the room turned on Ranson. The older man choked down a fit of coughing that lasted too long to be fake.

"It should've been done months ago, my lady," Ranson rasped, looking slightly defeated.

"You are too kind," Heather said. "Thank you for your support."

Ranson nodded graciously.

"Our zyn'ight are ready, Wilfred the Wise," Heather said.

"What?" Ranson asked in more than a whisper. "These aren't knights! These are children, women, old men...what am I seeing?"

"You are seeing patriots and heroes, Lord Ranson. Wielders giving their lives to protect the people of Unsel," Wilfred said. "The Fulk'han are already at the border, and these are the heroes who will save us."

* * * *

Nordruaut

The air was so fresh, it was practically intoxicating. Rose had been stuck in the room with the very ripe princess for far too long. Not only did she want out to breathe, she really needed a break to think. A lot about Alloria didn't sit right. She'd appeared out of nowhere with half a foci, and instructions to kill them. In a matter of hours, the princess's mood had changed from cornered animal to flirty waitress. It was unnatural, as if someone else controlled the puppet. Or she was just a crazy bitch.

CHAPTER THIRTY THREE

"Thank you for letting me go outside," Alloria said with an innocent smile.

"You aren't a prisoner," Dallow said. "Well, actually, we all are."

"You're sweet." She giggled and brushed his cheek with her hand. "And cute."

Dallow smiled like a child given candy, blushing furiously. He adjusted the memndus stone on his temple, Rose could only imagine what he was focusing on.

"Where do you bathe?" Alloria asked.

"In the creek," Rose said, struggling to keep hatred from her words. "It's cold, really cold, but that's all we've got."

"Oh, okay," Alloria said. Without warning, she wiggled out of her corset and tossed it to the ground. Before anyone could object, she squirmed out of her tight leather riding pants. "I hope you don't mind."

"Nope," Hector said, wiping his mouth.

Dallow shook his head, but said nothing.

Alloria's hips swayed hither and to, her walk mesmerizing even Rose. She deftly hid the long triangular dagger in front of her thigh. Goosebumps rose on the young woman's pale skin as she went ankle deep into the clear water with a high-pitched, "oooh." When she was waist deep, she turned around and shivered, the chilled water making her goosebumps, and everything else perky, quite visible. "You're right. It really is cold."

Rose smacked Dallow in the back of the head.

"What?" he asked.

"She's sixteen," Rose admonished quietly.

"I'm not sure I believe you," Hector replied, turning away as slowly as humanly possible.

"Right," Dallow said with a stiff nod, staring off into nothing.

Rose took the memndus stone from his temple.

"Hey," Dallow said defensively, grasping at the air. "I can't see."

"Good," Rose replied.

"This water feels wonderful," Alloria said. "I could probably stay in here forever."

"Good plan," Rose said.

"Could you toss me my clothes so I can wash them?" she asked.

Rose picked up the leather leftovers and walked to the creek. No wonder Angst was so fond of this one. Alloria's breasts were so large and perfect that Rose wanted to slap her. What had her parents fed her? She was just a teen, but didn't look like one. Had she really kissed Angst? He must've been overwhelmed. Rose knew well enough that that was never his goal. He prided himself on having friends who were beautiful women, but never crossed the line. He kicked at that line, jumped on it and stomped around, but the line was still there. That line versus that kiss must've been a whole new challenge. And this girl must've known that. She was dangerous.

"While you're being all naked in front of everyone, could you tell us how it is that you're dead?"

"We'd really like to understand," Hector called out.

"Turn back around, old man," Rose said under her breath, returning to the others. She couldn't roll her eyes enough. There was only so much bathing and goosebumps she could take.

"Oh, and I'm not sixteen," Alloria called out. "I'm seventeen now!"

Dallow and Hector both grunted, mostly facing away from the spectacle.

"Sometimes I really hate Angst," Rose huffed.

"What did he do now?" Dallow asked defensively.

"This is all him," Rose said, glancing at the gorgeous young woman wading in deeper. "Wow, she's really perfect. Too bad you guys can't see."

"I hate you," Hector said.

"Go find some towels," Rose demanded.

"Some?" Hector asked.

"One for her body, one for her hair," she explained. "And one for both of you. You'll need a cold bath after this."

"Ha," he said, rushing off.

After much splashing, a few too many giggles for Rose's taste, and one invitation that was quickly denied, Hector finally returned. He walked right past Rose's hand and brought an open towel directly to the princess. She exited the creek and pulled it around her. Rose wanted to barf. In all her years, Rose had never had that much fun taking a cold bath.

"Thank you, Hector," Alloria said.

"My pleasure," he replied, looking back at Rose with a wry smile. "You were going to tell us why you think you're dead."

Hector laid another towel across the warm walkway. Alloria sat down and began drying, leaving very little to the imagination. They all sat. Dallow held out a hand and Rose placed the memndus stone in his palm. He shoved it under the blue kerchief covering his eyes, adjusting it until the stone was against his temple. He sighed in relief.

"What happened to your eyes?" Alloria asked.

"We were killing a dragon, and their blood is like lava," Dallow said with a shudder. "That blood sprayed across my face..."

"You poor thing," she said, resting a hand on his knee.

"He's fine," Rose said, brushing the hand off. "You're the most alive dead person I've ever seen."

"Yeah," Alloria said, staring at the corner of her towel. "My father, stepmother, and I were visiting Cliffview. They'd left me alone for a social gathering, and I was going to sneak out with friends." Her face twisted like she suddenly had cramps. "So many of my friends had gone there to meet up with me. All dead now. Cliffview, my friends, my family."

She shuddered and held herself. Rose wanted to say something, but didn't know if this was an act or the truth.

"Water attacked, the city began falling into the ocean, and I fell too," Alloria said with a white-knuckled grip on the towel, as if it kept her breathing. "I stopped falling and so did everything around me. I just hung there, over the ocean, waiting to fall to my death. A tall, bald man appeared. He called himself Vivek."

"As in, 'by the Dark Vivek'?" Dallow asked.

"The same," Alloria said frantically, her voice shaky. "He

told me I was already dead, and I knew he was right. He offered me a ruby ring and said it would keep me alive if I did what he told me. Dark Vivek said he would always know where I am. He told me I would be queen of Unsel if I followed his command."

"In all your nakedness, Your Highness," Rose said sarcastically, "I don't remember seeing a ruby ring."

"Angst has one on a necklace," Hector said in a panic. "This Dark Vivek didn't kill him—"

"No," Alloria said. "He carries mine. I put it around his neck when I kissed him." She looked as if she'd stolen pie from a baker.

"That's why you kissed him," Rose said.

"No," Alloria replied abruptly. "I kissed him because he's Angst. I want him to be my champion, and not hers, and... It doesn't matter. I just hoped that if he had my ring, I'd be safe, and it worked."

"Right," Rose drolled, hoping it sounded politer than calling her a liar.

"I swear, he'll be my champion!" Alloria said, holding up the dagger. "Angst and I are close, and we'll...he'll love..."

"Alloria!" Hector snapped.

"I'm sorry," she said, her voice becoming small as she set the dagger down. She took deep, calming breaths. "I think about Angst a lot. He was always nice to me, when nobody else was. He protects me every day without knowing it."

"You said the Dark Vivek would always know where you are when you wore the ring," Dallow said. "That means he always knows where Angst is."

"I'm sorry," Alloria said, covering her mouth with a hand. "I'm sorry. I never meant to put him in danger."

"That explains a lot," Hector said.

"It wasn't just coincidence that the elements could always find us," Dallow said. "The attacks on Victoria, the battles at sea... I don't even know how we made it."

"Angst," Alloria said, looking at them all sheepishly.

"Tell us more," Rose said, frustrated she couldn't strangle the tramp.

"A lot of people died. Vars killed Queen Isabelle and Captain Guard Tyrell," she began. "I was queen, for a while, and then Unsel was attacked by Water. Half the castle was destroyed, the woman with light wings threw two daggers at the battle, and the Dark Vivek told me to pick them up." She held up half of Jormbrinder. "It hurt so much, but then I saw Angst kiss some woman."

"Heather," Rose corrected.

"No," Alloria said. "A fish woman. She was covered in scales like a mermaid but had legs."

"Moyra," Hector said, peering with his wolf-like eyes. "She had legs?"

"Yes," Alloria said in a disapproving tone. "And when they were done kissing, Water killed her."

"Oh no," Dallow said.

"Angst crossed a line with that one," Hector said to Rose, shaking his head. "I never understood it. Why her out of everyone? But there was something between them."

"Because she was a mermaid," Dallow explained. "It was someone he couldn't actually be with, something he couldn't have. So sad, and very Angst."

Rose didn't understand, and it appeared Alloria didn't either.

"He kissed her back," Alloria said. "I kissed him, and he didn't kiss me back."

"There's a difference?" Rose asked.

"Yes!" Alloria said. "I was so mad, I did what Vivek told me. He loved that stupid mermaid, and he loves his princess. The mermaid was dead, so I went to her chambers and killed her."

They all stood. Hector and Rose looked at each other, and her heart raced.

"Who did you kill?" she asked.

"I stabbed Victoria through the chest with Jormbrinder," Alloria said, tears welling in her eyes.

Before Rose could blink, Hector's sword was at the princess's neck. Alloria lifted her chin even as she sobbed.

"You killed our queen?" Hector growled.

"She's alive," Alloria said, sniffing deeply. "Vivek said that Angst saved her, that she's stuck in time."

"Anderfeld's spell!" Dallow said proudly. "Angst cast it. Wow!"

"He's on his way here now," Alloria said.

"Finally," Rose said. It was the first good thing to come of this conversation. "Once Angst gets here, he can free us."

"I still wonder if the dagger could help" Hector said. "At least we should try..."

"No!" Alloria said frantically. "Don't you see? I've finally escaped. Vivek can't come here. He can't come into the mage city. He told me none of the elements can enter mage cities either."

"Wielders found a way to protect themselves from elements," Dallow said, scratching his chin. "That's amazing."

"That's why I'll never leave," Alloria said. "I'm finally safe, and I'll do anything to stay."

34

Gressmore Ruins

"Angst, you need to concentrate," Aerella said, her husky voice stern. "I'm not old enough to do this myself."

"I am concentrating," he said in frustration.

"On the spell," she replied. "Not on me."

To Kala's disappointment, Aerella had aged and was now somewhere between her older teens and younger twenties. She'd bloomed overnight, and was every bit as lovely as when they first met at Gressmore. She was petite, very busty, and with a mane of brown hair you wanted to run your fingers through...

"Angst!" she shouted.

Faeoris and Maarja laughed. Jintorich sighed deeply, shaking his head in dismay. Kala marched over to Angst, crossed her arms, and took a deep breath. She looked like his wife just before a verbal beating.

"Yes, I know," Angst interrupted before she even had a chance to speak. He bent over, crossing his arms and staring at her. "You're going to tell Heather."

"Everything!" she said defensively.

"Well, go ahead!" he said.

"I will," she replied, stomping off to the other side of the camp. Scar scrambled to keep up, lying down at her feet with sad, droopy ears as if he'd just been yelled at too.

"Angst," Jintorich squeaked, gently admonishing him.

He was right. Kala hadn't deserved that. Angst should've let her vent. She was more upset about losing her playmate than his lack of focus. There was so much pressure that anything became distracting, especially Aerella suddenly looking drool-worthy. The last time Angst had used the memndus stones to create a map of Unsel, he'd been surrounded by friends, which made it easier, somehow. Angst had experienced so much with his missing friends—everything from boozing to battle. They'd seen him make mistakes, stood beside him when he failed, and knew him to be emotional...and distractible. Angst looked around, and it struck him: these companions were becoming his friends, too. They weren't pressuring him to get it done; they were here to support him. There was no judgment, except a little from Kala. Maybe, rather than giving her something to judge, he should've been helping the prodigy learn.

"One sec," he said to Aerella, who rolled her eyes. Angst approached the sniffling girl and knelt beside her. "Kala," he said softly.

"What?" she snapped, staring at Scar as if willing the dog to bite Angst. The dog's head became skinny with guilt.

"I'm not doing this right. I need help casting this spell," he said. "Would you help me, please?"

"Really?" she asked, facing him with wide, excited eyes.

He nodded, and she hugged him around the neck. It was probably one of the best hugs he'd ever gotten. They walked hand-in-hand to the others. Angst let go and placed one hand on the flat of Chryslaenor, which rested upright on its tip. He nodded encouragingly. Kala studied him for a moment as if through new eyes. She sucked in her lips and reached out hesitantly. Her eyes widened as she touched the foci, and a broad smile crept across her face.

"He sings really pretty, Mr. Angst," she said.

"Yes, he does," Angst said. His heart skipped a beat, and he met eyes with Aerella, who smiled knowingly. He hadn't expected that. What did it even mean? Could she actually pick up his foci? He could sense Kala's connection, both to Chryslaenor and to him. The girl had an incredible amount of raw power that seemed to mirror his own. It wasn't identical, or nearly as strong, but it was there. She also emulated his magic, creating a tiny thread of connection to the sword.

The foci warmed to this, more determined than ever to share knowledge. Angst could see her nodding from the corner of his eye before she let out a giggle.

"What?" Angst asked.

"Chryslaenor is funny," she said with a smile.

"Huh," he said, wondering why the sword had never shared anything funny with him. He'd need time to fully understand what Kala could do, and her new relationship with his foci. Throughout this mission, he had only thought of her as a stowaway, and a potential snitch. If she was going to imitate Angst, his heroics weren't really just for him. Instead of trying not to be noticed by this unwanted conscience, maybe he should start acting like a mentor, and lead by example.

Angst had invited Kala to cast this spell as a ploy to cheer her up, but they actually were going to do this together. "Now, do just as I do."

Aerella looked at them dubiously, but still held out a palm full of small, clear stones. Angst nodded at the twelve-year-old, and she scrunched up her face and nodded back, her dark, pretty eyes sincere.

The stones rose from Aerella's palm. They spun in a vertical oval, faster and faster. Angst and Kala drew from the foci to create a picture of Ehrde, like viewing a map from high above in the face of an oblong mirror. Blue and white lights appeared on the map like distant stars. The others closed in for a better look.

"It's so shiny," Faeoris said, her voice filled with wonder.

"A-mazing!" Jintorich squeaked, his ears and eyebrows at full attention. He pointed a stubby finger at the lights on the map.

"The white lights are mage cities," Aerella said excitedly. "The blue ones are other memndus stones."

Angst recognized a couple of the mage cities, Gressmore and

Azakthra, but only two locations shone bright blue. Where they stood at Gressmore ruins, and far, far north in the middle of another white marker.

"Enurthen!" Aerella said in amazement. "How on Ehrde did they end up there?"

"I can find this place if I had a better look," Maarja said, leaning forward.

"Closer," Angst said to Kala, and her fists shook with the effort. "Just follow my lead."

"I don't know if that's a good idea," Aerella warned.

"Hold steady," Angst said. He remembered the struggle of focusing on one place with the memndus, but it was so much easier with Kala's help.

The image came closer, and closer still. What had once looked like a distant map soon became the view from a mountaintop. Angst willed the map to slide up and to the side, seeking the source of blue and white dots. It blurred until they finally held it still. Dark spots spread across a white background, the opposite of bright stars in a clear night. There was a glimmer of light from an enormous city that stood over a cliff. Blue lights shone brightly inside that city. Enurthen.

"Hurry," Aerella urged, her hand trembling as the stones spun faster.

"What's that, below the city?" Faeoris asked.

"It's too much," Aerella said, her voice strained.

"Almost done," Angst said. He could feel Kala's focus waning from exhaustion and drew in power from Chryslaenor to compensate.

The shaky image closed in to show a snowy battlefield littered with Nordruaut bodies. Hundreds of dead scattered about the frozen wasteland, covered in blood and ice.

Kala screamed in fear.

"No," Maarja said. "I'm too late!"

"Watch out!" Aerella cried as something snapped, sounding like a whip cracking.

Tiny memndus stones shot from her hands in all directions.

CHAPTER THIRTY FOUR

There were several *thwap*s that sounded like hail on hard ground.

"Faeoris!" Jintorich said.

The Berfemmian's hand was inches in front of Kala's face, a stream of blood flowing freely to the ground. She'd been fast enough to catch it. Without a word, she handed the memndus stone to Aerella.

"I'm sorry," Aerella said, her hand already glowing yellow. "It was too much."

The injury didn't seem to faze Faeoris, she merely looked at Maarja with concern. The Nordruaut's face was torn between pain and hurry.

"We go north as fast as we can, Maarja," Angst said, not sure of the best way to console her. "We get on our swifen and race straight through Rohjek all the way to Nordruaut."

Maarja nodded but said nothing, her great fists clenching. Jintorich hopped up to her shoulder and spoke into her ear, patting her long platinum hair. The tenseness in her face slowly abated.

"Angst, I..." Aerella began, pressing against her temples. "There's something, something I can't remember."

"What is it?" he asked, placing Chryslaenor on his back with a solid click.

"We should avoid Rohjek," Aerella said. "At all costs."

"Why?" he asked. "Can you tell me why?"

"No," she said after a long pause, her young face contorted with an aged worry.

"Then we don't have a choice," he replied. "Summon your swifen."

* * * *

It was as if someone had drawn a line in the sand, with fire. The border of black and gray soot was disturbingly straight, as if that same someone had determined, everything beyond this point should be burned to ash. On one side was spongy spring grass. On the other side was death that stretched into a shadowy expanse of more death. They'd stopped just before the edge, and

Angst could only guess that this was the border between Unsel and Rohjek.

Angst and Faeoris dismounted his steel ram swifen. Kala and Aerella remained on her white, flowery tiger, Jintorich and Maarja on his oversized six-legged...dog thing. They all stared in awe, and Kala coughed as a dry breeze blew wisps of ash at them. Angst was wary of actually stepping across, instead leaning forward to look up and down the border, with Faeoris's firm grip on his shoulder keeping him from leaning too close. It went far beyond his vision.

"Wyrms," Aerella whispered, her voice heavy with sadness.

Faeoris and Maarja looked at her quizzically.

"We first called the minions of Fire wyrms because they were slow and crawled on the ground," she explained. "They were still deadly, belching fire and almost impossible to kill. To save Gressmore, we raised the city high on stilts so they couldn't reach us. The wyrms grew wings, and we called them dragons."

"I've always wanted to kill a dragon," Faeoris said hungrily, a dangerous glare in her eyes.

"Yes," Maarja said nodding vigorously. "But later, after Nordruaut. We will hunt them together."

"It's not as fun as you'd think," Angst said. "Scales like volcanic rock, blood like liquid fire, and they're hungry."

"You killed a dragon?" Maarja asked, scoffing in disbelief.

"I thought I killed *the* dragon," Angst said. "It was as large as a city. Victoria flew me up on her swifen—"

"The pink unicorn," Faeoris interjected, dryly.

"Oooh," Kala said, her eyes wide before glaring over her shoulder as Aerella began braiding her long black hair.

"Hold still," Aerella said.

"Yeah, so, the dragon," Angst said. "I leaped off the pink unicorn and onto the dragon's back, carved a big hole into it with Dulgirgraut, and then jumped off. Fortunately, Victoria caught me in time."

"That sounds like fun!" Faeoris said.

"Without wings, it was...exciting," Angst said, licking sweat and ash from his dry lips. It tasted awful.

"You're making this up," Maarja said. "The good stories come from truth."

"Does this look like I'm making anything up?" Angst held out his hand as if presenting the scorched horizon for the first time.

"Were there other dragons?" Jintorich asked, his thick eyebrows raised high.

"Of course," Angst said, looking over at him with a smile. "The gamlin are impervious to dragonfire, and they killed many. Unfortunately, Fire wasn't happy with that and attacked. Earth came to our defense. My friends and I tried to help, but Fire threw a sun on us."

"Is that...is that what happened to Melkier?" Jintorich asked in shock. "There were many rumors, but nobody really knew."

"Ouch!" Kala cried.

"I said hold still," Aerella said. "You don't want stray hairs burning off."

Kala frowned but said nothing further, holding Scar close.

"I've seen the ruins," Aerella said. "I even remember reading about it once, I think."

"He's telling the truth?" Maarja asked, wide-eyed.

"Yes, Fire destroyed half the capital city in Melkier, and there was nothing I could do," Angst said, staring off at the wasteland. It felt like the guilt and frustration and panic had all been combined to create a protective barrier of numbness between his heart and grief. "I only had time to try and save my friends, but half the city, and all those people, were lost."

"I'm sorry, Angst," Jintorich squeaked. "That sounds like a terrible burden. You must know it isn't your fault."

"And Fire must hate you for killing his dragons," Maarja interjected.

"He must hate you a lot!" Kala agreed, nodding vigorously, now playing with the end of a long braid.

"It seems to be going around," Angst said. A familiar knot of tension stabbed between his shoulders.

"That's why you didn't want us coming with," Jintorich said, his voice even higher, the excitement of understanding lighting his eyes. "Because of Fire."

"Fire, and Magic," Angst said. "I wasn't able to defeat Fire, and Magic escaped my trap." Chryslaenor pulsed a bright blue light, and he glanced over his shoulder. "I know you tried, but Magic isn't predictable. Really though, I'm glad to have you back." The foci's song hummed nicely in his head as if grateful for his understanding. "I'm not sure how I can destroy both elements, find my friends, and keep all of you safe."

He saw the panic in Kala's eyes.

"Except you," Angst said with a wide grin. "I know I can keep you safe."

"Oh, good," she said with the instant relief only a child could enjoy.

"That makes sense, Angst," Faeoris said dryly, crossing her arms and peering at him. "Trying to save Ehrde by yourself since it took you, your friends, and an element just to survive last time."

"Well, uh..." Angst stumbled over words, his cheeks warming.

"She means it's a good thing we're here," Jintorich said, his long eyebrows dangling over his cheeks. He held his toothpick staff up defensively.

"Mostly what I meant," Faeoris said irritably.

Angst looked them over. Aerella was the most knowledgeable mage he'd ever met. Kala, a child prodigy with a dog that turned into a giant monster. A Nordruaut—one of the strongest beings in Ehrde, and a Berfemmian, who was stronger yet and could fly. They gave him hope. Maybe together they could make it through Rohjek alive. They had to!

"You're right," Angst said. "We have a chance."

"I'm scared," Kala said.

"Being a hero doesn't mean you aren't scared," Jintorich said. "Being a hero means you face your fears and do what must be done."

"My friend speaks truth," Maarja said. "As always. Now let's move."

But she didn't step forward. None of them did. With a deep breath, Angst placed his foot on the ash as if dipping a toe in water. It felt like he was stepping on a pile of feathers. He took a step forward, and another. It was as if he'd entered the wrong house by accident, and the owners liked to burn things. Only ten feet into the mess, smoky air dried his throat, and his armor was becoming a steam room.

"We should stay mounted, and ride through this," Maarja said, coughing several times.

"You're right," he said. "Faeoris, would you fly ahead?"

"Of course," she said, her wings already out, the colorful feathers of light blurring through the smoke.

"Not too high," he said, gripping her hand, "or too far. Please be careful."

"I'll try not to kill too many dragons on the way," she said with a wink.

"Please stay here," Kala asked, her eyes flashing red. Scar yipped several times.

Faeoris looked at the child with barely an ounce of patience. Before she could say anything, Scar hopped off Kala's lap and began sniffing at the ground.

"It's okay," Angst said. "Maybe I can send some gamlin ahead, and... Wait."

As if he'd already called for them, gamlin of all sizes popped up out of the ash, directly in their path.

"What's this?" Faeoris asked.

"Mah boys!" Angst said as he knelt. "What's up, kids? We're in a bit of a hurry."

Angst focused, leaned forward, and aimed an ear at them. He heard the gentle buzz that could've been their odd method of group communication, or remnants of his hangover ringing away. Scar growled, and Angst glanced back to see his dog's eyes flash a brighter red. Was the dog genuinely sensing a problem, or merely picking up on Kala's own anxiety?

"Scar, no," he called back before returning his focus to the gamlin. "You're mine, remember," he said firmly to them, concentrating on whatever magic tethered his mind to theirs.

The connection felt strained, like muscles that needed a good stretch after running around the world. He usually ignored that buzzing of communication like background noise, and sometimes felt it wouldn't take much to cut it like a string, but the creatures made far better allies than enemies. They were invulnerable to everything but water, and his foci. They were the only creatures he'd seen successfully kill dragons. Not only were gamlin good little fighters, but they were everywhere, making them an invaluable source of information when he remembered to tap into it. But, they were also the first monsters he'd faced with Chryslaenor, so he didn't completely trust them. They belonged to Earth, and even though she said the gamlin were his, how could he ever believe an element would be totally honest?

The smallest gamlin dove into the ground and popped out again mere feet away, the dirt rippling around it like a pebble thrown into water. He somehow sensed this one as Tori's favorite. The cute little creature had traveled a long way to be here. It opened its small, human-like mouth and strained until a sound came out that sounded like, "Hort." Its little head shook as it tried again. "Hort."

"Yes, hort," Angst said. He felt impatient, but there was something going on. "This isn't how we usually communicate, buddy. I don't speak hort."

"How do you communicate with them, Angst?" Aerella asked.

"Not with any sort of language," he explained. "It's more a sense of things. You know that feeling like you're being watched, just much stronger. Honestly, I haven't had much time to explore—"

"*Dort!*" it called out, stomping its tiny feet in apparent frustration.

"Well," Angst said, almost laughing at the funny sound "That's new. Look, guys, I'm sorry, we really need to keep going."

"Dor...dan..." it strained, shaking its head violently. "Daaanger."

Angst's eyes went wide and his mouth opened. "What?"

The gamlin was gasping from the effort, but a small smile appeared on its tiny face. "Danger."

"Danger," the other gamlin replied. "Danger."

"Not creepy," Faeoris said sarcastically.

"What danger?" Angst asked.

The gamlin shook his head, merely repeating the word, "Danger."

"I guess explaining the danger is a bit much, if that's their first word," Aerella said. "Is there anything else? Do you sense anything?"

"Yeah," Angst said. "They're scared."

"I'm scared," said Kala.

"I'll protect you," Faeoris said.

Everyone turned to look at the Berfemmian. She blushed at the attention and shrugged.

Angst knelt, his knee sinking into the soft, moist ash. He placed his hands on his thighs and leaned forward.

"Thank you for the warning," he said. "I don't know how much you understand, but the Princess Victoria, my friend...your friend. She's in danger."

"Danger?" it asked.

"Yes." Angst nodded. "The only way to save her is if we go that way."

The gamlin shook their heads, several horting and the others straining to say danger. They all dove in and out of ground until they ended up in a huddle. Now that he was paying attention, the buzzing in Angst's head made him wince. As suddenly as they'd appeared, they dove back into the ground without another word, or hort.

"That was thoughtful, I guess," Angst said. "But we should keep going."

"Thoughtful?" Jintorich asked. "You think their effort to say words we could understand was just being thoughtful?"

He was right—right enough to make Angst's stomach gurgle. They should still scout ahead. Kala had asked Faeoris to wait, the gamlin said danger, and he couldn't shake the feeling that his Berfemmian friend should stay behind. Not to mention, Maarja was much better at direction than anyone. Still, he didn't want his friend to be upset.

"Faeoris," Angst said. "Would you keep them safe while I run ahead with Maarja to look around?"

"Of course," she said. "But hurry, and be careful. Both of you."

35

Rohjek

Despite her size, Maarja moved with the grace of a gazelle, quick and silent. Angst in his armor on top of his steel ram swifen sounded like the precursor to Armageddon. They'd tried walking, but Angst had the stealth and tact of a dropped dinner plate. Maarja said it was pointless when the smallest steps created plumes of ash that were only sometimes hidden by random pockets of dark smoke. Now his traipsing was a combination of armored everything and larger plumes of ash but greater speed. They must've looked like an oncoming storm.

Maarja stopped abruptly, holding up a hand that almost knocked Angst off his mount. She waved him closer, so he dismissed the swifen while still mounted and dropped to the ground. He'd never remembered it being quite so loud.

"We're close to something. If you can't be quiet, you should remove your armor and sword," she whispered sharply.

"Did you want to just feed me to the dragons raw?" he asked. "Or is this a ploy to get me naked?"

She actually smiled, sort of, before pointing to a red glow in the distance. It was impossible to make out through the thick air, but the light seemed inconsistent. Flickering in and out, reminding Angst of a darkening campfire. Without words, Maarja moved forward at a pace he could follow. He snorted at the thought of them stalking, only to be instantly shushed by the enormous woman. But it really was funny. She couldn't fit in his house, and he had a sword the size of his own body. They weren't sneaking so much as walking with hope.

"Maybe the dragons nearby are deaf," he said, frowning with determination at her glare.

She shook her head, and they continued forward.

Normally he would welcome a quiet moment such as this. Scar wasn't yipping, Kala wasn't nagging, and Jintorich wasn't squeaking out questions. He liked Aerella, but found it frustrating that she said so much without getting to the point. Faeoris was his favorite distraction, when she wasn't beating on him. Maarja was always the quiet one, but it was impossible to appreciate that in their eerie surroundings.

He had the vain hope that this short time with the Nordruaut would bridge a gap. Angst didn't get the sense that she hated him. Intolerance may have been a better description. But here they were, traveling together, their means combined to the same end. He really felt they should get along on the same level as the others. That there should be a connection of some sort, if not a friendship. And she was pretty.

Ash hung in the air, making it feel close, like they were in a small room with people he didn't like. Angst's eyes watered, blurring his vision. Something crunched noisily underfoot, far louder than it should have. Her large head turned to face him with the look of his very patient mother just before pulling out her hair. She shushed him again, and he fought the urge to sigh.

"Walk heel to toe," she whispered brusquely. "Try not to step hard."

"Right," he said. "Thanks."

There was a noisy crunch as he shifted his weight. He smiled at her with all his teeth, and she sighed as she turned around and continued toward the red glow. How was it possible that a woman so large could move so quietly? Was it even necessary right now? They were completely alone out here, their target was a long way off. This was really his only opportunity to talk, even though she may shush him to death.

"Were you in Unsel to see Tarness?" he whispered, far too loudly.

"What?" she whispered sharply, turning to face him again. "No."

"Then why were you there?" he asked.

"To find you," she said, looking about nervously.

"Me?" he asked. "I thought you liked Tarness."

"I wasn't there because I *like* you!" She took a deep breath to compose herself. "I think of him, but I was sent on a mission from Nordruaut—"

"So, you weren't there to see Tarness?" he asked, not believing her for a second.

She stared at him now with the combined impatience of his mom, his wife, and Faeoris. "I did hope to see Tarness. It's why I volunteered."

"I knew it," Angst said cheerfully.

"Yes, you're a bright human," she said. "Now can we go back to being quiet?"

"He talks about you," Angst answered.

"He does?" she asked, her lip almost curling into a smile.

"More than he means to," Angst said. He'd always sensed that Tarness longed for Maarja more than anyone. Maybe this was a chance to put his buddy in good standing. "He's one of my closest friends. I can tell that he wants something more with you."

"Why do you tell me this?" she said, crossing her arms. "Why does he not tell me this?"

"I tell you because he would want you to know," Angst said. "He doesn't tell you, because he's not here."

"Then you are a good friend," she said crisply.

"I try," Angst said. "Always."

"Then try to be my good friend," she said. "And walk quieter."

He made the mistake of wondering if there was a spell to walk quietly. There was, and Chryslaenor shared a complex revelry of earth and air and magic that made his head spin. Out of nowhere, Dulgirgraut suggested another spell that combined just air and magic. The swords argued, and his head wrenched. The only thing that saved him was the noisy crunch of another step. Maarja said nothing, but her broad shoulders tensed.

"Please, Angst," she said, with surprising politeness. "You need to be quiet from here, or you need to stay behind."

He took her words in stride and nodded sincerely. As quietly as he could whisper, he said, "Wave me off if I make too much noise, and I'll wait. I promise."

She nodded appreciatively and took a large, silent step forward.

There is an art to certain skills, that Angst had always appreciated. Whether it's painting, or bricklaying, or singing, or walking silently when every step screams for attention. It requires more than knowledge. There's experience and ability behind those endeavors, and almost a passion that can make it come to fruition. Maarja had all of those and sounded like she walked on feathers. Angst sounded like he was kicking the feathers off a bird. But the rest of his steps were careful enough not to bring a bevy of dragons down on them, and she only winced with every third step. Progress.

A hot breeze cleared enough smoke to reveal a mass of enormous red crystals rising from the ground. Rohjek was known for using small crystals in jewelry, and Angst vaguely recalled Heather wanting a necklace or something, but he'd never heard of this. It was a structure, of sorts, that easily took up the space of the Unsel training grounds, maybe 75 or 100 yards across. Chryslaenor sang in his head, a tune that brought him chills despite the heat. They moved forward slowly, studying the mass of crystals in awe. The shards varied in size—the smallest no larger than most men, the largest rivaling his Nordruaut companion. From a distance, the crystals appeared to jut out randomly, but up close, they seemed almost organized, as if circling around something that glowed brightly.

"What is it?" Maarja whispered, so quietly he barely heard.

"It's what we're looking for," Angst said, pointing at it accusingly. "That's got to be the danger my gamlin were warning us about, and exactly what we need to avoid. Now we can head back to the group and lead them through Rohjek while staying away from everything giant, red, and glowy."

There was a loud crunch, and Maarja frowned at him.

"It wasn't me," he said, holding both hands up defensively. "I didn't move."

Someone moaned from the other side of the crystals. Were there people ahead? Could there possibly be Rohjek survivors in this thing? His jaw set as he reached for Chryslaenor. Something about this wasn't right. The gamlin warning them away, Chryslaenor's wary song, giant red crystal structures, and now crunching and moaning. He moved forward and bumped into Maarja's outstretched arm.

"This is a trap, human," she whispered.

"It would be their mistake," Angst said through clenched teeth.

"Let's not make it ours," she said, lowering her arm.

"There could be survivors," he said, no longer whispering.

"Yes," she said, looking around worriedly. "But we can't save everyone. Our job is to find a safe path to Nordruaut. We don't have time to save your friends, your princess, and what's left of Rohjek."

He fought back his growing frustration with grinding teeth. This situation was setting him on edge, and her reluctance made it worse. She was right. They couldn't save all of Rohjek. But maybe, just maybe, they could save some of Rohjek.

"I need a way over," he said. "People are on the other side of this thing."

Maarja's eyes darkened, and she made fists like she was going to pummel sense into him. They heard another crunch followed by a weak cry, and her expression softened.

"We can't climb it," she said. "Can't you magic yourself there?"

"I don't know how to create portals," he said, his mind racing. He reached into the earth for something solid enough to lift him. "I can't make a platform out of the ground beneath us. It's too soft and would break apart."

She looked at him curiously.

"If a rock or boulder is solid enough, I can stand on it and lift it into the air for a short distance," he explained.

"You can fly?" she asked, her pretty eyes wide with wonder. "Do you need rocks? What about using your armor?"

"I can't fly, I can make rocks go up and down, and make air shields to stand on," he explained. "But I can't guide them. And I've already tried using my armor to fly."

"What happened?" she asked.

"It, uh, well, it left bruises for weeks," he said, glancing at his crotch. "I almost couldn't sit down."

She covered her mouth and closed her eyes, her stomach clenching as she held back waves of laughter.

"Please don't tell anyone," he whispered.

"What do we do?" she asked, her eyes glossy but her demeanor becoming more sincere.

"This looks like a wall," he said. "Can you toss me over?"

"That would be a bad idea," Maarja warned, her large eyes bearing down on him. "How will you land?"

"I'll figure something out," he said.

"I've wanted to throw you many times," she said, now very serious. "But not like this."

"Hey," he said confidently. "I've got this!"

Maarja shut her eyes and shook her head before looking around. They were still alone. The large woman cupped her hands and bent over. He stepped onto them and crouched to jump. She looked at him with concern, and he felt self-conscious standing on her palms, so close to her face. The Nordruaut may've been larger than him, but that certainly didn't take away from her beauty. Angst brushed a platinum blond strand of hair from her eye and nodded.

"Not too much," he whispered. "Go!"

She stood fast and lifted up. Angst jumped from her hands at an awkward angle, launching high into the air.

"Too much," he cried. "Too much!"

His flight turned into an ungraceful somersault as he descended, landing with a noisy crack that must've been his spine. Whatever he'd landed on made him roll over several times until he stopped on his side. The object that had broken his fall made the hairs on his neck rise. A slick, diamond-shaped leathery head popped out of a glowing red egg the size of his bedroom. The head lolled to one side, like a chick unprepared to leave its shell. He wanted to stare on in wonder, but Chryslaenor's song said go! Without hesitation, Angst blurred forward and sliced off the creature's head. Liquid dragonfire spilled from the monster's neck, melting the side of the egg. There were easily twenty more, all wiggling with anticipation. His heart raced as he searched for an exit. This place was large enough that he couldn't see all the way across through the smoke. He carefully backed away to the edge of the enclosure, his gaze darting from egg to egg, until he bumped the edge. The crystal behind him was warm and smooth to the touch. Could he climb over? He didn't want to turn his back to the eggs.

"Kill me," a raspy voice whispered in his ear. "Please, kill me."

Angst whipped about to see the face of a woman. Her cheeks were puffy and her eyes orange with sick. Those eyes begged him to set her free. Hers wasn't the only voice—there were more. People, trapped in red crystals, begging for death. They surrounded him with their nightmarish pleas. One voice was cut short with a disgusting wet gurgle.

"Angst," Maarja called out. "Are you all right? What is this?"

The diamond-shaped head of a young, red dragon turned away from a distant croaking wail. Unlike the mother of all dragons with her insanely thick hide, this creature seemed fragile. Fragile like an elephant. He heard a crackling sound, followed by several more. Baby dragons' heads reached out from their eggs. Some yawned, some licked lips, but eventually all eyed Angst as their first meal.

"It's a nest!" Angst shouted, his words clipped.

"Angst," she cried. "Get out of there!"

A burst of wind crashed down on him, kicking up ash and dirt. The wind settled as a fully grown red dragon landed on the edge of the nest, its enormous claws clutching shards along the top. Mom was home. Her scaly head lowered to nuzzle the dead hatchling. Angst swallowed hard. The beast was so large he could barely take in its entirety. The baby dragon didn't move, and two wide, golden eyes peered at him. It reared back, taking a deep breath.

"Maarja," Angst called. "Run!"

36

Enurthen

Hector and Dallow sat beside the noisy brook, water flowing and bubbling from somewhere to nowhere. Hector threw stones into the creek, all skipping expertly to the distant bank. This had to be the most peaceful, boring place on Ehrde. After finding balance between worry and grief over Tarness, he'd figured out how to relax, which was something he'd rarely experienced. But now, with a potential way to escape, anxiety crept closer like distant stormclouds. It was time to leave, and he had the patience of a toddler being told to sit still.

"You've found nothing else that can help?" Hector asked. "I'd hoped that your trips to the library with Alloria would produce something."

"She read a few titles under her breath, so I think that foci can help her translate," Dallow said in frustration. He threw a stone that landed on a distant path, far from the water. "But she doesn't want to leave, so she plays dumb and flirts a lot."

"I've noticed," Hector said with a grunt. "If she's not going to help, why does she go with you?"

"I think to stay away from Rose," Dallow said.

"Or to piss her off, which doesn't take that much," Hector replied with a half-smile. "Ever since Alloria's naked bath, Rose hasn't held back."

"I'm learning new curse words every day." Dallow laughed. "I'm not even sure what some of them mean."

"You really don't want to know," Hector said. "What makes you so sure the foci can get us out?"

"I was hoping for a translator, but there's another way," Dallow explained. "Rose told me that Chryslaenor cracked the shield in Azaktrha, and she wasn't Al'eyrn. The foci was just stuck to her, like Jormbrinder seems to be stuck to Alloria. Even if she can't wield the foci like Angst, it's powerful enough on its own to poke a hole through the shield."

"But she doesn't want to leave," Hector said. "And if anything she says is true, I can understand why."

"According to Alloria, the elements aren't able to enter the mage cities," Dallow said, lying on his back in the soft grass. His eyes glowed dimly beneath the blue silk kerchief. "You know, I bet that's the primary reason the cities were created. Not just to give wielders a sanctuary from non-wielders, but to protect them from elements and their minions."

"Don't be distracted," Hector *garumph*ed.

"Right," Dallow said excitedly. "But it makes sense. The only place we can be safe, from elements and from humans."

"What about Rose?" Hector asked.

"What *about* Rose?" Dallow asked.

"Can she pick it up?" Hector asked. "If so, she could probably take Jormbrinder away from Alloria."

"I don't know," Dallow said hesitantly. "Probably."

"Go on," Hector said. He had known Dallow for years, and even without eyes the man couldn't gamble, his face gave too much away.

"I shouldn't say." Dallow's throat tightened, and he licked his lips.

"This is more important than your affair," Hector said.

"We aren't sleeping together!" Dallow snapped defensively. "Not until I get a divorce."

"You kissed her," Hector said.

"Just the once," Dallow said. "More or less."

"Look, I'm not judging..."

"Of course you are," Dallow snapped. "That's what Angst hates more than anything! It's in your nature to make quick decisions, about situations, and people. You judge!"

It was true, he had to size people up fast in order to assess any situation and plan for the outcome. Whether it was training soldiers, leading troops, or at a dinner party. That foresight and planning had always given him the edge, and allowed him to survive.

"You're right," Hector agreed. "It's instinct, and my instinct wants to leave this place. Alloria didn't appear by accident. So far, all she has done is piss off Rose and try to manipulate us."

"I haven't been manipulated," Dallow said in mock sincerity.

"No, never, never," Hector shook his head. "But I've got a feeling that if we don't act soon, we're not going to be leaving. So what aren't you telling me about Rose?"

"She can hear music from Jormbrinder," Dallow said hesitantly.

"How?" Hector asked, cocking his head to one side.

"It's just a theory, but recent events seem to have changed her. Chryslaenor practically kidnapped her from Unsel and dragged her to that mage city. When we found Rose, the Dark Vivek tried forcing her to bond with the foci," Dallow said with a heavy frown. "Now, she can hear a song from Jormbrinder, just like Angst can from his foci."

"Huh. I always thought Angst was just going crazy," Hector said. "But that sounds like good news. I'd feel a lot better if she took the dagger away from Alloria."

"It's not that simple. This has been traumatic for Rose, and we've spent a lot of time discussing it," Dallow said. "I think the time at this mage city has been good for her, but the last thing she wants to do is touch another foci."

"Have you asked her?" Hector asked.

"Well...no," Dallow said.

"Would you?" Hector asked.

"Yeah," Dallow said reluctantly.

"We should do this now and get out of here," Hector said. "I'll grab Alloria and wait for both of you."

"Gee, can you manage?" Dallow asked.

"I'll try to be gentle," Hector said with a sheepish grin his friend couldn't see.

"Your job sounds easier than mine," Dallow said.

"And more fun," Hector said slyly.

* * * *

Eastern border of Unsel

A spot under Andec's arm itched. It was impossible to reach wearing zyn'ight armor, and unflattering to scratch even if he could. The dramatic rush here on swifen had not only made him sweat, it had kicked up dust that found its way under his layers of armor and aketon. The dust must've burrowed into the pores of his old, dry skin, making him itch. Or maybe it was something else. Anticipation? Anxiety? It felt wrong being here. Wielders shouldn't be fighting a war for people who hated them. Now, with a city of their own, they should've been learning and teaching. They should've been spending more time understanding exactly what they could do with "the magics." With the crown involved, there just wasn't enough time for anything. Now, he was always in a hurry to do something for someone else. That was the culmination of his brief experience as a wielder for the throne: an itch he couldn't quite scratch.

Andec sensed he'd been chosen to lead the other eleven zyn'ight because he was old. He had twenty years on Angst, and would gladly let that be known, once all this nonsense was done. Unlike the others, his magic, the ability to create portals, was both defensive and offensive. According to Wilfred and Mirot, this gave Andec an advantage. That, and people listened to him because he complained loudly. Most people, except for the young ones. Bastards.

With a noisy whistle, he urged his goat swifen to a halt in

front of a young page standing alone in the middle of the road. The teenager looked like a target in his burgundy tunic and pale leggings, staring at them like a deer in candlelight. His eyes opened wide, not in fear but disbelief. Andec dismounted his goat, petting the rough tree-bark hide before dismissing the beast. He wanted to admonish the kid, but shook his head disparagingly as he looked at the other zyn'ight.

Trailing close behind was a zoo of animals and their armored keepers. They rode everything from glass gazelles to birds made of tall grass. The zyn'ight armor appeared sturdier than the heroes wearing it. They were a mishmash of men and women of various sizes and ages who could talk to animals, throw dark bolts of power, or any sort of chaotic, unspeakable things. It was a lot of power in an unflattering package and must've been a fright to look on, so he decided not to admonish the page, for now.

"Where's your captain?" Andec said, his chest heaving from the long ride. "Mirot and Wilfred sent us, and we need to talk before splitting up."

"We've been waiting. We weren't sure what to expect and—" the page cut himself off. "Please, this way. Hurry." He took off at a sprint.

"I don't run," Andec called out.

"Do you need an arm, old man?" Nikkola teased as she dismounted her swifen.

"You're welcome to carry me," he said, before turning to an emaciated young man. "Sean, where's your armor?"

"He won't wear it," Simon replied. "I keep trying, but he just shakes his head."

"Being gutted is a bad way to die, son," he said with a sincere frown.

"Don't worry, Sean," Simon said. "I'll heal you."

"Stop being a grouch," Nikkola said under her breath. "They're all scared enough."

"Right," he replied, not feeling leaderlike. "Come on."

They walked up a tall embankment, his knee questioning

loudly why he wasn't still on a swifen. He was too old for this, but too stubborn to believe it. A flop sweat made him itch again, and he was short of breath, but he still refused to take Nikkola's arm. The view at the top stole his remaining breath. A great field stretched out before them—it would've been pretty if not for the two armies lined up on opposite sides. At this edge of the field, armored Unsel soldiers stood side by side, with weapons and shields and bows and banners at the ready. Far across the way was a noisy, threatening horde of gray figures. In the middle of them stood an enormous beast that beat the ground like an ape. Andec was ready to go home.

A tall man with perfect blond hair and perfect white teeth approached with the overconfidence of an ambitious thirty-something leader. His gleaming breastplate appeared untouched, practically glowing in the sunlight. His sharp blue eyes looked down on them from high over his cheekbones.

"What is this?" he asked.

"These are the zyn'ight Wilfred promised, Captain Kyle," the page said with a short bow.

"The zy..." the Captain said dubiously. "I was expecting knights, not old men, women, and children."

"Who said we were knights?" Andec snapped, holding out an arm to keep Nikkola back.

A dangerous dark power bubbled around her hands, making Captain Kyle and his stalwart page take a step back.

"You're right. We aren't knights, we aren't fighters," Andec said. "We're patriots, and we came to protect Unsel."

"Right," Kyle said, staring at Nikkola's hands.

"How many are there?" Amay asked, staring off at the other side of the field. "It looks like a lot!"

"We have a brigade of 1,500, and as best as we can tell, they have at least as many," Captain Kyle said confidently, sticking his chest out. "It's an even enough match. We probably won't even need you."

"An even match?" Andec scoffed. "Do you know what they're capable of? Have you heard how fast their wounds heal?"

"Anyone can die," Kyle retorted.

"Have you met Angst?" Nikkola asked.

"I...no, I haven't." He coughed uncomfortably. "I've heard the stories."

A bird landed on Sean's shoulder and began to sing. He leaned over and whispered something to Simon.

"What is that thing in the middle?" Simon asked.

"We, uh, we aren't sure," Kyle said, his shoulders drooping as if his pride were slowly trickling out of a tiny leak.

"Ugh," Andec grunted in disgust. He stepped away from the others. "Be right back."

Gasps and the rattling of swords filled his ears as he created a portal appeared beneath his feet. Andec fell, his stomach lurching into his throat for the briefest of seconds before he landed hard on the other side of the battlefield. A hundred yards from the monster wasn't far enough. Andec couldn't begin to fathom how a creature like that could even exist. It was the size of a large building, with six muscular arms, a long, hairy torso, and mottled skin. Its charcoal black face looked squeezed until its lower jaw stuck out and teeth thrust upward in all directions. The ground shook every time a great fist struck the earth. The shaking stopped as two intelligent eyes fell upon him.

"Guldrich, a wielder who can create portals," a purple woman said from beside the beast.

"Lurp," Guldrich commanded. "Kill him!"

Lurp launched high into the air, giving Andec only panicked moments to create a small portal and fall through. He landed beside the other wielders and collapsed, his heart racing wildly and his head pounding. Shakily, he pushed himself up to one knee. Nikkola knelt beside him, and Simon placed a hand on his forehead.

"He's fine," Simon said.

"I'm not fine!" Andec muttered, pushing away the young man's hand.

"What is it?" she asked. "What did you see?"

"That isn't just some Vex'kvette monster," Andec said through rushed breaths. "A Fulk'han named Guldrich called it Lurp. It looked...it looked intelligent."

"What are you saying?" Kyle asked.

"I'm saying they don't need an army," Andec said. "Their beast is enough to destroy all of us."

37

Rohjek

The ground shook and plumes of ash billowed behind the quickly approaching figure. Still safely on the grassy border, Aerella stepped in front of Kala and held out her hands. A yellow hue surrounded them as she summoned an air shield. It was an invisible dome large enough to surround all five of them. Scar barked anxiously, but remained in puppy form.

"Do you think you can you cast this spell, Kala?" she asked.

"Yes, ma'am," Kala said confidently.

"Remember it," Aerella said. "This one will save you."

"What's coming?" Jintorich squeaked, raising his tiny staff. "It's moving too slowly to be a swifen."

Faeoris leaned forward, squinting in concentration. "Maarja," she said. "And she's alone." Wings of light appeared from her back, and she launched, smashing against the shield, and crashing back to the ground. "Let me out, wielder!"

"Sorry," Aerella said, releasing the shield, her heart racing.

"Faeoris!" Maarja called out.

Aerella had seen Faeoris fly fast, but now she practically blurred like Angst. Picking up Maarja like a bird with prey, she rushed back as if the Nordruaut weighed nothing. She threw Maarja to the ground as they landed. Maarja crashed onto her side with a grunt, gritting her teeth.

"Where is he?" Faeoris shouted, drawing her longsword.

Maarja's eyes were dark and her fists balled up to fight, but she remained on the ground. Her large hand shook violently as she reached for her ribs. Was she scared, injured, or both?

"Tell me now, Nordruaut!" Faeoris cried. "Where is he? I swear I will tear off your arms if you let him die."

"Faeoris, stop," Jintorich said. "We don't have time to fight each other. My friend, what happened? Where is Angst?"

"We found..." Maarja was interrupted by a cough that made her wince. "We weren't sure what it was at first. There was a wall of giant red crystals that appeared to circle something."

"A dragon's nest," Aerella said with a gasp.

"We heard moans," she glanced at Kala with a worried frown, "and eating. Angst wouldn't leave them behind and asked me to throw him in..."

"Of course he did," Aerella said, raising a hand to Maarja's side.

"I'm fine," Maarja said, pushing her hand away. "Save your strength."

"At least there was no sign of the mother," Jintorich squeaked.

"There was. That's when he told me to run," Maarja said, her eyes were wild. "We need to hurry."

"Point the direction," Faeoris said baring her teeth, her temper barely restrained.

"We go together," Aerella said, summoning her tiger swifen, white flowers blooming as it appeared. "You can't find it without Maarja, and this will take all of us."

"I can't believe you left him!" Faeoris looked angry enough to split Rohjek in half.

"He told me to!" Maarja snapped.

"Since when did you listen to him?" she asked. "I don't."

"Faeoris," Aerella reasoned, wondering if the Berfemmian could focus enough to listen. "There is little she could have done. She can't protect herself from dragonfire, and neither can you."

"What do we do with the girl?" Jintorich asked politely from his six-legged bear-mount-thing.

"We can't leave her," Aerella said. "She'll ride with me."

"I'll be safer with Scar," Kala said.

"How?" Maarja asked, coughing as she stood. "Oh."

Kala leaped onto Scar's shoulders as he grew from tiny lab pup to giant six-eyed monster. She somehow found a nook behind his head free of the spiky knives that had replaced his fur.

"Ride with me," Jintorich said to Maarja, his ears now flat against his head. "We will lead the way."

Maarja winced as she mounted the creature, letting out a brief gasp of air, but otherwise said nothing.

"Go!" Faeoris commanded.

Jintorich sped forward, and Aerella followed, keeping a close eye on adventure girl and her giant pup. Kala was every bit as reckless as Angst. Maybe he was actually twelve too. Dusty ash filled her nostrils and made her eyes water, and she struggled to remember a spell that could clear the way.

A flash of light and an explosion made Jintorich rear his mount. They all stopped, staring on in horror. Bolts of lightning cascaded across low-hanging clouds before crashing to the ground as if beating it into submission. There was a furious roar followed by another, and she couldn't tell if it was the dragon or Angst. A flash of light that made them all cover their eyes was trailed by the sounds of another explosion, blowing her hair back like the wind.

"What is going on?" Maarja asked in awe.

"No time," Faeoris said, her voice shaky and eyes wide. "Hurry!"

They rode forward, but at a gallop instead of full swifen speed. Despite all Aerella's travels throughout the millennia, she couldn't imagine anything more horrific than what lay before her. It was, indeed, a dragon nest. Blood-red shards of crystal rose from the ground, randomly jutting out like stakes shoved in sand. The group approached from behind. The sounds of battle were gone, and smoke billowed from the center of the nest like a signal fire. They rode around it cautiously. The red shards appeared cloudy at first, and then cracked and singed. As they neared the other side, the remaining crystals were melted away or entirely gone.

The air was thick with soot, making it hard to see. She finally remembered the spell and summoned her will, clearing the air around them. Her heart skipped beats, and she forced herself to breathe. How was this even possible? This half of the nest was entirely gone, blown away from the inside. Bodies were everywhere, some human, most dragon. Almost all the wyrms were horse-sized. Babies. And in the distance, the silhouette of a frighteningly large, decapitated dragon. Black smoke rose from its shuddering figure as it collapsed in on itself, melting away in its own dragonfire.

"Angst?" Faeoris asked in wonder and worry.

He shouldn't have been menacing. He was short, and stubby, and old. Edges of his red cloak had burned away. One arm hung limp at his side, the armor torn away and blood flowing from deep wounds. Frightening gashes had split his leg armor like ripped paper. Angst's face was a mess, his wide eyes and bared teeth practically glowing white beneath a thick layer of dirt and blood. With his good arm, he held Chryslaenor high. Lightning surrounded the enormous blade, flowing down his arm in streams that danced on the ground all around him. Angst took a step forward, and the hundred men he faced took a step back. There was a loud thud, and the ground shuddered as the dragon's head landed nearby. The men took another step back.

Faeoris landed beside him, the earth shaking on impact. She placed a concerned hand on his shoulder, but he said nothing. Aerella dismounted her swifen and approached with the others. Without a word, she grabbed his arm and began healing what she could of the mess. Angst didn't wince, or say anything to her, so focused was he on the men before him. He grimaced, taking another step forward. Aerella followed, grunting in concentration as she tried to continue her healing, but there was so much damage. She glanced up to see the small army of men he faced shuffle anxiously. He pulled his hand free from her grasp.

"I think I could do more," she said.

"It's enough," he said, wiggling his fingers. "Save your strength."

She didn't agree, but this wasn't the time to argue. Angst had to be exhausted after that fight; his chest was heaving, and his gray hair matted with sweat, but he showed no sign of weakness. It was hard to tell through the haze how many bare-chested warriors stood before them, but they looked dangerous. Not only that—they were perfect, every one of them tall and muscular, all holding long two-bladed staves.

"The tribes," Faeoris said in surprise, her voice quavering. "What are they doing this far east?"

The mass of Vex'steppe tribesmen parted, making room for a dark man who led a dragon larger than Scar. The man's head wasn't right, half of it caved in over his right eye. It was hard to believe he was even alive. His left eye glared at Angst, fierce and full of danger. Scar growled deeply, and many of the tribesmen took another step back. Angst raised his healed hand to keep the enormous dog at bay.

"ANduaut!" Faeoris said, shocked.

"Yes," ANduaut said with a malicious smile.

"You're dead." Faeoris shook her head.

"I died a long time ago." He held up a hand bearing a ruby ring.

"ANduaut," Angst said. "What have you done?"

"Welcome to my new world, champion," the tribesman said, turning around with a flourish as if presenting all of Rohjek.

"You destroyed a nation. You're feeding people to dragons. You're helping the bad guys win!" Angst said, trying to make sense of it. "This is madness!"

"Fire is going to win this time, Angst. You've seen how strong he is," ANduaut said. "When the world is reborn in fire, I will rule it, and the tribes will win the prize!"

The Vex'steppe tribesmen cheered as if ANduaut's claim was

significant. What prize was he talking about? Something nagged at the back of Aerella's memories, and it was important. If she only had more time.

"A prize?" Angst shouted back. "Have you lost your mind?"

ANduaut roared like a crazy man, shouting and stomping around.

"A little sensitive about that, isn't he?" Angst whispered to his friends before calling out again. "You realize I'm going to have to kill you. You can't just destroy a nation and get away with it. Crazy or not."

"I get to kill ANduaut," Faeoris growled.

"Fine," Angst said, the lightning around Chryslaenor growing to a frenzy. "I get the rest."

"And you think you can do battle with us?" ANduaut taunted. "With your giant, and your midget, and your child. Maybe I will keep the child when you are all dead."

"Can I kill him, Mr. Angst?" Kala asked.

Angst smirked but didn't reply. He seemed unmoved by ANduaut's taunt, as if this were a game. It was far from a game, and yet, they remained still as if each waiting for the next move. Aerella didn't understand. They were completely outnumbered. What could Angst possibly gain by threatening them? Was this bravado? Did he have a plan?

"What are you doing?" she whispered, shaking her head in frustration. There had to be a way out of this.

"They're already afraid," Angst said quietly. "The more they fear, the worse they'll fight. Hector taught me that."

"That's it?" Aerella said in disbelief. "You're posturing."

"Trust me," he said with a wink. "I've got this."

"Oh, that's not good at all," Jintorich said.

"Before we get started," Angst shouted, his voice mocking, "I have one question."

"Oh?" ANduaut asked.

"What happened to your head?" Angst asked, circling the corner of his forehead with a finger. "Is that why you've gone crazy? Because your brains are mush?"

CHAPTER THIRTY SEVEN

In a fury, ANduaut cried for his troops to attack, but didn't move. None of them moved. They all looked at their feet. The dragon looked around as if waiting for something to happen. It didn't. Angst had anchored their bones to the ground, and Aerella shuddered in awe of the raw power that must've taken. The strain showed in his pale face, and he was gasping for breath as if being chased, but that didn't seem to dent his confidence.

"See?" he said with a self-satisfied smile.

"Angst?" Faeoris pointed into the sky. "Dragons!"

* * * *

"Bring it!" Angst said through gritted teeth.

"Are you the one who's crazy?" Aerella asked.

"Like a silver fox," Angst said, pointing forward. "Gamlin! Get some!"

Horting noises came from everywhere even before the dragons could land. Dozens of gamlin, large and small, leaped up as if flung from the ground. They dove into the dragons like fingers shoved into a plum. Liquid fire poured out of the dragons as they crashed to the ground.

"Faeoris," Angst called out. "Kill ANduaut!"

"Yes!" she cried, flying forward.

"Aww," Kala said.

"Sorry, kid," Angst said. "She called dibs before you."

Commanding the gamlin to attack was enough of a distraction that he'd released the tribesmen. They raced towards them, screaming an annoying battle-whine that made him wince.

"Maarja, to the right," he commanded, pointing at the charge with his long blade. "Scar, to the left. Kala, keep him safe!"

"Affirmative!" she said as the large dog launched into the air.

"Me?" Aerella said, sucking in her lip.

"You didn't come with to fight," Angst said. "Keep your eyes open, let me know if someone is in trouble...well, more trouble than they can handle."

"I can wield magic you can't even fathom!" she snapped defensively.

"As a teenager?" he asked. She was too young right now, maybe only five years older than Kala, who was protected by Scar. Aerella held way too much knowledge to be injured in a battle he knew they would win. He placed a hand on her shoulder and looked into her eyes. "Our survival may hinge on what you know. Let's save your power and use it as a last resort. That's an order."

Her grimace became a pout as she crossed her arms and stared at the ground. He sighed. This was not the time to think Aerella was cute, and he was glad she wasn't reading his mind like Victoria.

"Not to mention," Angst let go and pointed to the battlefield. "Look around, they're already doing great."

Faeoris's broad grin was visible, even from this distance. ANduaut's attacks were quick, but it was obvious she was toying with him. Every time he lunged, she slapped him across the mouth, her sword held high and away. He swung wildly, and she leaped into the air, hovered, and landed again, giving ANduaut a shove. Angst smiled until ANduaut made a quick cut across her ribcage with his double-bladed staff. Angst fought the instinct to blur to them and hero the crap out of him, but she deserved the kill. If things got too rough, Maarja was nearby.

A dozen tribesmen surrounded the Nordruaut in a wide ring, wary to approach. Angst tapped Aerella's shoulder and pointed at them.

"Wow," Aerella said. "I knew she was strong..."

Tucked neatly under Maarja's giant arm was the diamond shaped head of a young dragon. It reminded Angst of a dog that had gotten its head stuck in a fence, except the dragon was continuously being punched in the face. While these dragons weren't the largest Angst had ever seen, by far, it could have eaten him in a mere bite or three. Every time Maarja's punching bag drew in breath, she would point its mouth at the nearest tribesman. Right before the dragon spewed flame, Jintorich would leap up from behind the target and strike him with his staff. In spite of his size, it was just enough momentum to move the man into the line of fire. Jintorich would bounce away to safety, leaving another toasted body to squirm and smolder with the rest.

"Yaaaah," squealed Kala from the other side of the battle, her little war cry followed closely by a bone-rattling bark.

Scar picked up men like chew toys, shaking them ruthlessly before tossing them into the air. Most remained still when they finally landed; the unfortunate ones who tried moving were crushed by the giant dog's enormous paw. Several were peed on—territorially, of course. The tribesmen were deft enough to avoid Scar's three wagging tails covered in steel blades. Occasionally, one would try attacking from the sides, only to be knocked away. Small bolts of darkness shot out from Kala's hands, something she must've picked up from her mother. The blasts were just strong enough to strike approaching tribesmen down. New chew toys for his dog.

"This can't be healthy for a young girl to see," Aerella admonished, still flustered. "You should be out there instead of her. What are you doing?"

"Catching my breath." Had he been that belligerent as a teen? He mopped sweat from his forehead, his chest still heaving from his own battle with dragons, which had been as rough as any he remembered. There were no friends, no time to summon an army of gamlin, just him and his beatstick. It had been close.

"Don't you dare get old on me now," she snapped.

"Not today," he said, pointing his sword at a dozen tribesmen who'd decided to rush them. It didn't matter. He could do this. One more breath, that was all he needed. After two, he blurred forward. This wouldn't take a minute, and then he could get back to the breathing thing...

"Angst, watch out!" Aerella cried.

Crushing, wet jaws lifted him off the ground. Hot breath like falling on a campfire cooked the side of his body. He couldn't breathe. His chest felt like he was wedged between two cliff walls, but these walls had very large teeth. The dragon landed, spitting him out like he was bad food. He stood slower than he normally would've. Everything hurt. His joints creaked, his muscles strained, and his chest felt dented inward. He was shaking from exhaustion. Maybe a third breath would've been wise. The dragon took a step back, and then another, giving him just enough time to gather power from Chryslaenor.

The sword didn't sing, it screamed and cursed a song that made Angst turn his head. His eyes went wide, and his heart suddenly bounced around the inside of his chest as panic took over. A ball of flame from nowhere, far too large to be dragon-fire, was heading straight toward him. He froze. There was no time. His mind raced, but it was too much and too fast. He thought of Heather, and he thought of his kids, and he wished he could've held them again.

The tiniest of shadows leaped before him, squeaking a cry that pierced his ears. The enormous ball of flame engulfed Jintorich. There was a high-pitched scream and a blinding flash of bright white. When Angst could see again, he found Jintorich at his feet, lying still. The fireball was gone. The Meldusian's small body was smoldering, but miraculously seemed untouched. His tiny, white robes hadn't even been burned, and he clutched the little staff like a beggar would bread. Angst's senses hesitantly returned as if peeking out from under covers one at a time. His heart slowed to a race. He could see the battle around him. He could once again hear sounds other than the foci song. He breathed.

"I don't know how you did it, but thank you," Angst said, kneeling beside Jintorich. With two fingers on the Meldusian's shoulder, he gently shook the tiny man. "Wake up, buddy, we're not done yet." Jintorich didn't move. Angst placed a hand on his chest. "Jintorich?"

"Wake up, my friend," Maarja said, suddenly beside them. Her white furs were scarred with black singe marks, and she held her side. Maarja brushed Angst's hand aside and pressed a finger to Jintorich's unmoving chest. A moment passed, and then another. Her eyes squeezed shut.

CHAPTER THIRTY SEVEN

"Jintorich, no," Angst said, his throat tightening. Angst gripped the man's tiny wrist but felt no life. "I'm so sorry," Angst said, shutting the Meldusian's eyes.

Maarja roared.

38

Eastern border of Unsel

"Going over there may've been a mistake!" Simon shook Andec's shoulder. "Sean says they're coming!"

He already knew. In spite of collapsing to the ground in panic and exhaustion, Andec heard the distant battle cries and felt the ground vibrate. Nikkola and Simon helped him to stand so he had a much better view of their onrushing slaughter. The horde of Fulk'han gray men and brightly colored women charged across the wide battlefield in a V formation, like a flock of geese. Lurp lumbered forward slowly, staying far behind at the center of the V.

"I thought you were here to help," Captain Kyle said sharply as he mounted a great white stallion. He rode off shouting, "To arms, soldiers of Unsel! Archers at the ready! Pikemen, brace for impact!"

"What do we do?" a young, dark-haired wielder in homespun asked.

"We wait, Jace," Andec said, struggling to keep his voice steady.

They only had minutes, and he couldn't imagine surviving this. There were so many Fulk'han, a sea of gray rushing toward them, roaring in challenge. He licked salty anticipation from his lips and hoped his face was braver than his heart.

"We should fight!" a heavyset woman shouted, a deep purple hue glowing around both hands.

"Hold, Misty." He pointed out to the battlefield. "We don't even know where to go yet."

As the Fulk'han closed in, the two ends of the V shape came together to form a double-file line. They shouldn't have been able to move this fast on foot; it was as if someone had shot an arrow of Fulk'han at the Unsel army. Guldrich stood atop his building with legs as they raced alongside the new formation, all the while shouting orders and directing them.

"Now! Go to the middle of our soldiers, we face this head on," Andec shouted. "Keep track of your partner, protect the soldiers, and try not to get blood on your armor."

They all looked at him in surprise. This was why he rarely joked—nobody appreciated his humor. He summoned his swifen, and raced to the center.

Unsel soldiers had been standing in rows along the field, making them too spread out to face the attack that would puncture the heart of their formation. Both ends of the Unsel's long line rushed toward the middle, but they would never make it in time. The sparkly captain and his knights would be long gone before backup arrived. The charging arrow of Fulk'han would slice through them like an apple. Even if Unsel soldiers managed to kill one or two, or a dozen, the thin line would only last moments.

"Fire!" Kyle called out.

A thick volley of arrows screamed through the air, each made solid *thwipping* sounds as they struck their targets. Not a single Fulk'han fell.

"Fire!" Kyle called out again, his voice strained.

More arrows flew like migrating birds, most connecting with their target to no avail. The two Fulk'han lines split into four as the arrow widened. Andec didn't understand what they were doing, and from the look on Captain Kyle's face, neither did he.

A dark, vertical circle appeared with a loud pop a mere hundred yards away from them. It grew, spinning faster and faster like a hungry cyclone forming on a mirror. The Fulk'han army raced toward it as if it were merely a cloud.

"Stay away from that!" Andec called as loudly as he could. "It's a portal!"

"One of yours?" Nikkola asked.

"Are you kidding?" he asked. "I don't have that sort of power. Nobody does!"

"Fall back!" Captain Kyle shouted. Soldiers down the line echoed his command.

The Fulk'han army rushed straight into it. The circle grew, gaping open like a mouth that devoured hundreds and hundreds of them in one large bite. Two hundred yards away, Guldrich and a purple woman stood on top of their champion. Her arms were held out as if ready for a big hug, and dark clouds hovered around her hands.

"Zyn'ight! Kill the beast!" Andec commanded.

Without hesitation, the wielders attacked. Black bolts flew from Nikkola's hands. A beam of incandescent light shot from Jackson's mouth. A large rock rushed toward their target, closely followed by a dozen more. All their spells were sucked into the portal like debris in a whirlpool. It was as if their magic was for show.

"Everyone to me," Andec said. "I'm porting us out there!"

The zyn'ight, Captain Kyle, and a dozen soldiers moved in close as he cast his own portal. His stomach dropped with his feet. It was like missing a step. His heart skipped painfully, and they landed behind Guldrich and Lurp.

Guldrich whipped about. "Go, now!"

The creature leaped into the Fulk'han portal. It closed behind them, slicing several Fulk'han in half. Their screams were cut short as the dark whirlpool disappeared.

* * * *

Enurthen

Dallow had never really been given the chance to finish the

transition to blindness, thanks to the constant state of emergency they lived in. But, maybe it was his reluctance to believe there wasn't the hope of regrowing eyes burned away by dragonfire. Angst had died and come back many times; what was growing a couple of new eyes compared to that? His unwillingness to give in also meant that he avoided his own potential. He'd read that the blind experienced things in such a different way. When sight was lost, other senses took over. Taste, smell, touch, and sound all tried to fill in the blanks left behind by the void of color and image. On a rare occasion, Dallow would be teased by these extra senses, experience something more, like a hint of things to come. Right now, he was overwhelmed by the tangy scent of copper.

"Rose?" he asked.

No answer, but it wouldn't be the first time she'd teased him with silence, sneaking up on him with a kiss or a caress on his face. It was always intoxicating, and his heart skipped at the thought of her finding him in his darkness. She wouldn't do more until his marriage was over, and it would be over when all this was done, but he didn't need more right now. His senses were always on high when Rose was near, and the experience couldn't have been more intimate.

Dallow wished the memndus stone pressed against his temple worked inside. He would've loved to see her lurking about, and thought fondly of that curvy figure covered in smooth, pale skin. Her large, dark eyes were probably inches away, looking at him, and all he could do was trust.

Nothing. He listened close, forcing his hearing to reach beyond the confines of his thoughts. Breathing, shallow breathing from the far side of the room. Maybe she was sleeping, and he could sneak up on her for once. The very thought of a blind man sneaking up on someone in their own room made him smile mischievously. Dallow inched forward carefully until his feet bumped into a heavy mass of something.

Rose had only been in this home for a week, but he'd been here twice and didn't recall any obstacles. His nostrils flared at the scent of copper once again, and the husky breathing came closer.

"Rose, this isn't funny," he said, kneeling down and patting the lump.

Cloth. Warmth. An arm. A body. Whose body? His hands grasped leather leggings, reached up a tiny torso, felt thin arms like sticks until finding a face. He'd touched that face countless times with its strong jaw and kissable lips. Rose. It had to be. Her chin was damp. He felt along her throat which was warm and wet, bubbling out hot blood. Her body began to jolt and shudder.

"No!" he cried, shaking her. "Rose, no!"

"I won't leave this city," Alloria said, her voice distant and damaged.

"Please no," Dallow said. "What did you do?"

"I was told I'd rule all Unsel if I killed her, and you," she said, her voice shaky. "The elements told me so."

"You...you killed Rose?" he asked in disbelief. His hands were covered in her warm blood; they were shaking uncontrollably. "All so you can rule?"

"No," she said. "I don't want to rule."

"Then why?" he asked. Rose's body convulsed violently. Dallow reached deep down inside, past layers of worry and panic, seeking a healing spell that would be enough.

"The elements can't come in here. They can't enter Enurthen," she said. "This is the only place I'm safe, and you can't make me leave!"

Dallow heard Alloria circling him as he found the spell. He couldn't imagine how much damage had been done to Rose, tried not to think about it as he placed his hands on her wet neck.

"You want to leave, all of you," she said, her eyes wild. "But why would anyone leave paradise? You think this half of a foci can release you? It won't. I won't let it!"

There was something in what Alloria had said. Something about the word Enurthen. He'd seen it so many times in so many texts, but dismissed it as gibberish. It had to be the key. It had to be the code that unlocked the older Acratic, the Ughcratic.

"I know what needs to be done," Dallow said. "I know how what I need to do so we can get free!"

His cry was silent as pain seared through his chest. Something inside felt cold, and his heart rushed to compensate. He let go of Rose and grasped the triangular blade that had been thrust through his midsection. His own blood covered the blade now wrapped in his hands, and that was fascinating. She jerked it back, and Dallow fell to his side. His breathing slowed, and his heart stopped its race.

"I won't let them kill me! The elements can't get me in this place," Alloria said. "So I will never leave!"

* * * *

Unsel

The first day Mika had taken his turn as guard for his cousin, Victoria, the guards watched his every move as if he were planning to steal her away. He'd spent that day absorbed by her. Even near death, she was so very lovely. Memories of her kindness filled his chest with pain and his eyes with tears. His princess appeared in dire pain, and how could she not be? Her tiny blood-soaked hands clutched the end of the triangular dagger Alloria had shoved through her chest. It filled him with hurt, and a deeply buried fury.

In their youth, Victoria had always been reserved until the day he'd brushed her cheek. She'd grabbed his hand and held it there, staring on at him and finally saying, "You will have a choice: to be a killer or a protector. If you try, in time, you can be a hero, Mika." These words had haunted him for years. He remembered them from his dreams, could hear them whispered in his mind. When he'd discovered she could wield, that she could see a person's future, he'd known what had to happen. She stared out from her prison, right at him, her eyes begging to be set free. He could hear her whisper. "It's time to be a hero."

Mika did not like people and wanted nothing more than to

stay away from them, all of them, except Victoria. His father had taught him how to interact, to feign courtesy even when he felt nothing. The guards assigned to the hall ate up his attentions. A funny, embarrassing story from royalty went a long way with soldiers. After several days of guard duty, they relaxed their watchful eyes, even going as far as wishing him luck. Who didn't want to help their future queen?

Today, he would not be distracted by her lovely eyes. Instead, he would listen to her whispers, begging him to save her, to free her. Today, he would listen to the other voice, that of the man who'd saved him from a fiery death. That tall man certainly had to be Time himself. And that man wanted her free.

Mika placed a shaky hand on the shield separating the princess's chamber from the hallway. There was a red spark, and the palm of his hand numbed. The giant sword glowed red inside the doorway. Not a guardian, but rather a jailer barring his access. He concentrated. This wasn't really a shield. It was time, a wall of time. Mika had a relationship with time that allowed him certain...privileges. It wasn't easy—time was very demanding and required gifts—but ever since his rebirth through flames, he could do more than he'd thought possible.

He focused his will on the soldiers. They stopped shifting in their armor, staring off into nothing, frozen like Tori. It would require concentration to keep them in place while breaking through this time wall, but she needed saving.

Mika pressed his remaining will against the barrier. It was unmoving. He tried reaching through it slowly. Nothing. He begged it to set her free. It didn't reply. Mika kicked at it until he heard a toe crack. He hopped up and down, wailing in pain. Fortunately, the soldiers remained still. It was so infuriating he felt like killing them, but she wouldn't approve of that. How could he save Victoria from this trap?

He dropped to his knees, beating against the shield with the base of his fists. He could only see red through his fury and collapsed, slapping the wall with the palm of his hand.

Tink.

CHAPTER THIRTY EIGHT

A flash of red.

Was it the sword? His hand hurt, and he shook the soreness from it. He struck the wall with his other palm, but nothing happened. He looked down and was struck with realization. The ring! The tall ageless man who'd kept him alive was helping him even now. What a friend that man was, to make him the hero who freed the princess.

Mika turned the ruby ring around so the stone fit in the palm of his hand. He reached back with all his might and smacked his hand against the time wall.

Tink.

A flash of red.

A drop of Victoria's blood fell to the floor.

39

Rohjek

Maarja's wail was deafening, and for a moment, Angst feared for his life. She shook with rage, her eyes glazed over as if sense and reason had been entirely washed away. She moaned between breaths, looking around in jerky motions. The pain she was unable to contain needed an outlet, fast.

The fireball had cleared a path. The tribesmen who hadn't been able to scatter fast enough were either gone or smoking remains. Those who'd lived were a Nordruaut's stone throw away. They huddled in a group, holding their wooden staffs with a knife attached to both ends, like that could possibly protect them from the end of all things.

Almost reluctantly, Angst jerked his head toward the mass of frightened men. It was enough. Maarja leaped into the air, so high Angst was surprised she hadn't sprouted wings of light. In a single bound, she reached the Vex'steppe tribesmen, landing so hard that several fell. Maarja didn't tear them in half or punch them into the ground like Angst had expected; she picked two men up and began swinging them like weapons.

Angst winced, swallowing hard at the grotesque sounds of skulls smacking together and bones crunching. Bodies flew away like arrows loosed from a bow. When her weapons were too limp and broken, she tossed them aside and grabbed two more. It was a berserker rage far beyond anything Angst had seen or experienced, and it made his heart ache for Maarja. She was too lost in her fury to even let the tribesmen run away, chasing them down, all the while screaming her pain. She killed everyone nearby until there was nothing left but a broken, bloody pile. Maarja dropped to her knees and sobbed. He didn't want to be next, but wouldn't be any sort of friend if he didn't go to her.

"Angst," Aerella said, placing a hand on his shoulder. "There's something you need to know about Jintorich."

"I know," he said sadly. "I know he's dead. And even worse, he's the last Meldusian."

"No," she began. "Something else."

"Tell me later," Angst said. "Right now, Maarja needs me, and... Oh no."

A whirlwind of flame grew behind the few remaining tribesmen, who scrambled off to nowhere. The flames quickly formed into the shape of a burning man the size of a mountain. Raw heat cooked Angst's face. Fear gripped his heart and tried punching it through his chest. The remnants of bravado and victory washed away completely in a torrent of hopelessness. Faeoris returned to his side, as did Scar and Kala. Maarja lumbered over, her arms covered in others' blood. She wept uncontrollably, dropping to her hands and knees beside Jintorich's body. Faeoris immediately went to console her. Kala remained on Scar's back, but sobbed at the realization that their friend was gone.

Fire didn't attack, but instead seemed to revel in their pain. The fear reached from Angst's heart, crept up his spine, and danced around his head. What could the element possibly be planning? Last time they'd fought, Angst had lost. Fire had thrown a sun at his friends. They'd only survived because Earth had sacrificed herself while he buried them alive for protection. He may have wielded two foci, more or less, but he wasn't Earth, and sacrificing himself would mean all would be lost. One friend was already dead. How could he possibly keep the rest of his companions safe from an element this powerful?

"I'm not ready for this," he said under his breath.

"Not ready? I thought you were one of us, Angst?" Fire said, his voice low and resonating with power.

"He wasn't supposed to hear that," Angst whispered.

"I did." Fire laughed, but the laughter wasn't contagious. "Aren't you the element Human?"

"Am I?" he replied, not really feeling it.

Angst looked at Jintorich, and wanted to weep, but there was something else. It was like tasting something bitter that shouldn't have been in your mouth. A taste that made Angst's jaw set. Jintorich hadn't deserved to die, Marissa hadn't deserved to die...none of them did. His swords agreed, clashing in his head with a rage of music that made no sense. It really didn't matter how tired he was, or how old, or even how frightened. He was pissed. Angst raised his hand and spread his fingers.

"Maybe I am! Let me count down how many of you I've gotten rid of. Earth, Air, Water...didn't she usually win? Magic, mostly. Hmm, who's left?" His middle finger was the only one left standing, and he raised it high in the air.

"Oh, Angst," Aerella said, sounding defeated.

"Yes!" Faeoris said.

Fire shouted curses, giving Angst enough time to hoist Chryslaenor and create an air shield. The barrage of fireballs that struck the shield was relentless. He winced at each blast, feeling the strain deep in his muscles. It didn't just take will to defend; it required physical strength and mental focus. It was as if Fire wasn't just blasting them with flame but with pure hate. His shield became stronger. Aerella's hand glowed yellow, and there was something else. Kala was grunting as she emulated their spell.

The element roared like a volcano. Plumes of black and gray smoke shot up from the being. Angst set his right foot back to brace himself and stretched out his arms. Blast after blast struck their shield, the sound deafening.

"I can't..." Kala said, falling from Scar and landing in Maarja's arms.

The shield weakened by a third. Angst couldn't believe how much the kid had helped reinforce it. It was almost as if she'd been channeling his foci again.

"Angst," Aerella said, her voice strained. "I don't have much more either."

"Weakening already, element human?" Fire mocked. His flames burned brighter, and the element leaned in with both arms stretched toward them. "You're not one of us!"

The barrage of fireballs became a steady blast of red flames, and Aerella collapsed. The element roared in anger, but Fire hadn't seen Angst's fury yet. He thought of their prior battle, when Fire had thrown a sun on his friends. He thought of the element war, and the victims of Rohjek, who were dead or food for Fire's dragons. Angst thought of his princess, slowly dying. And poor Jintorich lying on the ground. He wasn't ready to die. He deserved to know his daughter's name! He may not have been ready for this fight, but he had enough angry and bitter to fuel his shield and more.

The lightning began as a few sparks, crackling like tiny fireworks, and growing until it forked all around him. He held it in close until his arms shook, until his teeth rattled, until he glowed like a distant star. A stream of fire slammed against his air shield, and he released it. The lightning struck out as a single thread that wrapped around the pillar of fire, splitting and splitting again until it was a blue mesh of power forming around the flame like a barrel. Angst willed the lightning surrounding the torrent to close, squeezing until there was more lightning than fire and it shrank to a trickle. He then pushed with all his might. This wasn't a fight of fire versus lightning; this was a battle of will. He struck out with the lightning, and Fire was thrown from his feet.

"I can do this!" Angst said.

"Angst, we should run..." Aerella began.

He ignored her, attacking Fire with bolts of lightning. He pulled blast after blast down from the sky. Fire stood but backed away, holding his arms out defensively, his dark shadowy eyes wide with surprise.

"You've hurt my friends!" *Crash.* "You've destroyed a nation!" *Crash.* "You aren't welcome here anymore!" The wild anger in his mind fueled his power as he continued his onslaught. The element became smaller than a mountain, smaller than a graymowl tree, and smaller yet as the attack continued.

"No!" Fire shouted. "You can't do this! You aren't an element!"

"I am!" Angst growled. He squeezed his eyes shut, reaching deep into himself, and found something. It was power like nothing he'd ever wielded, so raw he couldn't fathom it. It was the trickle that becomes a river, the cloud that forms a devastating tornado, and it was inside him. This great power was frightening, and maddening, and exactly what he needed, no matter the cost. Opening his eyes, the moment before cutting loose, he saw it. A mere flash in the corner of his eye made him glance up. And there it was, high above: the sun. A sun. A star. Something enormous coming closer, getting larger, and racing toward them. Fear scared his newfound source of power away, and he choked out a tiny, "no."

"No Earth to protect you this time, little human!" Fire shouted. "More companions destroyed by your folly. You're no element. You're nothing. Die!"

"I..." he stuttered. He didn't know what to do. Should he dig a hole and cover them? Could he blast the falling star from the sky? They only had moments. "I can't!"

"Angst!" Aerella shouted, pulling him to face her. "Do you trust me?"

"Yes!" he said, without hesitation.

"Maarja," she cried. "A hundred miles from here. Think of a place."

"What?" Maarja said slowly.

"You were guiding us," Aerella said. "Focus on a safe place, far from here. Now!"

"Yes, I've got it," Maarja said.

"I need all your power, Angst," she said, reaching for his

hand. "All of it!"

Angst took her hand and fed her everything he could. Her eyes widened with shock, and blood trickled from her nose and ears. She aged, and within a breath appeared two hundred and then twenty again as the power of an Al'eyrn with two foci flowed through her body. Somehow, she gathered herself enough to reach out for Maarja. The Nordruaut didn't hesitate, taking the tiny hand in her own and squeezing her eyes shut. Aerella muttered some words, and a black vortex formed beneath them. Angst's stomach sank as they fell. Powering the spell was exhausting in a way he hadn't expected. A cold, numbing sensation coursed through him, followed by a flash of intense heat. Almost as if someone had grabbed him by the nape and shoved his head in freezing water, and then boiling water, again and again. Angst landed hard on his back, like an inverted belly flop.

"Never done it like that." Aerella grunted. "Do better next time."

He propped himself up on his elbows. Everything spun like a sweaty nightmare right before the worst hangover. In the far distance, there was a bright flash of light. The light of a star dying in the middle of Rohjek. It was a silent explosion, which made it all the more terrifying. The light faded, and everything went dark.

40

Eastern border of Unsel

"Whoa," Captain Kyle said, his face pale and sweat dripping down his cheeks. "I thought enlisting wielders was a terrible idea. I take it back. I take it all back!"

Andec simply nodded, staring at the empty battlefield in shock. Every thrum from his tired heart was a reminder that he was too old for this. His breathing steadied once he realized they hadn't been trampled by the angry horde of Fulk'han, or skewered in a sword fight he didn't belong near. Soon after, reason pried the fear from his brain, it began to start working again, and it had a question.

What was that thing? Sure, it was a portal, but nothing like the ones he could make. His were horizontal, lying on the ground like a dark lake of oil. People would fall through, for what felt like a foot, and end up where he wanted them to. Porting himself around town didn't take much effort. Moving a group of people several miles reminded him of his age; anything more would probably kill him. That could mean the Fulk'han army was nearby. A sudden, sharp slap on his back was a brisk cue that the shiny captain was still talking.

"...and you all deserve commendations for this bit of magics!" Captain Kyle pulled back his slapping arm. "I was ready for battle, of course, but you just saved a lot of lives."

"That wasn't me," Andec said, his low voice shaky.

"Oh," Kyle said, looking around coyly as though he'd maybe said too much. "Well, if it wasn't any of you, then what happened?"

"They made a giant portal and the entire Fulk'han army ran through," Andec explained.

"To where?" Nikkola asked, looking several shades paler than normal.

"Anywhere," Andec said, grabbing the captain's arm. "We need an immediate sweep of the area."

"You don't give the commands here." Kyle jerked his arm free.

"Captain," Andec said, attempting to rein in his growing panic. "They could've taken that portal and appeared right past us. Those creatures could be racing toward the castle ten miles down the road."

Kyle's eyes went wide.

"No wielder has the power to move an army like that very far," Andec explained. "Ten miles, best guess, in any direction."

"Okay," Kyle said with a crisp nod. His eyes became so cold, it was almost impossible to see the worry in them. The captain barked out orders, making everyone nearby scurry to follow commands.

"Andec," Simon said. "It's Sean. My brother says there's still something alive out there. The birds told him. We should hurry. They're getting ready to feed on the remains."

"Mount up," Andec said, summoning his swifen.

"What's this?" Captain Kyle asked, looking around irritably at the menagerie of animals that suddenly appeared.

"One of the Fulk'han was left behind," Andec said. "We're going to see if we can learn what this was about."

"When you're done, we're going to have a discussion about the chain of command," Kyle said sternly and immediately followed up with an answer to Andec's rolling eyes. "It's for your safety, and for theirs." He pointed around at all the soldiers, his finger finally landing on the wielders.

"Fine," Andec said gruffly. "We should go. There may not be much time."

Kyle whistled and waved over eight soldiers. Most of them approached with hand on hilt, wary of the magics at play and the dangerous looking swifen. When Nikkola tapped one on his shoulder, he turned around and she blew him a kiss, making him jump back.

"Commander Mirim, you and your soldiers stay close to Andec, and follow his orders. Remember, we're on the same team," Kyle said sternly before turning to the wielders. "Be patient with them. They aren't comfortable with magics. Neither am I. Listen to the Commander. She knows what she's doing. And remember, we're on the same team."

They waited for the soldiers to mount their war horses and then waited for them to keep up, unable to maintain the swifens' pace. At Andec's command, the soldiers and zyn'ight spread out to search the area.

Dark wisps of thick purple and orange smoke drifted from the remnants of the portal, looking like everything you wouldn't want to breathe. The front, and back, of several Fulk'han carcasses lay scattered about, like remnants of a battle, one that hadn't taken place. The top half of a blue woman crawled away from the center. She moaned softly, her body unwilling to let go of life. A pair of dismembered, bone-encased, gray-man legs, and several other appendages, squirmed helplessly like earthworms cut in half.

Jace scrambled off his swifen, dropped to all fours, and emptied his stomach. A soldier dismounted beside him and placed a hand on his shoulder.

"The bodies shouldn't be moving," another soldier said, swallowing hard.

"No, they shouldn't," Andec said, dismissing his swifen and taking a hesitant step forward. "This is wrong."

"Look there." Nikkola pointed.

A breath of wind lazily brushed thick smoke away, revealing a Fulk'han gray man. One remained. Out of the entire army, one

Fulk'han stood his ground. The gray man looked bewildered, like a puppy dropped out of a wagon and left behind. He was a third taller than the largest Unsel soldier, and covered in dark gray leathery protrusions like a turtle's shell. The Fulk'han's hands resembled a monkey's paws with three fingers and sharp claws, and his muscular arms reached his knees. Silvery eyes peered out from the shadow of a diamond-shaped bone helm that matched the bone armor around his chest. When he saw them, the beast didn't panic. He braced himself. His chest heaved as he crouched, ready to charge. Just as the Fulk'han *rawr*ed, Andec opened a portal beneath his feet.

After a tense, hushed moment, the commander asked, "Where did he go?"

Andec pointed up but said nothing.

"I don't understand," she said.

"Wait for it," Andec muttered.

There was a quiet wail that quickly grew louder. Mirim tried stepping forward, but Andec held out an arm.

"Wait for it," he said.

The desperate cry became louder yet until it ended abruptly with a disconcerting crunch. Nikkola jumped back with a squeak. The Fulk'han splattered, dark blood spraying from the impact of his landing like a waterfall on stone.

"What did you do?" Nikkola asked. "He could've told us what just happened!"

"She's right, we could've used..." The commander's breath caught and her eyes grew wide. "What's this?"

The Fulk'han pushed himself up to his hands and knees, blood dripping from his face and chest like a wrung towel. Awe overtook them like a barrier they were reluctant to push through. Breaths passed as the gray man shakily stood, his bones reforming and his skin knitting shut.

"I think I'm going to throw up again," Jace announced.

"Me too," said the soldier who'd assisted him.

The Fulk'han shook his head as though waking from a dream, crouched, and prepared to leap forward.

"Oooookay," Andec said, rubbing his hands together. "Calm down or it'll be worse."

He was answered with another *rawr* and sighed. The gray man yelped as another portal sucked him into the ground.

"This will take a little longer," Andec warned. "Stay back. I'm not completely sure how big the impact will be."

"Did he just come back to life?" Nikkola asked.

"I don't know. After seeing these moving remains, I assumed he'd live through the fall. I didn't expect him to heal so quickly," Andec said in disbelief. "I never intended to kill him."

"You almost killed me," Nikkola declared. "I almost had a heart attack!"

"You meant to incapacitate him," the commander said, her tone filled with admiration.

"How are you able to drop him in the same spot?" Amay asked. The young woman watched the skies nervously.

"Practice," Andec said, unable to hold back a smile.

"Incoming!" Jace said, holding his arms over his head.

The gray man flattened on impact, striking the ground hard enough to create a small crater. Those nearest were sprayed with dirt, bone, and blood. The remains of the Fulk'han's body were almost unrecognizable, but everyone inched forward cautiously. When they arrived, mere feet away, Nikkola gasped.

"I don't believe this," Andec said, closing his eyes.

The mass of bone and skin moved. White sinews crept out, grasping for parts that littered the ground and reabsorbing them into the whole. The reforming body looked like a wet, sloppy puzzle that already had arms and legs. It shuddered as bones clicked, setting back into place.

"We don't have much time," Nikkola warned.

"Allow us," Commander Mirim said, nodding to her soldiers.

The commander and three of her guard unsheathed their long-swords, each finding a place around the sprawled body. She kicked the gray man over onto his back, his healing arms sprawled. With a nod, they simultaneously stabbed their weapons into an appendage, pinning the Fulk'han to the ground. The

Fulk'han screamed, his head rocking back and forth as the soldiers threw their weight down on top of the weapons, jamming them into the earth as deeply as they could.

"I'm glad we're on the same side," Andec said dryly.

"Me too," Mirim said with a wicked grin.

"Hey, ugly," Andec said, kneeling beside the body. He twirled a finger in the air. "What was all this about?"

"I'll tell you nothing," the Fulk'han muttered around his quickly reforming jaw.

"You moan like a baby when your body splatters across the field," Andec said. "I'm guessing that even though you heal, it still hurts."

"I won't talk!" he screamed, bloody spittle spraying from his mouth.

"Commander," Andec said calmly as he stood. "Would your soldiers mind terribly running back to camp and getting lunch? I'm going to drop him from that cloud about a dozen more times. It's going to take a while."

"Wait," the gray man said, looking about frantically.

"Bread and cheese?" the commander asked.

"Dried meat sounds good. I don't mind field rations. Would you happen to have a chair?" He plopped to the ground and crossed his legs. "This cold ground isn't good for my old bones, and that's a very long way to fall."

"Sorry, no chairs," the commander said. "We do have blankets."

"That'll do," Andec said with a grin.

"Maybe towels too," Nikkola requested, wiping Fulk'han off her armor. "He makes a big mess."

"Angst!" their prisoner cried out. "We brought our champion to capture Angst!"

"So, all of you, that entire army, came to nab Angst?" Andec asked.

"They really hate him, don't they?" Jace asked. "How many people did he piss off?"

"Our champion will break Angst for killing Takarn-Ivan!" the gray man spat.

"I think he's telling the truth," Commander Mirim said.

"But not all of the truth," Andec said.

"Do they realize that Angst isn't in Unsel?" Jace asked.

Everyone looked at him with admonishing eyes.

"Uh, you know," Jace said, his cheeks reddening. "Because that was supposed to be a secret."

The gray man's eyes were wild, and he began to struggle against the restraining swords.

"I don't think it was a secret, Jace. I think the Fulk'han already knew," Commander Mirim said. She stared at the Fulk'han quizzically. "But how would you know where Angst went?"

"More importantly," Andec said. "Why capture him, unless Angst has something they want?"

There was a crunch of bone as one of the gray man's arms pulled through a sword.

"Drop him!" the commander said.

Andec squinted as he focused on the size of the portal. It slowly grew beneath the man's rear to encompass his calves and torso, and then stopped. The gray man cried out in fear, the three swords pinning his legs and arm the only thing keeping him from falling through.

"The prize!" he cried out. "Angst knows where to find Prendere. The most powerful weapon on Ehrde. Fulk'han will win it and control everything."

Andec released the portal, and the gray man yelped before blacking out.

"Oops," Andec said apologetically, standing up and moving back.

"Oops?" Mirim asked as everyone followed.

A glob of gray man landed with a squishing sound on top of their captive. The spine writhed like a snake, even while the gray man's body convulsed.

"His, uh, back end must've still been in the portal when I let it close," Andec said with a wince.

CHAPTER FORTY

"Gross," Nikkola said, turning away and covering her mouth.

"Gather the other body parts. We burn them all," Mirim said to the soldiers. "And look for more survivors in the area. We need to understand what the monster was talking about. What in Ehrde is Prendere?"

41

Rohjek

Angst woke to the sounds of deep sobs. He'd heard Tarness cry like that, in his low, booming voice. This wasn't Tarness; it had to be Maarja. But why sobs? His mind tried to slowly creep from its slumber, but his body rebelled. It was like one giant cramp that encompassed every muscle, even his brain. Angst winced through the pathetic struggle to push himself up, his muscles begging him to stop, and his tendons wrenching as if never used.

An enormous dragon had bitten down hard on his arm, almost tearing it off. His limb sort of worked, after Aerella's quick patch job, but didn't feel right, or whole. His entire chest throbbed in pain from another dragon that had carried him off like a puppy's bone. At least that meant he was alive.

He'd apparently gotten away with a brief nap after they'd ported to this place. But it wasn't nearly enough to cleanse the bone-deep exhaustion that threatened to shut his eyes, if only for another minute. His eyes opened wide at Maarja's cries, even if his brain was still half asleep. But, why was she sobbing? And then he remembered. Jintorich.

His friends sat around the maw of a large hole in the ground. Kala held Scar, and both nestled comfortably into a middle-aged Aerella's lap. Faeoris held herself, perhaps for warmth or cour-

314

age as she looked at Maarja. The Nordruaut woman rocked back and forth, clutching the small bundle of Jintorich in her arms. Angst stood shakily and wobbled over to Faeoris, placing a hand on her shoulder. She turned to face him, her large eyes glassy and her lip trembling. Faeoris gave him a crushing hug and sobbed loudly into his shoulder.

His heart felt cold, another death washing over him like a frozen river. That cold numbed his brain, as if there was no use even trying to make sense of anything anymore. His life was becoming as tragic as everything happening on Ehrde. The only warmth he felt, deep down, buried in layers of his onion, was a burning rage. That fury struggled to be set free, the yearning to let it loose was almost uncontrollable, but the numbness was so much safer.

Angst patted Faeoris on the back, stroking her fine hair. He was sure she wiped her nose on his cloak before pulling away. He touched her tears with the back of his hand, and she nodded gratefully. He broached Maarja, and she stopped rocking. She took a deep breath, and held the sobs in. The pretty, young Nordruaut looked more human, more vulnerable than he'd ever seen her.

"His will be a great story," Angst said, his throat dry and scratchy. "The greatest."

"It will be the best, Angst," she said, her voice filled with pride. "I don't cry just because I lost a friend today. His was a great hunt. I cry because he is the last of a people. The last Meldusian."

"Yes," Angst said solemnly. "One, one of many." He'd never understood what Jintorich meant by that, and wished there was another moment left to ask. "How would you like to honor him? In Unsel, we bury our dead."

"No," she snapped. "When this is done, he will be honored as Nordruaut."

"If it's permitted, I would like to attend," Angst said gently.

She only nodded, but seemed amicable, her composure returning. Kala sniffled loudly, and Scar gave her hand a lick.

Angst approached them and knelt, petting the lab pup.

"How long have I been out?" Angst asked Aerella.

"It's been a day. Maybe longer," she said softly. Her olive skin was blotchy and her bloodshot eyes hovered over dark, tired circles. She didn't just look older; she appeared wasted away. "We landed by the Ruautu river several miles to the west and walked here. Faeoris carried you."

"Thank you," he said over his shoulder. "Aerella, you look...I don't know how to say it. Not older, but maybe drained?"

"That portal took a lot out of me, Angst," she said. "I don't think I could do that again, even with your help."

"There's something I don't understand," Angst began. "Andec, in Unsel, can move groups of people short distances with ease."

"Maybe you should've brought him," she snapped.

He reached around Kala and Scar to give her an awkward hug, and the tension in her shoulders relaxed. He pulled away, brushing her mane of brown hair from her face.

"I didn't mean it to come out like that," she said, her husky voice hoarse from exhaustion. "Magic changes, over the years, and I can only do what I know. That portal spell exhausted me as well."

"Thank you," he said. "You saved us."

"We need to keep moving," she said. "We only have days before we have to turn back."

"Injuries?" Angst asked.

"Maarja's ribs. Faeoris has some burns," she said. "And your arm. I'm sorry, I've been too exhausted."

"No need for apologies," Angst said. He'd learned a little about healing from Dulgirgraut when he first found Moyra in a mermaid trap. Chryslaenor was ecstatic to provide him more spells, to the point that Angst had to be more specific about what needed healing.

Maarja set the bundle down and lifted furs as he approached. Taut muscles were covered in angry red and black bruises. He gently placed a hand on her side. She was burning up, and he wondered if that was from the injury, or just being Nordruaut. Maarja winced at his touch, but said nothing as he concentrated. A gentle hue of blue light surrounded his hand, flowing through it into her skin. He didn't completely understand everything he was doing; it was a spell borrowed from the sword, but he did understand bones, and he knit three of her ribs back to whole. Most of the bruising diminished, and he drew his hand away.

"Thank you," she said, her voice softer than he'd ever heard it.

"Of course," he said. "I'm not good at this, but at least your ribs aren't broken anymore."

"Now, where were you burned?" Angst asked, turning to face Faeoris. "Oh no."

Boils and scorch marks covered her chest from shoulder to shoulder. How could he have missed this when he hugged her? Even the hug must've been excruciating, but she'd shown no sign of weakness. Fortunately, her armored top appeared untouched, but for the first time since meeting her, he wished it had covered more than her breasts.

"Heal your arm first," she said, her eyes stern. "I have a high tolerance for pain."

"Apparently. Now shut up," he said, turning Faeoris around to face away from the others.

"Why are you turning me around?" she asked, her words clipped.

He glanced toward Kala before gently placing his hands on her chest.

"Oh," she said with a small smile. She leaned forward and whispered. "To get you to touch me, all I had to do was burn myself?"

Angst tried not to smile as power coursed through his hands and into her chest. She had been burned deep, and he found himself drawing power from Chryslaenor. After long moments, the damage was mostly healed, except for a long scar over her left breast that didn't want to give in. He frowned, trying to figure out how to mend it.

"Angst," she said, placing her hands on his, "it's okay."

"I think I can fix this," he said, unable to keep the shaky exhaustion from his voice.

"Not all scars go away," she said, gently pulling his hands away. "I feel better, thank you."

"But..." he said.

"And I think it's sort of cool." Faeoris poked at the scar and smiled. "It could use a little color, though."

Angst sat hard on the ground, more tired than he would've expected. Healing definitely wasn't his gift, and the wave of dizziness was overwhelming.

"Why here?" he asked. "Why the cave?"

"It will lead us under the river, all the way to Nordruaut," Maarja said. "All the way home."

For the first time since waking, Angst took in their surroundings. A hundred yards from the rocky cave entrance was a river unlike any he'd seen. It seemed more like a lake than a river, in the sense that it was incredibly wide. But rivers flowed, and an old tree the size of his house rushed by. He was a strong swimmer, but wouldn't even consider trying to cross this.

"I could try finding a stone large enough to carry us across," he suggested.

They all looked at him like he was a crazy old man. Maybe he was.

"Even Al'eyrn need to rest," Aerella said gently. "Why push yourself when there's already an easy path?"

"Well, yeah," he said reluctantly. "I could still do it."

"What about me?" Faeoris asked. "I could fly everyone over, one or two at a time."

"My ribs still hurt from our last flight," Maarja said, practically spitting out the words. She wouldn't look at Faeoris, and it was apparent that she would put up a fight before letting the Berfemmian fly her over.

"We should avoid splitting up," Aerella said, instantly calming the tension. "Is the cave safe?"

"Mostly," Maarja said. "It's hard to explain, but some claim to see ghosts and visions in these caves."

"Is this...is this *sotherscra?*" Aerella asked in wonder.

"You speak our old words," Maarja said in surprise.

"A few," Aerella said, her brow knitted. She chewed her bottom lip, looking down into the cave, lost in thought. "I've heard things. Stories."

"The stories keep thieves and spies away," Maarja said, looking down guiltily at the bundle of Jintorich in her arms. "Everyone I've known has made it through alive, and sane."

"Every Nordruaut?" Aerella pressed.

"Well," Maarja said hesitantly. "Yes."

"Sane?" Angst asked. Chimes from both swords rang through his mind, pressing against his skull. Now was not the best time to struggle with this battle between foci. It was almost too much effort to concentrate and he didn't need another discordant note in his thoughts. Angst willed them to hush.

"The cave is a beautiful place, filled with crystals," Maarja said encouragingly. She looked at Faeoris. "They are pretty, like you."

"Oh," Faeoris said, smiling at the Nordruaut, maybe for the first time ever. "I want to see."

"And..." Aerella urged her to continue.

"It is a great story, but very long and we are in a hurry," she said, apparently reluctant to cut it short. "It is said a man entered the cave, looking for an easy way to cross the river. In each crystal, he saw a different future, and lost himself in the one he liked most."

"He got lost?" Kala asked, a sincere frown on her face.

"A Nordruaut found him, sitting by a crystal, talking of love and happiness," Maarja said, looking around nervously. "When she tried to remove the man, he became wild, and then like a *durr.*"

Faeoris looked at Angst in confusion. He hadn't heard of a *durr* either and shrugged.

It seemed Aerella had. "*Durr* are maybe the dumbest animals that exist. They basically lie about on the shores of Nordruaut waiting to be eaten," she explained. "Basically, his mind was gone."

"It is said that humans lose their mind to the crystals," Maarja said. "But this is only story. They do not affect Nordruaut."

"Why not just have Faeoris fly us over?" Angst asked, pressing the issue again.

"I will not be flown around like prey by the Berfemmian!" Maarja snapped. "She already injured me once."

"Well, you shouldn't have left Angst behind like that!" Faeoris said, balling up her fists and shifting into a defensive stance.

Angst held out his arms and moved between the two women.

"We must hurry, and this is the fastest way. I will see you through safely," Maarja said, her words rushed. "Do you trust me, Angst?"

He thought on this, blocking out the quiet warning songs between his ears and ignoring the awkward tension between his companions. He knew Maarja least of all, but she'd never strayed from their goal. She'd been very close to Jintorich, who he'd liked. Tarness was practically in love with her, and he didn't trust anyone more. Angst studied her pretty face, noting the white vertical lines painted under her large, light blue eyes. Those eyes pleaded, but were sincere. She was really pretty. He nodded.

"I trust you, Maarja," he said.

"Angst," Aerella warned. "I trust her too, but this may not be the best idea. Especially considering you and the swords."

He glanced at the others. Faeoris frowned at him prettily, on the verge of saying something, but kept it to herself. No doubt she would ask what Aerella meant later.

"I think Maarja knows the danger everyone would be in if the crystals drove me crazy. She wouldn't put you all at risk like that, so let's go." He tried to sound positive. "What could possibly go wrong?"

42

Enurthen

Hector spent thirty minutes looking for Alloria. He searched the pond she bathed in, her quarters, the kitchen they all ate in, and the pond again. Unfortunately, she wasn't in the pond. She tended to follow Dallow around, mostly to irk Rose, so he also checked his friend's room and the library. There was no sign of her, not even the faint scent of her. He returned to the riverbank and paced.

After an impatient wait of ten more minutes, worry crept into his thoughts. Dallow was supposed to grab Rose, figuratively, while he grabbed Alloria, literally. Dallow felt that Jormbrinder was the key to escape this prison. This beautiful, amazing, luscious, vacation spot where nobody got killed and he'd actually learned to relax. Kind of. Hector snorted in frustration, not only for his love-hate relationship with this mage city, but that he had to go find his friends.

He knew which building Rose called home this week, but didn't know which floor, or room. That was Dallow's job, and he was slightly uncomfortable showing up unannounced. Hector's relationship with Rose was much different than everyone else's. Rose was Angst's friend, Dallow's something, and his... She was young enough to be his daughter. This made it feel inappropriate to even spend time with her, socially, but Angst and

Dallow seemed to forget this small fact. Maybe he should too. He had no kids, that he knew of. He liked Rose, and they had much in common—neither of them enjoyed hugging.

Each floor of the building seemed to be its own home. There were no locks on any doors, and he walked into the first-floor entryway like a guest. Hector cautiously wandered through a kitchen, dining room, bedrooms, and a great room for gathering. At one time the main room must've been welcoming and cozy. It featured a spacious fireplace with a mouth wide enough to warm Nordruaut. Cushioned chairs were placed neatly around an oval stone table. The room felt comfortable, made for entertaining a small group of friends or family. Games must've been played here, conversations had—he could practically hear the ghostly echoes of friendly laughter. People had lived lives in this room, and he felt like an intruder.

Someone screamed, jerking his thoughts back to present. He remained still, waiting, and listening. A woman's cry made him sprint back to the entrance. Was it Rose? No. It had to be Alloria. Hector rushed upstairs, not caring for stealth or silence. The center of the building was a wide spiral staircase that annoyingly leveled out at every floor. Two screams weren't enough to find them. He stopped on the third floor and breathed deeply through his nose. His ability to follow scents wasn't quite as good as a trained hunting dog's, but it was far better than a regular human's. Copper. The coppery scent of blood was close, but not here.

He sprinted to the fourth floor, pausing to smell once again. It was strong enough to make him wince. This was it, and he pushed through another unlocked door. The layout was identical to the first-floor home, and he hugged curved walls while searching the rooms, peeking around each corner as quickly as he felt was safe. Around the way, at the farthest point from the door, he heard quiet sobbing.

Hector entered a small bedroom to see Alloria lying unconscious on the floor. Rose held Dallow close, her hand on the deep red spot of blood soaked into his jerkin. There was so much blood it was pooling on the floor. She rocked back and forth, and when she looked up, it dribbled from an open wound on her neck. He was too late; they were both as good as dead.

"Rose... I'm so sorry I wasn't here. Can I do anything?" he said, dropping to his knees beside them.

Rose shook her head, and he was at a loss. Long moments passed; he didn't know what to do. He was used to death, but not like this. They'd become family, and he felt closer to Dallow than anyone. His military-disciplined emotions slipped, and his throat became so tight Hector lifted his chin to stretch it. Breathing shouldn't have been this hard. He reached out to place a shaky hand on Dallow's chest.

The blood dribbling from her neck slowed, and finally stopped. She swallowed hard, still rocking. Dallow gasped for air as Rose let loose a racking sob. They were breathing. Dallow was breathing. Alloria was breathing. He wasn't crying. That had to be sweat. From his eyes.

"What on Ehrde is going on?" he demanded, his voice strained.

Dallow's glowing eyes were wide with panic, and his head rocked back and forth as though searching the room for an answer. Rose made calming noises, patting his hair until he stopped.

"It's okay," Hector said, his gravelly voice low. "Rose and I are here."

"Rose!" Dallow coughed, reaching up with a hand. His voice was weak, barely audible. "You...you're alive! I stumbled on your body. There was so much blood."

"Alloria stopped by for a visit," Rose said. "The bitch cut my throat the minute my back was turned."

"Oooh," Hector said, his whisper low. "I'm surprised you didn't heal through it."

"She kept the dagger against my throat. Jormbrinder must've dampened my wielding, and I lost too much blood," she said through gritted teeth. "But somehow Dallow *was* able to heal me, a little. It was enough."

"How did you, uh..." Hector pointed at Alloria's unmoving body.

"I think the dumb cow slipped on all that blood," Rose said. "She must have struck her head on the wall."

"It sounded like she was screaming," Hector said.

Rose shrugged, all of her focus on Dallow. He tried speaking and instead gurgled, turning his head aside to expunge whatever had entered his lungs. He rolled over to his hands and knees, gasping, coughing, and vomiting. Hector placed a hand on his friend's shoulder.

"I've seen you in worse shape after a good night at Graloon's," he said, trying to sound cheerful. "You'll be fine."

Dallow nodded, pale and dry-heaving, but alive. Rose, free from holding Dallow, stood. She rushed over to Alloria and kicked her in the ribs. The princess didn't even grunt, and Rose kicked her again.

"Rose," Hector said softly.

She held her next kick mid-air. "I'm going to make it hurt before I kill her."

"We're better than that," Hector said then replied to her wry expression. "Okay, we're not better than that. But, we may need her."

"She tried to kill us," she snapped, but lowered her leg. "I've never pulled someone back so close from the edge. I almost couldn't."

"I'm glad you did. Thank you," Hector said.

"Then why let her live?" she asked.

"The foci," Hector said. "She's the only one who can wield it. Dallow thinks we need Jormbrinder to leave, and I don't think cutting off her hand or dragging her body to the wall is enough. I don't think we could do that with Angst and his foci. The weapons are too smart."

"He's right," Dallow wheezed then sighed deeply. "I never thought air could taste so good."

Rose knelt and went back to petting his hair. "I get to kill her when we're out, right?"

"Fair enough." Hector bowed his head.

"Good, then we need to get out of here now," Rose said. "I can't stand this place any longer."

"You said I only healed you a little?" Dallow asked, rubbing his chest.

"Yeah," she said, peering at Alloria. "It was like you flicked my ear, but I guess that was enough."

"I thought I healed more than a trickle," he said. "The dagger must've affected me too. I had completely forgotten it could do that, which could explain something else."

"What's that?" Hector asked, scratching the scar along his chin.

"Alloria read some book titles while we were at the library. It should've been enough to let me figure out the rest of Ughcratic," Dallow said. "The dagger may have caused some sort of disconnect with my ability to absorb information."

"That's why she kept going to the library with you," Hector said. "Hoping to slow you down."

"I thought she was following you just to piss me off," Rose said.

"Even after her run-in with the elements, she'd be too afraid to do that," Hector said with a broad smile. "I would be."

"You should be," Rose said, punching him in the arm.

"Enurthen," Dallow said.

"What?" Hector and Rose asked.

"This place, this mage city is called Enurthen," Dallow said, sitting up with a wince. "That's what she said before killing me...almost killing me."

"Pretty name for a prison," Hector said.

"Why does that matter?" Rose asked, crossing her arms.

"Because she had to have read it somewhere. Maybe in the library," Dallow said.

"So..." Hector said, impatient for the punchline.

"Every lost language has keys. Words that help unlock the rest," Dallow explained with a tired grin. "I don't think the little liar is bonded, or even knows how to use her foci, but it helped her understand at least some of Ughcratic."

"So what do we do now?" Hector asked.

"What you should always do when you need to figure something out," Dallow said, his face brightening. "Go to a library."

43

Sotherscra

Faeoris flew Aerella down first, followed by Kala and Scar. Maarja climbed down on her own, mumbling something about the Berfemmian dropping her. Faeoris peered down the hole after the Nordruaut coldly.

"We'll wait for you to finish climbing, so it's not too crowded," she said with a little bitchiness in her voice. She looked at Angst and sized him up. "Will you ever tell me the full truth?"

"Fine, I'll admit it," he said after a long sigh. "You're the most beautiful creature I've seen in all of Ehrde. There! Please don't be angry."

She smiled, in spite of herself, and gave him a quick hug that only hurt a little. "Quit teasing," she said, her cheeks pinking prettily.

"I'll tell you anything, Faeoris," he said, and he meant it.

"Why is Aerella worried about your swords?" she asked.

"She's right. I struggle with them. They both want the same thing, exclusivity. They want me, but they have to share."

"I don't like sharing," she said darkly.

He smiled. "Neither do my foci, and together, they probably have enough power to split this world in half. They also help me a lot, though usually too much. The swords talk to me through song, in my head, all the time. That music is sometimes loud,

327

rarely in harmony, and the information is often more than I can handle. Since bonding with another, it's a constant battle to hear my own thoughts. It would be maddening, if I let it."

"How do you manage?" she asked, her thin brows in a furrow.

"Let me tell you about this gorgeous friend of mine," he said with a wide grin. "She doesn't wear much, and is the best distraction ever."

"Stop," Faeoris said. "You're making me blush."

"Well, it's true," he said. "But really, I've got it under control. I can't imagine what could possibly drive me over the edge. A silly cave certainly isn't going to."

"If you say so," she said, frowning.

"Hey, I've got this," he replied, not feeling quite as confident as his words. Really, though, what choice did he have? There seemed to be a constant cost to being a hero, and this was just one of them.

Maarja grunted something, and it mingled with Scar's bark echoing up the cave entrance. He smiled.

"Ready?" he asked.

"Wait until you see this cave," she said, moving behind him and wrapping her arms around nicely, resting her hands on his chest. It was more of a hug than a hold, and he liked it.

"Are you sure I shouldn't be behind you, holding on?" he teased.

"Sure, go ahead," she said, her voice a little sultry.

"Uh, this will work fine," Angst grumbled. He hated being out-flirted.

The cave entrance was mud, and rock, and roots, and everything you would expect to see when looking at a hole in the ground. It went straight down for half of forever, and Faeoris's wings of light provided him an excellent view of brown dirt, and then red clay, followed by boring limestone. What was she so amazed by? They had to have limestone and dirt in Angoria. He enjoyed the hug far more than the view.

Something glittered like a distant star, soon followed by more lights, now like fireflies. It was as if they were diving through the colorful burning ash of a campfire. The sparkles became blue and white and yellow, shining all around them. Dim at first then eventually brighter as crystalline formations grew out of the cave walls. The crystals became larger as they descended, until they were the size of Maarja or taller.

Faeoris placed him down as gently as ever and, unfortunately, let go. She extinguished her wings, but a steady light from the crystals still surrounded them. Everyone but Maarja seemed as awestruck as he felt. The cave ahead was a wide trail of translucent, gently glowing crystals jutting out in all directions from the walls and ceiling. It was almost like being in the middle of a snowflake. A path along the floor had been stomped flat from centuries of foot traffic, wide enough for three humans, or one Nordruaut.

"Are you okay?" Aerella asked. "That took a while."

"I had to pee," Angst said.

Kala giggled, and Angst winked.

"Oh." Aerella shook her head. "Well, now that business is taken care of, Maarja and I have been discussing strategy."

"Let me guess," Angst said. "We walk to the end."

"Don't be an ass," Aerella snapped, her face, and temper, younger than when they'd entered the cave. "If any of the stories are true, we need to be careful."

"Angst," Maarja said sternly. "Don't look directly into the crystals."

"What if I do by accident?" he asked.

"Then look away," Maarja said, her face even more sincere than usual.

"What about blindfolds?" Kala asked.

"Great idea, little genius," Angst said with a nod.

She beamed at the recognition.

"They could still affect you, just slower," Maarja said, looking around nervously. "It would be better to run through then walk slowly and expose yourself longer."

"You can't let yourself be drawn into the visions," Aerella

urged. "Let your mind go blank. If you see something, remember that it isn't real. Don't get lost in fantasy."

"First time for everything," Angst said, winking at Faeoris.

She replied with a short, nervous laugh.

"Angst, we're going to have a buddy system in case we get separated. Maarja will lead Kala and I, and you will stay close to Faeoris. We're hoping Faeoris doesn't get affected by the crystals just like Maarja, since they aren't exactly human," she said gently.

"I couldn't be happier about that," Faeoris said with a sniff.

"That way, if the rest of us are drawn into the crystals, they can quickly pull us free," she said.

"Sounds good to me," he said, looking at the Berfemmian. "Think you can handle my fantasies?"

"I look forward to it," she said with a broad smile.

Maarja and Aerella sighed.

"Should I tell Heather about this, too?" Kala whispered.

"Definitely," Aerella said, not whispering.

"What are we waiting for?" Angst asked, ready for a few moments away from the ethics committee.

"Run," Maarja said, holding out a large hand for Aerella to grasp.

Maarja kept her pace at a slow jog, which meant Angst was gasping for breath and sweating within a minute. He held hands with Faeoris, his grip slick with perspiration. She didn't say anything, but he certainly thought it. Could he be any older at this moment? A little endurance fed to him by the swords would've been nice, but he was pretty sure they laughed at this thought. Jerks.

The cave seemed to go forever. They'd already been jogging for easily three entire minutes. He wanted to suggest that they ride swifen, but was trying to keep his lungs' desperate pleas for oxygen as quiet as possible.

"Mom?" Kala called out.

"Kala," Aerella said. "Look away."

"Mom, I'm sorry," the girl said. "What? You're not angry?"

CHAPTER FORTY THREE

"Faster," Maarja urged.

"I can't," Angst wheezed.

He didn't understand the need to hurry; beauty surrounded them. His lungs burned, and he just wanted to slow down and admire the pretty rocks. His eyes were drawn to them like he was drunk and couldn't take his eyes off a beautiful woman. He practically leered at a large crystal, and his feet slowed to a shuffle.

"Tori?" he asked.

"Yes, my king," she said, wrapping her naked body around his.

"Go," Faeoris snapped.

He dragged himself out of the delusional quicksand and made a mental note to finish that fantasy later. But, why did Faeoris sound so stern? There was something he shouldn't be looking at, but not this. This had to be a daydream. He wasn't really so exhausted from this short run that he was starting to see things. Not wanting to anger her again, Angst focused on Maarja in the distance, who slowly pulled away from them.

"Father," Aerella said, her voice echoing down the cavern. "You're still alive! It's good to be home."

"No," Maarja yelled. "Get up. Keep going!"

Angst continued to stare at the Nordruaut, but in his periphery were visions he longed to be real, and some he feared.

He was under the sea, Moyra was alive, and his exotic mermaid placed her mouth against his so they could breathe.

He left himself chained to a bed so Faeoris could finish what she'd started.

Tori lay next to him, soft, and warm, and very, very naked.

The twins, those beautiful young women, grasping at him, reaching into his pockets, asking about a foci.

Ivan, alive and well, walking beside him and Alloria, making him long to beat the man's face to a pulp one last time.

He lay on the edge of the maiden's courtyard, looking off into madness. The sinkhole that had eaten part of the castle was now filled with orange Vex'kvette that flowed away from Unsel like a river. Dragons of all size flew overhead.

A creature Angst didn't recognize, like a giant gamlin in a collared shirt, handed him a notched coin. Hadn't Aerella called it a gear?

It was getting harder and harder to concentrate through the onslaught of images that could happen, and some he wished would. He needed to keep moving, but the images were glue to his feet, and he was so tired. His pace slowed with Faeoris, and she let go of his hand.

"Mom," she said. "You made it. You're alive. We're back from Vex'steppe. I am? I'm pregnant?"

"Faeoris, no," he said weakly as Maarja ran out of sight. All he could see was crystals.

"Angst?" Heather called out. "Angst, you're home!"

"I am," he said in wonder.

He took her in, and she looked incredible. They were still older, he was still chubby, her hair still teased some grays, but it didn't matter. Heather looked hungry for him, the passion in her eyes the same as when they'd fallen in love. She wasn't angry, or ready to argue; she was simply happy to see him.

"I heard about all of it!" she said. "I'm so proud of you for being a hero. Not just a knight, a zyn'ight. And now that Unsel is safe, we can be together."

"I did it for you, for them," he said, feeling more fulfilled than ever. "Are they sleeping? Is Thom and..."

"Both are in bed," she replied with a hungry smile. "We should be too."

He heard something, a distant chitter, but ignored it. Nothing could be more important than this. He'd lived his destiny, fulfilled his dreams, and his reward was family.

He was a zyn'ight of Unsel. He could wield magic freely. He knew in his heart that all his friends lived and were safe. Weren't they meeting for drinks at the Wizard's Revenge tomorrow night? It had to be after seeing Queen Victoria. It didn't matter, nothing else mattered as he began unbuttoning his wife's blouse.

"All I ever wanted to be was your hero," he said.

CHAPTER FORTY THREE

He looked into her eyes, but pulled back as her face distorted, becoming larger, finally transforming into... Maarja?

"Angst, I'm sorry," she said.

The blur of her enormous fist raced toward him, and all went dark.

44

Nordruaut

While a loud thump and some rude jostling woke Angst, the smell was what made him open his eyes. He was face down in thick fur, his nose buried so deep, he felt like he was bobbing for apples in a haystack, and hoped he wouldn't find one. His head throbbed from Maarja's punch, and he needed air like he'd never breathed. Pushing himself up was impossible, his arms and legs were firmly tied to his smelly host that rocked back and forth at a vomit-inducing pace. The thick scent of animal made his nose drip and his throat scratchy.

"At least I'm not on the inside," he mumbled, certain it sounded more like, "Af leaf fur fur fur."

"Hold," Maarja said from somewhere nearby. "Angst, do you want me to set you free?"

"Mf fur fur cough sneeze," he replied.

The familiar sound of guttural laughter surrounded him. She apparently wasn't the only Nordruaut nearby. That was good, but why was he tied up? Blood began to flow into his fingers and toes as the bindings loosened.

"Hold still," Maarja said, as if he had a choice.

Something gripped his waist and plucked him free from the great expanse of coarse fur. He gasped at the blast of freezing air before immediately coughing and sneezing out animal. It was so cold he couldn't catch his breath. Angst looked down. Maarja's large hand was wrapped around his chest like she was preparing to throw a javelin. He pushed frantically at her fingers as panic overtook him. The strength in her hand was enough to crush his armor like an egg.

"Set me down!" Angst commanded, unable to keep the quaver from his voice.

More laughter didn't help.

"As you wish, human," she said, placing him on top of the snow.

"Thank—" He sank into deep snow until it reached his nose. "—you."

The laughter was hard to hear through his frustration. Throughout their entire journey, she'd barely cracked a smile at one of his jokes. Now she was the biggest comedian in Nordruaut, and at his expense. Wasn't there a line in the hero book that read 'something something something...it's okay to kill people who mock you?' He raised his arms without a word, and held onto Maarja's outstretched hand as she lifted him up. She placed him once again on the enormous mass of fur. He stood on the beast, shakily, and stared at her. His Nordruaut friend wouldn't make eye contact, avoiding him like he'd suddenly become the least popular kid in school.

"This prisoner is supposed to champion us?" a Nordruaut woman called out. "The bokeen he rides on couldn't even make a meal of him!"

More laughter. They were certainly a lot heartier than he remembered. Yup, killing sounded about right, and then realization struck him, in the gut, with a cudgel.

"Prisoner?" Angst asked, staring at his 'friend.' "Maarja?"

She still wouldn't look at him. Her fair cheeks reddened, and she sucked in her lips.

"I deserve an explanation," he said. "What's going on?"

"I was sent to retrieve you from Unsel," she said in a hushed tone. "One way or another."

"Another way would've been better," Angst growled. He was

so disappointed it hurt, especially after all they'd been through. "If anyone else has been harmed..."

"They're unconscious...after the cave," she said. "You should still be as well."

He covered his mouth with a hand. "That's why you wanted to go in there so badly. Is that why we didn't wear blindfolds?" Disappointment escaped his lungs in a deep sigh. "What I saw in there...was so real. Maarja, I don't know if I'll ever get over some of those visions. How could you think that was okay?"

She shrugged and stared intently at the snow around her ankles. It was like talking to a teenager who'd stayed out too late...and kidnapped all his friends. Although, he supposed, she sort of was a teenager in Nordruaut years. That was still no excuse.

"Where is everyone else?" he asked sternly.

"You want me to quiet him?" a burly Nordruaut said from behind her. He was easily a head taller than Maarja.

"And you would be the smallest monster I've killed yet," Angst said, reaching for his sword.

"Angst, no," she said, a slight quaver to her voice. She placed a warning hand on the man's chest. "Please, Angst, everyone is fine, I promise. They are spread out too far for you to reach in time."

"In time for what?" he asked.

"She said you could destroy all of us," the man said in disbelief.

Angst lifted his chin in the briefest of yup gestures.

"But they would be dead before you found them all," the man continued.

For the first time since waking, Angst looked around. Standing atop the stinky bokeen mount, he had a good enough view to spy a caravan of one hundred or more Nordruaut and maybe twenty bokeen. But really, hiding in the blinding white of snow that formed tall mounds as far as he could see, there could've been more. It wasn't comforting, and agitation rested at the base of his skull.

"Yup," Angst said.

"Yup what?" the Nordruaut man asked.

"I could kill every single one of you," Angst said, crossing his arms.

"No!" Maarja shouted, grabbing the man's arm before he could wield a wicked looking staff that was wider than Angst.

"Hey," Angst taunted. "What's your name?"

"Gose," the Nordruaut grunted. "Why?"

"Just making a list," Angst said, staring Gose down.

"Go on, Gose," Maarja said firmly. "Go cool off."

The large, angry Nordruaut stomped off through drifts of snow, Nordruaut winter steaming off his skin like a hot spring.

"Shouldn't be too hard to cool off out here," Angst called after him. It had sounded much less stupid in his head.

There was a shout from far ahead, and the caravan lumbered forward at a painfully slow pace. The bokeen must've immediately broken into a sweat, because the smell became the scent of sour towels left in the wash too long. He wanted to sit, and maybe eat something, but knew this wasn't a good time because the stench would've ruined his meal. Instead, he stared at Maarja until she looked at him.

"I'm sorry I hit you," she said. "I tried to be gentle."

Gentle like a boulder, he thought.

"That's what you're sorry for?" he said pointedly. "When will we get to wherever we're going? I feel like I should hop off and push."

"By nightfall, if we don't stop again," she answered sullenly. "You're small. It's hard to tell in the snow, but we're moving faster than you think."

"You promise everyone is alive?" he asked.

"Faeoris woke up outside the cave and flew off," she said, licking her lips.

"Oooh, that's not good," he said darkly. "For you."

"What do you want from me?" The words poured out in a desperate plea. "We're being killed off! If you can't save us, my people will die."

"So will my friends," he said. "So will Victoria."

"There's time," she said, choking on her words. "Angst, there's still time to save your princess."

"There'd better be, or I'll destroy everyone in Nordruaut," he said firmly. "Except you."

She nodded, sniffling now. Was she crying? He hadn't even known she could produce tears.

"Did Jintorich know?" he asked. "Or did you lie to him too?"

"He did not know," she said, now sobbing.

"He would've been so disappointed in you," Angst said.

She looked at him as if he'd pierced her heart. Maarja rushed away in tears, a bundle still held tightly in her arms.

45

Enurthen

"He's been in there for days!" Hector said, unable to completely keep the whine out of his voice.

"He's been in there for hours," Rose replied snappily.

"Close enough," Hector said. "How long is this going to take?"

"Let's see," Rose began. "He's reconstructing an unknown language from one word and then finding the right spell to set us free. It will take more than a few hours."

"Knowing Dallow, probably more than a few libraries," Hector said with a sigh. "Hopefully it'll be easier without the dagger nearby."

Alloria made several muttered whimpering sounds. She was bound like a sack of potatoes and gagged with a small towel. Her eyes were wide with panic as she struggled against her restraints. There were a lot of them. Hector had offered to help tie her, as he was familiar with knots, but Rose had stared him down. Too many bindings and one set of sheets later, Alloria looked more like a mummified corpse than a beautiful young princess. Impractical, but effective. It was like Rose didn't trust her or something.

"She's awake." Hector said. "Thanks for not killing her."

"The bitch said she couldn't die anyway," Rose said with a

sharp glare. "I'd still like to try."

"You're more than welcome to," he said with a nod toward the bound woman. "Once we're out of here. She's only good to us as long as she holds that half a foci."

Tears welled in Alloria's large eyes. Was it from the death threat or just the thought of leaving Enurthen? Had she really tried killing Dallow and Rose just to stay here? Maybe there was a way they could leave her behind. She'd already been through so much.

"How is it she's even able to hold the dagger?" Hector asked, nudging the bulge with a toe.

"Dallow has theories he'd be glad to share with you in great detail," Rose said with a patient sigh. "In short, either that crazy bald guy did something to her, like when he tried forcing Chryslaenor to bond with me. Or Dallow thinks she may've had some latent magic ability."

"I wonder what?" Hector asked.

"She seems gifted at lying," Rose said.

"Oh, she's gifted," Hector said with raised eyebrows.

"Boobs aren't magic," she said, rolling her eyes.

"I completely disagree," he said, his tone light.

"You sound like Angst," she said, giving him the barest of smiles. "Making inappropriate jokes at the worst times."

"Boobs are no joking matter," Hector continued.

Rose whacked him in the arm, and then leaned against him for a hug. Hector held her close, and she broke into a sob against his tunic. He could relate, all too well. In spite of all his close calls and brushes with death, he'd never walked away without some sort of emotional reaction. Laughter, anger, hope...he even remembered longing for sex (that had only happened once). It was as if the body reacted to death's cold touch with the need for as much life as possible. He understood her sobs, even more than she did, so the two people who hated hugging the most held on for long moments.

"I was thinking of Angst when I said that," he explained. "Not only because he loves boobs, but even when I hated it, I needed his humor."

She nodded, her head still on his chest. "Don't tell him, but I miss him."

"Me too," Hector said, nodding in agreement.

"Do you think he's okay?" Rose asked, finally pulling away.

"Probably surrounded by beautiful women," he said with a smile, "as determined to impress them as he is to save us."

She snorted while dabbing at her eyes. "He's probably replaced me already."

"Don't believe that for a second," Hector said.

"But, that Berfemmian..." her voice trailed off.

"Faeoris? She's perfect," he said then quickly moved on past her glare. "But, that's the thing about Angst. He's had beautiful girlfriends all his life. Nobody really gets it, but neither does he. It just happens. Anyway, a lot of them move on. They get married, or move away, or they realize he can only give so much and just give up. I've seen him practically grieve over some, and then, somehow, he meets another beautiful young woman and is happy again. It's sort of sad, and kind of funny, and very Angst."

"See," she said darkly, shoving him away. "He's going to move on."

"No, you don't see," Hector said, his tone fatherly. "If you don't leave him, he'll never leave you."

Rose's thin brows furrowed in thought, one cheek curled up in a half smile.

"I found it!" Dallow said excitedly from the library entrance.

"Finally," Hector said, rushing over to his friend and taking an arm. "We can get out of here!"

"No, not that. Not yet." Dallow shook his head. "The alphabet! I learned their alphabet!"

Hector's shoulders collapsed, and Rose smiled.

"So, what next, oh learn-ed one?" Hector asked.

"Just one more book," Dallow said. "This library was mostly engineering and science. It was fascinating..."

"Where can we find you the right book?" Rose asked quickly, to hold back the oncoming tide of information.

"Oh," Dallow said. "There are a few more libraries in En-urthen. I need the one over where we found Alloria."

"I'll lead the way," Hector said. Both Hector and Alloria grunted as he threw her over his shoulder.

Two additional libraries later—totaling four—and many hours—totaling too many—brought them to the center of En-urthen. It was a large building that looked as official as any. They'd never been able to open its enormous steel doors, so had mostly ignored it.

"All I need is..." Dallow began.

"We know," Hector said, unable to hold back his exhaustion.

"One more book," Rose said, finishing his sentence.

"This is it, though," Dallow said. "There really isn't any-where else to go. This is the archive where they kept all the information on how this city was built, its history, and the power that's kept it going."

"You're loving this, aren't you?" Hector asked.

"You know it!" Dallow said with a broad smile. "Am I facing the door?"

"Yes," Rose said, sounding tired.

He raised a hand, his long fingers spread, and his eyes glowed bright white through the blue kerchief. Dallow frowned in con-centration, finally saying something that sounded like 'clamchowder' but was pronounced more like, "Cremkouchder." Nothing happened, and Hector threw up his arms. Rose rested a hand on his shoulder and shushed him with a finger to her lips. Dallow tried again and again, his pronunciation changing each time. After his fifth try, there was a tiny click followed by the gentle creak of old hinges. A small door within a much larger door opened wide enough to slide fingers in the crack. Dallow sighed and collapsed on the stairs.

"Great job!" Rose said, sitting close to him.

"Yes," Hector agreed. "But I would've expected some-thing...bigger. Horns, maybe a parade, or possibly monsters."

"Heh. I'll try harder next time," Dallow said. "Who knew figuring out a language that old would be so hard. Do we have anything to eat?"

Alloria cried out through her cloth gag. Hector looked at Rose, who apparently had no plans to remove it. He knelt and gently removed the binding from her mouth.

"What?" he asked.

"Please...please," she said, gasping for breath. "I have to pee!"

"Go ahead," Rose said.

"No, that's gross," Alloria begged. "Please, no."

Rose jerked the cloth from Hector's hand and tried jamming it back into Alloria's mouth. The princess rocked her head back and forth until Rose slapped her. Alloria sobbed as she jammed the gag back in place.

"What?" Rose snapped at Hector. "She shoved that dagger into Dallow's stomach and cut my neck open. I don't trust her, at all. She can pee on herself for all I care."

"Oookay," Hector said.

Dallow shrugged, stood, and slowly made his way up the stairs. Rose took his arm while Hector picked up Alloria and followed. The princess squeaked but fortunately didn't pee all over him.

"I can't see anything in here," Rose said as they entered. "There aren't any windows."

"No problem," Dallow said, raising a hand again. He fumbled through more words until finding the right pronunciation of 'horsemuck,' and then there was light.

Hector gasped as the room filled with light. This wasn't the spotty light from candles or torches; this was like light from the sun that filled everything in brightness and warmth.

"How did you do that?" Rose asked.

"See what you can learn from books?" Dallow said haughtily. "Please describe the room."

"No books here," Hector said quickly. "We should probably go."

"What?" Dallow asked in surprise.

"Dallow," Rose said in wonder. "You'll never want to leave.

There are enough books in here for a lifetime."

"Maybe your lifetime," he scoffed. "I wish I could see."

"It's at least twice the size of your library in Unsel," she said.

"My library," he whispered longingly.

"The walls are shelves and shelves of books, reaching stories tall to the ceiling," she said, her voice filled with concern. "But there aren't any walkways, not even any ladders. How can you possibly get to the one you need?"

"What else is in the room?" he asked, trying to sound calm but his voice shook.

"There are a dozen desks, each with a wooden chair," Hector said. "It's as boring as any school I forgot to attend."

"Hurry," Dallow said, reaching out and grasping at the air like a toddler reaching for a toy. "Bring me to one."

Rose guided him to the nearest desk, wiping away dust as he awkwardly found his way into the chair. A white hue was already glowing from his eyes, and he lifted his hands, wiggling his fingers excitedly. Hand prints had been carved into the desk. As he lowered them, Rose helped guide his hands to the carved-out impressions.

"Ahh," he cried out, jerking his head back.

His eyes glowed so white that Hector couldn't look directly at them. Rose tugged on Dallow's arms but they were stuck. Hector set the bundle of Alloria on the floor and went to help. His friend was stiff as a board, as if rigor mortis had set in.

"Wait," Dallow whispered. After several labored breaths, he lifted his hands and smiled. "It still works!"

"What, Dallow?" Rose asked.

"I'm not the only reader who's ever existed," Dallow explained. He pressed his hands together and pulled them apart several times. "They tingle," he said, his voice filled with wonder. He was out of breath, as if he'd run around the room several times, and his words tumbled out with excitement. "This was a library for people like me."

"Oh, good," Hector said, rubbing his thumb along the scar on his chin. "What does that mean?"

"This desk...these desks are connected to all the books on the shelves," Dallow said. "I don't need to go to the books, they come to me."

"Huh," Hector said, feeling incredibly stupid. "So what does that mean?"

"I need three hours," Dallow said. "It should be enough time to learn their system for cataloging books, finding the ones I need, and reading them."

"That's it?" Hector asked.

"Food," Dallow said. "I'm famished."

"I can bring us dinner...or breakfast," Rose said, rubbing her eyes.

"Hector, are you done sewing blankets?" Dallow asked.

"Sewing?" Rose asked with a raised eyebrow.

"I wasn't just watching Nordruaut beat each other to death in that tower," Hector said proudly. "I made some protective gear we can wear outside. It's not pretty, but should be enough to keep us warm. I even made some for Alloria."

"How thoughtful," Rose said dryly.

"Speaking of, what do we do with her?" Hector asked, nodding at the bundle.

"She's not going anywhere," Rose said. "If she could've escaped by now, she would've, just to pee."

"That's a lot of confidence in embarrassment," Hector said with a frown.

"Have you ever seen a woman pee?" Rose asked.

"Well, uh, no," Hector said, his cheeks warm.

"Exactly," Rose said.

"I can handle her," Dallow said nonchalantly. "I've learned a lot today and could turn her into a puddle if needed."

"I think she'll make her own puddle," Rose said with an evil laugh.

Alloria sought Hector, her eyes pleading for compassion.

"Harm him, and I'll put a body part in every room of this city," Hector said, staring Alloria down. "That would be an awful thing to live through. Understand?"

Alloria's nodded briskly, crying and sobbing through the gag.

"We're going, Dallow," Hector began, but his friend was already in the throes of books.

Rose gave Dallow a brief peck on the cheek, and they left.

* * * *

Unsel

"You look exhausted," the guard said. "Are you all right?"

Two soldiers stood at the top of the entrance to the royal hallway, watching Mika lumber slowly up the stairs. They were the same two who stood here every day, the same two he spoke to in his friendliest tone, and the same two he had told most of his best stories. He couldn't remember their names.

"I think I figured out how to hold back the deterioration of this shield," Mika said with his most winning smile. "It seems to be fading fast, but I can keep it going for just a bit longer."

"Hurry," Victoria's distant voice whispered in his head, making him wince.

The second soldier's face went askew at the wince, as if he'd never seen anyone with a headache. Of course, this headache made Mika's cheek twitch, forcing his eye to squint uncontrollably. The two guards looked at each other nervously, and the distrust in their eyes made his teeth grind. This wasn't the time. She needed him, and he had to save his energy. He would've explained, but they just wouldn't understand.

"I'm not all right," he said, making his voice quiver and letting his shoulders droop. "I didn't think it showed."

"Maybe some food?" one of them said, practically offering to fetch some. "Or some rest?"

"I ate before coming, but thank you," Mika said. "I don't mind being exhausted. It's for Victoria. She's family, and sometimes it's necessary to sacrifice for people we love. Several years ago, there was a blizzard that struck our township. It came in the early winter and was devastating. My father—"

"What's wrong with your hand?" the first guard asked.

CHAPTER FORTY FIVE

Mika must've been tired, for he'd meant to keep his hand with the gift, the ruby ring, hidden. The entire palm was blotchy with dark purple and yellow bruises. Cracks of dried skin crept around the edges like shattered glass. Dark fissures of blood seeped out if he flexed his swollen palms too hard. His ring finger was darker than the rest; the swelling had almost completely cut off circulation.

"The magic to keep her alive has a price," he said. It was easy to explain this part; it wasn't a lie, just not the entire truth. He raised the mess of a hand, a dark orange glow throbbing from the cracks. "I can explain it more..."

Both soldiers took nervous steps back, and stopped. They didn't move, or breathe, or speak. They simply remained frozen between moments. Mica could've killed them, but that would make things even more complicated. Instead, he turned away from the frozen guards and approached the shield.

"Yessss," Victoria whispered in his ears.

"I'll save you, my love," he said, gritting his teeth. Mika winced again as he turned the ring around, moving it with hesitant jerks before it lined up with his palm. He took a deep breath and struck the shield.

Smack. Mika couldn't refrain from yelping out every time his hand connected. *Smack*. The shield flashed a sharp burgundy that made him wince. *Smack*. It stung all the way up to his shoulder. *Smack*. Was that what it felt like when you decided to cut off your own hand? *Smack*. Love required sacrifice, and they were in love! He collapsed to his knees. *Smack*.

Hours passed. Mika's mouth was dry and his bangs damp with sweat. His ring hand was a bloody mess, splattering red every time he hit the shield. It was so frustrating! It made him so angry that she was locked in there, stuck in time. Time was supposed to be his! Was he even making progress? He wound up for one last strike and, with all his will, slapped the shield.

Victoria blinked.

"Thank you," he heard her whisper in his mind.

He coughed in exhaustion. She was still in there, but blood

now dripped from her like dew from a leaf. One more day. His princess would be free in just one more day. Mika shakily pushed himself to stand and shuffled over to the frozen guards. He willed them back into present time and rushed into exposition.

"...my father invited the entire town into our keep, so they would be safe and fed. He tended to the sick and elderly. Gave up his own food so they wouldn't go hungry. He sacrificed. I learned that from him."

The soldiers nodded at him, smiling at each other, though their eyes were disoriented.

"Your father is a good man," one of them said. "And you do him honor."

"I try," Mika said with a genuinely shaky breath. "But I think you're right. A little rest and I may be of more use."

"After all you've done," the soldier said, "you deserve it."

46

Nordruaut

When Angst had first moved to Unsel, he was young and had little in the way of money. Very little. The shoddy room he'd rented was far from a palatial estate, and its location over a barn hadn't improved matters. Now, this campsite for warmongering Nordruaut brought back memories of that stinky, run-down room.

In his twenties, Angst had thrived on optimism. He'd considered that downtrodden, poverty-struck, and rat-infested barn a challenge, a stepping stone on the path to better things. These Nordruaut weren't twenty, and not a single pair of eyes greeted him with an ounce or pluck of hope. These eyes seemed to be waiting for inevitable death. His heart went out to them. They looked so depressed that he instantly wanted to help. Until he remembered...he was a prisoner.

Once the caravan stopped, a horde of tired Nordruaut surrounded them. It was like a gathering of curious onlookers gawking at two horses that had collided on the street. They stared, some pointed... Was he supposed to start juggling or something? Jarle pressed his way through the crowd and bared a cautious smile at Angst, until he saw the scowl.

"Thank you for coming, Angst," he said, crossing his thick arms.

"It's not like I had much of a choice," Angst growled.

Wielding Chryslaenor, Angst dramatically leaped off the bokeen mount and was grateful there was enough soft snow to cushion his landing without making him cry out in pain. Maarja led Kala and Aerella to him, not roughly, but they were bound and gagged. Aerella nodded that she was okay, while tears streamed down Kala's cheeks. Who could blame her? He was scared too. Scared for them, and so angry he shook.

"Where's my dog!" Angst demanded, lightning crackling along the edge of his sword.

"I don't know," Maarja said, holding up her hands defensively. "We looked after attaching you to the bokeen. We were hoping Faeoris took him."

"Perfect," Angst said coolly. He whistled. Normally, his whistles sounded like someone spitting corn from their teeth. With Chryslaenor's help, Nordruaut around him winced and covered their ears.

"Incoming!" Faeoris shouted from overhead.

Angst looked up to see Faeoris throw Scar toward the Nordruaut, giving him barely enough time to put up an air shield. The lab grew mid-air before crashing to the ground. Like dropping a boulder in water, everything within twenty yards, from snow to Nordruaut, was blasted away from the point of impact. He pointed at Jarle, hoping Faeoris would see. She didn't disappoint.

She rushed past Angst in a trail of light, knocking over standing Nordruaut until she arrived at Jarle. He was already up but unprepared for flight as Faeoris lifted him into the air and brought him to Angst. The Berfemmian dropped him hard enough that he was forced to his knees.

"Kill him?" Faeoris asked.

Angst knew she wasn't joking. "Maybe," Angst said, his jaw clenched. "Jarle, by the Vivek, this had better be a good story."

Jarle remained on his knees, his expression downcast. Faeoris removed the bindings from Aerella and Kala. To Angst's surprise, Scar leaped into the air and shrank to puppy size before landing in the snow before the young girl. Giggles battled hysterical sobs as she dug him out of the snow and buried her face in the lab's soft, wet fur.

"Get up," Angst said, extending an arm and anchoring himself to the ground for leverage. Jarle took his arm and stood, apparently surprised that, despite his size, Angst could help him. "What's this about? I'm in a hurry."

"The Nordruaut have tended to Ehrde for two thousand years," he said, his voice low but his words rushed. "We are hunters, gatherers, and farmers, having left war far behind us. King Rasaol has gathered the eastern tribes. They believe the nations of Ehrde will soon battle, and want to go on the offensive. It could be bad, Angst. The last time we did this..."

"The Mendahir died," Angst said.

"Yes," Jarle said with a frown, cocking his head to one side.

"He may be right," Angst said. "Ehrde may face war, and soon."

"But Nordruaut shouldn't go to war for domination!" Jarle said vehemently, spit flying from his mouth. "If we have to fight, it should be to defend our people or end it mercifully! Nordruaut should not rule other nations. We hunt, and tend, nothing else."

"And you need me because why?" Angst asked testily.

"We need a champion," he said. "Their champion, Niihlu, wields a foci."

"Wait, what?" Angst asked. When he'd first met Jarle and company as nomads on the hunt for Vex'kvette creatures, Niihlu had longed for Chryslaenor more than Angst wanted sex. And that's a lot. Niihlu had challenged Angst for the sword based on some Nordruaut law, and Tarness had represented Angst in battle. Tarness took a beating, but still won the fight, leaving Niihlu a bruised lump. "He couldn't even pick up my blade. How could he wield a foci?"

"I don't know," Jarle said. His hands were out, and his eyes held no answers.

"Rose," Faeoris said. "At that mage city, underwater, that odd

351

man tried to do something with Rose and your sword. Could it have been like that?"

Angst lowered his head in thought. That tall, bald man had tried to force a bonding between Chryslaenor and Rose. What if he'd forced another bonding, with another foci?

"That's it?" Angst asked.

"Um," Jarle said, a perplexed look on his face.

"You *kidnapped* us to fight *Niihlu*?"

"Well, yes," Jarle said, clearing embarrassment from his throat. "He now has a foci, and an army."

"I have two foci," Angst said. "And a Berfemmian."

"That's right," Faeoris said, crossing her arms and looking stern.

Jarle's face brightened.

"I also have one of the most knowledgeable wielders in history." Angst nodded at Aerella. "A dog that turns into a giant steel-covered beast, a child who can wield magic better than I can, and a Nordruaut who's been an incredible ally and friend—though I do question some of her recent choices."

"I...I..." Maarja's eyes were sad, and she took a deep, brave breath. "I thought you would hate me."

"What you did was wrong. You shouldn't have tricked us, and I really don't have time to fight your war. I'm busy fighting my own," he said, struggling to keep anger from his voice. "But I would've done the same thing to save my people. We're friends. I wish you'd told me, but really, I understand. I do stuff that pisses off my friends—"

"This is true," Faeoris said with a nod.

"Indeed," Aerella confirmed, raising an eyebrow.

"All the time," Kala piped in.

"Hey," Angst snapped at them before turning to Maarja. "But you forgive friends and move on. We are friends, right?"

Maarja looked uncomfortable, tugging at her platinum blond braid. After long moments, finally, reluctantly, she nodded. "Yes, Angst, we are friends."

"Right," Angst said, not quite feeling the love. "You owe me a drink, and a hug, maybe two, and then we're good."

Maarja nodded with surprised eyes and a grateful smile.

"So, Jarle," Angst said, facing the skaadi. "You want me to kick Niihlu in the shins while you guys sit back and watch."

"I don't like how you describe being our champion," Jarle said darkly. "But yes."

"Okay," Angst said.

Jarle looked at Maarja in confusion, as if seeking translation. She smiled warily and nodded.

"You'll do it?" Jarle asked.

"This is ridiculous!" Gose barked, shoving past Marja. "He's so tiny, I could take him—"

"You can take my order for lunch," Angst snapped.

Gose's cheeks reddened, and he tried to move forward. "I can't move."

It took some effort to hold the Nordruaut's bones in place— the man was large and powerful, and there was a thick layer of snow and ice between the Nordruaut and actual ground. Angst's anger swelled as he shuffled through the snow. Standing before Gose, he was face to waist with the large man. He looked up, all the way up, until they made eye contact. His voice came out in a rumble.

"I came here to save my friends, to save my best friend—the future queen of Unsel—and I'm in a hurry!" The last word came out a sharp yell that made everyone nearby jump. "You tricked us, kidnapped us, threatened my friends, and in spite of all this, I agreed to be your champion. What else do you want from me?"

Cold air steamed from his nose, and his armor suddenly felt so close, he wanted to rip it off before tearing Gose apart. Angst hadn't been aware of the power he'd summoned until sparks crackled from his glowing blue hands. He could barely see the Nordruaut through his blind rage, and considered making an example of this one. Tense moments passed, the only sound coming from his lightning and a gentle, cold breeze.

Aerella placed a hand delicately on his shoulder. "It's been a long trip," she said softly.

Angst was unsure if she said this for him, the Nordruaut, or everyone.

"He is not the enemy," she whispered softly in his ear.

Angst took deep, labored breaths as he released the gathering power. Cold air snuck into his armor, chilling the sheen of sweat brought on by the flash of anger. He nodded once, and Aerella patted his shoulder.

"You hold much power," Gose acknowledged hesitantly. "I would not wish to hunt you."

Angst couldn't help the half-smile that lifted his cheek. He almost chuckled, overwhelmed by a sort of giddiness from the sudden build-up and release of so much power. He muffled it as best he could; they needed to see him as strong, not crazy.

"You can be my warm-up, or my teammate." Angst set him free and held out his hand.

Gose looked around, his cheeks ruddy as he squeezed his hands into fists and let go several times. With a deep breath, he tried clasping forearms with Angst but Gose's hand enveloped his from elbow to fingertip. Angst choked down a whimper at the blow to his arm.

"I'll do it, Jarle," Angst said. "But it has to be soon. I have people who need me, yesterday. Let's get this done."

"This will make a fine story, Angst!" Jarle said proudly, slapping the back of his armor and making his spine pop.

"Hopefully it's a story about how the little guy beats up the giant," Angst said warily.

Every Nordruaut within earshot laughed in that guttural way, and Angst sighed through a forced grin. He really hadn't meant it as a joke.

"Can...can we talk?" Aerella asked, her voice quavering.

"Now?" Angst whispered from the corner of his mouth.

"Now," she replied firmly.

"I, uh, I need a place to meditate," Angst said to Jarle.

Jarle, who hadn't appeared surprised or offended by Angst's outburst, now looked at him like he'd just requested a last dinner of fish and custard. That thought made him realize how famished he was.

"It's a wielder thing," he lied through his teeth. "Aerella needs to help me prepare to be champion."

"Of course," Jarle said. "Nordruaut don't usually mate before battle, but I respect that. You can use my tent."

"What?" Faeoris snapped, her eyes bearing down on Angst.

Aerella shot her a wide-eyed glance that the Berfemmian may or may not have understood. Her shoulders settled, but she still seemed wary.

"Now what do I tell Heather?" Kala muttered to Scar.

"Thank you, skaadi," Aerella said with a bow of her head.

She didn't give Angst even a moment to defend her honor, looping an arm in his and dragging him to follow Jarle. They walked down the path where the snow eventually gave way to ground. Angst felt more than a little awkward about their supposed reason for sneaking away, but couldn't think of an explanation that didn't sound stupid.

The tent was large, and separated enough from the others that nobody would hear them talk, as long as she didn't start yelling at him. This mere tent was approximately the size of his house, except taller, much taller. The round exterior was protected by taut leather made from enormous animals. Jarle pulled back a doorway of heavy skins and nodded for them to enter like a good host. In the middle of the tent was a small fire, smoke billowing up through a hole in the center. It was otherwise sparsely appointed, with a small pile of weapons on one side, and a bed of furs on the other.

"I will send a messenger to the east that you will battle in two hours," Jarle said. "If that's enough time."

"It will be," Aerella said, pulling Angst into a hug. "Thank you."

Jarle winked at Angst as he let the leather curtain fall. The room became dark, and Aerella remained in his arms for several breaths.

"Kala is right. I really don't think Heather would approve of this," he said, jerking his head toward the furs.

355

"Good," she said, pushing him away. "Because neither would I."

"Well," he said. "If not the sex, what then?"

She rolled her eyes before they became stern. "What was that?"

"What was what?" he asked.

"I could sense the power you summoned," Aerella said, plopping on the furs near the fire. "That was enough to kill a dozen Nordruaut, not just Gose."

"Can't we go back to talking about sex?" he asked, wishing to avoid this conversation.

She patted the fur, encouraging him to sit. He wanted to take it as a cue to leave, but grudgingly removed Chryslaenor from his back and sat close enough to look at her without being too close. Sitting, and letting his guard down, allowed weariness to seep through. A nap sounded like a much better idea than a talk, and Heather would only be mildly irritated by them napping together. He needed his energy to save Ehrde, not to argue. She waited, and waited. He finally let loose a sigh.

"I'm frustrated, and Gose set me off," Angst explained. "The incredibly slow ride here, the constant worry that you were all in danger, that my friends are in that mage city, Heather being upset, and Tori... I got angry. I think I'm allowed to be frustrated after all of that."

"Yes, I agree," Aerella said, sounding more like a mom than the twenty-something she appeared to be. "But that's not why you were upset. Your anger came from losing Jintorich. You've been so certain this entire time that you can do anything, now that you're bonded with two swords. It must've been crushing to feel like you failed."

Her words were like a slap, with a giant icicle, and Angst reeled. He lay back and took several deep breaths, clenching his hands.

"And now this new challenge, that has nothing to do with the real reason we're here?" she asked.

"You're not helping," Angst said between huffs.

"I'm trying to make you understand that you're still human. In spite of all the power you wield, you still have limitations," she said softly. "Angst, even the elements have limitations."

"So, you're saying it *was* my fault. That my recklessness let Jintorich die?" he asked. The room was becoming blurry, and his eyes felt wet.

"No. I'm saying it wasn't your fault. I'm saying that Marissa dying wasn't your fault, either. I'm also saying that Kala sneaking with was not your fault," she said.

"And sleeping naked with Faeoris?" he asked.

"That was your fault," she said with a sigh. "But really, that's a great example. You're human. You don't always make good choices. Actually, you rarely make good choices."

"Not helping again," he said. "But I think I get it. You're saying that I believe I'm responsible for everyone else because I wield all this power, so I feel at fault when something goes wrong."

"You're smarter than you look," she teased.

"Thanks," he said, dryly. "So...it's not all my fault because I'm not all powerful so I shouldn't let it make me angry."

"But that wasn't anger you were experiencing when Gose threatened you, my friend," she said. "That was a blind rage."

She *was* right. Angst knew deep down that he'd almost lost control. He'd wielded an incredible amount of power, without even trying. But these Nordruaut didn't deserve to die. In spite of making Angst and his friends prisoners, they were as desperate to survive as he was to save...well, everyone. Angst felt fine, now, but that surge of anger, of rage, had pushed him to the edge of something he didn't want to revisit.

"Yes," he said, no longer justifying his actions.

"At this age, I don't know everything. When I'm older, I don't feel that I should tell you everything," Aerella began. "I've been traveling through years like a flat stone skipping across the ocean. I've spent more time with you than anyone. You're a good person, Angst, and a great hero. No matter how much you beat yourself up, you always try to do the right thing. A lot of people don't, and it speaks well of you."

"Thanks," Angst said, his cheeks warming.

"The rage isn't you," she said. "I believe it's something else."

"What do you mean?" he asked.

"You wield two," she said, her voice wary. "No human is supposed to wield two. I can't imagine the war that's happening inside your mind. Both foci fighting for the same space in you, it's unfathomable, and can come out in ways you won't be able to control."

"I only have one with me right now," Angst said.

"Which is probably why you're able to restrain yourself," she said. "But the battle inside has to be harder than the battle outside."

"Eh," he said, unwilling to agree, even if it might, maybe, be true. "What's your point? We could be napping."

She smiled, despite her worried frown. "I think I'm here for a reason. I believe you pulled me out of time because I could warn you."

"Of..."

"A choice," she said, sounding distant and staring off. "You are going to have two paths, Angst. One will save Ehrde, and the other will destroy it."

"Destroy Ehrde?" he asked.

"Not completely," she said. "But it will change into something unrecognizable, and everyone you care for will die if you choose that path."

"Okay," he said, frowning. "So how do I keep that from happening? Which path should I choose?"

"I can't answer that," she said.

"Can't, or won't?"

"Unfortunately, I don't know the specifics. I wasn't there," she said. "Something terrible happens. Something that triggers you to make a terrible decision, and that decision puts Ehrde into chaos for thousands of years."

"I'll try to avoid that," he joked. He could tell she wasn't joking, so he thought on it. "You're worried about my 'rage.' That the rage will take over, and drive me to make the wrong choice."

Aerella nodded, a sad look on her face. "I'm sorry I didn't do a better job of warning you not to wield both foci. I fear that you will lose control to their battle inside you. I don't want you to choose the wrong path when something out of your control happens."

"Okay," he said, pushing himself up to stand.

"What are you doing?" she asked.

"Well, you're not putting out," he said with a wink.

She shook her head.

"I need some fresh air, by myself, to think." He really needed out of here. "I do have a bad guy to fight, in ninety minutes or so."

"Of course," she said, also standing. "Will you think on what I've said?"

"You've made an impression," Angst said. "It's as clear as seeing through a thunderstorm, at night, in the ocean, surrounded by monsters..."

"I get it," she said with a wry smile.

"If something terrible happens," he said, "I'll try not to go crazy."

"Thank you," she said with a nod.

* * * *

"Is everything all right?" Jarle asked, apparently waiting creepily close to the tent.

"Sure," Angst said, and then wondered if he should provide an explanation. "Not really. She changed her mind."

"The way of women," he said, patting Angst's back more gently than ever. It only hurt a little. "That's good, though. Being angry will help with the coming battle."

"It usually does," Angst agreed with a sigh.

47

Angst wandered until the camp was mostly out of sight and dug out a place to sit in the deep snow. Setting Chryslaenor on its tip, he settled into his snowy throne and sulked. Nordruaut was a cold place, and his makeshift chair didn't help, but it was still good for pouting. The swords told him how to stay warm, but more than anything he wanted to be numb. Numb and alone to wallow in his worry. Minutes passed quickly before tall boots interrupted his staring. Faeoris had landed inches away.

"You don't look ready," she said, her eyes filled with concern and her lips tight. "If you give up now, he'll kill you."

"You're right," Angst said. She *was* right, he knew it in his head, but didn't feel like it mattered.

"You're going against another man with a foci, Angst." She sounded angry, but he sensed it was worry. "Aerella told me you could die, and not come back."

"Yeah, probably," he said with a sigh, poking at the snow with a stick.

"You're not even upset?" she said in frustration. "Do I need to try and kiss you again? That makes you upset!"

His laughter was wrapped in a sigh, but it was so much better than malaise. "That never upset me. I couldn't imagine a better compliment."

Faeoris tilted her head and frowned quizzically.

"I'll explain when this is over," Angst said. He was so grateful she was here, but Aerella's advice in the tent weighed heavily on him. She was right, he certainly wasn't unstoppable, even with two foci. No matter how hard he tried, Angst still felt guilty for failing. Not only for past mistakes, but the ones that hadn't happened yet.

"She said you're upset about Jintorich," she said, placing a hand on his shoulder.

"Yes," he said. "And Marissa, Moyra, Rook, Janda..."

"Kala, Maarja, me, Heather, your children, Victoria, and so many others need you," she said. "You deserve to mourn for the dead, but it's time to fight for the living."

"Yeah," he said, slowly dragging one foot out of his dark place as though it were sunk in wet clay. "I can do this. I'm actually not that worried about dumbass out there. It's the others. His giants outnumber our giants. What if Fire shows up to make another mess of things? While I'm killing him, who's going to protect you? Aerella's right. She was right all along. I can't save everyone. I need help, or a plan in the next ten minutes, or I'll be too distracted worrying that someone else will die. Just a tiny shred of hope, and I'll be able to focus. Give me something, and I'll be ready to throw down with Niihlu, Fire, and anyone else who wants to come and play."

She took a breath as if preparing to speak, but nothing came out.

He knew the feeling, and before either could say anything, the noisy crunching of feet on snow came toward them. Maarja, Aerella, Kala and Scar appeared. He'd asked Jarle to tell everyone he needed some alone time and wasn't really in the mood for more crappy pep talks. It was almost shocking to see broad smiles from everyone, especially Maarja. Were they drunk? That sounded like a good idea. Something hopped off the Nordruaut's shoulder, and Faeoris squealed, rushing toward them.

She bent over and scooped up a bundle that squeaked loudly. Angst would've recognized that squeak anywhere and leaped up from his seat to get a better look. Jintorich muttered something incomprehensible, his face squished into Faeoris's breasts as she hugged him in a death grip. Tears framed her eyes, and Angst's throat clenched. How was the Meldusian alive? Not that it mattered, but he had to know. Sometimes it felt like nothing good actually happened to him, and this might not be real. Jintorich's cheeks were becoming apple red, and Angst gently tugged at her arm.

"Don't break him," Angst said in wonder. "We just got him back."

Faeoris reluctantly set Jintorich down.

"Why do they all do that?" Jintorich squeaked.

"Because you're adorable!" Faeoris said with wide eyes.

"They don't do it to me," Angst said with a wink. "Consider yourself lucky."

Jintorich's flush subsided as he slowly sank into the deep snow. With a tiny grunt, he leaped up to Maarja's outstretched hand. Angst couldn't help but stare in wonder. He'd always avoided looking at the tiny man for too long, concerned it would be impolite to gawk, but something was different.

Jintorich's hair was now braided in delicate cornrows. Did Maarja do that? His eyes were now a deep blue like the sky before night instead of black. Had he lost weight? Was he a little taller? His ears seemed shorter, and less hairy.

"It's rude to stare," Maarja said defensively.

"Not this time," Jintorich said. "It's all right."

"I'm sorry," Angst said, moving closer. "But, is it really you?"

"It is, my friend," he said with a toothy smile.

"How?" Angst asked.

Jintorich glanced at Chryslaenor in the distance before holding his staff out. It was a tiny white toothpick that Angst feared would break if he picked it up.

"Yes," Angst said. "I see it."

Jintorich closed his eyes and lowered his head, shaking it. "Please, take it."

"I don't want it," Angst said, totally confused. "It's yours."

Jintorich's hand shook in frustration, so Angst reached out

and gently accepted the tiny weapon.

"*Maehtikyn*"

Angst gasped as the staff introduced itself with the music of a beautiful choir. Its great power resonated in his hand. Just holding it made him feel healthy and...happy. A foci! Jintorich had a foci, and he was alive, which meant...

"You're an Al'eyrn, like me!" he announced.

"Please don't make it your own, Angst." The Meldusian's voice was shaky. "Please don't bond with my foci."

"I would never take this from you. Never," Angst said firmly. "I would never intentionally try to kill a friend."

"Thank you," Jintorich said, tension leaving his tiny frame. He hopped off Maarja's hand and bounced to the giant sword, which towered over the Meldusian like a mountain. "May I?"

"Uh," Angst said, taken aback. "Of course."

Jintorich pressed the flat of Chryslaenor with his hand and scurried around to catch the hilt as it fell. Maarja rushed forward, and Angst winced in concern that the small man would be flattened. He wasn't. Jintorich lifted the blade as if it were light as feathers. He swung it about comically, making everyone chuckle.

"It's pretty big, Angst," Jintorich said as he rested the blade on the ground. With a grunt, he pushed the hilt upward, and it slowly rose to rest on its tip.

"And your foci is so small," Angst said. The foci had little to say, and little to share. It wasn't his, and he felt like he was meeting a friend's best friend. "How did you even find it?"

"It wasn't originally this size," he said, making his way toward Angst. "It became what I needed."

"I don't understand," Angst said in surprise.

"Maehtikyn was as large as your swords, at first, but when we bonded, it shrank to become usable. I theorize that the foci become whatever size you need," he said excitedly. "They compensate."

Maarja and Faeoris burst out laughing. Angst's cheeks warmed, and he looked to Aerella for solace. She turned away, covering her mouth.

"I don't understand," Kala said.

"Good," Angst said firmly, his cheeks and ears practically steaming. He wanted to bury his head in the snow. "I'm not sure it's completely accurate."

The women laughed louder, and Angst shook his head. He offered the tiny staff to the Meldusian. Jintorich smiled gratefully as he accepted the foci. Was the small man really so worried that Angst would steal it? He certainly didn't wield two by choice, and shuddered at the thought of bonding with a third. Angst nodded, urging Jintorich to continue.

"The Vex'kvette spread quickly across Meldusia, starting at a point in the north and reaching out everywhere like a spiderweb." He returned to Maarja's shoulder and sat down, resting Maehtikyn on his lap, petting it like a cat. "Our nation is large, like Nordruaut, and my people were spread across it in villages and towns. So many...so many were lost to the magic of the orange river."

Jintorich wearily placed a hand over his eyes. Maarja rested her cheek against him. He nodded and sighed.

"So many were dying, I didn't know what to do," he said. "I lived in the capital, the city farthest south. We, too, had a monument near our castle. It held this staff. The Vex'kvette was destroying everything in its path when I heard a song, felt a song, a calling, and I ran. I could also hear my people crying out. I had to fight my way through the orange goo. It was killing me, and I only barely made it. Even as I bonded, I began to change."

His breathing sped up, and he rested a hand on his chest. They were all respectfully silent, giving Jintorich time to regain his composure. Angst gritted his teeth in anger at the elements, especially Magic. Angst had watched animals die in the Vex'kvette. It was horrific. He'd also watched them change. It was a violation.

"I bonded, I lived," he said as he stood, looking down at his own body. "And I became this."

"I'm so sorry, my friend," Maarja said. She was visibly shaken.

Aerella was pale, her lips thinned and her eyes filled with pity. Faeoris seemed upset, both tearful and angry at the same time.

"What happened to your people?" Faeoris asked.

"They are no longer there," he said simply, his weighty brows dipping low. "But they are with me."

"All of them?" Maarja asked, her lip quivering.

He merely nodded.

"Why are you...different?" Angst asked. "When I die, I always come back looking like this...unfortunately."

"Stop it," Faeoris admonished.

"We are one," Jintorich said, pounding his chest with a tiny fist. "We are one of many."

"I don't understand that phrase," Angst said, struggling through his own frustration to grasp at a straw. "What do you mean, 'one of many'?"

Jintorich tried saying something but his face soured like he had bitten into a lemon laced with poison. After several moments, he gave up and shrugged. "That is all I can tell you."

Angst sought Aerella's eyes. She frowned, shaking her head. Kala held Scar close, the puppy licking her face excitedly. Maarja continued leaning her head against him, having no other way of showing affection to the small man.

"Thank you," Jintorich said, patting Maarja on her cheek.

"That's why you came to Unsel," Angst said, wondering now why he hadn't put it together sooner. He was always surprised at Jintorich's prowess on the battlefield. The little guy was just so little, but he packed such a wallop. He also seemed to retain an uncanny amount of knowledge, about everything. Healing, fixing armor, history. It explained a lot. "You came to ask me about being Al'eyrn."

"Yes, but there is something else," Jintorich said.

"Go ahead," Angst said.

"When you bonded with Chryslaenor, Angst," Jintorich began. "When you bonded with Dulgirgraut...did no one perish?"

"What?" Angst asked in surprise.

"Everyone around you," Jintorich continued. "When you bonded with your foci, did they live?"

"Well, yeah," he said. "I mean, there have been deaths, too many. But nobody died because I bonded. That usually happens after I'm done," he said darkly.

"Good," Jintorich said firmly.

More mystery than answers prompted Angst to seek Aerella's counsel again. If only his gaze could've drawn something from the future she visited. It would've been nice if Tori were here to gleam something off the Al'eyrn. Aerella continued to say nothing, pursing her lips tight.

"Is that all you wanted to know?" Angst asked

"There was one other thing," Jintorich said, scratching his chin. "Why didn't you pick it up sooner?"

"Pick what up?" Angst asked, distracted by his thoughts.

"Chryslaenor," he said. "You said all new employees of Unsel were hazed into lifting the sword. That they would become a knight if they held it aloft. You must've tried, when you were young. Why didn't you pick it up? Why didn't you bond with the foci then?"

"I...it..." Angst bit his tongue. It was a question he didn't want to answer. "It must not have been the right time."

"Timing is everything," Jintorich said wisely.

"Something my dad used to say," Angst said appreciatively. "And you're right, it is time. Jintorich, can you protect everyone in case things fall apart?"

"Indeed!"

"Then you're exactly the hope I needed."

48

Enurthen

Hector and Rose arrived at the library door three hours later. He clumsily dumped a large armful of equipment on the stairs then stood and watched Rose drag an enormous bag almost larger than her.

"Is that enough fruit and nuts for one meal, or do I need to go back for the other bags?" Hector asked sarcastically.

"He said he was hungry," Rose said, blushing furiously.

"You really do love him, don't you?" Hector asked.

"Shut up and take this bag, strong guy," Rose said, setting it on the ground as gently as she could.

"Woof," Hector said as he lifted the dense bag. "I didn't think those stick arms were that strong."

"Don't make me beat you up with them," she warned, leading him into the library.

Rose gasped as she walked through the door, and Hector dropped the bag of food. Dallow was lying over the table, heaving and gasping. Alloria stood above him, one hand on his shoulder and the other holding the dagger near his head.

"Get away from him, you felking bitch!" Rose roared as she ran toward them.

Hector sprinted past Rose, a longsword in both hands. He leaped up onto the table and pointed the blades at her head.

"Stop," Dallow gasped, lifting his head from the table. He sniffled and wiped tears from his cheeks, his voice was raspy. "Both of you, stop."

Alloria looked up at Hector's swords, both now inches from her eyes. For the moment, she looked sane, and...sad? More importantly, Dallow was alive and well. Hector lowered the blades and jumped off the desk, but didn't put them away.

"How did she get free?" Rose demanded.

"It was me," Dallow said. "I cut her loose."

"Why?" Rose asked, her hands balled up into fists. "She tried to kill us."

"She's been tortured by elements for months and dropped into one of the few places they can't enter," Dallow said, his voice tired and his face sincere. "It was a mistake, done out of desperation. Yes, she's broken, but she won't do it now."

"How do you know?" Rose snapped, her tone filled with venom.

"Because we'll all die if we stay here," he said softly. "And she claims to love Angst. I explained to her how upset killing us would make him, especially after what she did to Victoria."

"Oh, come on," Hector said, putting the swords away.

"You love Angst?" Rose rolled her eyes.

"He's always kept me safe," she said, her eyes slightly dilated. "I know he'll feel the same once he understands."

"You try to kill three of Angst's closest friends, and you think he's going to love you?" Hector couldn't even fathom the level of crazy she'd reached.

"We have a special bond. He's my champion." Alloria suddenly glared at them in a way Hector was familiar with. It was the ferocious gaze one might see from a mountain lion protecting her young, right before she ate you.

"Sure, whatever," Hector said dismissively, shaking his head. "Whether it's all true or just a bucket of crazy, why would that keep her from killing us?"

"And why were you crying?" Rose said softly.

"It will take a while to explain," Dallow said. "But it's the saddest story I've ever read."

"I knew reading too much could make you cry," Hector said. "I'm getting the food."

The daggers coming out of Rose's eyes may've actually killed the young princess had they made contact. Alloria avoided that gaze and led Dallow from the desk to sit on the floor. Rose followed closely, hate practically seething from her. Hector dragged over the bag and placed it in the center before plopping down. They took turns grabbing handfuls of nuts and berries out of the sack. Rose handed Dallow a flask of water, from which he drank deeply, before passing it to Alloria.

"Do you remember the story Jarle told us about the elements?" Dallow asked.

"I remember the storyteller," Rose said with a thin smile.

"Of course you do," Hector said dryly.

"The story is more or less true," Dallow continued. "Everything that Jarle, and Aerella have told us is confirmed in this library. The five elements go to war every two thousand years. Typically, they embody hosts that manipulate the races around Ehrde to fight for them. When the war is done, and the humans and other races are thinned out, there's a final, deciding battle.

"History states that Water usually wins, but sometimes it's Fire, and once in a while, Magic. When Water wins, Ehrde is mostly covered in ocean, like it is now. When Fire wins, it's horrific. When it's Magic, it's madness. Angst broke the cycle by killing Ivan the way he did. Ivan was Magic's host."

"Because Angst is so powerful," Alloria said wistfully.

"Because he doesn't know what he's doing," Rose said, rolling her eyes.

"With the help of the Mendahir, the wielders built these mage cities," Dallow said. "They were meant to offer protection from these wars, but in each situation, Magic manipulated all of them into cursing themselves. Azaktrha was buried in the ocean, Gressmore Towers was lost to time..."

"And Enurthen?" Hector asked.

"Someone cast a spell to destroy all who enter. The spell

worked." Dallow lowered his head, shaking it. "Slowly, almost methodically, everyone living in Enurthen was destroyed, having already 'entered' the mage city. What they experienced didn't translate well, but they just seemed to fade out over a long period of time. As far as I can tell, we haven't experienced the effects, but it will eventually happen to us too. The people of Enurthen didn't learn of this until it was too late."

"That's terrible," Rose said.

"It's worse," Dallow said. "This city, Enurthen, has been here for over four thousand years, maybe even six, and Magic was still able to trick them into self-destruction."

Hector wasn't hungry anymore, and returned his handful of lunch to the bag. "Is that all?"

"I didn't have time to go through every book," Dallow said, his shoulders slumping. "It would take a lifetime. An amazing, glorious lifetime. But I have learned some things. It's strictly forbidden to mess with time."

"I'll try not to," Hector said. "What else?"

"The Mendahir created the foci," Dallow said. "And no one should try bonding with more than one."

"Say that again?" Rose asked, her voice filled with concern.

"It shouldn't even be possible for a wielder to bond with two foci," Dallow said, his fingers pressed together and tapping his chin. "But doing so will drive the Al'eyrn mad. It's just too much power for one person. Eventually, it will drive Angst crazy, and then kill him."

"I can't imagine Angst being crazier than he is," Rose said with a thin smile, though her eyes were filled with worry.

Dallow coughed several times and took another draw of water. In spite of claiming to be hungry earlier, he hadn't eaten a thing.

"It could be one little thing, or maybe one big thing, that triggers it," Dallow explained. "But it will happen."

"We have to help him," Alloria said firmly, still shoving food into her mouth.

"And why are we letting you live?" Rose asked the young

woman. "Because you suddenly want to help Angst?"

"No," Dallow said. "I think the only way to save Victoria is with both halves of Jormbrinder. Since nobody else is bonded to the dagger, she's the only one who can remove it. This is just a theory, of course."

"But she stabbed you with the dagger too," Hector said. "How is it different?"

"She didn't leave it in my chest," Dallow explained. "Without Jormbrinder, and Alloria, the princess is dead."

"By the Dark Vivek," Hector swore.

"That's the last piece," Dallow said, pushing himself up to stand. "There is no Dark Vivek."

"Of course not," Rose almost spat. "It's a turn of phrase. There is no Vivek, or Dark Vivek. It's just something people say."

"Vivek may actually be someone, or something," Dallow said hesitantly, as if unsure he should correct Rose. "It's a greater force that we don't understand."

"Fine," Hector said, feeling uncomfortable in his own skin. "But why did you say there is no Dark Vivek. What difference does that make?"

"There is someone who calls himself Dark Vivek. He's the one who tortured me. He's the ageless bald man who tried bonding Chryslaenor to Rose," Alloria said, dismissively. She made a sucking face, pulled a half-eaten berry from her mouth, and threw it behind her. She looked up to notice everyone staring at her and tossed her head to one side. "He just calls himself the Vivek to confuse people, but usually he says he's the Dark Vivek to scare everyone. He's actually the element Magic."

* * * *

Eastern border of Unsel

"The Fulk'han remains have been burned," Commander Mirim reported, standing at attention with her helm tucked smartly beneath an arm. "I don't believe they'll live through that."

"You don't believe..." Captain Kyle asked, shaking his head.

"The appendages are no longer moving," she said, her dark forehead scrunching in concern. "But the fire turned orange, and the smoke was black. I've never seen anything like that."

"Understood," he said with a nod.

"No sign of the Fulk'han army?" Andec asked, grinding his teeth. There were too many unknowns that needed to be understood, and right now.

"We searched a twenty-mile radius," Kyle said. "Unless they ported directly to the castle, it's unlikely they're nearby. I sent a regiment of soldiers back to the capital just in case."

"Good plan, but I don't think they are headed to Unsel," Andec said.

"What makes you say that?" Kyle asked.

The wielders all turned to stare at Jace. The young man coughed uncomfortably and shuffled his feet.

"While the wielders were interrogating the remaining gray man, we discovered the Fulk'han plan to hunt down and capture Angst," Mirim stated. "They seem to be aware that he's not in Unsel."

"I still have a hard time believing they need all those soldiers to chase down one man," Kyle said.

"According to what I've heard," Andec said, "they killed Angst and locked him in a dungeon, and he escaped. I'd send more than a few soldiers after him."

"The gray man said something about a prize," Mirmim continued. "He called it 'Prendere' and said it was a weapon."

"Isn't Angst a weapon?" Kyle scratched his chin.

"Military," Nikkola scoffed. "Angst isn't a weapon. He's a person. A friend."

Captain Kyle rolled his eyes, looking to Mirim for relief.

"It was my impression that Prendere is something else. Something that could destroy Angst, or the rest of us," Mirim said. "They believe he knows where this weapon resides."

"That's good," Kyle said with a nod.

Nikkola shook her head with a disbelieving sigh, and Andec balled up his fists.

"It's good that they don't know where the weapon is," Kyle said defensively. "The last thing we want is for them to destroy Angst. My weapon, your friend, is needed by Unsel."

Tensions calmed, and Andec plopped down to sit. It wasn't completely on purpose; he felt that tired. The ground was freezing, and he longed for the blanket Commander Mirim had offered.

"Please, sit," Kyle said, his tone impatient.

"What?" he snapped huffily. "I'm old."

"How would they know where to find Angst?" Kyle asked, shaking his head.

"Fulk'han have been spotted along the border towns," Mirim said. "They may have seen him leaving."

"That crew would be hard to miss," Nikkola said. "The giant sword, a Nordruaut woman... you couldn't exactly hide them in wagons."

"Nobody would be that foolish," Kyle said thoughtfully.

Andec stood and paced, nudging people out of his way.

"What's this?" Kyle asked in a mocking tone. "I thought you were old."

"I was uncomfortable," Andec grumbled. "Something doesn't make sense."

"I'm pretty sure none of this makes sense," the captain said.

"Most of Unsel's forces were drawn to this battle that didn't happen," Commander Mirim said, her eyes on the old man. She paused and stared at him before continuing. "It would've made sense to lure us from the castle if they were going to port past us and attack, but they didn't."

"If there actually had been a fight, it would've been a massacre without the zyn'ight," Nikkola said, and then quickly followed that with, "No offense."

Kyle drew in a breath to retort.

"She's right, sir," Mirim said before he could speak. "The Fulk'han can survive almost anything, except maybe fire. Maybe."

"Fine," Kyle said. "If what you say is true, they're throwing a lot at an individual target. That entire army hunting down just one person. Drawing out our army..."

"And our zyn'ight, sir," Mirim said.

"Victoria," Andec said abruptly. He immediately began to summon his goat.

"What about the princess?" Mirim asked sharply, turning her entire body to face him.

"Wielders were taking turns guarding her chambers," Jace said, mounting his swifen. "Wilfred commanded us to come here."

"It will take my regiment the better part of a week to get there," Kyle said, his cheeks ruddy. "How long will it take you?"

"A day, maybe two," Andec said, reeling. He was very pale and seemed hesitant to mount.

Nikkola flashed Mirim a worried look, shaking her head.

"I'd like to accompany them, Captain," she said. "If these mounts can handle two people."

"They can," Jace said hopefully, patting a spot behind him.

Kyle nodded and walked to Andec. Without asking, she mounted the back of his goat and offered him a hand.

"I'm fine," he muttered, but took it and sat behind her.

"I'll steer if you keep it alive," she said. "We'll do this together."

"Just hurry," he said.

49

Nordruaut

Hope is an amazing force. Hard to capture, harder to keep, but far more powerful than hate or anger. Angst had always known this, and right now he felt it. The fact that Jintorich was alive fueled Angst's confidence. This kicked his distress hard enough to clear the foreboding darkness that had been overwhelming his thoughts. Their journey was far from over. By his calculations, they still had days to save Victoria. More than enough time to defeat this nimrod and find his friends. And, he didn't have to do this alone. Another Al'eyrn had his back. Jintorich would keep his new friends safe. Yeah, he had hope.

Unfortunately, he didn't have long legs. Snow drifts reached his thigh, making his journey across the battlefield less than heroic. Every step was a knee-high march, each more exhausting than the last. The gaps in the light and well-designed zyn'ight armor worked like tiny shovels, sucking in snow with every step. His proud charge to meet the eastern Nordruaut champion was initially accompanied by clapping, cheers, and the stomping of feet. Angst could only imagine that this trailed off to impatient sighs, eye rolling, and maybe even some snoring.

He mostly didn't care about the long haul, appreciating the hope more than begrudging the trek. And what should he do with that hope? That elusive gift had provided him with enough lift in his stride to traverse this thick ocean of snow, and distract-ed him enough to mostly ignore the cold—but what next? Blurring forward and effecting a humiliating defeat on Niihlu seemed like such a waste of this positive energy. He could let loose that fury buried deep inside, just as Aerella feared, but it seemed to counter what he felt. Angst had battled his way through this entire ordeal, and it just kept going. Maybe, just maybe, he'd been doing it wrong this entire time. And after twenty minutes of walking and thinking, he arrived with a fresh perspective.

Niihlu towered over him, though "tower" was an understate-ment. Angst never really gave much thought to being shorter than most men. What was the point? He couldn't do anything about it. His friends didn't care, and bullies bled no matter how tall they were. But this was different. Niihlu was just...really, really tall. This Nordruaut easily stood a head taller than Maarja, who could pick Angst up and throw him.

Where Chryslaenor "compensated" for Angst's height, the enormous war axe Niihlu held looked about the right size in the big man's grip. Angst was suddenly grateful for his sword's size, despite the uncomfortable teasing he had suffered.

"'Sup," Angst said between gasps, clouds of breath pouring from his mouth. "I see you finally got one of your own. Good for you."

"Huh?" Niihlu asked.

"Nice axe." Angst nodded at the thing.

It looked vicious. The long-handled battle axe rested in a mound of blue ice that looked like a tiny mountain. The curved blade was the size of Angst from head to knee, and it glowed an incandescent white. Ice formed around the handle, cracking off in brittle sheets to shatter on the blue mountain. Slush dripped from Niihlu's bare arm, and then his bare torso. His opponent grimaced through a shiver, was it from cold, or pain?

"I will destroy you with—" Niihlu began.

"One sec." Angst held up a hand, leaning over to catch his breath. "That was a long walk."

"You are weak!" he scoffed.

"No, I'm short," Angst replied. "Your thirty-second skip across the field was my six-day hike."

"I don't skip," Niihlu said.

"You should try it," Angst said.

"It's time to battle!" Niihlu cried, tearing the giant war axe from its icy stand and lifting it high.

"Not yet," Angst said, waving his hand dismissively. He was still breathing heavily, but his heart had slowed to a jog as cool air vented through his armor.

"What?" Niihlu asked in surprise. "Why do you delay? What is this?"

"Exactly," Angst said. "What on Ehrde are we doing?"

"We are champions, battling to decide who will lead Nordruaut, the east or the west," Niihlu explained. "And I will beat you—"

"No, no, I get why we're here," he said, pointing between the two of them. He then swung his arm in a wide arc, pointing all around. "Why are we *all* here? Niihlu, look at those Nordruaut. What do you see?"

"I see the western tribes," he said with sneer-laden glance over Angst's shoulder.

"And behind you?" Angst asked.

"I know who is behind me," Niihlu said, every word clipped with impatience.

"Don't be afraid. I'm not even holding my sword yet. Just look!" Angst said sharply.

Niihlu's gaze briefly flicked over his shoulder. He shook his head. "What is your point, human?"

"From here, they all look the same. That's because the Nordruaut are all one people," Angst snapped.

"You're trying to distract me," he said, wiping icicles from his confused face.

"I'm trying to save you," Angst replied.

"There is a war coming," Niihlu said, his voice uncertain.

"There doesn't have to be a war if nobody fights," Angst

pleaded.

"You're afraid to fight me," Niihlu said, rattling his axe.

"Do I look afraid?" Angst asked, slowly removing Chryslaenor from his back and setting it on its tip. "Shouldn't you ask yourself why? There can only be two reasons. Either I'm crazy, which I'm told is possible, or I hold so much power now that you wouldn't stand a chance."

Niihlu studied him for long moments, his constant leaking of ice slowing as he leaned forward and looked into Angst's eyes. Something about the enormous head within inches of his body made Angst steel himself. Now would be a bad time to show fear, and he repeated that in his mind over and over.

"You, me, Jarle, your leader...we can all sit down with some ale and figure this out," Angst said. "I could really use a drink or seven."

"Drinking does sound like a better idea," Niihlu agreed hesitantly. "But it would be shameful not to kill you, Angst. Nordruaut do not walk away from the challenge."

"There is no shame in peace," Angst said, reaching out with a hand.

"It will hurt," Niihlu said, holding up his palm.

"Less than the alternative," Angst said with smile, and the two men clasped arms.

It did hurt, a lot. Ice formed along Angst's forearm, and it felt like he'd shoved it into a frozen lake. The change that had overcome Niihlu from bonding with the axe wasn't right.

"I don't know that they will come to an agreement," Niihlu said.

"We can persuade them. These tend to help," Angst said, nodding at the sword.

"What's that?" Niihlu asked, gripping tighter to Angst's forearm. "What *is* that?"

There was a noisy pop in the distance that made them turn to look. A portal, larger than any Angst had seen, formed about a mile away. Hordes of creatures rushed through the black hole, charging toward the center of the battleground.

"It...it looks like a portal" Angst said, trying to tug his arm free.

"Did you do this?" Niihlu said.

"No," Angst replied. "I don't know what's going on."

Niihlu wouldn't let go, his face twisted with anger as he turned to him. Angst grasped for Chryslaenor, which was just out of reach.

"You lie!" Niihlu cried. "It's a trap!"

50

"What have these warmongering fools done now?" Jarle asked.

"It's a Fulk'han army being led by a giant creature," Faeoris said as she landed, her bright wings disappearing.

"I don't believe it," Aerella said, her eyes wide. "I don't think even an Al'eyrn could maintain a portal of that size to move so many. They had to be close."

"We receive scout reports every day," Gose said firmly. "There have been no armies within a hundred miles of this battlefield."

"No," Aerella gasped, reaching back shakily to lean against Maarja. "Magic. The element Magic had to bring them here."

"What do we do?" Maarja asked, placing several calming fingers on Aerella's small shoulder. "That monster is charging on Angst, and the Fulk'han army follows."

"We fight," Faeoris said, drawing her long sword. "We protect Angst!"

"We can't take the battlefield first," Jarle said firmly. "Not during a challenge. We would be in forfeit. Those are the rules."

"If we don't fight, Angst will die and you will lose!" Faeoris said, her cheeks flushed with anger.

"Skaadi," Jintorich squeaked respectfully. "Is that your army of Fulk'han?"

"No, Al'eyrn, it is not," Jarle answered.

"Then someone else has taken the battlefield first," the Meldusian said from Maarja's shoulder. "They could be working with the eastern Nordruaut."

Jarle stared at the army as it rushed forward. Clouds of snow billowed into the air around the Fulk'han, and the charge sounded like distant thunder. With the lightning that sparked around the portal, it looked like a storm had landed on the battlefield.

"Then we go to war," Jarle said darkly. He turned to Gose. "Tell our brothers and sisters that we take the field at my command. Ready the archers. I want them to draw the Fulk'han to us and away from Angst."

They clasped arms, looking into each other's eyes. Gose nodded and marched away, barking orders to the Nordruaut.

"What of Angst?" Jarle asked. "Can you help him?"

"With Jintorich's help, I can create a portal that will bring us to him," Aerella said.

"I am at your service," Jintorich said with a bow.

"I will stop the giant before you get there," Faeoris said, her wings appearing. She leaped into the air and flew toward the charging Fulk'han.

"Wait for the second volley of arrows!" Jarle called out after her. "Maarja, with me. We are going to hunt down King Rasaol and end this madness."

"I will stay with my friends," she said firmly. "Jintorich and I battle well together. We are a team."

"Fine, keep them safe," Jarle said. He hefted a pike the size of a small tree and held it aloft. "And let's end this war."

* * * *

Anger crashed through King Rasaol with every wave of Fulk'han soldiers that charged out of the enormous vertical hole. It looked like a cave mouth filled with dark swirling clouds. Yellow lightning leaped from the edges, striking the ground and kicking up snow. A giant beast with six enormous arms, a blotchy colored gorilla creature the size of ten Nordruaut, led the army.

"I knew the West couldn't be trusted!" Rasaol shook a fist in the air. "Jarle would rather fight his Nordruaut brothers and sisters than see the challenge through!"

"They have no honor," Dark Vivek said, placing a hand on the king's shoulder. "But it's not what you think."

"Where did you come from?" Rasaol asked, jerking his shoulder away. "And where have you been?"

The odd-looking man, who typically appeared ageless, now showed his years. His cheeks were sunken and his eyes drawn, as if the Dark Vivek hadn't eaten in a lifetime. He lowered his hand shakily and gasped in a short breath.

"I thought you were going to be here to help," Rasaol said. "To advise."

"Then pay attention while I advise." The tall man pointed to the dark circle. "Look."

The shadowy hole collapsed into itself until nothing remained. Rasaol's fear of the black hole was soon replaced by fear that a Fulk'han army had taken his battlefield.

"Your help is too late. I've seen what one gray man can do," Rasaol said, unable to keep the shaky edge from his voice.

They'd captured a gray man named Guldrich. After almost killing their champion, Niihlu, without a foci, he'd murdered a dozen Nordruaut and escaped. That was one man; this is an army.

"The Fulk'han aren't here to fight you," the Dark Vivek said. "They're here to help you."

"What?" Rasaol snapped. "After killing my people?"

"Would you rather have them as enemies, or allies?" the old man asked.

Rasaol nodded reluctantly as the militia of western Nordruaut charged the field.

"Angst will now have to battle two Al'eyrn," the Dark Vivek went on. "Your Niihlu, and the Fulk'han champion, Lurp."

"Why would they do this thing?" Rasaol asked, feeling helpless. "Why would they be our allies?"

"They are after knowledge that Angst holds," the old man said. "That is all you need to know."

Rasaol spun around and grasped the old man by the neck with two fingers, lifting his limp body high into the air. This advisor had done little to help his cause, providing the eastern Nordruaut with nothing more than a broken Al'eyrn. He was done being treated like a servant.

"Tell me!" he roared.

The Dark Vivek didn't fight his fearsome grip, his legs didn't kick, he merely hung on. He raised what would've been an eyebrow, had the man had any hair, and stared at the grasping hand in annoyance. Rasaol lowered him slowly and let go. The Dark Vivek angled his head to stretch out his neck.

"There is a prize they wish to win. It is called Prendere," he explained calmly. "Angst knows the location of the weapon. It has enough power to win this war, and he will give it to the West."

"The prize should be ours," Rasaol said with a grimace. "But how can we trust these creatures? I would feel better if they were dead. And how do we fight the wielders that travel with Angst?"

"I'll take care of his wielders," the Dark Vivek said. "And when the West is defeated, I will tell you the Fulk'hans' weakness."

"Yes," Rasaol said, the bloodlust flowing hot through his veins. "And then the prize will be ours!"

"Of course," Dark Vivek said with an indulgent smile. He snapped his fingers and was gone.

"And once the prize is mine, I will see an end to you," Rasaol said.

* * * *

Enurthen

The fifth time Dallow attempted his pronunciation of a word that sounded like "cornblower," Hector lost it. Frayed nerves, excitement to leave, and concern for his friends and what they were facing—all of it exploded out of him in a fit of laughter. Rose chuckled while Dallow faced forward irritably.

"You're not helping," Dallow snapped, swiping at perspiration on his forehead with the back of his sleeve.

"I'm not sure I could," Hector said, struggling to control himself. "I would've laughed the first time I said it!"

Dallow's thin lips curled into a reluctant smile. He walked over and placed a hand on Hector's shoulder. "I don't want to leave, either."

"What?" Hector asked in disbelief.

"It's been sort of...nice," Dallow continued. "No crazy monsters, no magical weapons, we aren't being hunted by anyone, all wrapped up in paradise."

"But we can't stay," Rose said.

"This city will kill us," Alloria said shakily.

"Yes, and I'd rather die out there than sitting around in here," Hector said, now calm. He looked at Dallow and Rose, wrapped up in their blanket armor. There was an odd feeling of warmth in his chest, one he barely recognized.

"As a soldier, I don't often let myself get close to people. Too many deaths, and grieving is a distraction. Maybe that's one of the reasons I'm often at odds with Angst. His heart is exposed to pretty much everyone, and mine is buried under layers. But for all our arguments, I would have to agree with what Tarness said. I'm glad we went on this adventure, and I did enjoy this time with you, my friends." He gave them both a brief, firm hug before stepping back and coughing uncomfortably into his fist.

"Speaking of Tarness, what do we do...you know..." Rose said, looking uncomfortable.

"We bring his body with," Dallow said darkly. "Angst should have the opportunity to say goodbye."

"Of course," Hector agreed with a nod.

"Can we just go?" Alloria asked with an impatient sigh, wrapping herself in a protective hug.

"One more word, and I'll bond with the dagger and jam it down your throat!" Rose snapped.

CHAPTER FIFTY

Alloria swallowed hard, tugging nervously at her honey-brown hair, but said nothing.

"It's time for another adventure," Hector said, placing a hand on Dallow's shoulder and walking him toward the barrier.

"It's time to leave," Rose said.

"You can do this," Hector encouraged, taking several steps back.

Dallow took in a deep breath, said the words, and the doorway opened just where it had been months ago. Hector expected to be blasted with freezing Nordruaut air, but the cold merely seeped in like a door had been cracked open. It was as if something blocked the wind, but Dallow merely looked satisfied, nodding to himself.

"Took you long enough," Tarness said, walking through the doorway. "I was getting bored waiting"

Hector drew two daggers, Alloria screamed, and Rose leaped forward. She wrapped her arms around as much of the enormous black man as she could. He patted her on the back with one large hand while reaching out with the other. Dallow and Hector stepped forward to join the embrace.

"I knew you'd make it," Rose said.

"What?" Hector said in surprise.

She stuck her tongue out at him.

"Do you people ever stop hugging?" Alloria asked.

"What's she doing here?" Tarness asked, his head cocked toward the bound girl.

"We figured there was a better chance that Angst would come looking for us if we had her nearby," Hector teased.

"Makes sense," Tarness said with a smirk. "I'm pretty sure she's why I'm here."

"Heh," Hector said with a grin. "It is good to see you! How did you survive?"

"I...I can't say," Tarness said, staring at the ground. He briefly looked at them all again and grimaced out a smile. "I can't say right now. We don't have time. Angst needs us!"

"What has he done now?" Rose asked, shaking her head.

"Niihlu is an Al'eyrn, Angst is going to fight him, and the entire Fulk'han nation just showed up through a portal."

"Angst doesn't mess around," Rose said in disbelief.

"A portal, for that many?" Dallow asked. "How—"

"No," Alloria said, tugging on Hector's sleeve. "No. It's the monster. The element Magic brought the Fulk'han with their monster, Lurp. He'll kill Angst. We have to go now!"

"I guess we're crashing a party," Tarness said with a grin.

51

Nordruaut

Angst hung by one arm in Niihlu's icy grasp. How long would it take to freeze completely and break off? Chryslaenor was so infuriatingly close that lightning hopped from the sword to his reaching fingers. A steady thunder boomed around them, growing ever louder. An army approached, but with greater speed than humanly possible.

"What is that?" Niihlu asked in alarm, whirling Angst about to face them. He pointed at something large in the center, approaching faster than everything else. "What did you bring here?"

From elements to giant Ivans, Angst had faced a lot of larger-than-life threats. There was something nightmarish about any creature that grew to the size of a small tree. He'd gone toe-to-toe with things that made the Nordruaut seem as small as Angst on his first day of school. The existence of these creatures, any of them, didn't make sense. Sense would be giants that moved slowly, but this thing, this behemoth galloping toward them on six legs, hurtled forward. It didn't blur around like Angst could, but it was like a boulder rolling down a mountain.

"Let me go!" Angst shouted. The song from Chryslaenor blared through his head, a staccato of sound that raced his own heart. "We need to defend ourselves!"

Niihlu just stared like a cat facing a mirror, in awe of this force of nature that would inevitably overtake them. The Nordruaut had hunted creatures along the Vex'kvette. He'd seen monsters, but had likely never faced elements. Angst had felt the same sense of awe and fright during that first battle with the one-eyed creature who'd abducted Rose.

Something about that thing running toward them reminded Angst of the fight with the one-eyed monster. It had been a messy win, and after, Hector had told him to stop trying to brawl, to use the sword and magic. Chryslaenor's song virtually sang "yes," and Angst listened.

Angst couldn't get Niihlu's attention, and breaking free might break his arm, which was now mostly numb and covered in ice. Niihlu was practically made of ice himself, and would probably let go if he was burned. There was no wood...but Angst didn't need wood. He'd made fire from nothing when sitting on top of that mountain with Faeoris. How much could he make?

He knew the spell, but needed fuel to make it more effective and something to help him focus. Earlier, Angst had been filled with so much hope, he'd almost—accidentally—done something peaceful by offering Niihlu a truce. Now that pandemonium had broken out, he was feeling irritated and helpless—not the best source of power. Challenging roars surrounded them from all sides as Nordruaut from the east and west took to the field. Chaos approached fast on many, large legs.

Bright, colorful lights dove at the large creature, slowing its approach. Faeoris! As always, just what he needed.

Angst focused on the spell, straining to draw in enough power to summon a lot of fire from nothing. Faeoris flew around the creature, weaving in and out of his swings like a hummingbird. It stopped, rearing up on two...arms? She swooped low, and it batted her away like a gnat. The Berfemmian was thrown high into the air, soaring in a long arc until landing in the snow, unmoving. "Faeoris!" Angst shouted.

Fire exploded before them, throwing Niihlu off his feet and freeing Angst from the Nordruaut's hold. Angst landed in the snow, and stared in surprise at the ten-foot-wide orb of flame he'd created. It wasn't what he'd intended to cast. It was more like the fireball he'd thrown at Water on the ocean, but stationary, and hovering. There was no time to figure it out. Angst rushed to his sword and hefted Chryslaenor high.

Niihlu looked like a melting snowman, taking panicked steps away from the fire as the icy sheath that covered his body steamed. He screamed in pain, stumbling back through the thawing snow. The fire blazed like a desert summer; snow around it pooled into a boiling pond beneath the ball. It had been the distraction Angst needed to free himself, but it was too much. The ball of light was slowly growing, but before he could ask the swords how to stop it, the ground began to shake.

"Now what?" he said, turning away from his fiery creation.

"Lurp!" the monster roared as it launched himself high into the air, blocking Angst's view of the sky.

* * * *

"Jintorich, I need you to come down and hold my hand," Aerella said, beckoning him off Maarja's shoulder. "I'm going to cast the spell to create a portal, but you'll need to fuel it."

"I can help," Kala said nervously, practically petting the hair off Scar.

"I know you can," Aerella said impatiently. "But I can't make a portal large enough for Scar at his full size, and it wouldn't be safe for you to be in the middle of that battle without his protection."

"I'll make my own portal," Kala said with a pout.

Aerella hadn't considered this. The child may have had the ability to duplicate spells, but she didn't have the strength to back them for long. The stress of it would probably kill her, or she would get stuck trying to go through and die in the process. She shuddered at the thought.

"Please, Kala," Aerella said. "The spell could kill you."

"Angst needs Scar," she argued.

"Angst needs Scar to keep you safe," Aerella said with a gentle smile. "Which is why he's staying right by your side."

The girl crossed her arms and stared off at the distant battle.

"Promise me you'll stay out of that fight," Aerella pleaded.

"Fine," the girl said in a tiny voice. "I promise."

"You look tired," Jintorich squeaked, still perched on Maarja's shoulder. "I'm having a hard time discerning your age."

"I am tired, but I sense that I'm in my forties." Aerella sighed deeply. "At this age, I knew the important spells and had the power to cast them."

"So you can control your age now?" Maarja asked. "That would be nice."

"No, my age is fluctuating fast. I'm not sure I have much time here, or should I say now," Aerella said. "I don't think I'll be staying much longer, either way."

"I don't understand," Kala said, taking her hand. "Are you going to die?"

"I believe I have one more adventure," Aerella said, kneeling to give her a hug. "So no, I'm not dying. But ever since I arrived, the more I wield magic, the more my age fluctuates. I can't choose my age, but I'm trying to hold onto this one for now."

"I bet Angst would like to do that," Kala said.

"Angst needs to worry less about his age and spend more time enjoying his years," she said. "I've certainly enjoyed all of mine, and this adventure with you has been one of my favorites. Unfortunately, I don't belong here anymore."

"That's what I said the last time I dismissed you," a tall, odd-looking man said as he appeared before them, waving an arm in a wide arc.

Everyone within view stopped moving. She could see and breathe, but her muscles were locked in place. It was like those moments between time, and between places, when she waited for the next unknown adventure. It was maddening, and she desperately tried to think of a spell that could free them.

"Don't bother," he said. "I'm no mere wielder, and you aren't

Al'eyrn."

Magic, she thought, her heart racing. In all her years skipping through time, she'd never faced an actual element without Angst. She didn't have the words to express her awe, or the breath to ask the millions of questions that came to mind.

Magic, the Dark Vivek, stood on the snow as though it were solid ground. He walked past each of them in their frozen prison, his arms down and hands clasped behind his back pretentiously.

"I'm returning you to timeless space," he said with a nod to Aerella. He approached Kala and Scar, placing a hand on the girl's head. "Having trouble growing, pup? When this is done, I'll make you mine again. And you, child, would make an excellent host, much better than Ivan."

Kala's young face was frozen in concentration as she took in everything around Magic, but never stared directly at him.

"Huh," he said dismissively. Magic stopped directly in front of Maarja and looked up. "I'm throwing you and your little morsel through a portal right into the middle of battle."

"I like your spells," Kala said from behind him. The twelve-year-old girl had broken free of the magical constraints and was now standing on top of a snow bank. "This is one I learned from my friend Angst."

A burst of blue lightning shot out from her two extended arms, slamming into Magic and throwing him through a deep bank of snow. His control released, Aerella gasped for breath, and had just enough time to create an air shield. Magic crawled out, black smoke rising from his chest where the lightning had struck. His eyes were wide with surprise, and his face contorted in a grimace.

"You dare..." he spat out.

"We dare," Aerella said, a blinding glow of yellow surrounding her hands, which shook from the force she held, ready to let loose.

Magic looked up from his hands and knees, and Aerella followed his gaze over her shoulder. Directly behind her, Maarja raised two giant fists while tiny Jintorich stood by her cheek.

Hovering over all stood Scar the giant dog, covered in steel, and six eyes glowing red. Kala peeked over the top of Scar's head, the blue lightning in her hand reflecting off Scar's steel fur. Magic burst out in laughter, pointing and laughing uncontrollably as if they were ants on the march. Jintorich leaped from Maarja's shoulder and cracked Magic in the head. White light flashed on contact, knocking Magic deep into the snow and far into the earth beneath.

"Not another Al'eyrn!" Magic wheezed from the bottom of the newly formed crater.

52

The creature's impact drove Angst deep into the snow. The tiny space was cold and dark like a cave, and there were already cracks in his air shield, which was barely large enough to cover him and his sword. How was that even possible? What was this thing that had smacked Faeoris away like a fly and could break an air shield created by an Al'eyrn bonded with two foci? Chryslaenor didn't know, and Dulgirgraut was almost too far away to hear. The shield wouldn't last long, and he needed out; he was getting a quick lesson in claustrophobia.

There was a muffled roar that sounded like "Lurp" again. What on Ehrde was a Lurp? Delicious sunlight reached his shield, revealing a cobweb of cracks; his protection was a sneeze away from shattering. With a weary sigh, Angst crawled out of his snowy crater to a vision of madness.

In an almost perfect one-hundred-yard circle, Nordruaut battled Nordruaut battled Fulk'han. The latter had apparently arrived through the portal. But how had they found this place, which had to be labeled "Middle of felking frozen nowhere" on every map? Arrows whistled angrily overhead, staves cracked upside heads, swords rang as they clashed. All around him, war wailed its ugly cry.

The ball of fire still burned and was even larger. He wondered if that was what had forced the attacker away, but his curiosity faded almost instantly. Niihlu's own battle cry pierced his ears.

The Nordruaut stumbled forward, striking down, his frosty axe slicing deep into the giant monster's shoulder. The creature roared in pain as ice immediately formed around the wound, coating the mottled black and white skin.

"Lurp," the beast roared, backhanding Niihlu.

Niihlu flew back, retaining a hold on his axe and tearing it free before crashing into Angst. He rolled until he could stand, finding himself in the middle of both giant and monster. Niihlu sprang up, and the two circled Angst at opposite ends. He held out a hand to warn off Niihlu, and kept his sword aimed at the moving house.

"We don't have to do this," Angst said, struggling to contain the quaver in his voice. "I'm tired of killing."

"I'm not," Niihlu said, wiping slush from his chin. Part of his face was covered in hard, blue ice, like a bandage over a wound.

"Lurp," the creature shouted, rearing back on two arms and beating its hairy chest with the other four. Apparently, it had six arms, as large as graymowl tree trunks, but no legs. Right.

Angst felt irritable. This was going to end badly, for him. These animals wanted to fight, and he was stuck in the middle, when he should've been checking on Faeoris and finding his friends. He knew the quickest way to stop this. It was an old trick he was very comfortable with. He willed magic into the ground and reached up to their bones.

"What is this?" Niihlu asked, looking down at his legs.

"Rawr?" Lurp blurted.

"I'm going to step away," Angst said cautiously, now that both were anchored to the ground. "When I'm gone, you two can work out your differences." He took slow steps back, watching them struggle in place.

"I'm...not...done..." Niihlu said, shakily lifting a foot and stepping toward Angst.

The Nordruaut forced his other leg forward, and for the first time, that old trick fell apart. Something about it made sense. Even as broken as Niihlu was, he was Al'eyrn, and his foci would've taught him how to escape. Fortunately, "Lurp" was only a Vex'kvette monster...who was also freeing himself.

"Oh, come on!" Angst said, as realization struck him like food poisoning. Lurp had to be Al'eyrn too, born of the Vex'kvette and bonded to a foci. They weren't going to give up, and Angst wasn't going to be able to sneak away and find Faeoris. He'd have to fight his way through, like always. "Fine then. It's on!"

* * * *

"Is this her?" a gravelly voice asked, his hot breath tickling her ear. His voice was filled with wonder. "The Berfemmian you were telling me about?"

Faeoris moaned as he rolled her over, exposing her cheek and ribs, still throbbing from the giant's swat. Her face was wet and warm, and she couldn't open her eye, which ached. Her entire side felt like she'd flown into a tree. She struggled to draw a full breath. What was that thing? Angst needed her help, now! They needed to end this so she could go drink booze, and heal, and drink more booze.

"I'm surprised she lived through Lurp's attack," he said over his shoulder. His eyes widened in surprise beneath the bone mask as he stood upright, looking around. "Felicia! That bitch is always disappearing when I need her. If she's not helping to destroy Angst..."

"Angst," Faeoris wheezed, reaching up.

"Oh, you're one of his," he said, kneeling down to grasp her throat. "I am Guldrich, and now you will be mine."

The world that had just started coming into focus was now hazy with spots. This creature was fiercely strong, his hold like a steel collar.

"This little war will end quickly. I've seen the Nordruaut savages fight, and despite all their great strength, they are not warriors. Angst can't defend himself against two Al'eyrn, and you've already experienced Lurp's strength and speed. Once Lurp softens them up, I will kill the Nordruaut champion."

He released his grip, and she coughed, gasping for breath.
The sadist was enjoying this; there was a gleam in his eye as he
thoughtfully looked at his hand. He stretched out his fingers and
balled them into a fist.

"The Nordruaut Al'eyrn cut this arm off. I will enjoy killing
him with it." Guldrich glared down at Faeoris. "I won't kill
Angst right away. After I defeat him on the battlefield, I will
take him as prisoner and break him, over and over. He will beg
to tell me how to find Prendere, the prize that will end this war.
When all is done, and Angst has witnessed his failure, only then
will I kill him."

Faeoris rolled over to all fours and began to push herself up.
She wasn't fast enough. Guldrich's bony foot lodged in her sore
ribs as he kicked her with a satisfied grunt. She flipped over as
she flew into the air, and he smashed down on her chest with
two fists, driving her into the hard-packed snow.

"I hear Berfemmian are quite strong," he said gruffly, stomping on her stomach. "It's a shame you are so damaged. I would
have enjoyed our battle. But now I'll just take you as my pet.
I've always wanted a bird of my own."

This Fulk'han wasn't just an enemy, he was an animal. His
words were madness that made fury flow through her veins. She
had never been so offended, so furious in all her life. Guldrich
raised his foot over her face and stomped down. She grabbed his
foot, twisted to her side, and slammed him to the snow.

"I am no pet bird," Faeoris said, standing over him and spitting a glob of blood in his face. Bright wings of orange, red, and
yellow flared over her shoulders. "I have no time for fools, my
friend needs me. When I'm done helping him, I'm coming back
to rip you apart!"

Before she could launch into the air, Guldrich grabbed her
ankle and jerked back with a twist. Faeoris screamed as something in her knee snapped. He rolled, pulling her with him. The
pain in her knee almost made her black out, but Angst needed
her, and she wouldn't fail him. They rolled together over and
over until he ended up on top and smashed his fist into her face.

Guldrich reared back to do it again, and she reached forward, grabbing his hand. She grasped the inside of his shoulder with her other hand, and with all her might and fierce determination, pulled.

She didn't stop pulling. He wailed in pain as muscles tore and tendons snapped. There was a noisy crack as his bony exterior gave way and she ripped his arm free. The Fulk'han fell onto his back, crying out in pain and gripping the empty socket of his shoulder. Blood darkened the snow, spoiling it like bruises on fruit. Faeoris stood and threw the wiggling arm to the ground in disgust.

Even before she had time to take flight, tendrils reached out from his shoulder. Red, fibrous ropes crawled across the snow until they reached the distant arm. In a blink and a gasp, the arm returned to its socket and he wiggled his fingers.

"Ewww!" she cried out. "What *are* you?"

The Fulk'han's laughter sounded like the choppy grating of stones. "Don't you see? We can't be killed!" He sat up and glared at her. "You *can* be, pet."

Angst would be fine, she believed in him, and this would only take minutes. She launched forward and grabbed Guldrich's hand, placing a foot against his chest and pulled. Guldrich cried out in pain as she tore the arm free once again. She smashed his head with the arm over and over, jerking it free any time it started to reattach itself. She stopped when he finally lay still, the bone armor gone from his face, and his eyes wide with confusion. Faeoris threw the arm far away.

"Let's see if you can live through this" Faeoris snarled, grasping his leg. She pulled.

* * * *

It was slow going along the edge of the cliff, even on the swifen. This snow hadn't been touched in ages and was waist deep. Horses wouldn't have lived through this, and Hector was once again grateful for their swifen. He led them while assessing

397

the battle four-hundred-ish yards away. His heart pounded in anticipation. The battle had gone on for too long, and Angst appeared to be losing. After far too many years on the battlefield, Hector had seen this time and time again. Honestly, Angst shouldn't have lasted this long against those odds, and he felt a pinch of pride beneath a shadow of panic. Angst was going to die.

"Faster!" Hector shouted. "He can't do this alone!"

"How can you see that far?" Rose asked.

"I just can!" Hector growled. This was not the time to discuss his skills.

"What do you see?" Dallow asked.

"Angst is trying to fight two...somethings," he called back over his shoulder. "A Nordruaut with an enormous icy axe..."

"Ghorjfend," Dallow said, his voice quavering. "It's a foci...he's fighting another Al'eyrn!"

"Great," Hector said, deadpan. "The other thing is just huge. A Vex'kvette monster with six arms, looks like an ape, holding its own against both of them."

"How is that possible?" Tarness asked.

"Lurp is Al'eyrn too. Magic said so," Alloria said. "We need to help Angst!"

"Tarness, how much longer will this take?" Dallow asked.

"It's just too much. I won't do this!" Tarness cried out, his fists pressed hard against his temples.

"What are you talking about?" Rose asked, shuffling her swifen over to place a comforting hand on his leg.

Tarness was practically hyperventilating, steam blasting out of his nose like a teapot ready to boil.

"Can you hold on?" Hector said. "Just a little longer?"

"We need to talk," Tarness said with a nod, his thick brows furrowing. "But it can wait."

"Tarness, you look angry," Hector said hopefully.

"You don't even know. What I've been through these last three months..." Tarness said with a grimace. "I'm...absolutely...furious!"

"Stop," Hector said, willing his panther swifen to a halt. He didn't know what was making his friend so upset, other than the thought of Angst dying, but that anger brought Tarness great strength.

"How's your aim?" Hector asked.

"I can hit a deer with an arrow from two-hundred-and-fifty yards," Tarness said.

"That'll do," Hector said. "Throw me."

"What?" everyone asked simultaneously.

"Even if Tarness can get you there..." Dallow began.

Tarness grunted.

"...and I know you can," Dallow went on quickly, "how will you survive that fall?"

"I've got this!" Hector said, drawing two long swords.

"Now you sound like Angst," Rose said, a bundle of shiver and worry.

"I believe in Angst," he said. "Let's give him what he needs to win."

Rose kissed him on a cheek. Hector turned and planted a full kiss on her lips. She didn't pull back. When they were done, he winked.

"This will be the best story," he said.

Hector hopped onto Tarness's outstretched hand with one foot and crouched low.

"Let your aim be true," Hector said.

53

Angst was one swing away from death. While the other two Al'eyrn didn't move in blurs like he did, they were fast as a sucker punch. Lurp's four tree-trunk arms came from all directions or all at once. Niihlu's strikes were viper-quick and strong like bull. It was less like a dance, and more like dodging arrows—angry arrows made from frostbite and boulders. Angst got short breaks, more like breaths, when Lurp and Niihlu attacked each other before remembering he was there. In the middle. Fighting for his life.

From a distance, it must've appeared that Angst knew what he was doing. He blocked Lurp's four-armed attacks with another air shield that shattered on contact. Simultaneously, Angst deflected the large icy battle axe with Chryslaenor. But he knew the awful truth. The only thing keeping him so barely alive was being bonded with two foci, and he only had one with him.

"Lurp!" the monster shouted.

"Oh shut up!" Angst cried, spinning wildly, his sword bouncing off two of the arms as if he were swinging a stick.

Niihlu launched toward him, leaping into the air with his blade raised high, ready to chop down. Angst had less than a second to recover from his failed blow at Lurp. Reeling from Chryslaenor bounce, he spun about to smack the Nordruaut with the flat of his blade. The strike vibrated painfully and hurt Angst to the bone, but Niihlu flew back, landing near the fiery orb. He

400

screamed and rolled away, giving Angst time to face Lurp.

The monster had too many arms and they all hit way too hard. Lurp struck the ground with four arms, making the ground shake and the remaining snow billow. Despite Lurp's great speed, Angst was faster. He blurred toward the closest arm and roared as he swung at the creature's wrist as hard as he could. Lurp wasn't quick enough to pull back. With a sloppy crunch, Angst sliced off his hand. Lurp stood on his two back arms and stared at the stump as gore poured out. He whimpered pathetically.

Fortunately, Niihlu was stupid and announced his approach with an ear-piercing battle cry. The warning gave Angst enough time to gather his strength and bat him away again. Niihlu flew several hundred yards, bowling over a bevy of Nordruaut warriors. For a second, Angst wondered if he was actually doing this. Was he going to beat down two Al'eyrn? He spun about to see Lurp pick up his hand with a confused expression. Under other circumstances, it would've been funny. Lurp held it to the stump, his eyes thinned with focus. Skin and sinew from the arm and hand sought each other like oil connecting in water. Angst sighed—of course it couldn't be this easy. Lurp wriggled his fingers, looked at Angst, and roared in fury.

It was the attack of a maddened gorilla, random strikes from four muscular arms pounding down like a landslide. Angst struck one with his sword, deflected the second with an air shield, parried the third with Chryslaenor, and was crushed by the fourth.

He was knocked to the snow, his sword thrown inches from his hand. Niihlu arrived in time to lodge his axe into the beast. Lurp lifted his freezing arm along with Niihlu, while placing a confining hand on Angst's legs. The giant slammed the Nordruaut into the ground beside him, and Ghorfjend landed across Angst's chest.

Songs. Music from Chryslaenor and Dulgirgraut rang through his head with spells that were blurry nonsense through the cold that seeped into him from the foci. He was conscious but could only lift his head and try blowing futilely at the creeping frost that reached for his neck.

Lurp reared back as if stung and roared in pain, freeing his hold on Angst and Niihlu.

Angst's vision was spotty, blurring in and out of focus. Niilhu pulled the freezing axe from his chest as he stood. Angst rolled over with a wheeze and grasped Chryslaenor. Something unexpected had happened, and that something was a miracle because Angst should've been dead. He pushed himself up to watch a man in dark leathers crash into Niihlu's face with two feet. His hero, his savior...his mentor? Hector bounced off the Nordruaut and landed lithely beside Angst.

"What are you doing here?" Angst said in between strained gasps. "I came to save you!"

"Funny," Hector said, his eyes wild and hungry for battle. "I came to save *you*!"

"Sounds like we'll save each other," Angst said, hope swelling in his chest once again.

"Just keep mind of those six arms, he's got a lot of power, and..."

"Hector, I've got this," Angst said with a smirk.

Hector rolled his eyes.

"What's that?" Hector asked, nodding at the ball of fire that was now the size of Angst's home.

"Leftovers. I'll fix it later," Angst said. They were now back to back as Lurp and Niihlu circled. "The others?"

"All safe," Hector said. "We made it."

"Let's finish this and go save the princess," Angst said.

"The queen," Hector corrected. "You get the big guy. I'll take the little one."

Angst almost burst out laughing since the "little one" was almost three times their size. Hector was the break he'd needed, the breath he'd needed to catch, and Angst blurred forward. With a grunt, Angst lopped off Lurp's hand again and rushed forward to remove another. The creature rose on its haunches, crying out in pain. Angst batted hands aside and sliced along his opponent's stomach, blurring away from the guts that poured out.

It gave him just enough time to check on Hector, who was holding his own. Niihlu may have been made an Al'eyrn, and was definitely a worthy opponent, but he wasn't a seasoned warrior. His friend took full advantage of this, leaping up to slice across the Nordruaut's forehead. Instead of blood pouring over Niihlu's eyes, a sheet of ice formed like a frozen waterfall that hardened to a thick blue mask. Even while Niihlu clawed at the ice, Hector slashed quickly across his midriff, shoulder, and hand.

"Hurry, Angst," Hector shouted. "I can only hold him off! Take out the giant then kill this one."

"Right," Angst said, turning to face Lurp.

A giant hand grasped Angst, slamming him to the ground again and again as if trying to crack open a coconut on stone. Lurp let go as Hector drove a sword into that forearm. He helped Angst up.

"Concentrate," Hector admonished.

"Behind you!" Angst shouted.

* * * *

Unsel

Andec led the zyn'ight through the castle gates at a gallop, waving away shouting guards like dismissing flies. He didn't have time, and really didn't have the energy to stop and explain their urgency. The wielders rode their menagerie of swifen through the castle entrance and along the main hallway.

He should've fallen off his mount during the long ride to the castle, but Commander Mirim kept him anchored and guilt kept him awake. It was as much his fault as Wilfred's that they'd left the princess unattended, especially after Angst had asked. They'd been drawn away like a bunch of amateurs. He was no tactician, but looking back at how easily they'd been led from the castle made him push harder than he should've.

When they reached the entrance to the royal hallway, Andec

cursed his age and frailty as he shook with exhaustion. Mirim helped him dismount while Nikkola grabbed his arm to provide stability on the ground. The younger woman appeared haggard, her black hair a tousled mass and her teeth gleaming white through caked dirt on her face. Andec stopped to take several deep breaths and look around. The other zyn'ight didn't seem any better off than he felt. They looked like they'd been dragged behind their swifen instead of riding the beasts. He patted Nikkola's hand thankfully, and dismissively.

"Nothing like ... a brisk ride ... to keep you sharp." Andec gasped between words. He couldn't catch his breath, and the sharp pains in his chest made him wonder if he ever would.

They laughed or chuckled, and something about this gave him strength. Finally, someone got his sense of humor. It was enough to make him fight through creaky bones and strained muscles and stand up straight. He wiped away thin wisps of sweaty hair and desperately hoped his heart would hold out just a little longer.

"What's up there, boss?" Jackson asked, her eyes fixed in a grimace from the long ride.

"We just faced down an army," he said with a wink. "Can't be much worse."

More chuckles.

"Please stop!" a man's tired voice carried from the royal hallway. "Don't do this, son. It's not too late to stop."

"Stay sharp," Andec said waving them to follow. "Let's go."

Stairs shouldn't exist some days, and there should never be more than two or three when you're exhausted. Not to mention, whose idea was it to put wielders in armor? After an eternity of climbing two flights of the cursed things, wearing too many layers of protection, Andec and the zyn'ight arrived. He shoved through a mass of soldiers to see Wilfred the Wise standing before the main hall entrance. A nudge away lay the withered remains of two soldiers, looking more like they'd been dug from an old grave than young men on duty.

"Stand back," a soldier snapped, grasping his arm. "It's a

trap!"

"I can see that," Andec said sharply. "If you don't let go now, I will magic you in there before you breathe another word."

"Hold," Wilfred said, staring down the soldier, who immediately let go. "They're here to help."

"What happened?" Nikkola asked. "Why aren't you in there with the princess?"

"My son, Mika," an older man said. "We thought he was on guard, and this whole time..."

"Ranson's son can manipulate time," Wilfred said. "Anyone who enters dies of old age."

Mika was on his knees in the hallway, facing Victoria's bedroom. He slapped at an invisible barrier, crying out in pain with every strike. Blood splattered every time his hand hit the barrier, covering his clothes and pooling on the ground.

"He looks exhausted," Andec said. "Maybe he let the trap go. Are you sure you can't enter?"

Ranson held up a hand that was too old to be his, covered in spots with grotesquely long nails.

"Let's see if we can wear him down some more," Andec said, moving away from the entrance. "Everyone back."

Wilfred nodded, waving the mass of soldiers down the stairs.

"Zyn'ight," he said pointing forward. "Attack that barrier!"

Bolts of light and darkness blasted the invisible wall and passed right through. It was like tossing a handful of flour into water, their attacks fizzling out a foot or two past Mika's spell. Minutes passed, and Andec raised a hand. Their attack subsided, and he waited for Mika to stop, or even slow down. The young man continued to slap the barrier, ignoring them.

"Now what, wielder?" a soldier asked.

"Probably human sacrifice," Nikkola said.

"It's the only way," Andec agreed with a nod.

"What?" the soldier asked, his face pale.

"Not now," Wilfred said dismissively, shaking his head. "Can you create a portal in there and pull him away?"

"The other spells didn't work, but I can try," Andec said

through gritted teeth. It took more strength and focus than he really had to give, but an oily dark circle appeared on the floor in the hallway. "His spell is making it almost impossible to aim."

The circle of darkness crept toward Mika like a drunken sailor unsure of the best path to take. The young man looked over his shoulder to see the portal approach and began striking the barrier blocking Victoria's room even faster.

"No!" he shouted. "You can't stop me! I'll save her!"

"Stop, Mika," Ranson called out. "Please!"

Sweat poured from Andec's forehead as the portal moved closer to the young man. His hands shook from the effort, and the portal made similar jerky motions. Mika roared maniacally, reared his hand back, and slammed it against the barrier. The invisible wall of time shimmered like a pond reflecting sunlight, and Mika fell forward into Victoria's room.

54

Nordruaut

The long, white blade of Niihlu's enormous axe buried deep in Hector's right shoulder, slicing down through his ribs and into his belly. Angst screamed as he reached forward, grabbing Ghorfjend by the handle and shoving it out. Ice formed along the edges of Hector's deep wound, threads of blue and white reaching through his leather armor. His gray, wolf-like eyes were wide with shock as he collapsed. Angst anchored his hand to the steel of Ghorfjend and tore the foci from Niihlu's grip. His arm numbed instantly, but he didn't care. He reared back and swung with all his might. The axe blade struck Niihlu's icy chest with a metallic ringing sound. Instead of slicing through, the Nordruaut was once again smacked away, this time with his own double-bladed axe. Niihlu flew far into the distance like a fly tossed by a tornado.

Angst threw the axe down in the snow. Grasping Chryslaenor with both hands, he called forth lightning until the sword glowed blue. He couldn't control the metal in his armor enough to fly, but with a nudge of will he was able to jump over the monster's head. Lurp pulled away, but not fast enough. Chryslaenor was too large to flee, and the blade sliced cleanly through the creature's neck with a sickening crack. Lurp's enormous head landed beside the orb of fire and burned, his face twisting in a silent scream, his enormous body collapsing with a thud.

Angst looked over Hector's twitching body and didn't know what to do. He dropped Chryslaenor and circled his friend, clenching his hands in frustration. Weren't they supposed to win? Weren't they the heroes? His mentor, one of his oldest friends was dying, and there was nothing he could do. It hurt—it was the worst pain he'd ever felt. The pain melted away the numbness in his heart, and a fury grew until he couldn't hold it back any longer.

Angst's emotions let loose in an explosion. His scream was overwhelmed by the sound and light that blasted from his chest. An air shield covered in red and blue lightning grew in all directions. As fast as a breath, the shield expanded to encompass the battlefield. Nordruaut, Berfemmian, Fulk'han, and human were all struck without remorse, blasted off their feet and knocked senseless by the spell. In that instant, all fighting stopped.

Angst dropped to a knee, took his mentor's hand, and willed. No one else should die because of him, because of what he'd started. He'd dragged his friends along, forced them to be a part of this adventure, made them all come with so he could be a hero. They weren't supposed to die, not for him, not for this. Angst drew in more power, pulling from the place that had scared him so much. He drew in power from the swords, all of it, every single bit. That power should be enough. That power, and will, and tears would be enough to keep Hector alive and—

"Stop," Hector whispered, gripping his hand weakly.

"I won't let you die!" he growled.

"This is how I was meant to die," Hector said with a cocky grin. Blood dripped from his mouth. "On the battlefield, impossible odds. It's the best story."

"Please don't," Angst said, panting at the exertion of keeping his friend alive. It was almost impossible to see through the blur of tears.

"I'm so proud of you Angst," he whispered. "I agreed to train you because I knew you could become a hero, and you did."

"I'm not a hero," Angst said, gasping for breath.

"Yes," Hector said, placing a hand on his cheek. "Yes, you are. And I'm the one who saved the hero. Best story ever."

"You did it, Hector, you saved me," Angst said. He could barely speak through the lump in his throat. He'd never felt so hurt. His body ached with despair. "Thank you for being my friend. I love you."

The old soldier placed a hand on Angst's cheek and nodded. "Angst," he said softly.

"Yes?" Angst leaned in.

"Angst," Hector whispered, almost too softly to hear. "You've got this."

They both let go, and Hector was gone. Angst wept like he didn't think possible. Tears flowed freely as he sensed those on the battlefield around him slowly come to. He stood, placing Chryslaenor on his back and brushed the ice from his old friend's body. Lifting Hector, he took slow, staggering steps to his fallen friends. His heart ached, his mind reeled, and the choices he'd made in his life weighed heavy with every movement. He kept saying he wouldn't lose anyone else, kept threatening the world with his empty words, but the ones he loved still died. They didn't deserve this, he didn't deserve this, and Hector would be the last. He had to be!

After a long, somber walk, Maarja stood before him, her face dripping with guilt and helplessness. Angst handed her Hector's body.

"Take care of him like he was your own child," he said, choking out every word. "Like Jintorich."

"I promise, Angst," she said, her voice trembling as she took Hector's body.

"Angst!" said a voice that shook the ground. "It's time!"

"It's him, Angst," Maarja said. "That ball of fire grew while you were walking back. Everyone else ran away. The Fulk'han, the other Nordruaut, are all gone. And, and, he's...oh, he's enormous!"

Angst ignored the element Fire, doing a mental count of friends. Dallow and Rose, Faeoris and Kala, Aerella and Jintorich, Tarness and Maarja. They were all there, including Scar. Especially Scar. The dog had retreated into his puppy form, licking Kala furiously as she pushed herself up. She was alive, they were all alive, and none of them would die. He would see to it. But Aerella was right; he couldn't do this alone anymore.

"Don't ignore me, Angst," Fire cried out. "I will destroy everyone you love if you don't face me."

"I'll be right there, dear," Angst shouted maniacally, raising his middle finger high. "Just give me one minute while I make myself pretty."

"Don't you dare mock me!" Fire blared. "Wait, what is this? I can't move!"

Whatever burning attack Fire threw forward was immediately snuffed out, and Angst did it with barely a thought. If it was possible to wield magic fueled by pain, Angst wielded all of it. His patience and tolerance were completely gone as the power of two foci flowed through him. He picked up Scar. The lab pup seemed so tiny. His tail stopped wagging and tucked neatly between his legs, and the dog's head looked a little skinny, as if he'd stolen a cookie.

"Look, I don't know how much you understand," Angst said as he held the lab up high. "You're a part of this. All of it. You always have been." Chryslaenor shone bright blue in the corner of his eye as if egging him on. "My friends are my family, and you've proven yourself time and time again to be my family, too. You've always been there." He paced along a snowy path as his friends around him watched. He wondered if the pup understood any of his words. It was impossible to tell, except for the skinny head that was blurry through tears. "But I can't do this alone, not any more. I can't lose anyone else. I need you to keep them safe, now more than ever." Scar whimpered, and the dog shivered in his hands.

"Are you done, Mr. Angst?" Kala called. "He's scared and wants me close."

"One more minute, Kala," Angst said, pulling Scar in for a hug. "Please stay back."

The lab didn't hesitate at accepting his love and petting, his tail wagging frantically with every long pull of fur. Angst was tormented by every loss. He thought of them all with every pet. Marissa. Captain Guard Tyrell and Queen Isabelle. His good friends Rook and Janda. Moyra...and now Hector. He choked at the thought of all that loss, his heart wrenched from so much pain. Angst knelt and set the dog on the ground. His hand held Scar's jaw, and he looked the pup in the eye.

"No more." His throat hurt, and he had to force the words out. "I don't want anyone else to die. You've proven yourself a defender, a protector." The pup's eyes become glossy, reflecting the red glow of his own eyes. "You've saved me, protected me and mine. Now I need you to protect them all."

Angst stood, letting go of Scar, who remained still, waiting.

"Protect them all, Scar. Protect everyone I love, now and throughout time. Protect them, Scar," he said, taking a deep breath. And with all his pain, all his remorse, with every ounce of will he could muster, he cast the spell, "At all costs."

Scar whined, and Kala cried out as sparks flew from Chryslaenor. The dog howled in pain, his eyes blazing as red as Angst's, his mouth foaming as power flowed through Angst into his pup. It felt like he was bonding with another sword. Power poured from his foci, from Chryslaenor, even from Dulgirgraut, through Angst and into Scar. The poor dog wailed and cried, shaking his head so fast it was hard to make out.

"What is this foolishness you miscast now, human?" Fire roared, his voice echoing loudly. "What is it you and your pathetic pet could...possibly...do..."

Scar grew. Muscles bulged and bones popped grotesquely. Clumps of fur combined to become sharp daggers, and then swords as his lab became larger than ever. The swords were now serrated, and lay flat like well-formed scale armor. His six eyes glowed bright red as his head reared back in a howl that shook Angst's eardrums. Scar shivered as if releasing water from his fur, the sound like a thousand sabers crashing together.

"Scar?" he asked.

411

"What have you done?" Aerella asked, her voice panicked.

What had he done? In his fury and despair, had he just damaged this companion, this friend with too much power? If the dog couldn't handle it, he may've just doomed them all.

Scar's enormous head lowered to make eye contact with Angst. Great clouds of steam puffed from the dog's nostrils, and it shuddered in anticipation. Angst reached up to place a hand on Scar's muzzle, swallowing a lump of fear. The metal coating of his nose was wet, and warm. Scar didn't attack, his three tails wagged, and Angst knew that all was well. That all was better than well.

"It's time to die, Al'eyrn," Fire called out. "Come out and face me."

"I agree, it is time," Angst said, lifting his hand. Scar's eyes followed as he pointed to Fire. "Scar...fetch!"

55

With a horrifying bark that sounded like a moon had crash-landed nearby, the steel-covered monster dog bounded toward Fire in long gaits. The element's smoldering eyes widened as he took several steps back. Fire raised his hands, throwing lava and flames at Scar, which were deflected by the dog's armor unnoticed. Scar leaned in, racing forward in a blur, giving Fire no further time to escape. He chomped down on Fire's burning leg, and the element roared in agony.

"Shouldn't you help?" Rose asked.

"He's got this," Angst said dismissively. His heart and mind hurt so badly he just wanted to crawl into a ball, but she was right. He knew Scar would win, but a little help wouldn't go awry. He lifted a hand and drew forth power.

Thick bolts of lightning crashed down into Fire even as Scar tore into the element's other leg. Fire tried backing away from the attack, shrinking with each step as his voice crackled with pain. The element sounded pitiful as he attempted in vain to beat away the enormous dog of steel reinforced with the power of two foci.

"Enough!" Fire cried out, his billowing flame throwing Scar aside. "I will come after you and everyone you love until the end of days, and you will forever regret—"

"Just die already!" Angst shouted, the thundering onslaught of lightning drowning out Fire's bravado. "Scar, back!" Angst

413

roared, pulling down as much as he could in one, final attack.

The blast of lightning that rained down from the skies was as wide as the castle at Unsel, and everyone turned away, blinking and rubbing their eyes. When his vision cleared, Fire was gone, and Scar was rushing toward them. His pup was frightening to look on with it's six wild eyes that blazed red, three steel tails wagging like swinging swords, and an enormous tongue that lolled to one side. The monster dog leaped into the air, shrank to puppy size, and landed in Angst's arms.

Angst petted Scar and rubbed his cheek into the dog's face. "I knew you could do it!"

After several gratifying licks, he handed the dog to an upset Kala. Her cold glare boring into Angst was soon melted by puppy love.

"You'll see," Angst said, wanting her to understand. "Scar will save everyone."

The tap on his shoulder made Angst spin about with raised fists, and his eyes went wide at the sight of Rose. She'd been there, he'd seen her, but it hadn't registered until now. Without a word, he pulled her into a hug she didn't fight. There was a pounding in his ears from the battle, and pain wasn't a strong enough word to describe how he felt. His tears weren't even close to coming, but she had plenty for them both. He petted her long, red hair and looked at Dallow and Tarness.

"Hector," he said, the word straining against his tight throat.

"We saw," Tarness said.

Tarness and Dallow joined the embrace while everyone around them remained quiet. Angst wished he could just cry this off to let go of the grief, but it was tainted with so much anger and guilt that he shook. Rose pulled away, looking up at him with a deep frown and tired eyes.

"I tried to save him. The wound was too deep," he said. It felt like a hollow excuse.

"Stop, Angst," Dallow said. "We know."

"This is what he wanted. The best story," Rose said before turning to Dallow and sobbing into his shoulder.

"We've got a lot to catch up on and only a few weeks to get back and save Victoria," Angst said. "I'll explain on the way, but we need to leave."

"We don't have weeks, Angst," Alloria said, shuffling into view from behind Maarja. "It may already be too late."

He rushed to her in a blur, lifting Alloria by her arms and slamming her down to the snow. He grasped her throat and squeezed. Her legs writhed beneath him as her pale cheeks became blotchy, but she didn't fight. After what she'd done to Victoria, she deserved this; she deserved to die. Angst looked into her eyes, and it frightened him enough to loosen his grip. They were filled with longing, eager to please, and completely submissive. He wanted nothing more than to kill this betrayer of Unsel. This backstabber. This traitor. And she would just lie there and let him? His stomach churned as he began to realize how broken Alloria was. It didn't make her actions right, but her death wouldn't be justice. It would be vengeance.

Angst pushed himself away as she took in gasping, choking breaths. He remained on his knees while glowering at his friends, expecting to see shock or disappointment. There was no judgment, only patience as if they wanted her dead too, and he wondered what had happened since they'd parted ways.

Faeoris offered to help him stand, which he gratefully accepted. It wasn't until after he'd brushed snow and dirt off his armor that he noticed. Her entire side, from temple to hip, was a bruised mess covered in blood. How was she even standing? Angst reached up, wanting to touch her cheek. Maybe he could heal her a little. She pushed away his hand and smirked.

"You should see the other guy," she said with a laugh that ended in a wheezing cough. "Is it time to drink yet?

"Almost," Angst said.

"Then you need to save your strength," she said.

"She's one tough bitch," Rose said, approaching from behind Angst.

"That's right." Faeoris nodded.

"Rose can heal you better than I can anyway," Angst said.

415

"Just enough to keep her alive, we don't know what else—"

"I know what I'm doing," Rose said, her lips thinning as she placed a hand on Faeoris's cheek.

"Dallow, I need the short version," Angst said, watching Rose heal Faeoris. He felt utterly helpless as the bruises and welts washed away from Faeoris and appeared on her.

"The portal brought us to a mage city, not far from here. We'd been trapped in there for months when Alloria arrived," Dallow said. "After Magic made her try to kill Victoria, the element sent her to kill us."

"Will this ever end?" Angst asked in desperation.

"There's more," Dallow said.

"Of course there is," Angst said, sighing deeply.

"Magic has been manipulating others. Just before they die, he gives them a ruby ring that keeps them alive," Rose said.

"Angst," Faeoris said. "Don't you wear one around your neck?"

Angst grasped the chain and ripped it from his neck, holding it out toward Alloria with a fierce glare.

"My champion," she said in a weak voice. "By wearing that ring, you kept me alive."

Angst threw the ring to the ground. She choked, her lip quivering. He felt a tug in his guts. Not the normal queasiness from anxiety; this was more like jerking out a serrated blade. What was that ring? Dulgirgraut's song was loud, trying to teach Angst about the rings. Wait, how could he hear Dulgirgraut so clearly? He reached out with his mind to find his other foci completely accessible, the song no longer distant or muffled in his mind. His spell protecting Tori was gone.

"What did you do?" he shouted, taking a step toward Alloria. "What happened to my spell? Why is Victoria free?"

"According to Alloria, Magic has sent a wielder who manipulates time to break down your spell," Dallow said. "We need to get back to Unsel. Now!"

"Even with my foci powering the swifen, it would take days!" Angst said fretfully.

"Flying?" Tarness nodded at Faeoris.

"Maybe a day?" she offered, not sounding at all confident.

"Um, Mr. Angst?" Kala said, tugging on his chainmail and pointing.

"Now isn't a good time, Kala," Angst said as gently as he could, glancing where she pointed.

Angst recognized the tall man from the cave; he'd been casting a spell to force Rose to bind with Chryslaenor. The man looked at him with a smug smile, his arms crossed. Angst also recognized him from somewhere else. Wasn't there a dream...?

"Magic!" Aerella shouted. A blinding beam of yellow light shot from her hands and crashed into the element. It was reflected toward the clouds.

"You showed up at the right time," Angst said, wielding Chryslaenor. Anger surged in his veins, and power swelled in his chest.

"How is that?" Magic asked, tilting his head curiously.

"Worst day ever," Angst said. "I'm ready to take it out on someone, and Fire seems to be dead."

"Fire is still alive, young Al'eyrn, and he's not done with you and yours," Magic said. "I don't think you have time to battle me, save your princess, and stop Fire."

"Wanna bet?" Angst asked. Lightning sparked along the edge of his sword.

"Nope," Magic said with a nod.

A noisy bang made Angst whip about to see a black spot on the ground where he'd thrown Alloria's ring. She screamed, her face horrified as the spot twisted and grew.

"Good luck saving anyone now," Magic said. He snapped his fingers and disappeared.

56

Mika scrambled out of sight as he entered Victoria's room. Wilfred looked at the wielders, who seemed as dumbfounded as he felt. Victoria, his princess, his queen, was supposed to be frozen in that room until Angst arrived to save her. Angst wasn't here yet, and they only had moments.

"Do something," Wilfred begged, frantically patting Andec's shoulder.

"I'm going in," Andec said.

"You'll die," Nikkola said, her voice shaky.

"He'll die with me," Andec said sincerely.

"Please don't kill my son," Ranson pleaded, grasping his arm. "He's confused."

"I'm not," Andec said, pushing the man to a guard. He pointed at Simon. "When you get in there, heal our queen!"

"I'll try," Simon stuttered.

"There's no time for trying," Andec said sharply.

The old man wielded a sick-looking dagger before falling into a dark swirling pool beneath his feet. Everything went quiet, and Wilfred could feel the anticipation around him, could hear it in the heavy breaths of everyone nearby. Was this it? Was she going to die? There was a loud cry and the sickening sound of flesh being torn.

"Come to me!" Andec cried, his voice wheezy. "Hurry!"

They hesitated. Was the barrier still there? Wilfred looked down at his zyn'ight armor. Did he really just wear this to win favor and impress Faeoris? No, he wore it because he, too, could be brave. Wilfred's heart raced and his body quivered as he reminded himself how much he loved Unsel, and how much Unsel needed a queen. Wilfred didn't really have a choice. There was no time to wait. Squeezing his eyes shut and holding his breath, he stepped forward into the hallway like diving into deep, unknown waters. Nothing happened, nothing hurt. The barrier was gone.

"Go!" he commanded, rushing down the hallway and into the room.

Victoria sat on her knees, hunched over and grasping the triangular blade of Jormbrinder. Red blood soaked deeply into the bodice of her white dress, pooling on the floor. The princess let out a tiny moan. She was alive, so barely alive, but alive. The top half of Mika's body lay near Victoria's bed, mere inches away from the bottom half of his torso. Blood stained the furry pink carpet beneath. Mika reached toward his legs with shaky hands. How could he possibly have lived through that?

"Heal her!" Andec said, his voice scratchier than normal.

"I can't heal all of this!" Simon cried, his hands shaking and covered in blood.

"Heal enough to keep her alive," Nikkola said, her tone strained. "Until Angst gets here."

Nikkola dropped to her knees beside Andec, who lay sprawled on the ground. He'd aged far past his years, and drew in short breaths. She rested a hand on his bald head and whispered calming words into his ear.

"Tried to kill him with the dagger, but he was too fast and only clipped his ring," Andec wheezed. "I ported him in half."

"Soldiers, zyn'ight, stay out of the room!" Commander Mirim shouted, pointing to a black mass that was growing from Mika's hand.

The portal wasn't anything like Andec's. This one was a hungry maw of darkness that sucked in every bit of life and light within breathing distance. It was like paint poured into a dark whirlpool as the pinks and lavenders of Victoria's chambers twisted into a void that drew in Mika. He screamed as his body stretched grotesquely, and Wilfred wanted to wretch. It sucked in both halves of Mika's body, taking its time as if enjoying a fine meal. The black disappeared with a pop, and everything went silent.

"Did I do it?" Andec asked, his voice so quiet.

"You did it," Nikkola said between sobs. "You got him."

"Bastard," Andec wheezed, and his breathing stopped.

Wilfred swallowed hard, his throat tight. He wasn't a hero, he didn't adventure, and he avoided death at all costs. This was too much. He turned away from Andec's body and dropped to his knees beside Victoria.

"Hang on," he whispered. "Angst is coming."

"I can't do this," Simon whispered. "I can't keep her alive!"

Wilfred slapped the young wielder across the mouth. "Angst is coming! You will keep her alive until he gets here. Do you understand?"

"Yes," the young man squeaked.

"Angst," Victoria whispered.

"He's coming, my queen," Wilfred said.

"...saw Mika's future," Victoria said. "Angst will destroy us all."

57

Nordruaut

The dark hole twisted light and images as it slowly turned, sucking away Alloria's life like a whirlpool emptying a small pond. Jormbrinder was already gone. The young princess's arm stretched like taffy as she was drawn into the vortex. She screamed in fright, or pain, or both, her eyes bulging unnaturally. Alloria clung desperately to a handful of chainmail that hung from Angst's chest piece. He stared down at her coldly.

Angst had never killed a friend, someone he cared about. He'd spent time getting to know Alloria and thought they were close. Alloria had kissed him in that hallway, something he'd dismissed to her flirty nature, not realizing that when she'd slipped the necklace on him with the ring attached, he'd also become her champion. Unwittingly, Angst had been protecting her this entire time. Maybe it was being Al'eyrn, but keeping that ring close had kept anyone from killing her. It may have also alerted Magic, and possibly other elements, of their location. That explained so many of their seemingly random encounters. He would've taken the ring anyway, had she just asked. Angst would've championed her, because he cared, because that was what you did for friends. She hadn't asked.

Alloria had betrayed him by attempting to kill Victoria, interrupting possibly the most important moment he'd spent with her.

Just before Tori was to be crowned, she'd been about to ask him something important. She never got to ask that question. The vision of Alloria standing behind Victoria, the long triangular dagger through her chest, Alloria's blood-soaked hands, and her pathetic apology was seared into his mind's eye like a branding. The memory made his fists shake and his teeth grind. All the manipulation, all the lies...he wanted to blame her for Hector's death, for all the deaths. Crazy wasn't a good enough excuse; she didn't deserve to live.

"Without the dagger, we can't save Victoria," Dallow called.

"You can't save Alloria, Angst!" Aerella cried. "You'll die, it's too late. We'll find another way."

Alloria's legs were now distorted horrifically, winding about the deathly vortex like paint stirring in a pot of dark oil. The tears streaming down her cheeks were sucked away, and the hungry black mouth of the vortex began dragging him forward too. Bright white flashes sparked behind her, lighting up her legs and torso like lightning strikes. Scar yelped, and the flashes stopped.

A dark hunger growing in the pit of his stomach longed to watch this through to the end. Maybe this was the madness Aerella had warned him about. He refused to believe anything would drag him into crazy, not even the death of his friend and mentor. He thought of Hector, closed his eyes, and decided that he'd seen enough death. She deserved to die, he wanted her to be punished for what she had done to Victoria, but he refused to give the elements another win. Today, he wouldn't let them have her; today, he would fight death and his own dark hunger.

Chryslaenor sparked over his back as he summoned power. The foci let him know that this wasn't a mere element, or someone pretending to be the Dark Vivek. This was death, and no mortal could fight death. Well, not most.

Angst anchored his armor to the ground beneath the snow, anchored his bones to the armor, and willed himself to be like the earth, to be a mountain. Death can't kill mountains. Alloria's hand was blurry; there wasn't much left of her. He grasped her forearm with both of his hands and held on for dear life, literally. Alloria screamed, and he winced in pain as a great force drew him forward. What started as a gushing breeze was suddenly a tornado that pulled at his skin and made it hard to breathe. His hold was slipping and, in spite of his efforts, it was a struggle to stand upright.

"She's already dead, Angst," Aerella said. "You can't bring her back."

"Yes...I...can," Angst growled, squeezing tighter.

It wasn't enough; he needed help. Chryslaenor was a frenzy of music, a panicked orchestra that made him wonder if this battle was already over. Dulgirgraut's deep tone sang clearly in his mind. A calm, low lullaby in the storm. A reminder that Victoria only had precious moments. Despite Angst's growing panic that chewed away at his gut, Dulgirgraut told him what he needed to know, and he listened.

Angst slowly, so slowly, anchored Alloria's bones to his own. He started with her hand and forearm, which mostly remained intact. Angst reached further with his will and reformed her shoulder, drawing the bicep back into shape. It worked, but the portal seemed furious, as though death knew what he had planned. Gently, Angst willed her chest against his and pulled her head forward so their foreheads touched.

"Hang on," he grunted to her.

"I like...this part," she said between pained whimpers.

"Then you'll like this even more," he said with a smirk.

He had little time, not only to save Victoria, but to rebuild Alloria before the death vortex closed. Angst willed the bones of her hips to reform, pulling them against his own like a magnet. The bones of her legs solidified as they intertwined with both of his, the blurred colors of her flesh becoming solid once more.

The swirling mass screamed as it shrank, fighting against his will as he forced the arm holding Jormbrinder to return. He sensed his own victory, and death's failure, and death was not pleased.

"Not today!" he yelled. "You've taken too much already.

This one is mine."

With a jerk, he willed her arm whole, dragging it out of the black. With an ear-piercing whine and a loud pop, the vortex closed. Alloria held onto him so tightly that Angst could feel her racing heart through his armor. His arms were wrapped around her bare back, and a quick glance down revealed almost everything—her clothes were in tatters. Her body shivered delightfully against him, and she giggled, and then laughed.

"A blanket," he requested.

"I don't care. It feels so good to be alive," she said through chattering teeth then whispered in his ear, "Thank you, my champion." She bit at it playfully, and his cheeks instantly warmed.

Maarja wrapped her in a white fur cloak that really didn't cover much. Angst would've appreciated the view under other circumstances, and on a person he didn't hate. He gently peeled her off and glanced at his friends. They all stared with wide eyes and slack jaws—everyone but Kala.

"I could do that," she said sincerely.

"Of course you could," he said with a nod, grateful she wasn't staring at him like some sort of aberration. "We're good like that. How's the mutt?"

"Resting," she said, petting the lab puppy in her arms.

That was a relief. Resting was so much better than dead. He wouldn't have minded some resting too. Aerella approached him slowly, taking cautious steps. She wasn't quite old, maybe fortyish, but pale and shaky. He needed her, and didn't have time for her to be exhausted.

"Are you okay?" he asked.

"What..." she began. "What are you?"

"Uh, well," he said. "Hi, you must be new here. I'm Angst."

Despite the apparent fear in her eyes, she couldn't help the lopsided grin. "No, I mean, you shouldn't have been able to do that. That was death. You can't stop death. You can't trick death..."

"Yes, you can," Dallow said smugly. "I tricked death once."

"You're all doomed." Aerella shook her head in despair. "Angst, an Al'eyrn shouldn't do these things. I don't remember hearing about this, ever, or reading about it in all my travels."

"I'm amazing," Angst said, taking her hand. "And I'm in a hurry."

"What?" she asked.

"My spell at the castle was broken. It was Dulgirgraut who told me how to save Alloria, which means it's time to save Victoria. I need you."

"You're so calm." Aerella's eyes were wide, her head rocking back and forth slightly. "After all that's happened, why are you calm? We thought...I thought you were going to lose it after Hec—"

"I'm calm because I have to be. That's what heroes do. I promise I'll go crazy later," he said with a reaffirming smile. "Really, if I can make it through Hector's death, I'll be okay. It will hurt, a lot, but later when everyone else is safe. A dear friend taught me to mourn for the dead after I'm done fighting for the living. Good advice."

"I try," Faeoris said, sounding stronger after Rose's healing.

"Aerella," Angst said. "I can't do this without you. Will you help me?"

"Yes," Aerella said, nodding.

"I need a portal to Unsel or Victoria will die," Angst said.

Aerella choked on her reply and began hyperventilating.

"Angst, she doesn't have that sort of power," Dallow said. "Nobody does."

"I do," Angst said, grabbing Aerella's shoulders. "We can do this together."

"Okay," she said bravely.

"Aerella, won't this kill you?" Dallow asked, pulling away from Rose.

"You've been to the mage city at the bottom of the ocean. Azaktrha," Aerella said to Dallow. "You've been to the library."

Dallow nodded, his face drawn.

"What does that mean?" Angst asked.

"Dallow can explain later," she said, her voice suddenly warm. "Angst, you will see me many times in the coming years, but for me, this is our last adventure."

"What?" Angst said. "I won't do this if it's going to kill you."

"It won't, I promise," she said. "I know how I'm going to die, and it's not here, and not today. But we have to hurry, and I just wanted to say thank you. You'll never realize the amazing life you gave me, all because you broke the curse of Gressmore Towers. I cherish my time with you as I cherish my life. Thank you."

She leaned forward and kissed him squarely on the mouth. It was like being kissed by a cousin, or maybe a second cousin, and Angst was taken by surprise. He didn't want to be rude, of course, so he kissed her back, sort of.

"Uh, you're welcome," he said, touching his lips.

"I never get to shock you," she said triumphantly. "I win!"

"Miss Heather won't like that," Kala said, a judging frown hanging over peering eyes.

"I did," Angst said, smirking.

"Everyone close," Alloria said. "Uncomfortably close."

"Not me," Tarness said.

"What?" Angst snapped. "We don't have time for..."

Tarness jerked his head toward Maarja.

"Oh," Angst said, dumbfounded. "Uh, then, okay. Will you...will you see to Hector?"

"With every bit of honor he deserves," Tarness said with a nod. "I'll find my way home soon enough,"

Angst took rushed steps forward to give his friend a hug. It was met with brief, crushing gratitude.

"Don't wear him out," he said to Maarja.

"No promises," she said with a nod and a wink.

"I'm staying, too!" Jintorich squeaked.

"Good! Someone needs to keep these kids alive," Angst said, kneeling. "And I'm so glad you are alive, brother Al'eyrn."

Angst tried his best to give Jintorich a gentle, one-armed hug. Faeoris was less gentle, picking up the little man and hugging him like a lost puppy. After a brief embrace, she pulled him free from her breasts and returned him to the snowy ground.

"I hate that," he said with a frown.

"No you don't," Maarja said.

Maarja and Faeoris stared at each other, nodded once, fist bumped, and said nothing.

Angst, Alloria, Aerella, Rose, Dallow, Kala, and Scar all grouped up in a huddle. Angst set Chryslaenor in the middle on its tip.

"No helping," he said to Kala.

"Aww," she whined.

"Just pay attention and learn," he said firmly. "That'll be help enough."

It was enough to make her stop complaining, even if her face was still sour. Angst placed two hands on the hilt of Chryslaenor and looked at Aerella. She intertwined her fingers with his. Angst nodded ready, as did Aerella, and he willed. As the power from her spell grew, he turned around for one last look at Tarness. His big friend's face was scrunched in pain, and he looked at the ground. One hand fidgeted relentlessly, spinning a shiny object wrapped around his finger. Spinning it until Angst could see the ruby ring on Tarness's hand.

"No," Angst whispered.

58

Unsel

There was a sudden drop, the unsure feeling of no ground beneath his feet, and a momentary lurch as his stomach caught up. But portal travel was fast, and the odd sensation was gone almost as quickly as it happened, leaving him disoriented. Had he really seen the ring on Tarness's finger? He glanced around. They were already in the great hall of Unsel, and his big friend was still in Nordruaut.

Faeoris, Rose, Dallow, Alloria, Kala, and Scar all stood with him, but Aerella was gone, just as she'd warned.

"Come on!" he shouted, jogging, not blurring, to Victoria's room. This level of exhaustion was new. Powering the spell that had gotten them to Unsel made him shake with the weakness of illness. At least the slow jog gave him time to think about Hector, remorse squeezing at his heart. So many had died, so many lost that he cared about, but Hector was different. He was family. Angst couldn't bear to lose any more family—he deserved for Victoria to live. He'd earned it. Hector had earned it for both of them. With every remaining fiber of his strength, he willed her to stay alive. He willed it. Angst could practically sense her pain, sense her desire to die and be done with it, but he wouldn't let her go.

The word forever couldn't describe how long it took to rush

down hallways in armor, breathing heavily, sweating in the late spring closeness of the castle. Had the great hall become longer since he left? Every guard looked at him with wary eyes—would they try to stop them?—then glanced at the giant sword and kept to themselves.

Chryslaenor hovered over his back, bright sparks of blue lightning flashed over his shoulders, popping and crackling noisily in his ears. The power thrummed like a second heartbeat that drove him, kept him from collapsing, and kept her alive. She would live, he wouldn't let her die, Chryslaenor wouldn't let her die! *Please, don't let her die.*

His friends were short steps behind him, most of them gasping in exhaustion. They sounded so fatigued that he could only imagine that their pain and weariness mirrored his own. They were at that point beyond tired, driven only by habit or a crazy man screaming, "Go! We're almost there."

Angst stumped up the stairs and stumbled to a halt before Victoria's room. The time barrier was gone, and he cursed himself for failing. Victoria's eyes were open, her hands on the dagger, and she blinked. She blinked!

He turned to Rose and Alloria, grabbing their hands and leading them forward. Angst shoved past several guards, pulling them to Wilfred and the young healer, who shook from exhaustion.

"I'm here," he said to Victoria. "We're going to make this right."

She barely nodded. It was enough.

"You, take out the blade," Angst said to Alloria. "Rose, heal her."

Rose looked at him like he was insane while Alloria followed his commands with surprising obedience. She pulled at the dagger, making Victoria squeak and gasp in pain. Rose placed her hands on Victoria's face and screamed, blood pouring from her chest. The dagger wouldn't move.

"Angst, I can't," Rose said, jerking her hands away. She was pale and shaky. "It's too much."

"The blade won't come out!" Alloria said.

"Try again," he demanded. "You put it in there. You take it out."

Alloria struggled with the dagger, being less gentle. Victoria writhed in pain, her chest unwilling to release the foci.

"I can't!" Alloria cried.

Angst shoved Alloria away, knocking her to the floor. She looked like he'd stabbed her through the heart and began sobbing.

"I thought she was the only one who could remove the blade, Dallow," Angst snapped.

"It was a theory, Angst," Dallow said weakly. "I'm sorry."

He turned to Rose.

"I don't know what to do, Angst," she said. "If I try to heal her, I'll die. Would you choose her over me?"

Angst's gaze danced between Rose and Victoria. Rose would do it if he asked. He loved them both so much, but in such different ways. Chryslaenor's song screamed that he couldn't hold onto Victoria much longer. He roared in frustration, making everyone in the room jump. Why did it have to be so hard? Maybe he could help heal. Both foci told him no, it wouldn't be enough. Healing wasn't his talent. Rose could heal, but it would kill her. If she could just...if she could...

"Rose," Angst said. "You need to bond with Jormbrinder."

"What?" she said, her entire body tensing.

"You almost bonded with Chryslaenor," he explained. "Can't you bond with Jormbrinder? It would give you enough power to remove the blade and heal her."

"I can't," she said, her eyes wide.

"Do you hear the song of the foci?" Angst asked, nodding at her wide-eyed reaction. "I think you do, and I believe that you can bond."

"I..." Rose said. She crossed her arms. "No. It changed you. I don't want to change like that."

"This is for Unsel," he said.

"I felking hate Unsel!" she shouted, her lip quivering.

"This is for me," Angst said.

"I felking hate you!" she said, tears welling up in her eyes.

"If you've ever loved me, Rose," he said, "you will do this."

A stream of curses spewed from her mouth, making the guards flinch, Wilfred blush, and Kala cover her ears. Rose leaned over to Alloria, grabbing the handle of Jormbrinder. "Give me that, bitch!" she said, jerking it from her hand.

Alloria reached for the blade, but Angst smacked her hand away. He spun Rose around to face Victoria.

"If you need to pass the wound to me," he said. "Don't hesitate."

"I won't," she growled. "I hate you."

"I hate you too," he said, his heart swelling with gratitude.

Rose placed her hand on the other half of Jormbrinder still in Victoria, and bonded with the foci. Angst knew she bonded. Not just because her hair lifted as if a breeze had entered the room, not just because the room itself seemed too bright, not just from her whimpers as she gave a part of herself to the foci. It was deeper. Maybe it was the songs of Chryslaenor and Dulgirgraut, harmonizing reverently. Maybe it was a deeper sense of everything that his foci gave him when he paid attention. Or maybe it was the fact that he was so close to Rose he could see the change happen, feel it.

"Yes," she whispered, her eyes rolled back.

What felt like an eternity passed within breaths, and Rose withdrew the dagger slowly from Victoria's chest. A forest green fire coated her forearms, pouring into Tori. The princess shook her head back and forth, her body tensing. Rose muttered words Angst didn't know or even recognize. Finally. Finally, it stopped. Rose and Victoria gasped.

Tears streamed down Angst's cheeks as he dropped in front of Tori. He placed her face upon his chest, and she collapsed into him, wrapping her arms around him. It was done. He was done. His princess lived. Rose was safe. Everyone was okay. From behind him, he could hear Kala's mom, Nikkola, sobbing. After many sorrys from Kala, there may have been a swat and

Kala began sobbing too. Wilfred was there, his hand resting on Duke Ranson's shoulder as the man wept into his hands.

"Rose, how are you?" Angst asked.

"I'm sorry, Angst," she said, her voice distant.

"What do you mean?" he asked, looking over Victoria's shoulder.

"I'm sorry I ever questioned this," she said with a wry smile. Rose stood and walked to Dallow.

"Are you all right?" Dallow asked nervously. "You sound...different."

"I'm better. I was able to heal the princess," she said, placing hands on his cheeks. "Now it's your turn."

Rose pressed her lips against Dallow's. Green light filled the room once again, and Angst felt warmth in his heart. If she could heal oldest friend, if Dallow could see again, it would be more than he could've hoped.

"Angst, you saved me," Victoria said weakly.

"I had help," he replied with a deep sigh.

"It hurt so much," she said, resting a shaking hand against her breast. "I should've died, but you wouldn't let me."

Angst looked at her for the first time since the attack, truly looked into those beautiful dark eyes. His heart swelled with love. She was okay. He would grieve for Hector, a loss from which he may never recover, but that loss hadn't been in vain. His mentor would've approved, mostly. Victoria had leaned in, she was a kiss away, her hands on his cheeks. He licked his lips as she inched closer, and then her eyes went wide.

Victoria pulled back and her jaw dropped. "Angst!" she cried.

"What?" he said. "What is it?"

"Your family!" she shouted. "Hurry!"

59

Angst grabbed Dulgirgraut and blurred out of the room, knocking over guards in his rush down the stairs. He leaped out of the corridor into the main hallway and landed on his swifen in one smooth movement. He couldn't have done that again if he'd tried, and barely even remembered summoning it in his panic. He was too far past the point of exhaustion to do anything but go. And go he did.

The midday streets of Unsel were bustling with business. Every vendor from every nation in Ehrde must've shown up to create a maze of food carts just for him. Between the carts were people chatting, walking pets, carrying children, and living life. Was he the only person in a hurry? They barely paid him heed, and he wanted to roar in fury. It was everything he could do not to blur straight forward and trample everyone in his path.

"Move off!" he shouted at a particularly thick gathering of mob that just seemed to stand still.

They looked at him with curious eyes or offended glares, taking his swifen and the two giant swords behind his back in such stride, it was surreal and maddening. They looked past him, several pointing up into the sky. Now what?

"I've got you," Faeoris said, lifting him off the swifen.

"Thank you," Angst said, his voice strained. He hurriedly dismissed his mount; it took two tries. He'd never been so scared in his life. That look in Victoria's eyes had told him everything, and he wanted to scream or cry or just get home in time to save them from whatever it was. "Just...please just put me down outside the city. I'll be faster on the swifen."

She didn't argue, flying so fast his eyes watered. From the wind, of course. He summoned his swifen again as she swooped down to the highway, and Faeoris placed him gently on the ram. Before he could grab hold, a giant, steel mass blurred by, closely followed by an excited, high-pitched squeal. Scar and Kala.

"No," he said, looking over his shoulder at Faeoris.

"Ride," she shouted, her face pale and her eyes wide. "Angst, ride!"

He drew in power from the two giant foci hovering over his back, their sharp hues of red and blue visible in his periphery. With a deep breath, he willed the ram forward. The first time he'd pushed his swifen this hard, he'd raced a dark beam of Magic across Ehrde all the way to the castle. It had taken a night and half a day fraught with worry and panic to reach Unsel. In spite of the frantic pace, he'd had time to think. Now he only had time to worry, and the half-day ride home was going to be done in twenty minutes. No, it would be fifteen. Ignoring his exhaustion, he willed the swifen faster yet.

Whatever he'd turned Scar into, the dog now moved like lightning. When the giant lab had rushed by with Kala on his shoulders, Angst could barely make them out. This wasn't the help he needed. Now, not only did he have to worry about the unknown nightmare placing his wife and children in danger, he also had to get there first. If losing Hector had taught him anything, it was that he had limitations. He couldn't save his family and keep Kala safe, especially without knowing what they faced.

Despite clear skies, water sprayed his cheeks. Angst wiped away a thick, foamy drop and rubbed it between his fingers. It was slimy. The spray wasn't rain; it was doggy drool. He was getting close, and could just make out the reflection of sun off Scar's hide, flashes of light as the dog passed trees. More slobber—enough that under normal circumstances, he would've laughed.

"Stop!" His cry was muffled by a mouthful of wind.

When he pulled up alongside the dog, Kala's eyes were glowing. She was wielding. What was she wielding?

"Kala, stop!" Angst tried again. "This is too dangerous."

"Scar says we need to be there!" she replied, her eyes flickering as she lost concentration.

Scar slowed slightly before picking up speed again. The girl was willing him to go faster, just like Angst did with his ram swifen. She must've watched him do it, and copied his magic. Angst shook his head in amazement. That young girl was going to be a force, and he looked forward to watching her become the hero he should've been. But something didn't make sense. After Angst cast the spell, at all costs, Scar was already able to run at a blur. How was she able to will the dog to run faster without some source of power to draw on?

A guilty song quietly entered his thoughts.

"Chryslaenor?" he asked aloud. "You've got to be kidding me!"

She'd drawn power from his foci when they cast the spell on the memndus stones, and was now leeching power from it to make Scar run faster. That sneaky little genius.

"Chryslaenor, you have to stop," Angst said. The sword actually whined in protest. It liked her. He couldn't believe it, but the sword apparently liked the girl, he could sense it. "This will put her in danger. She can have you when this is all done, if that's what you want, but I can't keep her safe and protect my family. Stop, now!"

With Dulgirgraut's help, Angst cut her off, and Scar slowed to a mere blur, but it was enough for Angst to pull far ahead. Chryslaenor wasn't happy with the decision, and the hairs on the back of Angst's neck bristled at the buildup of power. The swords wanted to have an argument now?

"I don't have time for this!" Angst cried out desperately. "Please!"

The songs in his head instantly stopped. The change was so abrupt it was jarring. He glanced up, and in his panic, almost reared his swifen to a stop.

"No," Angst shouted. "No!"

Dark, billowing plumes of smoke rose over the distant trees and blackened the horizon. Fire. Magic hadn't been lying. He'd assumed Scar had killed the element, and in his rush to save Victoria, hadn't given it any further thought. How had the element even known where he lived? Had they ever even made a fire in the fireplace? It wasn't necessary—his cabin was always hot. It was like they'd built it over a hot spring. And it struck him. Fire had threatened to destroy everyone he loved. Angst had thought it nothing more than noisy bravado, but the element had always been there. Fire had been at his home the entire time!

Angst wasn't going to make it. He was so tired. He hadn't counted on going into battle after feeding so much power to the portal spell. Feint remnants of energy drained from him like water out of a leaky bucket. He couldn't make the swifen move any faster. More smoke poured up into the sky. Cries and warnings followed him as he passed Rookshire. His heart raced the swifen, and Angst swallowed fear as he drew both foci.

Fire stood near his destroyed home. The element was smaller than Angst had ever seen it. Once the size of a mountain, it now looked more like a Nordruaut. But still an element, and still dangerous. Fire ignored his approach, holding a large ball of flame in one raised hand even as he stared down at Heather and his children. The babies cried, their screams like music because that meant they were alive.

"Angst!" Heather called out. "Stop! He's been waiting for you."

He *had* made it, and there was no time to waste. With a nudge of will, the swifen went from a blurred rush forward to a sudden and complete stop. Angst was somehow able to create an air shield as he was catapulted directly at Fire. He hoped the momentum would be enough to topple the element over before shredding it with his two swords. No matter how tired he felt, he knew Fire had to be depleted of power after Scar's attack. There was a chance. Hope swelled in Angst's chest, and he gritted his teeth in anticipation of the violent beat-down he was going to inflict on the element.

The ball of flames Fire had been holding struck Angst with such force his weak air shield disintegrated on impact. Bones snapped and tendons screamed for mercy as he was slammed against the remains of his home.

Instinctively, he held Dulgirgraut over his face and chest. He couldn't move the arm holding Chryslaenor; it must've been dislocated. That was the least of his pain. His back hurt so much he couldn't even scream. The fireball was gone, but behind it was a constant barrage of flame that melted away his armor and burned his legs. Angst couldn't move; he could only barely create another shield that kept his remaining skin from burning away. The attack stopped, and he lay there, smoke rising from his body like a freshly cooked turkey.

Angst lowered Dulgirgraut. His position against the rubble of his house provided a full view of everything. Heather held the babies close, boldly staring up at Fire. He had to save them, but he could barely move. The bones that weren't broken were locked into place by armor that had melted around his body. Fire stood beside his family, even smaller, now the size of Tarness. The element laughed maniacally, his crackling voice grating in Angst's ears.

Angst willed the melted armor into sand, freeing him. Hot grains of metal lodged in his burned skin. He whimpered, knowing he only had seconds. Pushing himself to sitting was like forcing a rusty, iron door open. But something else was wrong. He couldn't move his legs; he couldn't even feel them.

The element had shrunk again, now the size of a man. He held another ball of fire in his hand, smaller than the last but still large enough to engulf his family. Angst covered them in an air shield, but it was all him and not the swords. Dulgirgraut struggled to keep him alive while Chryslaenor kept him awake. It was everything they had to give. He was so weak, he hurt so much, it would have to be enough.

"I'm impressed," Fire said, the power gone from his voice,

sounding much like Angst felt. "I knew you could beat me if I held back, so I'm sacrificing myself to win. I'm using the last of my power to kill your family, and then you. I've never done that—since the dawn of creation I've never had to use the last of my power just to beat someone, but it is worth it just to destroy you, human."

"Please don't do this," Angst wheezed.

"Just enough left," Fire said weakly, raising his hand.

"Angst," Heather called out. "I love you!"

"I love you!" He coughed.

"Her name," she shouted. "Your daughter's name is Eila!"

"Heather," Angst cried.

Fire drew his hand back dramatically, as if stretching out that moment just to torture him. He took aim at Heather, Thom, and Eila. She stared up at the element with a fierce glare, as if her defiance would deflect their inevitable death. It wouldn't, and the element threw the ball of flame.

"What?" Fire called out as it left his hand.

The dog's bark was loud enough to make the ground shake. Scar and Kala blurred forward, straight into the path of the on-coming fireball. The fire struck Scar's steel hide, encompassing the dog, Kala, and his entire family.

In a blinding flash of light, all of them were gone.

To be concluded in book 5: Dying with Angst.

About the Author

David J. Pedersen is a native of Racine, WI who resides in his home town Kansas City, MO. He received a Bachelor of Arts degree in Philosophy from the University of Wisconsin - Madison. He has worked in sales, management, retail, video and film production, and IT. David has run 2 marathons, climbed several 14,000 foot mountains and marched in Thee University of Wisconsin Marching Band. He is a geek and a fanboy that enjoys carousing, picking on his wife and kids, playing video games, and slowly muddling through his next novel.

To learn more about David and his writing please visit his blog:
www.gotangst.com

www.ingramcontent.com/pod-product-compliance
Lightning Source LLC
Chambersburg PA
CBHW070930100726
47908CB00001B/165